THE RESURRECTION OF FULGENCIO RAMIREZ

THE RESURRECTION OF FULGENCIO RAMIREZ

A NOVEL

RUDY RUIZ

Published in 2020 by Blackstone Publishing
Cover design and illustration by Kathryn Galloway English
Book design by Joseph Garcia

Acknowledgments for permission to
reproduce song lyrics appear on page 337

Printed in the United States of America

First edition: 2020
ISBN 978-1-982604-61-5
Fiction / Magical Realism

1 3 5 7 9 10 8 6 4 2

CIP data for this book is available
from the Library of Congress

Blackstone Publishing
31 Mistletoe Rd.
Ashland, OR 97520

www.BlackstonePublishing.com

In memory of my father,
Rodolfo Ruiz Cisneros

PART I

ONE

1986

The obituaries were always the first thing he turned to in the newspaper. He started doing it the day he learned she'd married another man. There in the still cool blue of the breaking dawn, in the shadowy, unlit recesses of his dank and dusty old drugstore, he sat high behind the elevated counter, perched on the ripped vinyl cushion of an old stool. He wiped his black horn-rimmed reading glasses on his white guayabera. First the left lens. Then the right. He plopped them firmly on the prominent arch of his hawklike nose. As was his habit, one he learned from his grandfather (God bless his soul), he licked his left index finger religiously before turning each page. Although he knew from experience that the obituary section would be buried in the back, he still worked his way slowly through the town rag. World news, the national scene, sports: all he had lost interest in about twenty-five years earlier. The feeling of suspense coiled tightly in his chest, his heart beating a little harder as he paged to the last section, the one with the obituaries at the end. But still, he flipped methodically through the broad sheets. Floods, murders, elections: All these were irrelevant to him. All that mattered was the tiny newsprint on the last page, but still he flipped through . . . just in case the death he was waiting for had miraculously made the headlines.

For years he had wondered—sitting there beyond the fortresslike barrier of the pharmacy counter, in the shadows of the sun rising over the gleaming dome of Market Square—how the news would come. Would the man die suddenly of a massive heart attack? Would he be struck by one of the city buses that careened past his storefront day after day? Or would it come slowly? Would cancer or liver disease silently suck the life from his withering body? He did, after all, have a reputation for drinking tequila and smoking cigarettes of the filterless kind.

Or would he be killed purposefully by another man, a man bearing a grudge, perhaps? The husband of one of his jilted lovers, one of his *putas* or *queridas*. In the end it wouldn't matter *how* or *why*. All that mattered was *when*. And when the time came, he had told himself for years, he would not shed a tear for the man he once called his friend, for the boy he once ran with on the streets of La Frontera. *No señor.* Miguel Rodriguez Esparza deserved whatever pain the blessed Virgen de Guadalupe saw fit to send his way. He was a two-faced traitor. He had been a pampered little pretty boy his entire life. He had lied and cheated to steal his love when their youth was in full bloom, when their blood was still on fire for this adventure he once thought was life. And then he had betrayed the most holy of sacraments, his own ill-fated and ill-conceived marriage, with his womanizing and his gambling and his never-ending hypocrisy. Even though over the multitude of squandered years, he had come to realize that Miguelito was not solely to blame for his suffering, he still welcomed his old friend's death like the survivor of a heinous crime awaiting the final verdict and punishment of his or her assailant. No mercy for Miguel, the opportunist who had profited from—and cultivated—his misfortune. *No, no señor.* He doubted many tears would be shed at all when the twenty-two stinking letters in Miguelito's putrid name finally dried in black ink on the obituary page. Twenty-two: "M-i-g-u-e-l R-o-d-r-i-g-u-e-z E-s-p-a-r-z-a."

He lifted the penultimate page in the section to reveal his destination.

"Obituaries," the bold black letters sprawled across the top. Some scattered pictures. More than usual for a Wednesday.

"Maria de la Luz Villarreal, dead at the age of eighty-three . . ." La Señora Villearreal, hmm, better send flowers. That woman had been special, hadn't she?

"Dagoberto 'Beto' Treviño, dead at the age of fifty-five . . ." It was about time, the quack had been stealing the nest eggs from *viejitas* for years, long after he forgot whatever it was he learned in that medical school down in Panama. *Viejo sinvergüenza.* There was no question where he was headed.

"José Pescador . . . dead at the age of seventeen . . ." *Dios mio*, his thick, black brows furrowed at the thought. Why so many dead teenagers in this once sleepy town? But he knew the answer all too well. It shared a dirty five-letter name with the legitimate versions sitting in bottles on the shelves right behind him. *Las drogas.* Drugs. No self-respecting pharmacist called himself a druggist anymore.

And then . . . there, below the pregnant teen mother killed by her enraged boyfriend (of course, they never gave the true story in the paper, but over the years he had learned how to read between the lines), and right above Doña Eufemia Clotilde de la Paz San

Cristóbal, was an almost pathetic entry. One that he might have missed on any other day were it not for a bright reflection of the morning light bouncing off a passing bus, hitting his pharmacy degree from the University of Texas at Austin, and flashing ephemerally over a paragraph simply starved for words. His eyes blurred in disbelief at the sight of the name, and his left hand clutched hard at his chest as he leaned into the paper to stumble over the phrases. "Dead at the age of forty-six. Survived by his wife." No children. No pallbearers. His hands quivered as the paper slipped from his fingers, floating like a parachute toward his feet. No picture. No excuses. No glory. Just twenty-two letters sitting on the floor of the funereal drugstore. His glasses cracked when they fell on the tile.

Dazed, he searched his stunned mind for what to do next. For the first time in what seemed like forever, he would vary from his routine. There was no time to line up a relief pharmacist. He simply had to close the store for the day. His daily parade of *viejitos* and charity cases would no doubt be surprised by his absence. He had kept that store open religiously for two dozen years since he roared back into town with his *papelito* in hand. His little paper. The diploma, which kept vigil behind the counter, hung on the side of a shelf. Work was all he had known. Filling prescriptions. Helping the needy. Dispensing herbs when the Medicaid gave out. And now he stood mute and dumbfounded, gawking at himself—as if he were contemplating a complete stranger—in the small mirror over the porcelain pedestal sink in the corner. He watched himself lower his tan Stetson hat over his wavy, black mane. His hazel eyes squinted as he straightened out his thick mustache. His image passed like a translucent ghost across the glass pane of his storefront door swinging shut. Bus brakes exhaled their squeaking lament. And the doors to City Hall creaked open across the street as the beggars and drunks skulked into the ancient alleyways. In his khaki overcoat and matching hat, he stepped through the mist of his own breath like a smoldering beast rekindled and unleashed on that crisp December morning. He moved with an elegant determination past merchants sweeping their doorsteps. Their puzzled faces turned to follow him. Doing the mental math, it dawned on him that this morning marked twenty-five years since the day he lost her. And now, she was free again.

Turning the corner, Fulgencio noted the presence of Maria de la Luz Villarreal. Appearing sixty years younger than in her obituary photo, she accompanied her weeping daughter on a wrought iron bench beneath the Spanish arches of Market Square. Weighing whether to pay his respects, he decided it was more respectful to allow them time to grieve.

As he strode by, however, he overheard her tell her daughter, "There goes Don Fulgencio Ramirez . . . *que distinto se ve* . . ."

"How's that, Mamá? How does he look different?" She dabbed mournfully at her mascara-streaked eyes with an embroidered handkerchief.

"Maybe the *maldición* is finally lifting," La Señora Villareal whispered reverentially. "He looks . . . *pues* . . . He seems . . . alive."

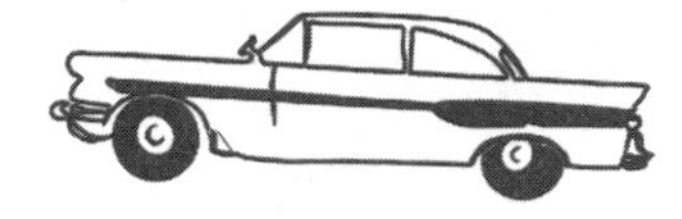

TWO

1956

The first time he saw her, she was stirring a vanilla milkshake with a red-striped straw, cheerleader legs demurely crossed as she leaned across the countertop at the soda fountain in her dad's downtown drugstore. Candy-apple lips and platinum hair in a ponytail, she laughed as she joked with her schoolgirl friends from the private academy run by nuns strictly for the border's elite, the daughters of La Frontera's wealthy Anglo ranchers and merchants as well as a handful of the richest Mexican students from across the river. It was summer, so they weren't in their navy-blue pleated skirt uniforms. Instead, they wore short skirts in pastel colors. Hers was pink. He'd never forget. Her coquettish and angular eyebrows danced with mischief as she glanced at him fleetingly, riveting his feet to the black-and-white checkered linoleum, right where he stood, silhouetted against the glass doorway by the golden haze of the setting sun. The shadows of the store's name on the display window crept across his shoulders as he mustered up the courage to amble toward the pharmacy counter, struggling mightily to not look her way, where she sat on the chrome stool with the lime-green seat. To his right, along the sidewall of the store, she giggled with her friends while Elvis Presley crooned "Don't Be Cruel" in the background. Were they giggling about him? He couldn't bear to think about it. Even Fulgencio, who was set to begin sophomore year at the public school, had heard of Carolina Mendelssohn, a freshman at the nun's academy. The pharmacist's daughter, the beauty they said looked like a movie star. You'd know her when you saw her because there was no one else like her in La Frontera. And now, thanks to his mother's ailing back, he'd finally gotten to witness her in person. Her beauty exceeded her legend, robbing him of his breath.

"Mendelssohn's Drugstore," the distorted shadow read on his back as he moved slowly up the aisle to the imposing pharmacy counter. He fought the urge to look her way again and failed. Her eyes flitted away playfully, sending a jolt of adrenaline through him. Another round of laughter from the girls. And his heart was in his throat as Elvis pleaded for mercy on truthful hearts.

Flushing fiery red as the *chile piquín* that grew wild in his mother's backyard, he avoided the pharmacy counter and pretended to browse through the shelves, sneaking back toward the front of the store, where he could steal another glimpse of her to confirm that, indeed, she was real, not a mirage of his hormonally charged imagination. As he fumbled with a canister of bandages, he traced her delicate feminine figure—now poised in perfect posture upon the chrome stool, her pristine hands dancing in midair as she engaged in animated conversation with her friends—from her impeccable legs all the way up to her radiant face. That face, it was so creamy smooth, and the angles were indeed those of the movie stars that beguiled him during Saturday matinees at the Victoria Theater. She was of that perfectly primped and coiffed, airbrushed and glossy world, not this flawed and filthy one on the border.

Suddenly, as he swooned for an instant in the magnetic pull of her charm, the canister slipped from his clumsy stone fingers and crashed loudly on the floor, scattering Band-Aids all around his frayed and scuffed charcoal-colored shoes. Startled from his reverie, he froze in terror. As if on cue, she spun around on her seat and arose like a living statue, bathed in the laughter of her entourage. She approached him with a sly smile, and the click of her heels would echo in his dreams and nightmares for weeks to come. He struggled to gather the bandages into the container, but one escaped into her grasp. As they both stood up straight, and his hazel eyes met her golden irises, her full lips parted like the Red Sea for Moses, and the words that fell from her grace caressed him like countless feathers over bare skin. "Be careful. You might hurt yourself." She held out the elusive bandage as cackles rose from her faithful onlookers.

At that moment, something took over, something he'd never known he had in him. Smiling coolly, swaggering a la Elvis beneath a grooved tower of Vaseline hair, his steady gaze locked firmly with hers. He gently pulled the bandage from her elegant fingers, deftly replying: "Well, I guess this might come in handy then."

A sincere smile spread over her angelic countenance, like a blooming gardenia, and all her coyness evaporated like morning dew beneath the rising sun. She blushed, and with the batting of a thousand eyelashes she and her gaggle of schoolmates vanished amidst a tumult of shrieks.

Old Vera behind the counter, in her pink uniform with the white apron, cleared away the mess, clucked her tongue, and shook her head at Fulgencio. "Smooth. *Bien* smooth." He wasn't sure if the venerable waitress was mocking or encouraging him, but the truth was he didn't care one bit either way.

That instant, he knew everything had changed. He realized he'd been sleepwalking through the first sixteen years of his life and now, suddenly, this magical potion found within the hallowed walls of Mendelssohn's Drugstore had awakened him. This mystical spell known as Carolina Mendelssohn, the pharmacist's daughter, had brought him to life for the first time. He knew she was an uptown girl. And he was just a poor Mexican boy from downtown. She was fourth or fifth generation German American. He was the son of immigrants. She probably didn't even know a word of Spanish, while at his home, that was all they spoke.

Her lofty ilk was considered off-limits for someone like him, for although Mexicans and Anglos worked side by side, they typically only intermarried when family fortunes favored the arrangement. But none of those traditional obstacles could dissuade Fulgencio from his newfound mission.

Determined, Fulgencio clenched his jaw and approached the high counter at the back of the store with a sense of purpose. His eyes scanned the pharmacist's pristine white lab coat, deciphering the embroidered words upon his left breast, "Arthur Mendelssohn, RPh." The drugstore owner exuded clinical confidence. He wore a crisp blue tie and gleaming golden glasses beneath clean-cut silver hair. Assessing him, Fulgencio shivered at the thought of how his father came home every night, slathered in soot from the tire shop, reeking of vulcanized rubber and stale sweat.

"How can I help you, son?" Mr. Mendelssohn asked.

He knew then what he wanted more than anything in the world. He felt a hunger twisting its roots deep inside him, deeper than when no tires were sold and no food found its way onto the table.

"Tell me, sir. What does *RPh* mean?" he asked, looking up beyond the countertop at the looming man.

"It stands for *Registered Pharmacist*." He pointed at the scripted parchment hanging over his left shoulder on the wall. "That's what I am."

"Then that's what I'll be!" Fulgencio Ramirez uttered in self-recognition and wonderment.

Mr. Mendelssohn startled a bit and leaned back, stroking his smooth chin. "It takes a lot of education."

Fulgencio frowned. The public schools in La Frontera were so impoverished he often went without textbooks to read or a desk in which to sit. "Where did you go to school, sir?"

"San Juan del Atole and then the University of Texas at Austin." He assessed him skeptically. "But those are expensive schools."

"I will find a way, sir. If you hire me, I'll save all my earnings for school. Will you give me a job here in your store, so I can learn?"

"Well," the pharmacist pondered, surveying the piles of half-opened boxes hiding behind the counter. "I do need a stock boy."

"When can I start? It's summer vacation, and I've got time."

"How about tomorrow? What's your name?"

"Fulgencio Ramirez."

"Full-hen-see-oh," Mr. Mendelssohn mouthed slowly, committing the name to memory.

"It's an honor to meet you," Fulgencio said. "I'll be here bright and early tomorrow morning."

With the pleasantries dispensed, and his first business deal closed, Fulgencio thanked Mr. Mendelssohn and bolted out the door, running all the way home to tell his mother the news. He hummed "Don't Be Cruel" as he passed a blur of bustling downtown shops and their shiny storefront windows: Zepeda's Hardware, J.C. Penney, Sears & Roebuck, Maldonado's café. He picked up his pace as he passed the line of moviegoers waiting to catch the evening feature at the Victoria Theater on Fourteenth Street. And he was practically running with excitement by the time downtown gave way to his dilapidated neighborhood. Hurriedly, he turned onto dusty Garfield Street with the faded clapboard shacks crammed with half-naked kids, rib-cage dogs searching desperately for a scrap, flaccid *abuelos* and *abuelas* dozing in metal rocking chairs on sagging porches. He burst into the cozy kitchen with the smell of refried beans thick in the hot and humid air, blurting out his news to his disheveled mother.

"¡Mamá! ¡Mamá! ¡*No lo vas a creer*! I got a job . . . I . . ."

His brother Fernando was wrapped around his mother's right leg, sucking on his thumb and crying, tears and dirt running down his ruddy face. She held a stirring spoon in one hand and the baby, Little David, in the other. Her eyes burned like coals as the rage that had been smoldering within her for the three and a half decades of her hard and tortured life drowned out every syllable of her son's rantings and ravings.

"¿*Trajiste mi medicina*? I don't see a bag. Where's my back medicine?"

His frantic words ("I'm going to be a *farmacéutico* . . .") trailed off, falling clumsily to the wooden floor like a child's broken toy as he realized in horror what he had done.

"You forgot! ¡*Eres un idiota*! You can't do anything right!" she screamed, bearing down upon him.

Even the wood tasted like burnt beans—in the corner of the cramped kitchen, under the rickety table they ate at—where he landed after the blow. Burnt beans and blood. Maybe a little dirt. Salty. Or were those just his tears? Splinters bristled like porcupine quills on his forearms from the violent slide across the floor. She must have hit him with the spoon too. Boy, the woman could hit. Not as hard as Papá, but harder than most men. He knew. He'd been in more than a few fistfights in his day. All he could do was crouch there beneath the table and wait for the storm to blow over. Pots and pans clanged. His mother yelled. Babies cried. Screeching. Shrieking. And he didn't even wonder his usual beneath-the-kitchen-table thoughts about whether his dad would let him have it again when he got home, and whether it would be with the hand or the belt, with or without clothes on. He just smiled dreamily through the bitter taste in his mouth. He bet Carolina never had to go through this. She probably didn't even know the taste of thrice-refried beans. *No señor.* All he could picture her eating were vanilla milkshakes so thick she required a silver spoon to scoop them into her mouth. There, in the elegant dining room of her two-story home with the white picket fence, surrounded by well-dressed family like he saw on the TV sets at his friends' houses. With her daddy's brand-new Buick shining in the driveway, rosebushes blooming beneath her window. And someday he could have it all. Because he was going to be a pharmacist too. So he could take care of her. And give her the life he hadn't even dreamed of until then. Not this life of a *pobre méndigo* dozing off on a dirty floor. No, the life of creamy vanilla milkshakes and gleaming soda fountains. His fantasies drowning out the din of the tumultuous household, he slipped into sleep to the sound of Elvis echoing in his ears: "Please forget my past. The future looks bright ahead . . . I don't want no other love. Uh, baby, it's still you I'm thinking of."

THREE

At 1448 Garfield Street, Fulgencio's mother, Ninfa del Rosario Cisneros de Ramirez, still lived there all these years later, surrounded by sons who had never amounted to anything. On a compressed block of receding huts and shanties, crammed between the rushing traffic of Fourteenth Street and International Boulevard. It had once been a quiet neighborhood of decent, hardworking Mexican immigrant families, people searching for a better way for their children. It had once been a sleepy little village, dirt road, the cry of roosters punctuating the dewy dawn. Now the state was erecting an elevated highway right over the block. The newspaper said it would connect Fourteenth and International with the Free Trade Highway running between Mexico and the United States. Instead of choking up Fourteenth Street every night with diesel fumes and smokestack filth, the colorful parade of tractor trailers would slingshot over that loop, down the Highway, onto a Free Trade Bridge to the south, over the Rio Grande and into Mexico. But in the meantime, the last five years, to be exact, dust and caliche polluted the once-clean air of his youth, blanketing the tiny homes and decrepit cars with the fine, powdery soot of construction. The rising shadows of the cement behemoth loomed over 1448 Garfield, threatening to block out the sun fully and forever upon completion. The gaping jaws of steel girders hovered overhead, promising change, politicans calling it progress.

But this morning, Fulgencio scarcely noticed the mess, the diaper-clad children slopping in the puddles of mud and cement muck, the flea-bitten, mange-ridden dog lying dead on the cracked, weed-infested sidewalk. The rattle and roll of his 1978 Toyota pickup deteriorated into a tired cough and sigh as he slowed down and stopped steps from the waist-high chain link before the old house. No, today was different after all. No time to let the thoughts wander. Just time for action. The metal pickup door groaned shut, the chain link gate swung open and he strode toward the porch. Stetson hat pulled low over his brow. Khaki coat flowing like a cape in the chilly Gulf breeze. The mist of a dragon enveloping him.

The kitchen hadn't changed much through the decades. It was perpetually permeated by a warm, moist atmosphere and a heavy air thick with the smell of something recently baked or cooked, fried or refried. He pulled the screen door open and let himself in unceremoniously. Of all the unassuming houses on the block, Ninfa del Rosario's was the neatest, the cleanest, and the prettiest. For though she had not hailed from money or high society, she was raised proud and strong on the ranchlands of northern Mexico. Steel ran through her veins, and fire still burned in the coal of her eyes. Outside of her household, she had never expected or demanded much of life or the world she lived in, but within her dimunitive domain, she reigned as undisputed master since the death of her husband, Nicolas Ramirez

Sr. So to appease her unbroken pride and untamed temperament, Fulgencio kept the house painted and the yard mowed. He had offered to move her into a newer house in a more respectable part of town, but she had refused time and again.

"Coming from El Otro Lado was enough of a move to last me a lifetime," she'd say, referring to the other side of the river. "And I'm still not sure that it was worth it but that's what your father wanted, *que Dios lo guarde*."

The widow Ramirez stood at her spot by the stove as Fulgencio entered. Spoon in hand. *Chorizo con huevo* on the skillet. Fresh *tortillas de harina* on the comal. Little David, whose disabilities prevented him from living on his own, sat at the table dutifully consuming breakfast tacos.

Fulgencio often thought in passing, if his brothers could still be physically attached to her appendages, they would be. He wondered if she ever moved from that spot, the place from where she had struck him that evening long ago when he forgot her back medicine. Maybe she just stood there, waiting for her children and grandchildren to come and go. Like a piece of furniture, maybe she felt this was the place where she belonged, beneath this humble roof.

"What are *you* doing here?" she asked casually. "Did you read the obituaries? Did you see who died?" She pointed at the newspaper spread open on the table he'd flown under as a teenager, propelled by the force of her rage.

His throat tugged on his heart again as he glanced at the page and his eyes landed on the twenty-two letters. But she spoke of someone else.

"La Señora Villarreal passed yesterday," she chattered, stirring the eggs and chorizo. "Do you remember her, *m'ijo*? She was the one that first told you about that ridiculous *maldición*. You were in high school. Scared you half to death. Our families were related, distantly of course, from the days when our people were out on the ranches toward the beach. That's how she knew about it. *Como pasan los años.* Eighty-three years old! I'll be going to the *velorio* tonight. Who would have thought? She looked so good last week when I saw her at Lopez Supermarket with her daughter, you know, the one that buys her medicines from you."

He nodded, maneuvering around her on his way toward the back of the house.

"*Pobrecita*," she carried on, oblivious to his machinations. "They say she died of pneumonia. *Ni modo . . . así es la vida*," she exhaled, sighing and making the sign of the cross over her chest, raising the dainty silver crucifix dangling from her neck to her lips.

He passed through her simply furnished bedroom into one of the two back rooms, where his older brother Nicolas Jr. snored on a couch in his wife-beater and boxers, a half-empty bottle of cheap Scotch sitting next to a coffee mug on the hardwood floor.

"It seems these days I spend all of my time either at one of the nursing homes visiting a dying friend from church or at one of the funeral homes paying my last respects," she rattled on from the kitchen in a slightly louder tone so he could hear her musings. "I don't know what's wrong with this town. Babies born without brains. Cancer as common as colds. It's all because of the pollution being dumped by those maquiladoras into the river. And those doctors are nothing but thieves. *Una bola de sinvergüenzas.* They just take your money, prescribe antibiotics, and collect your Medicaid till you die. I hear some of them keep collecting it even after you die. That's how they afford those big mansions on Palm Boulevard."

He reached up high in a closet for an old wooden box that hadn't seen the light of day in decades. Blowing a cloud of dust off its treasure chest lid, he opened it, revealing its red velvet interior. He rifled deliberately through the contents: a red, white, and blue Junior Citizen pin, three miniature plastic footballs dipped in gold, the years 1956, 1957, and 1958 etched on them, a mother-of-pearl teething ring with a silver amulet hanging black, the initials F. R. C. (Fulgencio Ramirez Cisneros) engraved on it, a tarnished Lady Liberty silver dollar collecting grime since 1925, a gold twenty-peso coin minted in 1918 still shiny as the sun, and the object of his search hidden at the bottom in a miniature onionskin sack. Delicately, he extricated it, closed the coffer, and slid it back into the shadows. His brother snored. His mother rambled. A fragile chain spun of yellow gold slipped like silk into his giant, callused hand. A tiny, circular medallion still hung from the fragile braid. His thumb traced its surface. Madonna and Child. He flipped it over, reading the inscription on the smooth, reflective back: "*With Love. For Carolina. 1958.*"

"Poor Maria de la Luz Villarreal," his mother continued as he brushed by her on the way back to the kitchen door. "I remember, a long time ago, she actually did get pneumonia. Was it 1958? You had just graduated from high school. The whole town was in a panic that she'd die and leave all those poor children *huérfanos. Ay pobre mujer . . .*"

The door closed behind him as his determined face met the cold morning air again. It was always too warm in that house. The floor fans had to run full blast for him to breathe, no matter the season. Always steaming, even when it was freezing outside and rock solid oranges plummeted from trees, shattering into bittersweet shards on the brick patio backyard.

"*Mira*, how rude! You don't even say 'hello' or 'goodbye' anymore! Is that how a son treats his mother? This isn't a revolving door hotel, you know. It's still somebody's home!" He could hear his mother's cries from the echo chamber of his frigid little truck.

He smiled. It felt good. Been a long time since he had worked those neglected muscles around his mouth. The truck sputtered to life with a big clap from the muffler and a cloud of smoke. As he shot down the pothole-ridden street, he could hear her parting salvo, "Good thing you don't live here anymore, Fulgencio Ramirez!"

No, no señor. He hadn't lived under his mother's roof since he'd left home at sixteen, following one of Papá's drunken outbursts of gratuitous violence. Instead, he spent his nights across the border.

Pushing the accelerator against the cold metal floor, he traversed the bridge and sped down the two-lane highway to the ranch on the outskirts of Nueva Frontera, Mexico. The wind ripped through the pickup's skeletal cab as he hurtled toward El Dos de Copas. The Two of Cups. No one else from the family had been out there in eons. They considered it a waste of space. After all, the Two of Cups was the lowest playing card in the Spanish deck.

Fulgencio's maternal grandfather, Fernando Cisneros, had bestowed the sorry name on this lonesome plot of salted, worthless earth when it became the last scrap of land remaining in his name after a lifetime of gambling away the vast land holdings granted to his family in the 1600s by the King of Spain. He'd managed to keep it only because nobody would accept its deed as a wager during a devastating string of losses in the early 1900s. The Two of Cups wasn't even a pair. Nor was it even part of a full house. It was just a lonely, worthless card. Like him, a widower with a daughter—Ninfa del Rosario—who he'd been too afraid to love and raise.

There, on El Dos de Copas, Fulgencio Ramirez lived to this day, tracing the outline of his grandfather's shadow on the adobe wall, humming the same corridos and boleros Fernando Cisneros had sung lovingly to him through the years, sensing the caress of the Gulf breeze on his skin and smelling the sweet fragrance of manure suspended in the air. This was the land from whence his family came. Here he felt most at home. A cluster of cattle. A smattering of sheep. No one but the ghosts to talk to, no one but the spirits to listen, nothing but the past to render judgment.

He rumbled over the bumpy dirt road—lined by the towering mesquites he and his brothers had planted long ago as a punishment for drinking Papá's tequila on the Fourth of July—to his crumbling adobe home. He'd made some improvements since the day his grandfather had passed to El Otro Lado (not the other side of the river, rather the other side of the border between life and death), but it was still rustic by modern standards. All he required, though, were the basics: running water (not hot), electricity (sporadic), and gas he lugged from town in rusted butane tanks. Two rooms. The one you walked into and the one next to it with the cot, a rusty stove, a rattling fridge, and a creaky wooden table. Bald bulbs hung overhead. A relief of La Virgen de Guadalupe protruded from an otherwise featureless adobe wall.

According to his grandfather, the image of the Virgencita had simply appeared there one morning in his waning days, during the summer of 1955. Campesinos and ejidatarios had trudged for miles in pilgrimage to witness the apparition on El Dos de Copas, at which time, Fernando Cisneros had decided the miracle must be a sign from God for him to repent his ways in preparation for his approaching death and subsequent ascent into heaven.

"The beauty of Catholicism," he had pontificated to his grandson, "is that even if you spent your entire life sinning, you can die moments after repenting and still get into Heaven. So live it up, Fulgencio. Just don't let death catch you by surprise."

Fulgencio still vividly recalled how his grandfather had prepared for his impending doom, even though he seemed to be in perfect health, much to the astonishment of the town doctors who had expected him to perish from lung cancer or cirrhosis of the liver decades earlier. He enraged his daughter, son-in-law, and other grandchildren by willing El Dos de Copas directly to Fulgencio. He charged the campesinos ten pesos a head to sneak a peek at the Virgen de Guadalupe. He hung around long enough to accumulate enough money to pay off his debts so the authorities wouldn't take the piece of land from his grandson. And he bid adios to the only person he had ever allowed himself to care for in the world after his wife's premature death.

Fernando Cisneros had instructed Fulgencio to sit next to him on a pair of rusted tractor-trailer tire rims at the edge of a serene pond on the solemn ranch. Young Fulgencio, still a year or more from that transforming epiphany in Mendelssohn's Drugstore, listened while chewing on a straw of golden hay.

"*M'ijo, como dice la canción: 'Canta y no llores.'* As the song says, 'Sing and don't cry.' For it's time to say goodbye. I drank life like you do a fine tequila. I savored it. I let it seep slowly into my veins. I felt its fire deep in my belly. And now the taste is fading. It's time for me to go."

His mottled hand reached out, patting Fulgencio's cheek tenderly.

"I never thought I'd love again." Fernando Cisneros stared into the sunset without contracting the deep cracks fanning out like bird wings from his bloodshot hazel eyes. "But I have loved you." The words tumbled from his parched lips inadvertently. As if he were realizing this for the first and only time, and his thoughts had materialized into words weakly seeping from his unwitting lips.

His grandfather stood slowly but deliberately and walked straight as a board back toward the hut with his grandson in tow. In the long shadows of dusk, by the flickering light of a gas lamp, Fernando Cisneros kneeled before the Virgen de Guadalupe, made the sign of the cross, and shuffled over to his cot, stooping to pass beneath the arched opening separating the two rooms. He sipped tequila from a bottle perched on a milk crate serving as nightstand. Laying himself to rest, he looked at Fulgencio, who sat with his tears at the table in the front room.

"*M'ijo*, don't make the same mistake I did. Don't be afraid to love. If you love, you'll never truly be alone. You'll see, *m'ijo*. Now, go home and tell your mamá I've died. The money for my burial is in the metal box behind the fridge. Promise me you'll come out here often to look for me. Because if I can, I'll return to keep you company. And maybe from El Otro Lado I can help you figure out a way to avoid the same cursed fate, *la fe maldita*, that has plagued me my whole life. I may have been unlucky in love and unlucky in cards, but at least I got you. So, I'm not letting you go that easy."

Fulgencio nodded, brushing away his tears, struggling to act macho.

"Don't say anything," his grandfather whispered as the gas lantern sputtered out and the room plunged into darkness. "I know you love me too. Now go. It's time."

Fulgencio tried to find his legs beneath him. Struggled to swim through the numbness of his grandfather's death enveloping. He fled from the shadow of the Angel of Death. He streaked past the row of freshly planted mesquites. He bolted down the highway to his friend Cipriano's humble campesino farm, where he knew they'd give him a ride to the border crossing in town. Night was falling fast. And the lament of the crows punctuated the air with dismay. His grandfather, Fernando Cisneros, was dead.

Standing in that same hut, all these years later, he fastened a bolo tie around his neck. He threw a black western jacket over his shoulders in one compact motion. He secured his gun in its shoulder holster. And he straightened his black Stetson with one hand while he combed his mustache with the other. He didn't need a looking glass to tell him how he looked. It was high noon and time to go to the funeral. To meet Carolina once again. He kissed the ghost of his grandfather playing solitaire at the table. He plucked a single white rose that had sprung from the image of the Virgen de Guadalupe on the adobe wall. And he ducked into the blasting sun.

FOUR

He clutched a white rose between his teeth as he wiped his palms on his tuxedo pants. This was it. He stood on her doorstep with his racing heart in danger of slipping through his slick hands. A full moon illuminated the generous porch of the two-story white house with rosebushes beneath the windows. A '54 Chrysler Custom Imperial (borrowed from his best friend's dad) gleamed—moonlight reflecting off chrome—beyond the white picket fence. He ran his fingers through his wavy hair, then had to put the rose back in his mouth to wipe the Vaseline off his hands on the back of his pants. All right, enough already. In a final effort to get a grip on his nerves, he reminded himself who he was and what he was doing. He was Fulgencio Ramirez, junior, football player, about to escort the most beautiful girl in La Frontera—and, as far as he was concerned, the known world—to San Juan del Atole's homecoming dance. He took a deep breath and gazed up at the heavens. "Don't abandon me now," he whispered, lifting the knocker as if it weighed a thousand pounds.

"Don't abandon me now," was a line he seemed to be uttering all too often those days. He wasn't quite sure to whom it was directed. It might have been God or maybe the spirit of his dead grandfather, but either way it helped him feel slightly less alone on his improbable quest.

This moment at the Mendelssohn's front door had been over a year in the making. Since that first day at the drugstore, Fulgencio had finagled himself into the Academy of San Juan del Atole, a revered institution typically reserved for the region's monied class, and he'd worked diligently for Mr. Mendelssohn before and after school. At the crack of dawn, he arrived at the downtown storefront eager to impress. He was always the first one there, striding urgently past the shuttered shops lining the streets, rousing the pigeons as he whistled the Mexican tunes he adored. The cobblestone streets had just been paved over with concrete, and there were no city buses to ruin them yet. He glided across their smooth surfaces. He admired the newness of downtown, frozen in the sleepy repose of the cool, blue dawn. In the distance, the mourning doves stirred, their lamentful cries breaking the morning silence. While he waited for Mr. Mendelssohn to arrive, he would find something constructive to do. Mondays, he would wipe the store's display windows with a bucket and rag stashed in the alleyway. Tuesdays, he cleaned up the mess left by the garbage men. Wednesdays, he hosed off the sidewalk. Thursdays, he ran a quick tour of the nursing homes in the downtown area, picking up new batches of prescriptions for the *viejitos* inside. And Fridays, he sneaked into the kitchen of Maldonado's Cafe and cracked jokes with the cooks while he made breakfast for the pharmacy's staff.

Several months after he'd begun working at the store,

Fulgencio was startled to hear Mr. Mendelssohn call his name from beyond the shelves. Mr. Mendelssohn was a quiet man who rarely raised his voice. Usually, he'd walk to wherever a person was in order to address him. So, it was with mild trepidation that Fulgencio hurried to the back of the store.

"Yes, Mr. Mendelssohn? How can I help?"

Mr. Mendelssohn sat in the small corner office where he kept the books. It was little more than a broom closet stuffed with a small desk and chair, stacks of paperwork lining the walls.

In the dingy light of the windowless room, Mr. Mendelssohn removed his reading glasses and motioned for Fulgencio to take a seat on a packing crate that doubled as his guest chair.

"Fulgencio," he started. "How long is it now that you've been working here?"

"Four months, sir," Fulgencio answered quickly.

"And in all this time, every single morning you've been here ahead of the other employees, haven't you?"

"Yes, sir."

"You've cleaned and organized. You've hustled to the nursing homes for prescriptions. You've even cooked breakfast at Maldonado's Cafe and brought it to us free of charge." Mr. Mendelssohn recited as if he were reading from a list.

"Oh, they don't charge me for the food at Maldonado's, sir." Fulgencio shrugged. "The cooks like to joke with me in Spanish. They say I remind them of life back home in Mexico."

"That's beside the point, Fulgencio," Mr. Mendelssohn continued. "You are the hardest working person I have ever known. If you continue to live by this work ethic, you will go far in life."

Fulgencio felt a rush of blood within his chest and head, a surprising swelling of pride. He wasn't accustomed to compliments.

Mr. Mendelssohn quietly slid his desk drawer open and pulled out a shiny key. Extending it toward Fulgencio, he continued, "I want you to take this. You are the only person other than me with a key to this store. You've earned it. You can open the store and get it ready for business. And since you're always the last one to leave, you can lock up too."

Taking the key, Fulgencio thanked him.

"Just remember. The medicines behind the counter can be touched only by me. Only a pharmacist can handle those. Don't trust anyone that tells you otherwise. If you ever have a question, just ask."

"I won't let you down, Mr. Mendelssohn," Fulgencio promised.

"I know you won't, Fulgencio."

Armed with Mr. Mendelssohn's trust, Fulgencio was poised to pursue an even more precious prize: his daughter's heart.

Throughout the course of that first year, Fulgencio took every chance he could to chat with Carolina when she came in with her friends. She, in turn, seemed intrigued by him, his olive skin, his dark hair, his boundless energy. She had even gone as far as telling him that none of the other Mexican boys in town ever dared even look her in the eye, much less muster up conversation with her.

"I hope you don't find me too bold," Fulgencio had responded.

"I find you refreshing." She smiled mischievously. "My parents say it's okay to be friends with all kinds of people, but I've never tested their resolve."

"Friends?" Fulgencio pondered aloud. He hoped to push the boundaries of her parents' principles as soon as possible. To that end, he offered to help Carolina with her Spanish homework, right there at the soda fountain beneath her father's watchful gaze.

Gladly, she began availing herself of his tutoring services. She loved listening to his tongue roll the *r*'s, and his accent swept her imagination away to more exotic lands.

After Mr. Mendelssohn gave him the drugstore key, Fulgencio began to draw upon his entrepreneurial instincts to make the business increasingly profitable. Before, the soda fountain had never opened for business prior to lunch, but now—thanks to Fulgencio's budding culinary gifts, breakfast was served bright and early. And unlike at Maldonado's Cafe, Fulgencio's patrons could complement their breakfasts with any of a number of herbal concoctions he had learned from his mother.

Pancho the Carpenter came in every morning at 5:30 a.m., ordering *chorizo con huevo* with a *te de yerba buena*. He'd leave with a full belly, the town paper, and a candy bar for the midmorning hunger pains he experienced. The *yerba buena* soothed his troubled stomach (and if that didn't work, the Milky Way would).

Cruz the Plumber religiously ordered *chilaquiles* with a side of *papa cocida con hoja del chile piquín*. Fulgencio's potato *piquín* production cleared Cruz's mind, enabling him to see plumbing problems more clearly. Of course, now that he was stopping by Mendelssohn's Drugstore every morning, he also filled his mother's prescription there, instead of at Riley's Pharmacy uptown. Just like Pancho and Cruz, a steady stream of other hardworking immigrants found comfort in Fulgencio's soda fountain breakfasts. Fulgencio would recount stories his grandfather had told him on the ranch. He began singing the songs his grandfather had taught him. Old Mexican favorites like "Sin Ti" and "Cuatro Vidas," tunes from the golden age of romantic Mexican songwriting. Soon, Fulgencio was bringing in more money for Mr. Mendelssohn before he rushed off to school than the store made the rest of the day. Such was the trend that one day even Old Man Maldonado from the eponymously named Maldonado's Cafe poked his head in and—gawking at the crowd assembled at the soda fountain, the trio strumming their guitars, and Fulgencio Ramirez flipping an omelet while belting out "La Barca de Oro"—shouted, "So, this is where everyone went! Well, what the hell, Fulgencio Ramirez. You can have the morning. I'll take the rest. Now serve me up some *chilaquiles*, and I'll pay you a buck to sing 'Veracruz.'" The crowd burst into laughter as Old Man Maldonado pulled up an extra chair and slapped a George Washington on the countertop. Even some of Maldonado's cooks emerged from the shadows of the store's shelves to share a cup of *te de yerba buena* with their jovial boss, who had shown such graciousness in the face of utter defeat.

Inspired by Fulgencio's zeal, Carolina designed new menus for the soda fountain, featuring Fulgencio's yearbook picture in the upper right-hand corner. She began to visit the drugstore more frequently, eating breakfast with her father at the counter while listening in wide-eyed amazement to Fulgencio's singing, and later returning after school to seek his "help" with her Spanish homework. Fulgencio was beginning to suspect that she was more fluent in his first language than she was letting on, and this possibility of her growing attraction thrilled him.

Stirred by her presence, he added more romantic ballads to his repertoire, thinking of her as his voice sailed through the rafters. And he worked harder than ever to impress her father. Motivated by his desire to be embraced not only by Carolina but also by her family, Fulgencio developed a strategy to generate an unprecedented increase in prescription referrals. Every morning, he cooked extra breakfast tacos. These he wrapped in foil to keep warm and bagged in simple brown bags. In exchange for a meal, he managed to motivate El Perico Juarez (widely regarded as the town lunatic) to run around town delivering the bags to all of the doctors' offices, nursing homes, and hospital administrators. "Compliments of Arthur Mendelssohn, RPh," he scribbled with a fountain pen on the bags.

During that year, at both the drugstore and the Academy, Fulgencio's spirits soared. Pouring every free moment and extra ounce of energy into lifting weights at the school gym, Fulgencio had transformed himself into a formidable football player. While on the field, Fulgencio was driven by the hunger of Carolina's eyes boring into him from where she stood at the foot of the bleachers with the other cheerleaders.

As Fulgencio's confidence boomed, Mr. Mendelssohn's books ballooned. The astute pharmacist expanded the drugstore the moment the saw shop next door cleared out. Fulgencio was given new kitchen equipment to work with and carte blanche on the ordering of food products from Lopez Supermarket.

As summer approached, the *La Frontera Times* announced that Riley's Pharmacy would be closing its doors. Fulgencio Ramirez had sent Old Man Riley packing back to Waco to work for a regional chain.

The evening Riley's closed for the last time, Fulgencio appeared with a trio of guitarists at the front door. The shelves had all been cleared out and the store gaped cold and cavernous. Fulgencio's powerful voice reverberated through the vacant metal of the fixtures. They sang Mr. Riley songs of farewell. Fulgencio gave him an amulet dipped in a special holy herbal potion of his own invention, shook his hand, and wished him well. The vanquished Irishman took it on the chin, knowing the young boy—though filled with hubris—meant well. But he could not bear to be as generous in retreat as Fulgencio Ramirez was in victory. As the door closed shut behind the trio, Fulgencio could have sworn he heard the pharmacist bitterly mutter to himself, "Damn Mexicans."

The day he came home from serenading Mr. Riley, Fulgencio's smile was so broad it barely fit through the door as he burst into the unusually quiet kitchen. Without warning, his father's hand flew from where he sat with his back to the door, striking Fulgencio across the face so hard he flew straight out the kitchen window, rolled off the porch, and landed in a muddy bed of rosebushes out front. Covered in thorns and scattered rose petals, Fulgencio tasted the tears of his childhood resurfacing against his will on bloodied lips. His mother's frenzied screams and the sound of furniture breaking and dishes shattering emanated from the house. How could such a small space generate so much noise and pain? He sat helplessly in the muck, listening to his younger siblings cry in panic. Would they be next? Of course, this was why his older brother, Nicolas Junior, had enlisted in the army the first chance he got, shipping out to Korea months shy of finishing high school. It seemed his brother's absence only served to expand the target on Fulgencio's back.

"Why?" Fulgencio pondered. Was it the song he had been whistling as he skipped joyfully up the steps? Was it the cologne he was wearing? Was it the crispness of his white linen suit contrasted with his father's filthy tire shop overalls? As he pulled himself up by the thorns on the towering bushes, more blood pouring from his dirty hands, he finally realized it didn't matter why. He simply couldn't let it happen again. The blows had nothing to do with him. They had to do only with the man who dealt them. His father had yearned to give his family the American dream, to make up for the Mexican Nightmare he had lived as an orphan, roaming from town to town begging for food during the Revolution, sleeping wherever he could find shelter or work. And still he toiled in the darkness of his tire shop on the south side of the river to support the family he both adored and despised on El Otro Lado. But it was obvious to Fulgencio that his father's daily crossing of the river failed to cleanse him of his demons, failed to purify him of his tormented thoughts. There were times when his father just had to hit someone, anyone standing nearby. He regularly exacted revenge for the hand he'd been dealt, making it quite clear that at least his children had a father and a mother and a roof over their heads. And as far as he was concerned, that meant he had far exceeded his responsibilities in the world.

"You dare mock me with your English and your math. You taunt me with your pretty clothes and your private school. Feel a little pain so you can know your father," Nicolas Ramirez Sr. savagely intoned as he threw the screen door open and stepped out onto the porch, glowering down at Fulgencio who stood awkwardly in the mud. "This isn't suffering. This is easy. *Bola de llorones*, cry babies, *cobardes. Que se vayan a la chingada*," he yelled indignantly, climbing into his battered '49 Nash. The engine rumbled noisily as he drove toward the nearest cantina to drown his woes in the elixir of forgetfulness.

Fumes enveloped Fulgencio as he watched his father go from his spot in the mire surrounded by rose petals and pierced by the thorns. A searing pain twisted through his innards like a river of molten lava, his eyes smoldering with restrained rage as he squinted at the receding red taillights. How quickly his father could transmute joy into fury. Incensed, Fulgencio unleashed an unintelligible, primal scream, kicking the tattered rosebushes, tearing at them with his bare, wounded hands until the plants were completely obliterated. Cursing and spitting and grunting as he destroyed the bed of roses, he lost all sense of his surroundings. When he was finished, he fell to his knees panting, blood stained, and mud streaked. He looked up to see his mother, Little David, and Fernando gawking at him in a shocked mixture of horror and fear through the kitchen's screen door.

That night, Fulgencio packed a bag, an old leather suitcase left to him by his grandfather. He would have moved out to El Dos de Copas, but he didn't have a car. He would have ridden a horse, but they wouldn't have permitted him to cross back and forth with such a beast. So instead, he walked ten blocks west to the nicer part of downtown, where his best school buddy lived. Here the driveways were wide and paved with concrete, instead of narrow pairs of grooves worn in weed-infested dirt. Here the lawns were pristine and manicured, instead of overgrown and covered in forgotten refuse like rusted tire rims and crumbling barbecue pits. Here the houses were painted bright colors, instead of peeling and leaning and threatening collapse.

As he shuffled up the walkway to the front door, Fulgencio admired the fleet of gleaming cars parked in the driveway, one for each member of the family.

When Bobby's mom opened the door and witnessed his gruesome state, she seemed to understand his plight without posing any questions. He wondered if perhaps his family's reputation had preceded him.

"You poor boy," she soothed, taking his bag and guiding him

gently to Bobby's bedroom in the back of the spacious home. "Let's get you cleaned up and tend to those cuts."

That night, he slept on a blanket on the hardwood floor. The next day, Bobby and his dad brought another bed from his grandmother's house down the street.

Now his father could not knock him down from his place atop the world, Fulgencio thought lying in the darkness of Bobby Balmori's bedroom. He listened to the whir of the metal fan by the window, the rhythmic song of the cicadas oscillating outside. He felt the beads of sweat trickle down his face, onto his shoulders and back. He gazed at the distant stars and wished he could be out at El Dos de Copas singing a song with his grandfather. Practicing like he used to, sitting on the roof of the adobe hut and singing at the top of his lungs. This is how his grandfather had trained him to develop such a powerful vocal instrument. So strong had his voice become that people on neighboring ranches and farms would drag their rocking chairs onto their patios on the nights they knew he was visiting and listen to the corridos he and Fernando Cisneros sang, their voices carried on the gentle breezes of the Gulf for miles on end.

But now those days seemed long gone, as distant as the feeble stars dimmed by the growing lights of the city. And although his father would assault him no further with his fists or with his belt, a lonesome wrath twisted through him like a venomous knife, like the hunger he had known as a child, eating the thrice-refried beans that tasted like the dirt that mingled with the tears on the floor beneath the kitchen table. Maybe he had been given a chance at this *Sueño Americano*, but he felt inexplicably robbed of something greater.

Lying restlessly in the dark, Fulgencio was consumed by

longing. And then rage. It made him angry to want for so much and yet have nothing at all. For the first time, he felt overwhelmed by intense impatience. He yearned to belong to this world in which he did not even possess a dignified home. He desperately craved Carolina Mendelssohn's sanctifying love the way a pirate greedily thirsted for treasure to alter his position in the social order.

With the new school year approaching, he felt a sense of urgency to finally make his move. He would be a junior. Girls from both sides of the river were talking about him, flocking to parties and dances for a chance to hear him sing. Fulgencio determined it was time to reach for the ultimate prize. He resolved to invite Carolina to the homecoming dance as soon as the new school year commenced.

He caught her by surprise one evening amidst the towering pharmacy fixtures. He had just returned from delivering medicines on the store bicycle, and she was absorbed in restocking the shelves, teetering precariously two feet above the ground. Startled by his footsteps, she slipped and nearly crashed to the floor, only to be caught by his sturdy arms and eased gently down, like a feather gracefully floating.

As he held her close, their eyes locked. There was nowhere to turn, no way to avert each other's gaze. A wave rippled between them, like heat rising from a scalding highway. He asked her in a flurry of impromptu bravado.

"Yes, of course," she answered, her breath agitated. "I'd be delighted to be your date."

And now here he was, praying to his dead grandfather on the steps to Mr. Arthur Mendelssohn's well-appointed house on homecoming night, clad in a borrowed black tuxedo, white rose trembling in sweaty Vaseline hand, as the door swung open, bathing him in a warm and otherworldly golden light.

He was greeted by Carolina's mother, whose watery gray eyes scanned him skeptically as she motioned for him to enter the foyer. He'd never been in a foyer before, he thought. Rich white people had space to spare.

Frail by nature and rendered pale by chronic illness, Mrs. Mendelssohn radiated a gentle—if brittle—beauty. She guided Fulgencio to the plastic-shrouded sofa in the formal living room. His eyes wandered over crystal knickknacks and porcelain figurines and dowdy paintings bought in the town's uppity furniture store, Mr. Egglestein's Town & Country. Everything appeared so perfect to him, so otherworldy. This was a lady's room. A room for sitting with other ladies, eating finger sandwiches and drinking from teacups resting on doilies. He had never seen these kinds of things in person until he'd moved into Bobby Balmori's house. He'd only heard mention of them on TV shows glimpsed at the Sears & Roebuck, flickering in black and white on vacuum tubes encased in wooden consoles. But thanks to Bobby Balmori's family, he'd picked up knowledge to survive in this alien world, at least for a night.

Sitting on the edge of the sofa in Carolina Mendelssohn's formal living room, witnessing her float down the stairs like an angel in white, he also knew he would do whatever it took to learn what was required to qualify for permanent admission into her world.

Rising to his feet, the rose fell from his hands. Rushing to recover it from the red carpet, he pricked his thumb on a thorn. With the faintest of grimaces for all his awkwardness, his hazel eyes met her golden. Her lips unfurled into a conquering smile, "Be careful. You might hurt yourself."

He felt himself tumbling, lost in a tide of golden curls. He searched for words he'd never find because they'd never been invented. "You're beautiful," he whispered, drowning in the equally golden sea of her eyes as the white rose passed from his numbed fingers into her wispy white hands.

She leaned in as if to share a naughty secret with him, her face alive with mischief. He felt her sweet breath upon his lips as she mouthed the words slowly, "I know."

FIVE

Nobody liked a funeral, even if it belonged to someone they utterly despised. Not even Fulgencio Ramirez in his black Western suit and matching Stetson hat with the gun lurking beneath the jacket and the white rose firmly in hand. *No señor*. Death to him was not a welcome sensation. But, unfortunately, it was one that had seeped into his bones long ago. Therefore, he found the ceremony surrounding death to be a cumbersome custom. After all, he thought, you could dress up death any way you like, but in the end it would still stink.

Vultures circled over the small but obligatory gathering of perturbed relatives, weeping mothers, and black-veiled *abuelitas* who shuffled from gravesite to gravesite, arranging their funereal schedule in accordance with the timing of the shadows afforded by the clumps of trees scattered throughout the cemetery. Even on these wintry days, the sun worked its wondrous damage if one stood still too long. But beneath his broad-rimmed hat, Fulgencio was safe from the savagery of the light as well as from the vituperations of the vultures, which were renowned for vindictively directing their discharge at mourners concealing ulterior motives. He didn't doubt this local legend. Maybe a vulture could aim at those it discerned to be of its own kind. Maybe these women's mournful cries could blend with the vultures' shrieks into a final farewell song for the dead. Regardless, he was certain the vultures would not be shitting on anyone that day. This was a surety because the twenty-two lettered man had nothing to leave behind except a sour taste in the mouths of all whose lives he'd marred with his presence. There would be no anticipated reading of the will. No fighting amongst his heirs for coveted bounties and the spoils of a prosperous life. *No señor.* None of that on the campo santo today. Padre Juan Bacalao could pray all he wanted, but the church wasn't getting a penny from this worthless bastard's estate. The bishop would have to look elsewhere. The feast put on hold. And as for plotting to pilfer Carolina's heart, Fulgencio could not be blamed for reclaiming something that had been given to him in the first place, at least until Miguelito and Mexican black magic had meddled, muddled, and made a mess of their lives.

Miguel Rodgriguez Esparza had been one of the few individuals within whom Fulgencio could find absolutely no redeeming quality. In fact, Miguelito was so despicable that Fulgencio had determined long ago he wasn't even worth the cost of killing, putting a premature end to his life. No, that would have been both too easy to accomplish and too costly in the aftermath. Sure, Fulgencio had at times employed violent means to accomplish just ends. Blood had been spilled. Wives transformed into widows. Children into orphans. But not Miguelito. No, it would be too banal, too crass, to be expected. If he had allowed his jealous rage to guide his retaliatory actions against Miguelito, he would have spent the rest of his life in a maximum-security prison. And then he would have never had a chance to set things right with Carolina. So he had chosen to wait for the inevitable. Let nature take its course. Let Miguelito slowly squander his own life away on liquor, cigarettes, and whores. Besides, he knew Carolina would never accept him as a convicted murderer. Unlike the Ramirez and Cisneros clans which long had run wild on the highlands of Mexico, the daughter of Mr. Arthur Mendelssohn, RPh, was a civilized lady whose love was destined to operate within the limits of proper society. So, he had patiently waited, watching from afar. Just as he did now, standing beneath the oscillating shadows of a mangled mesquite tree on a mound, tortured limbs extending toward the heavens. The faint aroma of incense wafted past him on the breeze. He witnessed El Padre Bacalao making all sorts of signs and gestures with his robed arms in the wind as the wooden box was lowered into the ground. *¡Adios, amigo!* A fate sealed in soil, in *saecula saeculorum*. The priest and his cross vanished, fleeing like the vultures. The crowd scattered like ashes, and only a small cluster of hobbled women draped in black propped up the veiled Carolina in her solemn promenade back to the limousine.

He moved hastily from the shadows of the mesquite, on a trajectory calculated to intersect her path.

He didn't heed the murmurs rising from the widow's entourage.

"*¿Quien viene allí?*"

"*Dios mio, ¿Quien es ese hombre?*"

"I can't believe the nerve. It's Fulgencio Ramirez."

As the women protectively circled the wagons, his eyes struggled desperately to penetrate the veil concealing her face.

"Carolina, I brought you this . . ." He held out the rose, his eyes melting for an instant, pleading for a sign.

As the women pushed her into the waiting car, he heard her speak for the first time in those long and excruciating twenty-five years. He heard her agonized cry as clearly as he'd heard his mother's exhalation of rage, passion, and boundless pain the day they had lowered his father into the ground.

"No," Carolina Mendelssohn sobbed. "Not him. He's the one to blame. He's the one that ruined my life."

The dilapidated funeral home limo rambled away, past the towering wrought iron gates to the burial ground. The white rose dropped to the grass beneath Fulgencio's shiny black boots. He clutched his chest as he watched her go, his fingers finding the delicate medallion he still carried in his shirt pocket.

"It's okay," he told himself, his head rocking back and forth ever so slightly beneath the late afternoon sun. "I've waited this long. I can wait a little longer. After all, without love we're dead." He watched her vanish around a bend in the road, a heap of fresh dirt punctuating the death of his treacherous friend in the background. Fate and time finally on his side, Fulgencio hungered to begin again.

SIX

Disrupting the spell of Fulgencio's enchantment with Carolina, her father emerged from his den on the opposite side of the foyer. Fulgencio nearly jumped in surprise at the sight of Mr. Arthur Mendelssohn, RPh, in casual clothes. He resembled one of those golfers he'd seen in the *gringo* magazines—polo shirt, plaid slacks, all-American. As Fulgencio sought to rediscover his ability to speak, Mr. Mendelssohn rescued him from further embarrassment.

"Fulgencio." He smiled tersely. "What a surprise to see you outside of work."

"Yes, sir." Fulgencio fumbled nervously. "It's quite a surprise to see you in anything but your white lab coat, Mr. Mendelssohn."

"Yes, well, life is about more than just work, Fulgencio," Mr. Mendelssohn said, slinging his arm around Carolina's bare shoulders as if he wished he could transform it into a scarf.

That statement by Mr. Mendelssohn would jostle about in Fulgencio's mind for years to come, taunting him through those long stretches when relentless toil would be his only refuge from failure in love.

"Yes, Fulgencio. There's work and then there's play," Arthur Mendelssohn continued, "And you better play it safe with my daughter. I want her home at a decent hour."

Fulgencio snapped to attention, "Yes, sir. You have nothing to worry about. Your daughter will be safe with me."

Her eyes twinkled with mischief as she took him by the hand and pulled him toward the door. As they headed down the walkway to Mr. Balmori's gleaming vehicle, Fulgencio looked over his shoulder at the silhouette of Mr. and Mrs. Arthur Mendelssohn, standing arm in arm in the doorway, expressions of concern clouding their faces glowing white in the moonlight.

"The real question is: will *you* be safe with *me*?" Carolina whispered as they approached the showboat car, her glamorous reflection on the spotless window. He pulled the massive metal door open for her and helped her step in, her long dress rustling in tow. As the engine roared to life, Fulgencio and Carolina waved goodbye through the car window.

***

The air in the black '54 Imperial was tense and chilled. Cold metal. Vast vinyl. And the endless expanse of the dash. Carolina's preferred way of dispelling tension was frantic activity. Whenever she was not fully at ease, she simply buzzed like a bee. Flying from one side of the room to the other, messing with things, rearranging sweet nothings. Of course, in the car she couldn't quite do that, so the radio was her best recourse. As Fulgencio cautiously steered toward the San Juan del Atole campus, she played with the chrome knobs set squarely in the center of the dash. The tiny red line danced around as she twirled the knobs, cutting from one song to another, crackling static between.

"*Rancheras*, no!" she exclaimed, skimming past a station from El Otro Lado. "*Conjunto.* God, no!" She jumped in disgust at the awkward accordions. "Oooh, Elvis . . . yes!" she delighted, her hands in the air, her smile quickening Fulgencio's pulse. He was trying to remain calm, but all this energy was more than he could handle at the moment. He yanked the steering wheel to the right and pulled the car to an abrupt stop by the side of the abandoned road. As she turned her head to either side wondering what was going on, he extinguished "Hound Dog" with resolve.

"What?" Carolina protested, wide-eyed, unaccustomed to such contrary behavior from anyone, especially a boy. "I liked that song!"

He furrowed his brow, rubbing his temples and eyes with his right hand to clear his mind.

"Carolina," Fulgencio said. "There's something I've been wanting to tell you for a long time. But it never seems to be the right moment at the pharmacy. Old Vera is always keeping an eye on us. I think maybe your dad asked her to."

"What is it? You're talking in circles."

"Someday, I want to marry you."

Her eyes opened wide, and she began laughing nervously. "Are you crazy? We're on our first date."

"I've known since the day we first met."

"You need to slow down and loosen up, Fully," she said.

"Fully?" Fulgencio's face contorted in a mixture of surprise, amusement, and disgust.

"Yes, for Fulgencio." She continued, "If all you ever think of is work, marriage, and the future," she waved her hands in the air as she talked, moonlight bouncing off the diamonds adorning her wrists and fingers, "you'll never enjoy life itself."

"Life itself?" he echoed in a daze, as if the concept had never occurred to him. He had conversed with Carolina in her father's drugstore many times over the last year, but it was always with his heart beating so hard he could hardly breathe or maintain his balance. He could barely listen to whatever she was saying because of the tremendous amount of concentration required to maintain his cool, calm exterior while also absorbing the magnetic power of her beauty. Now, it seemed to Fulgencio as if she were speaking to him for the first time. Here in the dark refuge of Mr. Balmori's car. His heart still raced, but for a moment he was not playing a role. He was listening.

He sensed the masks were about to drop. He was on the verge of connecting on a deeper level with her, to seeing beyond her looks and her money and her Anglo ways, to touching something noncorporeal, something intangible yet real. And then, suddenly, her genuinely spoken words washed away like the surf on the beach near El Dos de Copas, their meaning receding from his grasp, a low rumble of white noise rising up in his mind and drowning them out, the static interference growing into a thunderous sound, the reverberation of a thousand waves churning tempestuously. He heard words, but they were not Carolina's. Her lips were moving, but instead of hearing her, all he could fathom was a distant, ancient voice speaking in an unintelligible alien language. Strange words. Mystical incantations. Menacing iterations brimming with the kind of power that lurked beneath the deceptively calm waters he'd seen at the spot near the old family lands where the Rio Grande flowed out to the Gulf. Waters that would seduce you with their docile surface only to drown you in an instant, his grandfather had once warned him as a boy. And something he never thought possible happened as he gawked at Carolina and struggled to listen to her through the waves of disembodied sound flowing through him. Before his very eyes—shining greener than ever with astonishment—Carolina Mendelssohn physically and spiritually transformed into something even more beguiling, angelic, and captivating. She was more than the boss's daughter, more than the prettiest girl in town, more than a person; she was a dream, a goddess in his eyes. She was something to aspire to, to reach for, but could he ever possess her like a macho was supposed to possess a woman? Could he ever hang on to her? Was he worthy of her? Just a poor son of dirty, refried-bean eating immigrants, like him? Could he ever stand a chance?

Suddenly, he snapped out of his surreal waking dream, alarmed and perplexed. Was he suffering from a bizarre medical condition? Should he turn the car around and rush back to Mr. Mendelssohn for help? He struggled to refocus on Carolina's conversation.

"You know, Fulgencio," she said with a tone of authority, as if she'd read it in a book, "we're not machines. We're not gods. We don't have to waste all our time trying to reach some perfect image we've dreamed up for ourselves. We're just people. Human beings. Surviving. We have to let things be. Enjoy. Relax."

"Relax?" Fulgencio was not familiar with this word.

"Oh, Fully," she went on, "what is it you're working so hard for?"

The answer was—of course—her. But he couldn't say that. No, not yet. That would be showing his hand way too early in the game. On the other hand, he had inadvertently proposed marriage, sort of. He winced from the pain in his head. What an idiot. He'd been preparing for this moment, body, mind, and soul for an entire year and he had not planned his script for their first date. And now, he was hearing things and doubting himself at the worst possible moment.

He stared at the speedometer beyond the chrome-coated steering wheel.

"Well?" she asked. "What are you trying to accomplish?"

In lieu of the truthful answer, Fulgencio resorted to one of the truisms and *dichos* he often heard fly from his mother's mouth. "¡*Trabaja . . . sin cesar . . . trabaja*!" he said. "That's my philosophy," he added trying to regain his composure. "Work is all I know. It's in my blood. It's the way I express myself!" he declared triumphantly.

"Hmm." She frowned, leaning in toward him, looking intently into his eyes. "I don't know about that, Fulgencio." She shook her head slowly. "The way you sing, that's how you express yourself. The way you make people feel good and special when they come into the pharmacy. They know you have love in your heart. They know you're a generous spirit. You always give your all. I think that's how you express yourself."

He was taken aback, speechless. He'd never been analyzed to this degree. It was flattering but also disconcerting.

Suddenly, her face lit up. "I know!" she shouted, jumping up and down in her seat. "Maybe you can be a singer when you grow up. You have the voice and the looks. You could be like that guy in the Mexican movies . . . Pedro . . . What's his last name?"

"Pedro Infante?" he ventured, somewhat stunned. Sure, he'd mused once or twice about singing, atop a horse, with a charro hat in hand, but that wasn't the life for Carolina Mendelssohn's husband. That represented the old way of life south of the river, not the American dream. In Mexico, audiences saw a hero in Pedro Infante, a Mexican cowboy, an icon on a horse with a hat, a pistol, and a celestial voice. In America, the gringos would only see a fall-down-drunk Mexican fool, a pauper, someone to shoot at.

"Yeah," she said excitedly. "You could be the Mexican Elvis!" Her hands landed firmly on his shoulder as she looked up at him, her golden eyes glimmering in the moonlight.

"But . . ." He paused. "I'm going to be a pharmacist like your father." That was the only way he knew of giving her the life to which she was accustomed. And if it wasn't what she wanted, it was surely what she needed, not some *pobre diablo* scraping out a meager living singing in cantinas, praying for an improbable shot at fleeting fame. *No, no señor.* Sure, he loved to sing, but he would be a pharmacist. And that was all there was to it.

"Pharmacy?" she thought out loud. "It doesn't sound quite as exciting, but you seem so determined. I like that about you."

"I hope that's not the only thing you like?" he asked, hope filling his voice.

She smiled slyly. "Fully, you don't expect me to spill all my secrets, do you?" Her tide of whimsy subsided as she sighed reassuringly, "Pharmacy is a good profession, or so my father says."

He smiled as his world settled back into its familiar order, into the comfort of his illusory dreams. He breathed a sigh of relief because for a moment Carolina had frightened him (as had the mysterious incantations he'd heard). Somehow, the door had been pried open just a crack for the demons of doubt to slip in momentarily. But now all was well. He could feel her soft, sweet breath on his neck as her head rested on his shoulder, quiet now, calm now. For the first time, he felt truly comfortable in her presence as he guided the car around the corner and onward toward the homecoming dance. She now knew his intentions and she had not fled from the vehicle. Instead, for once, she was quiet and at peace. He angled the rearview mirror downward so he could look at her unobtrusively, finding her ruby lips curved into a gentle smile. Her long sloping eyelashes fluttered shut, and she chuckled softly to herself for a moment.

"What?" he asked.

"Fully."

SEVEN

The previous evening, Brother William's boys from the Academy of San Juan del Atole had fully demolished their opposition at the homecoming game. "Fifty-one to zero," the scoreboard at Canaya's Field had read. The score reflected the infinite mercy of Brother William, who played the freshmen during the fourth quarter to avoid further rolling up the score.

"Never kick an opponent when he's down!" Brother William would lecture the boys in his booming voice. He was half-German, half-Irish, and 100 percent devoted to winning football games. Tall and athletic despite his age, he snapped his commands like a seasoned field general, carrying a long reed, his whipping stick. No one had ever seen him use it in public, but legends and rumors of both his disciplinary fervor and his unusual provenance had circulated the dimly lit halls of the Catholic school on Elizabeth Street for decades.

No one knew exactly how long his tenure at the Academy had endured, but its longevity was unprecedented within a brotherly order that typically transferred its members every few years. Some theorized the true reason Brother William had eluded this virtuous vagabond's life was that he wasn't really a member of the Order anymore. These heretics posited that Brother William had been kicked out of the Brotherhood eons ago, shortly after his arrival in La Frontera, over a confrontation with the school's headmaster at the time. This legend had it that in the days of the Mexican Revolution, Brother William arrived fresh-faced and still wet behind the ears. Like most of the other brothers in those days, he had sailed on a boat from Ireland. But to the chagrin of the headmaster, and unlike any of the other religiously punctual members of the Order, Brother William arrived four months behind schedule. Looking disheveled in linen pants and a sky blue guayabera, Brother William burst into the headmaster's office without knocking.

According to most accounts compiled from the recollections of the school secretary, who listened through the keyhole while crouching at the door, the conversation that followed set the tone for what would become La Frontera's most triumphant sports legacy.

"You are four months and two hours late, Brother," the headmaster spoke, straining to conceal the anger his reddened face betrayed. "What do you have to say for yourself?"

"I apologize if I have inconvenienced you in any way, Brother," the tardy one responded, "but I assure you I was delayed in the service of God."

"I understand you made unscheduled detours and stops in the ports of Yucatan and Veracruz before resuming your course to La Frontera. Those ports are hundreds of miles south of here. Why have you done this?"

"The answer to that question is simple," Brother William replied. "To learn."

"Expand."

Brother William leaned forward in the uncomfortably rigid chair. "Have you ever been to Mexico? Beyond Nueva Frontera?"

"No. Nor do I care to. It's a filthy backwater." The headmaster turned up his ruddy nose.

"Ah, but from that backwater come the ancestors of over ninety percent of our students. More than half of our boys speak the language of Cortez in their humble homes here in our own little backwater. And the soccer teams of the Mexican villages from whence their forefathers hailed are among the best in the world."

"So, you're telling me you went to Mexico to learn Spanish and watch dirty kids play soccer in the mud?" The headmaster's voice rose in tandem with his generous body. "I have half a mind to excommunicate you right here, right now!"

"How can we teach, when we ourselves do not know?" sought Brother William. "How can I communicate with someone whose language I do not speak, whose customs I ignore?"

"You've ignored a great many things, Brother William," the headmaster spoke in a tired and pompous tone, extracting a sheet of parchment his desk. "Most importantly, you've ignored your obligation to me."

"I'll make you a deal, headmaster," proposed Brother William, his voice soaring with emotion. "Excommunicate me as much as you want but let me do the work of God here at San Juan del Atole. I bring victory in my veins. I will teach these sorry children from this miserable border town how to win! I will show them how they can find within themselves the strength to overcome obstacles that would daunt a giant. I will show them how, together, they can bring glory to the Lord through their communal actions, rising beyond the meager hand that fate has dealt them!" The room hung in suspense, the velvet curtains held their dusty breath. The school secretary crouched at the keyhole, biting her lips nervously.

"Clearly, Brother William, you are inspired," the headmaster conceded. "But inspiration does not suffice within the halls of this institution. Discipline is the key to achieving success. It is a necessary and vital element within any decent Christian life."

"I couldn't agree more!" Brother William leaned over the desk, his nose nearly touching the headmaster's. "It shall take both discipline and inspiration to rally the spirits of these lackluster boys."

"Still," the headmaster continued, twirling a quill in his hand and waving it in circles over the parchment on his desk. "You broke the rules."

"Indeed," admitted Brother William, returning to his awkward chair, perplexed by the dilemma. "I tell you what, Brother. You excommunicate me, but you allow me to remain here at San Jan del Atole Academy as long as at least one of the school's teams wins a championship each year. I don't care about the formalities anymore. I just want to do the work of God and I know that this is where I'm meant to do it."

"So be it then." The headmaster nearly yelled in jubilation at the compromise Brother William had devised. "You're excommunicated." He signed the certificate with a flourish of the feathered pen and slid it across the desk. "Just sign here." He pointed at a spot on the parchment.

Brother William gleefully obliged. Both parties were pleased. The headmaster knew that under the pressure of being booted onto the spare streets of La Frontera, excommunicated from the order, and with no return ticket to Ireland, the penniless coach would be compelled to deliver the goods. And for him, as he would later confess to his gossipy secretary, his lifelong dream had come true. He had excommunicated someone. This Brother William had surely won his heart. As he walked him out the door arm in arm, they chatted of the green meadows of Ireland and the places they'd both been. The school secretary stumbled hurriedly back to her desk. Later they would meet for some of that fine tequila Brother William had smuggled in from the Yucatan, and those spicy shrimp tacos he'd learned how to make in Mérida. And since Brother William had managed to field not one but at least two championship teams every year to date, he was still there. He may not have been a real brother anymore, but he ran the place, acting as *ex-oficio* headmaster. (The leaders of the order reputedly accepted this oversight due to the tremendous influx of funds Brother William's teams generated, as well as to the simple fact they could convince no other headmaster to accept an assignment in La Frontera.) He'd been there nearly forty years. He'd grown old and gray. And he eloquently taught the ways of winning to boys who previously knew nothing but loss and hardship.

As for the headmaster, the official story put forth by the order was that he "drowned" in the river the year following Brother William's excommunication, leaving the latter in charge. But it was rumored that in reality, he'd been found dead in a Mexican brothel after a long night of drunken debauchery.

"Funny," Brother William had mused to the dutiful secretary as she helped him move into the deceased headmaster's office and quarters, tearing down the red velvet drapes and replacing the ornate mahogany furniture with rustic Mexican basics, "somehow, our holy headmaster's sense of discipline slowly slipped away in the murky waters of the Rio Grande."

It was there, in the once musty and dark office that Brother William had stripped down to light and white some four decades earlier, that the coach had seen for the first time—from behind the ranch table he used as a desk—a pleasant-looking boy named Fulgencio Ramirez.

It had been the summer of '56, weeks before the start of the school year. He had arrived unannounced, but the school secretary—feeling a tinge of pity for the boy—let him in anyway. In those slow and lazy summer days when the boys were not in school, Brother William did not mind one bit. He could use some company since all the other Brothers were away at a retreat for the members of the Order in upstate New York. And, besides, he was always scouting talent for the school teams.

He motioned for Fulgencio to take a seat opposite him at the table.

"So, Fulgencio Ramirez," Brother William asked. "What can I do for you?"

Direct and to the point, as he'd always been, Fulgencio Ramirez stated: "I wish to go to school here, Brother."

"Have your parents put in an application?" the brother inquired.

"My parents . . . are not that interested," Fulgencio ventured.

"Why do you say that?"

"Well, they don't think school's that important. They say work is what matters. School is for the rich, the ones that have forgotten how to speak Spanish, and the Anglos."

Brother William shifted in his chair.

"They send my brothers and me to the public school,"

Fulgencio continued, "but I don't like it there. I need to come here, to the Academy."

"Why's that?"

"For the love of a woman, Brother," said Fulgencio. "I must make myself worthy. This is where her father came to school before going to the university to become a pharmacist. So, this is where I must go too. Besides, at the public school, everyone speaks Spanish all the time, even the teachers. I don't feel like I'm learning anything there. Then I see the older brothers of my classmates, the ones that already graduated, and they're still as poor as my father, working in tire shops and picking onions in the fields. There has to be more for us here in America, don't you think, Brother William? I know I want more. I want to become good enough for Carolina Mendelssohn," he asserted sincerely.

"You seem to have given this a great deal of thought," the Brother mused. "In all my years at San Juan del Atole, I have never met a youngster quite as reflective—or obsessed—as you."

"This is my destiny, Brother William." Fulgencio spoke with conviction, a distant fire burning in his eyes.

Sizing him up, Brother William conceded, "With some exercise, you might make a promising addition to our football team."

"Whatever it takes for me to enroll here, Brother William, I will do it."

"Your determination is rare, Fulgencio. You would not be the first man propelled to greatness by love," Brother William snapped. "But, tell me, how do you propose to pay for your tuition? As you know, the Academy carries upon its blessed shoulders a rather heavy cross which we must all help to bear."

Fulgencio had known all along this would be a major obstacle to overcome, and by no means did he wish to be treated like a charity case. *No, no señor*. The Ramirez Cisneros clan may have suffered from a lack of wealth, but they came from a long line of ranchers, minstrels, gamblers, and poets. Beggars they were not.

"All I have, Brother William, is a piece of land my grandfather left me," Fulgencio said. "Although I do not wish to part with it, for it is my only possession, I would gladly offer it to the Church in exchange for my education here."

Brother William's right eyebrow cocked high as it sometimes did when he heard something intriguing. "Where is this land?"

"Across the river," Fulgencio responded. "About an hour outside of Nueva Frontera on the way to the *playa*."

"Near the beach." Brother William stroked his chin. "I would not call myself an expert in farming, but I have heard at times the land near the sea is rendered worthless by high levels of salt in the soil." He sighed, his gaze softening as he looked back at Fulgencio. "Nevertheless, when can we look at this land of yours?"

Surprised and thrilled that his offer had sufficiently intrigued Brother William, Fulgencio responded giddily, "Whenever you wish, Brother."

Brother William sat pensively for a while as Fulgencio fidgeted in his seat hoping that the man would not change his mind.

"I'll be honest with you," Brother William said, rising to his feet and guiding Fulgencio toward the door. "I'm as curious about your ranch as I am bored of sitting in my office. Summers are long and monotonous here. That said, I will entertain your proposition, having once benefited from an even more dubious deal struck within these very walls."

Standing in the doorway slightly bewildered, Fulgencio looked up tentatively at the towering Brother. He was unsure exactly what the Brother meant.

"Tomorrow morning right before sunrise," Brother William snapped, making Fulgencio's head bob with every word. "Meet me behind the school. We'll drive out to the land."

Patting Fulgencio on the back and nudging him gently out of the office, his eyes twinkled with mischief: "Remember. No promises. Don't get your hopes up and don't be late, Don Fulgencio. I don't tolerate tardiness."

Fulgencio felt a rush of excitement, thanking the Brother profusely as he exited through the waiting room occupied by the eavesdropping secretary now crowned by a head of white hair. As he left he directed a final question at the Brother who lingered in the doorway, "One thing before I go, Brother. Why do you call me Don Fulgencio? No one has ever called me that before."

"Well you are a landowner, aren't you?" The brother smiled and winked.

Fulgencio Ramirez smiled too as he skipped through the dark and vacant halls, the click of his heels echoing throughout the slumbering school. As he ran out into the relentless summer, he looked up at the cornflower sky and let it burn his skin as he made the sign of the cross in thanks to God, the Virgencita, and all the Saints above. He took his time walking home, passing in front of the downtown store windows, seeing himself in a different way for the first time. In the distorted reflections, he saw a boy that walked a little straighter and held his head a little higher than the others on the street, than he ever had before. Sure, he was poor and the son of a simple tire man with a bad temper. But like Brother William said, he was a landowner too.

The next morning, enveloped by the cool, blue light of the courtyard behind the three-story brick structure of the Academy, Fulgencio shook hands with Brother William. They climbed into the green jalopy the Brothers had shared since cars first arrived in La Frontera, and they rode through the slumbering streets of downtown toward the drawbridge. By the time the unforgiving sun burned at the horizon's edge—having rambled through the hauntingly quiet colonial streets of the still-dreaming Nueva Frontera—they rolled over the narrow road to the beach.

Outside the compact Mexican village, a vast expanse of meadows paved the earth green as far as the eye could see. The highway wound through the ejidos, communal farming parcels carved from the Spanish lands originally granted to the thirteen founding families of the region, the Cisneros clan included, and redistributed to the campesinos in the days following the Mexican Revolution. In theory, this was what the Revolution had been fought for, to return the land to its people, or so Brother William told Fulgencio as they headed due east toward El Dos de Copas. Fulgencio listened with interest, as he was unfamiliar with the history of his own land. The campesinos that worked the ejidos in unison were called ejidatarios, Brother William explained. They were a proud, hard-working stock, at least until decades later when the allure of easy drug money would steal the young boys away from their fathers, causing the lands to fall into desolate ruin. As they passed a bend in the road, Fulgencio pointed at a small hand-painted sign that marked a dirt path disappearing beyond a thicket of mesquites.

"That's where my friend Cipriano lives," Fulgencio informed Brother William. "We can get sodas there on the way back."

Brother William smiled as the warming wind whipped through his hair, rushing in through the open windows of the rattling and jostling jalopy. "We'll surely require some refreshment once the sun rises higher into the sky."

About forty-five minutes later, Fulgencio again broke the

tranquil spell of their repose, pointing at the dirt road that led to the ranch, off the left-hand side of the highway.

"There!" he exclaimed. "El Dos de Copas."

"I guess whomever named this ranch was a gambler," Brother William commented, veering onto the bumpy path. A cloud of dust trailed them as they passed the row of young mesquite saplings toward the unassuming hut on the edge of the ranch.

"How many acres?" he asked Fulgencio as he brought the car to a squealing halt in the clearing in front of the house.

"About five hundred," Fulgencio answered as they stretched their legs, stiff from the ride.

"Well, I'm curious," Brother William admitted. "Show me around."

A modest stable sagged behind some trees near the house. Fulgencio vanished for a moment around the corner and reappeared in what seemed like an instant, towing two horses behind him. "Do you ride, Brother William?"

"I sure do, Don Fulgencio," he retorted, taking a set of reins from Fulgencio's hands and admiring the amber tone of the horse's coat. "This looks like a Golden Palomino."

"It is, sir."

"This is a good horse," the Brother said, running his hand over the fine, short horsehair, stroking its creamy mane. "What do you call him?"

"That one is called Trueno," he said, motioning to the horse Brother William had adopted. "This one," patting the equally tall and sinuous black mare to the right, "is called Relámpago."

"Thunder and Lightning!" Brother William translated. "Great names."

"Thanks. I made them up," beamed Fulgencio.

"So, these are yours?" Brother William asked, his eyebrows arched high upon his forehead. "Who takes care of them?"

"My cousin El Chino, who lives nearby, watches over them," Fulgencio replied. "They were my grandfather's. He won them playing poker. But he gave them to me and let me name them. See here, they have the brand of the ranch." He pointed at a scar on each of their rumps in the shape of the number two followed by a goblet.

Brother William traced the brand on Trueno with his fingers and whispered, "El Dos de Copas." Then he turned with a boyish smile on his weathered face, his graying hair tussling in the Gulf breeze. "Let's ride!"

He looked as if he were about to jump on the horse's back that very instant, but Fulgencio restrained him.

"Brother William," he said, "we should saddle them first."

"Yes, yes, of course," Brother William stammered. "Let's saddle them up!"

Fulgencio disappeared around the corner again and emerged with a grimy, tattered saddle over each shoulder. He handed onc over to the Brother and proceeded to saddle Relámpago. The brother, pretending he knew what he was doing mimicked Fulgencio's every move, and in a few minutes they were mounted and ready to go. Fulgencio dug his heels instinctively into Relámpago's flanks and shot out of the clearing yelping.

Brother William, in his lime green guayabera and khakis sat motionless, stumped.

Circling back around, Fulgencio returned toward the Brother, "What's wrong, Brother William?"

"It won't go."

"What?" Fulgencio grinned. "Trueno loves to go. Just relax.

Trueno is a very tame horse. He used to ride in a charro show near the beach."

Brother William patted the horse with the slightest tinge of apprehension and flailed his legs in a futile attempt to spur it on, but Trueno stood still as a statue.

"Make a kissing noise," Fulgencio suggested. "He likes that."

Brother William puckered his lips and blew kisses into the breeze. Nothing.

"Loosen the reins," Fulgencio said, circling like a showman around the inert steed and his would-be rider. "Just don't let go of the saddle," he said, showing the Brother how he kept his right hand on the handle at the top of the saddle while steering the horse with his left hand on the reins. Just the way Fernando Cisneros had taught him as a young boy.

Flush with embarrassment at being tutored by a prospective pupil, Brother William did as he was told, flapping his legs against the side of the horse in frustration.

"Pat him on the back," Fulgencio said, "Like so." And he gave Relámpago a firm slap on the rump, at which point she gave a little spurt of speed, circling Brother William and kicking up a cloud of dust.

Sneezing, Brother William followed the example. And suddenly, Brother William burst into childlike laughter as Trueno sprung to life, chasing after Relámpago as they headed out of the clearing.

"I was a bit rusty," Brother William explained, as they trotted along the fence bordering the eastern edge of the ranch. "Thanks for the refresher course."

Fulgencio smiled. He liked Brother William. The Brother made him feel like he could do things, like he was worth something. He talked to him like an equal even though Fulgencio couldn't begin to believe that they were. And he respected Brother William's authority all the more for that very reason. He only hoped that Brother William would accept this piece of land in exchange for his education.

They circumnavigated the ranch, along a horse trail that Fernando Cisneros and Fulgencio had worn through the years on their long afternoons scouting the ranch, singing and talking. The land formed a north-south rectangle, with the house and clearing at the lower left-hand corner adjacent the highway, facing east toward the beach. The wrought iron gate, adorned by the same symbol found on the branding iron, was found on the lower right-hand corner, also facing east toward the sea. All along that lower line, between the gate and the clearing was the long line of mesquite saplings he and his brothers planted as children. And from that—most traveled—end of the ranch toward the north, the land rolled flat and green, tall, wispy grass flowing in waves. The farther north one headed, the closer one neared the Rio Grande, Fulgencio told Brother William.

Intrigued, Brother William asked Fulgencio to lead the way to the river. Beyond the northern fence, past a couple other tiny ranches, the dirt road eventually wound to a stop on a vast, open prairie. There, on that communal piece of land, the ejidatarios allowed everyone's cattle to roam, graze, and drink at the banks of the river.

"It is a desolate place," Brother William noted. "As is often the case in nature, one can feel the presence of God close at hand."

Resting atop Trueno and Relámpago, Fulgencio and Brother William silently admired the wide river flowing out toward the sea.

Then Brother William shot upright in his seat, startling

Trueno, who snorted and shook his head in protest at his rider's erratic actions.

"Who is that, over there?" Brother William pointed toward a dune in the distance, at the edge of the river. The figure of a lone woman stood at the crest, gazing north across the water.

"You see her too?" Fulgencio marveled. "Not everybody does."

"Yes, who is she?"

"I am not sure, but she is not 'alive' in the same way we are," Fulgencio explained.

"What do you mean?"

"She's been seen now and then standing there for about a hundred years. She never changes. She never speaks to anyone. She is a spirit."

Brother William rubbed his eyes and shook his head, realizing he had crossed more than a border between two neighboring countries.

Fulgencio continued, "They say that she is waiting for her husband to return, that she is part of a curse on this land placed long ago. People call it *la maldición de* Caja Pinta."

"Caja Pinta?"

"Yes, that was the name of all this land when it was one large grant from the Spanish King to the Cisneros family, before my grandfather and his ancestors sold off bits and pieces or lost them playing cards." Fulgencio paused. "Do you wish to go closer to her?"

"No, we must leave her be." Brother William made the sign of the cross. "Let's head back to El Dos de Copas. The heat is becoming unbearable."

As they headed back, Brother William rode deep in thought. After circling the entire perimeter of Fulgencio's ranch, the trail came to an end at the edge of the serene pond behind the hut. Brother William and Fulgencio dismounted and dove into the water for a refreshing swim. Afterward, Fulgencio showed Brother William the miraculous relief of the Virgen de Guadalupe, introduced him to the ghost of his grandfather Fernando Cisneros doing card tricks for the Virgen from his spot at the wooden table, and stepped out for a moment while the Brother prayed on his knees before the apparition. When the Brother emerged into the scorching afternoon sun, they felt like cows dying of thirst, so they rode the jalopy back up the road to the ejido of El Refugio.

There, in front of a modest wooden structure, they were greeted by the ear-to-ear smile of a wiry, dark-skinned ten-year-old boy.

"I've known Cipriano since he was a baby," Fulgencio explained to Brother William. "My grandfather was always friends with his family."

Brother William purchased some sodas, icy cold glass bottles of Joya Manzana pulled from a giant metal icebox by Cipriano. Then, they sat on the porch, quenching their thirst and wiping the sweat off their brows as Brother William told the boys and Cipriano's grandparents about his conversation with the Virgencita. She had advised him what to do about Fulgencio's proposal to exchange the ranch for his education.

"Fulgencio," Brother William said, "never let go of that ranch. It is in your blood and in your soul. While it may seem worthless to others, it is a precious piece of Heaven for you. Now, I still expect you to let me come out here and visit, however. Spend time with the Virgencita. Ride Trueno. Drink Joyas here at El Refugio with these good folk."

"So how can I pay you for the tuition, Brother William?" Fulgencio searched the holy man's eyes.

Sitting on the wooden planks of the porch, listening to the cries of the commune's boys as they endeavored to arrange a cock-fight in a corral across the dirt clearing surrounded by tiny pink wooden huts, Brother William dispensed the Virgencita's mandate.

"You will never have to pay me for anything," Brother William clarified, "but you can compensate the school by mowing the grass at the football field during the summer and in between football games during the season."

"Can I play football too?" Fulgencio became agitated with excitement.

"Yes. You will play football. And you'll win."

"Your teams always win, Brother William!" Fulgencio exclaimed.

"Yes, they do."

Cipriano chimed in: "It's because he has a deal with God."

"I'll be keeping an eye on you, Cipriano." The Brother tossed the boy's dusty brown hair, his eyes landing on the child's bare feet clad in dry mud. "You're an old soul."

As the sun set, they said their goodbyes. Brother William paid the extra peso so he could keep the empty Joya bottle for good luck and as a reminder of that special day. He paid for Fulgencio's too, so he could take it with him as well. Promising to return soon, Brother William drove westward toward town, squinting into the golden sun.

Fulgencio Ramirez faced Brother William, "So I'm in?"

"You're in, Fulgencio. I'm not sure what plan God has in store for you, but I'm glad to be a part of it."

Fulgencio smiled and fell asleep with his head on the windowpane. When the Brother dropped him off in front of his house, they made arrangements for Fulgencio to begin mowing the field and for a return trip to El Dos de Copas the following week. Brother William said he wanted to work on his horseback riding skills. But Fulgencio would always suspect that the true motivation for the quick return was the ear-to-ear smile on Cipriano's oval face when Brother William presented him with a giant box on the porch as they drank another round of Joyas. Inside, beneath the white tissue paper that Cipriano joyously tossed into the air, he discovered a shiny brown pair of brand-new cowboy boots.

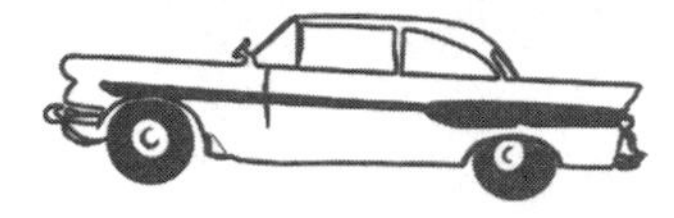

EIGHT

So it was that Fulgencio Ramirez joined the football team and grew into a formidable force under Brother William's coaching.

The first time he stepped onto the field for tryouts, he got creamed by a giant called Fat Victor. Fat Victor was a bearded boy so large that when they visited opposing teams, the children from the other schools would point and ask rhetorically how they could possibly be expected to win against San Juan del Atole when they were playing fully grown men cheered on by their wives and children in the bleachers.

Dejected by his poor performance at the try-outs, Fulgencio devoted himself to lifting weights and hauling sacks of flour across the field until he built his body into a frightening muscular force. Hours in the sweltering school gym built not only muscle, but tension. Every day he benched more weight, huffing and puffing and tasting the sweat as his chest heaved. All this time, Brother William watched, egging him on, slamming his whipping stick against the floor or the wall or anyone who got in his way as he shouted, "One more! One more! Don't do it for me. Do it for Carolina Mendelssohn. Imagine what she'll think when she sees you winning on that football field!"

A couple months into his first season, Fulgencio strode onto the freshly mown field without pads on, his muscles lean and tight. "Are you crazy?" his best friend Bobby Balmori cried in disbelief. "After what happened to you at tryouts? You're gonna get killed."

But Fulgencio marched straight out to the cluster of upperclassmen running drills in the center of the field, brushing by Brother William, clad in his robes and sporting his stick and his whistle.

Offensive and defensive players were lining up and rushing full force at each other. Fulgencio strode straight up to the biggest of them all, Fat Victor, and pushed his adversary out of the way. "You!" he snapped, Brother William–style, his pointer finger sticking into Fat Victor's chest. Fat Victor growled with a devilish smile on his face behind the helmet's mask.

Brother William played along. He knew Fulgencio had been toiling toward this moment. Now he would find out whether Fulgencio's destiny included a starting spot on the line of the 1956 championship team. He blew the whistle. Fulgencio lined up on defense directly across from Fat Victor.

Fat Victor winked at his buddies. "Watch this," he taunted with a cocky swagger to his voice.

Fulgencio fumed. His blood boiled. The quarterback called out numbers. The center snapped the ball. And all the rage blew like a volcano as Fulgencio smashed into every bone, every ounce, every cell of Fat Victor's existence. Propelled by the combined force of his legs, torso, arms, and spirit, Fulgencio hit Fat Victor so hard they both flew through the air landing in unison on the quarterback, who snapped like a twig and flattened like a pancake on the soft turf beneath. The circle of onlookers stood around them as Fat Victor struggled to regain his consciousness. Brother William waved smelling salts beneath the pulverized lineman's nose, struggling to control his laughter.

As Fat Victor's eyes recovered their ability to focus, the first thing he saw was the shadowy figure of Fulgencio looming over him. Gathering himself slowly, he leaned on Brother William to get back on his feet. Embarrassed, he growled angrily at Fulgencio, "Let's go again."

With the sun beating down from overhead, and the crowd of onlookers growing on the field, Fulgencio was happy to oblige. His body tingled with excitement from the delivery of such a massive blow. And he wondered if he could outdo himself.

As they carried the quarterback away on a stretcher, Brother William blew his whistle and said, "This is not necessary, boys. I think Fulgencio has proven his point."

Fat Victor glared at the Brother from his crouched stance. "Yes, but I haven't. Let's go."

"But we have no quarterback now," said Joe Lopez, the starting center.

Brother William assessed Fulgencio and Fat Victor, who were already in position and ready to clash yet again. "Very well," he relented. "If you're going to start on the same championship line together, you might as well work this out, here and now." Pointing at a scrawny player on the bench, he snapped, "You, what's your name?"

The pale boy, who looked more like he belonged in the choir than on the football team, glanced around, pointing at himself with trepidation, "Me?"

"Yes, you."

He sprang to his feet and walked timidly toward the coach. "My name is Miguel Rodriguez Esparza, sir."

"You play quarterback."

"But . . ."

"Just do it."

Miguelito lined up behind Joe Lopez, calling out a play.

As the ball was snapped, Fulgencio hurled furiously toward Fat Victor. The impact was so powerful and sudden that Fat Victor did not even feel the pain until he awoke fifteen minutes later splayed on the ground.

His friends told him that his body, all three hundred pounds, had been flung into the air, arching over Miguelito Rodriguez Esparza, and landing with a thunderous clap on the ground. For years, many of the townspeople—oblivious to the events at Canaya Field—believed there had been a freak earthquake that day in La Frontera, so catastrophic had Fat Victor's landing been. Cupboards shook for miles around. And shopkeepers clutched their most precious items to keep them from crashing to the floor.

Fat Victor could no longer bring himself to an upright position. "Again?" Fat Victor whimpered valiantly, tears streaming down balloon cheeks.

"No," Brother William concluded emphatically. "You're a lineman, not a football. I don't want to see you flying through the field goal uprights."

Players stifled their laughter out of mercy for the once-fearless behemoth. Fulgencio extended his hand to Fat Victor. And when the boy could not rise, he picked him up, slung him over his shoulder, and carried him to his house.

Fat Victor's mom screamed in horror at the sight of her vanquished son. "What have they done to you, Victor?"

"I fell," he muttered as Fulgencio eased him onto the couch. "I'll be fine," he slurred as a stream of drool oozed from his mouth.

Fulgencio could hear Fat Victor's snoring and his mother's sobbing as he let himself out and walked back to the school, where he showered and changed back into his street clothes.

Standing at his locker, Fulgencio turned to see the statuesque figure of Brother William looming in the shadows, golden sunlight filtering in through the windows above the wall of red lockers.

"Good job, Don Fulgencio."

"Did I make the starting lineup?"

"Yes," Brother William said. "Just remember. Direct your force in a positive manner. Don't dispense more pain than is necessary to get the job done. Your mission is not to kill the man across the line. Just stop him on offense and get past him on defense."

"Understood, Brother William," Fulgencio answered. "So does that means you're starting me both ways?"

"Yes."

"Only Fat Victor has ever done that."

"Yes, well, let's hope he lives to do it again," Brother William hollered as he strode out, leaving Fulgencio to his own thoughts in the silent room that always reeked of stale sweat.

He gazed at the faded and wrinkled black and white photo of his grandfather pinned on his locker door.

"Things are starting to happen," Fulgencio told his grandfather. "I can feel it. I'm on my way. Soon I will have her love, *abuelito*, the love of Carolina Mendelssohn."

A year later, Fulgencio was driven to unforeseen heights at the homecoming game by Carolina's cheers from the sideline.

Standing side-by-side, Fat Victor, Bobby Balmori, Joe Lopez, and Fulgencio Ramirez had formed the most powerful line in the proud and illustrious history of La Frontera football. They were the reason that San Juan del Atole was undefeated in Fulgencio's junior year. They were responsible for pulverizing the opposition 51–0 at the homecoming game.

Now, as Carolina and Fulgencio approached the school's dance hall, the other three linemen, dressed in black tuxes, stood illuminated by the headlamps of Mr. Balmori's '54 Imperial as the car pulled to a stop in the parking lot. The couple stepped out like royalty as Fat Victor opened Fulgencio's door and Joe Lopez opened Carolina's. Bobby Balmori helped her out, bowing like a gentleman.

"Mr. Ramirez, Miss Mendelssohn, allow us," they said, throwing the doors to the dance hall open and sweeping their arms in an exaggerated manner.

Fulgencio and Carolina walked in arm-in-arm, eyes only for each other, as the crowd parted and gawked. The DJ spun Nat King Cole's "Unforgettable." The golden glow of the Christmas lights strung overhead bathed the room in surreal warmth, a floating haze. It was the first slow song of the evening, and the tension hung in the air. The boys milled on one side of the dance floor in a sea of black suits, the Brothers bringing up the rear, like statues lining the wall. The girls stood shyly on the other side, chatting nervously, wondering if they would be asked to dance. The nuns tapped their toes and snapped their fingers as they kept a watchful eye on their charges. The only person not afraid at that moment was Fulgencio Ramirez, who looked deep into Carolina's eyes, smiled and uttered the few words he had gone over and over in his mind over the last year, "Miss Mendelssohn, may I have this dance?"

She smiled and curtsied, "Why, of course, Mr. Ramirez."

He escorted her to the center of the dance floor, where their bodies touched tenderly and glided to the rhythm of the romantic song. All alone on the floor. The music fading fast. The crowd a blur in the distance and vanishing. They moved in a trance, eyes locked, hearts pounding in tandem. Their motion was perfectly synchronized, as if they were one.

Fulgencio could feel Carolina's graceful form melting in his arms, her body floating at his whim. Then, suddenly, her eyes watering, she looked away.

"What's wrong," he whispered softly into her ear, his lips brushing lightly against her delicate curls, the warmth of his breath alarming her senses.

"I can't look at you anymore," she exhaled.

"Why not?" he asked, twirling her around in an attempt to recapture her gaze.

"Because . . ." she said.

"Because what?"

"Because I'm falling in love with you," she realized, lifting her angelic face toward his. A single tear overflowed from her golden eyes, past her long and curving lashes, onto the wooden floor. Fulgencio felt her embrace tighten as she buried her face in his chest. He held her. He wished he could hold her like this until the end of time and never let go.

Through slow songs and fast, Elvis and Frankie, Dean and Jerry Lee, they remained at the center of the dance floor in a steamy embrace, swaying gently with the music, surrounded by a sock-hopping throng laughing with abandon. After all, it was the night after the homecoming game. It was the big homecoming dance. They had emerged victorious yet again. And the souls of Fulgencio Ramirez and Carolina Mendelssohn had come a long way to find each other. Holding her in his arms, Fulgencio felt theirs was a destiny blessed by divine powers. His hunch was bolstered as he noticed Brother William watching them from afar, a subtle smile and a twinkle in his eyes.

NINE

Fulgencio reached into his shirt pocket and pulled out the tiny bag containing the gold medallion. He let it slip out onto his hardened hand. He stood in the entrance to his drugstore with the door locked behind him. Remembering. Wishing he could change the past. Twenty-five miserable years. Nearly three decades without her. How could he ever make up for the wasted time? And would she even allow him to try? At the campo santo, she had cried out in pain, accusing him of ruining her life. He could taste the bitterness of loss in his mouth. It was a flavor only tequila could mask. He ambled slowly up behind the counter to the office he kept in the back storage room, piled high with paperwork. Pulling a bottle of tequila out from his desk, he served himself a shot and leaned back into his wooden armchair. Mr. Mendelssohn's office had been much like this, he realized, a modest, cramped, and unadorned space as good for reflection as it was for getting work done.

Mr. Mendessohn. May he rest in peace. Back at the cemetery, after Carolina's limo had disappeared, Fulgencio had felt obligated to pay his respects to his old boss. Strolling somberly through the graveyard, Fulgencio made a beeline for the plot. He walked with the surety of someone who'd made the pilgrimage many times before.

His mentor had died too young, of cancer, about five years earlier. He remembered still opening the paper on that bleak winter day, alone in the shadowy damp chill of the drugstore at dawn.

Arthur Mendelssohn, dead at the age of sixty-two, survived by his wife and daughter. In lieu of flowers, donations could be sent to San Juan del Atole or the American Cancer Society.

Arthur Mendelssohn. Seventeen letters. Not the ones he'd been searching for during his daily ritual.

He had not attended any of the services for he did not wish to harm himself with the sight of Carolina standing next to her husband. He had, however, visited the gravesite over the years, wishing he could speak with Mr. Mendelssohn again, the way he continued to do with the spirits of his grandfather and Brother William. But he was never there. According to Fernando Cisneros and Brother William, ghosts demanded a particularly compelling reason to materialize. And when they did manage it, they did not loiter in mass, commercialized graveyards. They preferred to remain close to their bones only if they were buried in a place of personal significance to them. This was one reason why Brother William had been resolute in his wish to die—and be buried—at El Dos de Copas. He had figured it was a great place to remain for an eternity. And he had also harbored a hunch there was a mystery to the place that might provide him the kind of challenge he would need to avoid boredom in the afterlife. Plus, it came with the added bonus of open fields, a pond, the Gulf breeze, horses, a drinking and gambling buddy in Fulgencio's grandfather, and the expressive Virgencita on the wall.

Unfortunately, Fulgencio figured this meant that in order to spend time with Mr. Mendelssohn's ghost, he would have to be allowed entry into the special sanctum of his home, the one he had so often picked Carolina up from on their dates, the one with the rosebushes under the window, the one where he had sung so many serenatas for Carolina bathed in moonlight and backed up by Fat Victor, Bobby Balmori, and Joe Lopez on guitar. He had hoped maybe now that reconciliation with Carolina was a possibility, he might gain that access and see him once again. But the brief encounter with her at her husband's funeral had dealt a harsh blow to his dreams and desires, making him wonder if they might be mere delusions. It seemed Carolina did not have reconciliation on her mind. At least not yet.

Strange how life worked out, he thought, his eyes skimming over the dusty drugstore shelves. It was night now. The downtown streets had fallen back into their troubled sleep. The cross-dressers would be out roaming soon, their high heels clicking and echoing through the alleys. Cats banging through trash cans. Police sirens wailing their nightly lament. He had worked so hard to become a pharmacist. He had tried to follow Mr. Mendelssohn's footsteps. All for the love of one woman. And he had missed the mark completely. He had accomplished and acquired all the things he had believed would be necessaary to win and keep Carolina's love. And yet he'd lost her, not because the challenges of achieving the American dream had proven insurmountable, but because his temperament had mixed toxically—and explosively—with the haunting pull of his family's troubled past.

El Chotay cleared his throat and coughed from his rickety metal chair in the corner, reading Fulgencio's mind. "Don't be so hard on yourself, *patrón*."

Fulgencio nearly fell out of his chair. "Chotay. You almost scared me to death. I've told you not to do that."

"Well, maybe that's exactly why I do it." He flashed his jack-o'-lantern grin. "Maybe I want to scare you to death so I can put you out of your misery. If you were a horse, I'd just shoot you."

"*Pinche* Chotay." Fulgencio smiled, sipping his tequila. "Thanks for coming. I could use an old friend right now."

"Tell me about it," El Chotay said. "You look bad, boss. *Amolado*."

Fulgencio looked at his old sidekick with more than a tinge of sadness in his eyes. *Pobre* Chotay. Talk about *amolado*. He was a wreck, looking just the way he did on the morning of his death two years earlier.

Obviously, El Chotay was short. Hence the nickname, "El Shorty," which—when pronounced by the mostly Spanish-speaking coworkers, fieldhands, truckers, and drugstore clients that knew him—became "El Chotay." *Sí, señor.* Short. Thin as a rail. His dark, flaccid skin was that of a ninety-year-old woman. But he was just one year younger than Fulgencio Ramirez. His clothes always hung on him several sizes too big, presumably because he kept losing weight and couldn't afford to keep his wardrobe in step with his deteriorating physique. In his postmortem era, he sported brown polyester pants that looked like they were always about to fall off and a navy blue T-shirt with paint splattered all over it. His wily black hair streaked with gray, his bushy eyebrows and mustache punctuating his angular and animated face. Depending on El Chotay's condition at any given time, his looks reminded Fulgencio of either a dog, a weasel, or a raccoon. Black circles beneath his charcoal eyes. But no one had worked as hard as El Chotay in his time, nor for as little money. El Chotay, along with many of Fulgencio

Ramirez's followers and hangers-on, was a throwback to the loyal henchmen and vassals of medieval times. One day in the prime of Fulgencio's youth and business career, El Chotay simply materialized at the perfect time. Business was overflowing at the drugstore, the customers were lined up and down the aisles, pending deliveries were piled up to the ceiling in white bags, and Fulgencio was all alone. The delivery boy and the storefront clerk had both called in sick. It was the middle of flu season, and everyone in town was ailing, including his own staff. Surveying the chaos in Fulgencio's store, El Chotay walked in and climbed up behind the counter as if he'd worked there all his life.

"All right, boss, what do you want me to do first?" he'd asked nonchalantly.

Fulgencio, who was in the middle of concocting a convoluted medication for a woman who had three different tropical diseases plus diabetes, took one glance at the diminutive man, pointed at the mountain of white bags waiting to be distributed to the addresses scrawled on their surfaces, and knew instinctively that he could trust this man with his life.

As the elfin Mexican gathered the prescriptions in a cardboard box, Fulgencio Ramirez pointed to the service entrance at the back of the store. "Hey," he called out, "Shorty!"

El Chotay turned with a smile on his face and a white bag hanging from his mouth.

"Take the delivery truck out back. The keys are in the dash."

El Chotay nodded and scurried on out. El Chotay was at Fulgencio's side from then until the day he died of diabetic complications. It seemed by then that every system and organ in his body had simply fallen apart on him. And as he lay dying on the floor of the drugstore behind the tall counter where no one else could see, he whispered, "I'm scared, *patrón*." His black eyes jittered with apprehension as he gasped his last breaths. "What will I do up in Heaven without you to run errands for?"

Fulgencio lay his hands upon El Chotay's navy blue T-shirt. He had gotten it dirty that morning repainting shelves in the back. "*Calmados montes*, Chotay. It's going to be all right," he reassured his old friend.

"No, boss," El Chotay said. "This is it. No hospital can save me this time. At least the Medicaid people will be happy. They won't have to spend any more money on me."

Fulgencio forced a smile for his dying comrade.

"I just hope the drugstore makes it without my business," joked El Chotay, trying to ease the pain of his passage with humor.

He coughed violently, spewing a thick, black ooze onto the floor, his humor escaping him. "I'm scared, boss. I want so bad to live. To work like I used to. Remember, when I would drive a tractor trailer forty-eight hours straight without blinking once and then come back, make the deliveries, and drive you out to the ranch?"

Fulgencio remembered, shaking his head. El Chotay had never slept. He simply worked. And not just at the drugstore. As Fulgencio had diversified into other businesses, including the import of produce and construction materials from Mexico, El Chotay had been his top truck driver. Heck, he'd even become Fulgencio's personal chauffeur over the years, dropping him off at his home on El Dos de Copas late at night after they closed the shop. And then, when Fulgencio emerged from the arched doorway to his grandfather's hut in the wee hours of the next morning, El Chotay would already be there, waiting in the pickup, with donuts and hot coffee in hand.

As the years flew by and El Chotay's medical problems and

corresponding welfare check grew, he required less and less pay. Until in the end, El Chotay worked for free, for the fun of it. He had slowly transformed from trusted, zestful, and indispensable employee to cherished friend and supporter. Fulgencio Ramirez was his lord, his knight, and master. And he was proud to play the loyal vassal and serve.

When El Chotay lay dying on the drugstore floor, the banner slipping from his hands, he wheezed, "I'm not ready, *patrón*."

Fulgencio Ramirez reached deep within whatever meager reserves of healing power he still had left in his soul. He closed his eyes with his hands on El Chotay's chest and he hummed. It was the melody from a famous Mexican song, "Cielito Lindo." A smile broke across El Chotay's face, his body relaxed and his quivering voice sang the words clearly, *"Ay, ay, ay-ay . . . Canta y no llores . . . porque cantando se alegran . . . cielito lindo . . . los corazones . . .*" and his voice trailed. His lips slowed. His eyes drifted open. And he stared right through Fulgencio Ramirez.

"I see the Virgencita, Ramirez. I see your grandfather and Brother William. I see your Mr. Mendelssohn too . . . and . . ." he paused and Fulgencio thought for an instant he was dead.

"And . . ." he continued, "you, *patrón*. I see you! How can that be? You're still alive." He shook his head. It was as if he were asleep and merely experiencing a very vivid dream.

"You don't belong in this picture, boss," El Chotay had said, now looking directly into Fulgencio's emerald eyes. "You belong here among the living. Still alive. Stay alive. And you're right. Everything's gonna be fine. The Virgencita says I'll be back like the others. I'll still be able to help you, *patrón*." He smiled. That was all he had wanted, a reason to live for after his death. His eyes turned to glass, and his body sagged into the ground.

Fulgencio Ramirez looked wistfully at his friend of so many years. As a team they'd been in many battles. He made the sign of the cross, wishing El Chotay godspeed on this his last and final run, an errand for the Lord Himself, the delivery of his noble soul.

Unfortunately for El Chotay, however, the angels in Heaven may have performed miracles, but they didn't dispense make-overs. And both were looking mighty *amolados* about now.

"Tequila?" Fulgencio offered, pushing a glass toward his dearly departed friend.

"¡*Llénelo*!" El Chotay said. "Fill 'er up, boss!"

They drank together in the warm comfort of shared silence as Fulgencio's mind began devising a scheme to reclaim Carolina's heart, a plan to win her forgiveness and love.

TEN

After school dances in those days, it was customary for the boys from San Juan del Atole to swing by Maldonado's Cafe for a midnight snack before heading home. Roaring through the sleepy streets of downtown, their pack of gleaming cars pulled up in unison amidst a ruckus of laughter and victory yelps. Scrawled on their windows were the slogans of victory. "San Juan del Atole #1," spelled out the white shoeshine letters on the rear window of Fat Victor's father's metal green '54 Ford pickup. "God's on our side!" exclaimed the front windshield of Joe Lopez's shiny red Thunderbird convertible.

Of course, Fulgencio Ramirez was not about to deface Mr. Balmori's property, even if the vandalism was only temporary. Besides, it simply wasn't his style. Let others do the trash talking; he made his statements on the field.

As the other couples spilled out of their cars and bounced into the dimly lit coffee shop, Fulgencio and Carolina sat quietly in the car, glowing red under Old Man Maldonado's neon sign.

"I've had a wonderful night, Fully," she said, smiling sweetly. "I wish it would never end."

"Maybe I should take you home now, before I say the wrong thing or spill something on your white dress," Fulgencio wondered.

"No, let's make it last as long as we can," she responded, taking his hands off the steering wheel.

"What about your father?" Fulgencio asked. "Won't he be worried?"

"I'll call him from the payphone and let him know where we are," she said, pulling him closer. "Please."

How could he say no when all he wanted was to shout yes with all his might? "Okay, just for a little while," Fulgencio conceded, and they meandered hand-in-hand into Maldonado's Cafe.

Already stationed at a large table, the boys from Brother William's legendary line and their dates cheered and hollered as the two entered.

"What were you two doing out there?" Fat Victor's date, Maria del Refugio Gonzalez, asked in a salacious tone as the laughter rose.

"Now, you know Fulgencio," Joe Lopez reminded them. "A gentleman doesn't kiss and tell.

Carolina blushed as Fulgencio changed the subject with a glare at his friends that would have hushed a crowd on New Year's Eve.

"Sooo," said Bobby Balmori, taking his cue. "What's it gonna be?" He waved the tattered menu in the air.

"I'll be right back." Fulgencio winked at Carolina.

Several minutes later he emerged from the kitchen with Old Man Maldonado in tow. Behind them came the cook, pushing a cart heaped with food, *chorizo con huevo*, chilaquiles, *machacado*, and stacks of steaming flour tortillas.

Carolina loved the way Fulgencio always took care of everything.

She shifted giddily in her seat, her eyes devouring his every move.

They talked and they joked and they ate to their hearts' content. Old Man Maldonado, pulling up a chair, made his traditional request for Fulgencio to sing "Veracruz." And the boys on the line, who also doubled as Fulgencio's *serenata trio*, rushed out to the cars to pull their guitars from their trunks.

"A sheriff always carries his gun," Bobby Balmori used to say. "And a guitarist always carries his ax."

In the red neon glow pouring in through the big picture window, the girls swooned as the boys struck up their guitars, the chords resounding through the cafe.

Fulgencio Ramirez's voice rose purely and clearly toward the sky, nostalgically extolling the virtues of that distant coastal land of pirates and rumbas and star-filled skies beyond swaying palms.

Yo nací con la luna de plata
(I was born with the moon of silver)
Y nací con alma de pirata
(And I was born with a pirate's soul)
He nacido rumbero y jarocho
(I've been born a pathfinder)
Trovador de vela
(A troubadour)
Y me fuí
(And I went)
Lejos de Veracruz
(Far from Veracruz)

Veracruz
(Veracruz)

Rinconcito donde hacen sus nidos
(Little corner where the ocean's)
Las olas del mar
(Waves make their nests)

Veracruz
(Veracruz)
Pedacito de patria
(Patch of homeland)
que sabe reir y cantar
(Which knows how to sing and laugh)

Veracruz
(Veracruz)
Son tus noches diluvio de estrellas
(Your nights are a deluge of stars)
palmera y mujer
(palms and women)

Veracruz
(Veracruz)
Vibra en mi ser
(Resounds in my soul)
Algún dia hasta tus playas lejanas
(Someday to your distant beaches)
Tendré que volver
(I'll have to return)

The group exploded into applause as Mr. Maldonado rose to his feet and gave Fulgencio a giant bear hug.

"How I love that song, Fulgencio," he shouted, filled with joy. "And even more, how I love the way you sing it!"

"You see," the rotund old cook, in his white T-shirt and matching pants, continued, his eyes dancing over Fulgencio's young friends, "I was born there, in Veracruz, deep in the heart of Mexico! And I've never had a chance to go back, what with the coffee shop and my wife's rheumatism and all . . . And you, Fulgencio," he concluded, shaking him by the shoulders, "You take me back there even if it's only for a moment. You sing with such passion, *m'ijo*! Who could believe you've never seen the shores of my sacred birthplace?"

It was true; Fulgencio had traveled neither south of Nueva Frontera, nor north of La Frontera, with the exception of a few Valley towns where the football team had played away games. Yet he sang "Veracruz" as if he had been born and raised there. He could feel it in his veins, this distant land of adventurers and dancers, of coffee plantations and moonlit beaches. And it was his dream to someday go there with Carolina Mendelssohn, to dance beneath the deluge of stars in rhythm with the palms swaying in the Gulf breeze.

But for now, the audience chanted: "Encore! Encore!"

Fulgencio Ramirez whispered into Bobby Balmori's ear, who in turn whispered into Joe's and Fat Victor's. They huddled by the jukebox, plucking and tuning, nodding at Fulgencio when they were ready. Fulgencio took a long sip of iced tea, cleared his throat, and turned his gaze to Carolina.

He crooned "Ojos Café," a romantic Mexican ballad, as Carolina blushed and giggled, her hands clasped nervously in her lap.

Café de un café oscuro son tus ojos
(Brown, a dark brown are your eyes)

Con tintes luminosos de zafir
(With luminous tinges of sapphire)
Rubies son tus labiecitos rojos
(Rubies are your red lips)
Rojos y ardientes como el corazón
(Red and fiery like your heart)

Me miré en el fondo de tus lindos ojos
(I saw myself in the depths of your eyes)
En ellos ví mi adoración, mi fé
(In them I saw my adoration and faith)
Ese mi camino, vestido de abrojos
(My road filled with hardships)
Como linda estrella lo iluminas tú
(You illuminate like a star)

Al sentir mis labios cerca de los tuyos
(Feeling your lips near mine)
La emoción me llega hasta el corazón
(The emotion reaches my heart)
Y al contemplarte postrada de hinojos
(Contemplating you on your knees)
Me miré en tus ojos de color café.
(I saw myself in your brown eyes.)

As the impassioned roar of Fulgencio's voice echoed through the rafters, Old Man Maldonado and the boys yelled in jubilation. The girls shouted—"Bravo!"—fanning themselves with the menus and exchanging looks of disbelief.

Carolina was mute with emotion. And as Fulgencio sat back

down next to her, she could only speak with her tear-filled eyes. And these spoke volumes to him. He took her tense hands gently into his as the rest of the room subsided into the distant shadows.

"*No digas nada, mi amor,*" he whispered.

She shook her head, trying to hold back the tears. "I don't want to keep these thoughts and feelings bottled up inside. I want to share them with you. I never knew I could feel this way. Nor that it could strike so quickly and so ferociously."

"Like thunder and lightning . . ." Fulgencio agreed, cupping her face gently with his hands.

"*Truenos y relámpagos*, galloping straight into my soul," Carolina pressed her cheek against his, spurring his heart rate faster.

"Your Spanish sounds as good as mine," Fulgencio marveled. "I've been surprised by your eagerness to learn—and by your family's blessing to do so—because in your social circle, even the wealthy Mexican Americans shy away from speaking Spanish in public."

"I love how proud you are of your culture," said Carolina. "I've been practicing every chance I get. I've even been listening to some of the songs you sing at home. And I'm grateful my parents haven't dissuaded me, just like they haven't stopped me from spending time with you."

"Could they stop you?"

"They wouldn't dare."

"Speaking of which, shouldn't you call your parents?" Fulgencio suggested.

As Old Man Maldonado cleared the plates, and Fulgencio's friends danced to The Platters on the jukebox, she called home from the phone behind the counter. Standing next to her, his back to the window, a neon red halo illuminated Fulgencio's silhouette.

"Daddy, why did you take so long to answer?" Carolina asked, concern seeping into her voice, "Is Mom okay? Did something happen?"

"Oh, don't worry, angel," Mr. Mendelssohn's voice crackled over the line. "Your mother and I were just outside, looking at the moon. But you? Are you okay? What time is it? Isn't it getting late?"

"Yes, Daddy," she said. "I'll be home soon. I just wanted to let you know we stopped for some food, but Fulgencio will be taking me home in a minute."

"Good," he said. "I'll wait up for you."

"I love you, Daddy," she whispered into the clumsy black transmitter.

"I love you too," Mr. Mendelssohn said, his words punctuated by the click as he lowered the phone.

Fulgencio listened intently, his eyes entranced by her lips, yearning for the sweet and harmonious family life she possessed.

As the night's victors dispersed to their homes, Old Man Maldonado waved from his doorway, a white dishrag in his hand offering surrender for the night. After Fulgencio closed Carolina's door, the venerable cook walked around the car with him, placing his hand on his shoulder. "Together," Old Man Maldonado told Fulgencio, "you two could make a beautiful family, *m'ijo*. Beautiful children. A beautiful life. Don't let anyone tell you otherwise, just because you're not a gringo."

Mr. Balmori's black '54 Imperial rolled quietly to a stop before the white picket fence at Carolina's house. Holding hands, they inched up the walkway to the front door.

Standing beneath the bright moon, Carolina's eyes sparkled. Her bosom rose and fell in a steady rhythm. Her smooth cheeks were still flush with the evening's excitement.

"Tonight was like a dream," she smiled.

"Unforgettable," Fulgencio said, pulling her close.

"Did you ever think it would be like this?"

"For a whole year, I dreamt of tonight," he whispered into the cool breeze, watching her curls flow. "And still, being with you, it was more than I could have ever imagined."

Their faces tilted in unison, and gently, instinctively, their lips drew together as one. Their eyes floated shut as they kissed, delicately at first, then losing themselves in the depths of each other's souls. Time itself seemed to stop. And the rosebush beneath the Mendelssohn's window burst to life, dozens of red roses weighing the branches down to the ground.

As their lips parted, they knew their fate was sealed. When their eyes opened, everything looked different. In each other they recognized something unpronounceable, a yearning and meshing undefined. It was as if they had waited lifetimes for this moment, searching for each other through the ages, scouring distant lands under different names. And now, by the grace of God, here they were. Together at last.

Carolina reminded herself to breathe. And they collapsed back into each other's arms.

"I'd fall asleep standing here if we could," she whispered.

Fulgencio smiled, running his fingers through her curls. And then she skipped impetuously to the rosebush, plucking a flower from it and extending it to Fulgencio.

"For you," she said.

"No one's ever given me a flower," he said, sticking it into his lapel.

And when she said it would be the first of many to come, he believed her wholeheartedly. He watched her disappear into the house as he backed away toward the car. His eyes swept the starry heavens in gratitude, "Thank you, God. Thank you!" He shivered all over with excitement as he drove home, pounding the dash with his hands in disbelief, amazement, and joy. He saw the image of Carolina Mendelssohn everywhere he looked, her golden curls, her white chiffon dress, her ruby red smile. He yearned to sing from the rooftops. He was alive. He was alive. Thank God. He was alive.

ELEVEN

He had not felt so alive in years. Not since the days of his faded youth. And now, as he plotted the reconquest of Carolina Mendelssohn, he drew on the advice of those even less alive than he.

"Go see her in person," El Chotay said. "It's the only way."

But on seeing his black Stetson hat and thick mustache through the peephole of the Mendelssohn family's old two-story with the white picket fence sagging, the gaggle of grayed ladies protecting Carolina's health refused to open the door.

Funny, Fulgencio noted as he walked away. Everything looked different than it had that homecoming night so many autumns past. The rosebush that had burst with flowers now lay in ruins, gnarled and dry. The once immaculate lawn had become a patchwork of dirt, weeds, and crabgrass. And the white picket fence now wavered, hanging in a state of bleak disrepair. The entire neighborhood had changed, Fulgencio Ramirez noticed as he drove away. In fact, the whole city had slowly deteriorated around him, but it took coming to Carolina's house for Fulgencio to realize the transformation. What had once been the enclave of the rich was now a dilapidated running ground for widows and the vandals who would plunder the last vestiges of their dignity. The lonesome streets yawned, forgotten and cracked. And the downtown he still toiled in was comprised mostly of vacant buildings, secondhand clothing stores, and discount trinket shops. Long gone were the cotton boom days of the '50s. Those innocent and optimistic times had been replaced with a deep reliance on trade with Mexico, and the peso devaluations of the '80s had drained the life from the region's once robust economy, such that even the nice neighborhoods now seemed run down.

Back in the confines of the drugstore, Fulgencio recounted his brief expedition and observations to his deceased delivery boy.

El Chotay said, "One man's ghetto is another man's paradise. Why don't you try calling on the phone?"

But this effort went unanswered as well. Day after day, he left awkward messages on an infernal machine.

"I hate those things," he would exclaim, slamming the receiver down in disgust upon completing what he knew was yet another disastrous message.

Chagrined, he turned to Brother William for help during one of their evening horseback rides on El Dos de Copas. Brother William suggested writing her a letter. "There's something romantic and old-fashioned about a love letter, don't you think? Maybe she'll appreciate that. Maybe it will get her attention, remind her of how things once were between you."

Brother William was right, Fulgencio surmised. It had been rather presumptuous of him to think that Carolina would simply run back into his arms the first chance she got. A letter would allow him to voice his thoughts without being cut off or interrupted by well-deserved recriminations.

High up on a dusty shelf in his broom closet office, behind a forgotten Joya bottle, Fulgencio found a sheaf of ancient and yellowing stationary. Sitting at his antique pharmacy typewriter, he carefully articulated his thoughts.

Dear Carolina,

I never meant to ruin your life or bring you any pain. I have waited all these years to be able to speak with you and be your friend without bringing you any shame as the wife of another man. Now that your commitments and obligations have been fulfilled, will you do me the honor of allowing me to call upon you in your time of sorrow?

Sincerely,
Fulgencio Ramirez, RPh

He carefully folded the letter, sealed the envelope, and gave it to Little David to drop off with the evening deliveries. The next morning, he waited impatiently for Little David to report to work, hoping for a response. But his heart sank upon seeing the unopened envelope clasped in Little David's hand as he walked in.

"Sowwy, Fully," Little David drawled in a dialect only his immediate family could comprehend, his speech impediment a result of the cerebral palsy with which he had been born.

"Give me that," Fulgencio grumbled, freeing the envelope from Little David's tight grip. "And don't call me 'Fully.'"

"But that's what she call you, wemembah? When we was young and putty?"

"I was never pretty, Little David," sighed Fulgencio, stuffing the unopened envelope into his desk drawer next to an empty tequila bottle.

"She was," Little David whispered wistfully.

Ten years his junior, Little David had been a wide-eyed witness to Fulgencio's roller coaster ride with Carolina. The young couple had taken him—just a little boy back then—on their trips to the beach during those endless summer days before Fulgencio's senior year. Her hair as bright as the sun, they had all danced, holding hands in the shallow water. They'd built sandcastles for the relentless tide to swallow. Fulgencio belted out songs from the top of a sand dune as the sun set. Carolina melodramatically waved her hands in the air like an orchestra conductor, commanding the waves to spare their castle in the sand. And he, Little David, had marveled at them.

Fulgencio understood then—as he did now—that Little David loved them immeasurably and cherished his memories of them as a couple because they had been the only two people in the world that truly enjoyed his company. They invited him along because it pleased them, because they wanted him there, not because they pitied him, not out of some sense of obligation.

One night on the two-lane back from the beach, Little David had fallen asleep during the ferry ride back to the shore, waking to find Fulgencio and Carolina cuddled in the front seat as they cruised beneath the canopy of stars. Inspired, he'd blurted out: "Fulgencio, you aw da King of da Sea. And Cawolina, you aw da Queen of da Waves."

The two smiled and nuzzled, feeling new in their sun-baked skins, their arms touching, her cheek lightly brushing against his shoulder.

Carolina glanced back at Little David, caressing him with her sweet smile. "And you, Little David, you're the Prince of the Sand Castle!"

"I like dat!" Little David exclaimed, beaming proudly as if

the queen herself had anointed him with her scepter. "I've never thought of myself as a prince before." With a tranquil smile grooved upon his face, Little David fell back asleep as Fulgencio and Carolina wove dreams of marriage and children.

"Fully," she spoke gravely, "someday when we're married, if your parents were to not be there for Little David anymore, I would want him to come live with us."

Fulgencio pulled the car off the road and rolled to a halt. He made sure his brother was still sleeping and then turned his body toward hers, took her face in his hands, and kissed her passionately.

"I'll never be able tell you what your words mean to me," he said, gazing into her eyes. "You are so much more than the pretty girl I fell in love with in the drugstore. You are an amazing person."

She held him tightly, letting his love wash over her like yet another wave she had summoned from the sea.

As they resumed the drive back home, Fulgencio realized in astonishment how much his love had grown for Carolina that night.

"I never thought it would be possible to love you more," he said. "Yet every day you do or say something surprising, and I find myself falling even more deeply into your spell."

"I know," she whispered, laying her head on his shoulder. "I feel the same way, Fully."

"Fully, what next?" Little David asked Fulgencio in the gloom of the drugstore as El Chotay appeared, chewing on a breakfast taco. "Hi, Chotay!"

Fulgencio looked to the sky for an answer but his frustration grew into desperation as the weeks crawled by, and day after day Little David continued to return with his head hung low.

Unopened letters, unread cards, still-wrapped flowers, untouched chocolates. Four months had passed since the twenty-two letters had fallen to their final resting place on the pharmacy floor.

It was hopeless, Fulgencio began to believe. Until one night out on the ranch, Brother William appeared in the entrance to the hut.

"I spy the stench of defeat in the air," Brother William declared emphatically. "As hard as we've worked to fight *la maldición de* Caja Pinta, you cannot give up now!"

Always the master at devising winning game plans, Brother William joined his fellow ghost—the tireless, romantic descendant of troubadours, Fernando Cisneros—in helping Fulgencio concoct an inspired scheme.

On the day of Saint Valentine, Fulgencio gathered his favorite trio at El Dos de Copas. He rubbed a special mixture of herbs on the guitar strings as Fernando Cisneros and Cipriano repeated a set of obscure incantations in ancient Nahuatl. Brother William and the Virgen de Guadalupe looked on in prayer (just in case the Aztec gods needed a helping hand from Our Lord Jesus Christ). While the sun set over La Frontera, Fulgencio crossed the bridge over the river and shot toward Carolina's house, the warm, metallic spell of enchanted guitar strings filled the air.

Fulgencio's voice, instrument forged by the grace of angels and the torment of demons, rose as unfettered as a spirit on its way to heaven. And the words to "Sin Ti," an old Mexican standard he had often sung to Carolina in their early *serenata* days, sprung from his lips as he stood upon the thorns of the vanquished rose bush and raised his arms toward her bedroom window high above. Through that song he expressed the futility of living without her, the impossibility of forgetting her, and the sheer pointlessness of carrying on in her absence.

Sin Ti
(Without you)
No podré vivir jamas
(I can live no more)
Y pensar que nunca más
(And think that never more)
Estaré junto a ti
(Will I be beside you)

Sin Ti
(Without you)
No hay clemencia en mi dolor
(There's no clemence in my pain)
La esperanza de mi amor
(The hope of my love)
Esta lejos de aqui
(Is distant from here)

Sin Ti
(Without you)
Es inútil vivir
(It's futile to live)
Como inútil será
(As futile will be)
El quererte olvidar.
(To try and forget you.)

As the song drew to a close, Fulgencio Ramirez's heart jumped back into his throat. Just like that first day in the drugstore with the Band-Aids on the floor. Someone was at the window. A shadow rustled against the sheers. Could it be? He thought, his mind racing. Could his love finally have listened to the calling of his heart? To the siren song of their destiny in pending?

The trio held their breath in empathetic anticipation, ready to swing into a celebratory rendition of "Las Mañanitas," the traditional *serenata* opener. They tuned quietly, humming and plucking.

But Fulgencio Ramirez's heart plunged from its precarious perch as the hauntingly familiar voice of an old man floated down from above. The window cracking open, Fulgencio heard:

"Carolina says that—in deference to your younger brother's countless attempts to deliver your letters and gifts—she will grant your wish to see her. But you must wait at least a year from the date she became a widow, for her time of mourning to pass. Now go, son, it is not proper to serenade a widow so soon after her husband's death."

The window creaked shut as the disembodied voice dissipated upon the evening breeze. Their heads drooping like wilted flowers, the musicians gave Fulgencio Ramirez their heartfelt condolences and piled into their ramshackle van, headed for their next gig.

Fulgencio Ramirez did not know what he should be feeling anymore, as his pickup sputtered over the river toward El Dos de Copas. He felt rejected by Carolina's failure to appear at the window. He was devastated by the thought of waiting eight more months. But how could he not be heartened by the window of hope that had been cracked opened? Eight more months? What was a year in the scheme of things, at this point? But whose was that familiar voice which had floated down like a fog from heaven on high? What man dared be in the widow's room at this time of night on Saint Valentine's Day? His macho jealousy began to rise up, but he reminded himself to keep it in check, lest it be his undoing yet again. There's hope, he assured himself. Hang on.

As Fulgencio's truck bounced along the dirt road to his hut, in the darkness lined by the shadows looming of mesquites, he suddenly exploded with the realization: "I knew it!" He slammed on the brakes and slapped his hand on the steering wheel. "That voice!"

It had been none other than Carolina's father, Arthur Mendelssohn, RPh

TWELVE

Rage. At times, Fulgencio Ramirez could physically hear it, rising up from deep within him and drowning out everything else around him. It had begun in his childhood, been exacerbated by his father's torment, and escalated at an alarming rate from the day he met Carolina Mendelssohn. The rush of a thousand boiling bubbles, each carrying the bitter taste of pain, regret, and resentment into his mouth. In his veins. In his blood. Ascending from some forbidden and obscured chamber of his soul.

He could hear it, like a freight train rolling in from Mexico beneath the starry veil of night. Sometimes he sensed it from a distance, like when the train blew its whistle while still on the other side, then he shook with the rattle of metal wheels on screeching tracks. At times, it woke him terrified, an infernal brass band blasting in dissonance. In the pitch of night. Nerves frazzled and shaking. Disorientation. Running as a child through his parent's house, stumbling in the dark, searching for the comfort of his mother's arms in the middle of the night. The unrelenting train plowing blindly through his mind in a blur of random letters and digits stenciled in white on rust. Boxcars. Steel rolls. Containers harboring secrets imported from beyond, foreign to this land, yet native to his soul. Shrieking iron upon iron. Sparks and fireworks. Letters spinning and falling into place to form words that made no sense, words like *chahualiztli, nexicolhuiliztli, ellelaci, tlatzitzicayōtl.* The train would keep rolling, keep coming, keep twisting over slick rails like an endless serpent originating from a pit deep within the dark recesses of Mexico.

When he heard it coming, he could feel the fear racing by its side. What would he do? Who would get hurt? Who might pay the cost of his misdirected vengeance?

As a child, it had been schoolyard and neighborhood playmates, whom he had stunned with the surprising swiftness and sting of his fists. The wrong word, a miscalculated or misinterpreted glance or expression could set Fulgencio off. The normally cheerful and placid boy would erupt, punishing his victims until he was pulled away and punished himself. By the teachers with the paddle. And then again at home by his mother with the shoe. And then again by his father with the belt. Kneeling for hours outside before a bowl of *frijoles*, forced to stare at the food but denied for hours the permission to consume it.

He struggled to train himself to listen and look out for the rage, to cut it off at the pass and detour it away from his mind, to prevent himself from repeating his acts of hostility and violence, but more often than not, he failed. And when it caught him by surprise, in the aftermath of catastrophe, he flailed to stay afloat in a sea of drowning guilt.

It was this propensity to violence that made Fulgencio Ramirez a feared football player. Brother William had been quick to recognize the danger of Fulgencio Ramirez's condition. One afternoon, after an especially bone-crushing football practice, Brother William spoke eloquently on the subject, pacing in front of Fulgencio, who sat hunched on the locker room bench.

"Lurking in the shadows of your soul, there is a cauldron of tumult," he exclaimed, throwing his arms up in the air. "One way or another, that energy is going to escape. You can either channel it in a positive way, like a river that has been dammed and levied. Or you can allow it to be unleashed as a destructive force, one which kills everything in its path, like a river which has overflown, wiping out the cities built upon its banks. Which would Christ choose? Which will you choose?"

Fulgencio Ramirez was too young to take such philosophizing about his feelings to heart, but he trusted Brother William. He was willing to try anything to prevent his temper from tampering with the course he had charted toward his goals. For a brief time, it seemed to work. Whenever his anger or jealousy threatened to derail him, he focused his energy on football or work. It seemed for a moment during his sophomore and junior year that perhaps he could overcome these destructive tendencies. With Brother William's coaching and Carolina's companionship, Fulgencio felt invincible.

Only a person with a much broader perspective might have foreseen the drastic turn that Fulgencio's tortured psyche might force him to take. One day, a few months after Fulgencio had begun dating Carolina, he bumped into his mother at the grocery store. Standing in the produce section, weighing avocados on the scale, his mother's pained gaze seared his heart.

"Mamá!" Fulgencio exclaimed, yearning to be cradled in her arms just like he had as a child fleeing his night terrors.

"Fulgencio." She nodded curtly.

It was the first time he had seen or spoken to any member

of his family since the day he ceased sleeping beneath their roof months earlier.

"How is everyone, Mamá?" Fulgencio asked, stuffing the avocados into a large brown paper sack, inching closer. She wore a faded pink housedress and the weight of the world upon her shoulders. "How's Little David?"

"Everyone's fine," she said. "Don't worry about us."

"But I do, Mamá. I worry every night while I say my prayers to the Virgencita."

"Well, if you worry so much," she perked up, "when are you coming home?"

Fulgencio's face crashed to the dirty floor. He had no desire to return to that volatile world.

"I hear you've done very well at your fancy private school," she said, her stark eyebrows angled high as he eyes scanned him. "You look like you've grown."

"Yes, Mamá. And when I graduate I will go to the University of Texas at Austin to become a Registered Pharmacist like Mr. Arthur Mendelssohn."

"And then?" she asked.

"Then I will marry his daughter, Carolina, and live happily ever after." He smiled, reciting the plan he so often reviewed in his mind.

"It sounds like you have it all mapped out," Ninfa del Rosario said slowly. "It doesn't seem like we play a part in your life anymore."

"This is my new life, Mamá," he said, "but I still love you all."

"Well," she said, regaining her senses, "I have to hurry. You know how your father gets if dinner's not on the table when he comes home."

As she turned away, Fulgencio realized the extent to which he had abandoned his mother and siblings. Thinking only of himself and of his dreams, he had not stopped to consider that they were still living in that hell he'd found the courage to escape. He felt like something he'd never felt before, like a traitor.

Almost as if she'd read his thoughts, Ninfa del Rosario whipped her head around and stared at him vindictively, a flash of uncontrolled anger blazing in her dark eyes. "You can run as far away as you want, Fulgencio Ramirez Cisneros, but you will never be able to escape the dark side of who you are and where you came from." She opened her mouth to continue speaking, but then she seemed to catch herself, her hand flying to her mouth, her teeth biting down anxiously on her lower lip right before she covered her face in dismay.

Mother and son stood mere feet apart on the grimy linoleum floor, but they felt separated by the kind of vast chasm that was carved by rivers over millennia. Their tense silence hung as heavily between them as a thick drape being lowered between stage and audience. Just when both were about to retreat to their corners and vanish into the shadows of disparate aisles, they were startled by an unnoticed eavesdropper.

"*Tienes razón*, Ninfa," interjected La Señora Villarreal, a distant relative whose family also hailed from the lands near El Dos de Copas. Shaking her head despondently, she added, "*El pobre niño carga la maldición.* Just like his grandfather, and his grandfather's father before him, he has abandoned his family and never looked back. *Que Dios te salve, m'ijo . . .*" She made the sign of the cross as her avocados rolled across the hanging scale, "If you're not careful, the blood that you carry inside will turn those dreams that you so love into nightmares." She watched him gloomily, her watery gray eyes glimmering like crystal marbles set in the baked stone mask of her dark skin. Nodding politely at both of them, she swept her avocados into a brown paper bag and towed her endless string of children toward the butcher counter.

The blood had fled in a panic from Fulgencio's face, rendering him for a moment as white as a gringo. His arms hung lifeless. His mother left her cart in its place and exited without another word through the nearby entrance.

Later, in the back seat of Mr. Balmori's borrowed car, clasped in the tender embrace of Carolina's arms, Fulgencio asked.

"Do you think I have a dark side, Carolina?"

Pulling his lips toward hers, Carolina whispered, "It's what makes you sexy."

"How so?"

"When you kiss me," she said wistfully, "it's like putting a match to paper, a spark to kindling wood. And when you put your arms around me, I know you could either protect me or destroy me. Yes, you have a dark side, Fulgencio. Thank God, you have a dark side." She chuckled mischievously and pulled him down atop her on the sticky red vinyl seats.

Consumed by lust, Fulgencio cast aside his fears and doubts—thoughts of the family curse slipping from his mind like beads of condensation off a pane of glass—as the heat from their enmeshed lips and bodies steamed the windows.

THIRTEEN

Fulgencio and his friends elevated their games off the field to alarmingly violent heights. They rumbled for the bat of an eyelash, over the fickle whims of a girl, and—just as frequently—over racial insults hurled by the local White elites at the displaced and impoverished Mexican Americans whose land had been conquered a century earlier. Through that conquest, fortunes and social positions had changed hands, as had command over the laws and their enforcement. So it was that a place with a Spanish name was lorded over by Northern newcomers determined to exact their authority to maintain control and fill their coffers.

Penny loafers and sneakers clashed with boots and huaraches. Bowling shirts and leather jackets competed with guayaberas. Convertibles fended with motorcycles. Jeans, Vaseline, and back-pocket combs were universally appealing as jukeboxes played and hips swayed and fists flew. In the midst of it all, Fulgencio's senior year advanced in a frenzied blur.

As racial tensions boiled over throughout the South, along the border, the dynamic of discrimination and prejudice manifested itself in an ongoing struggle between gringos and Mexicanos. Certain establishments featured signs refusing entrance to Blacks, Mexicans, and dogs. Frequently, at the movie theater, the park, the beach, or even on the streets of downtown, Fulgencio and Carolina's romantic reverie was disrupted by a scathing racial insult, a crude joke, a snide remark, or a judgmetal stare. And not once could Fulgencio allow the affront to pass unconfronted.

At first, Carolina pleaded, "Why can't you let it go?"

"Because you deserve better," he answered.

"Someday things will be better," she insisted. "We just have to be patient. Times are changing, and people will change with them."

"Some people must be pushed toward change," he replied.

He admired her for looking to the future. He supposed that was why she could see past his last name, and the shade of his skin, and his family's poverty. But he could not resist the pleasure he extracted from the numbing impact of his fists thundering against giving—and deserving—flesh and bone.

As Fulgencio's opponents on the football field failed to provide a challenge, he increasingly turned his energies elsewhere. Dance halls, coffee shops, alleyways, to him they all seemed like stages for their taboo affair and his resulting acts of vengeance. The closer he grew to Carolina, the more aggressive he became. He became increasingly afraid of losing her, of others scheming to steal her away or come between them. He could not fathom life without her. And as his high school graduation neared, he dreaded the gnawing realization that he would be leaving for college while she would be staying behind to complete her senior year. Doubt crept into the dark corners of his mind, whispering ethereally in disembodied words that rang dissonantly and inexplicably in his ears. *Atle ipam motta* and *anel niteitta*, the ancient chants that had tormented him occasionally in the past, now washed over him with growing regularity. How could he possibly be good enough for her? Were the bigots who disapproved of their relationship fundamentally right? How could a *pobre méndigo* like him be worthy of her? And could he cling to her from afar? Inside his tortured soul, the insidious seeds planted by backward naysayers sprouted and grew into vines strangling his heart, undermining his confidence. Next to her, in their accusers' eyes, he secretly felt shamed and dirty while she gleamed glorious and clean.

God forbid an innocent boy flirt with Carolina, for he would be pulverized before he could even realize what hit him. And, of course, with Carolina's beauty blossoming daily, the formula was an equation for disaster. When people spoke of her looks, elegance and style, they often compared her to Grace Kelly. How could he, practically a *mojado*, a wetback, cling to the likes of her? Didn't she belong with one of the rich white boys with Anglo names that flowed in English and matched those of the heroes in the schoolbooks and movie stars on the silver screen?

His insecurities and jealousy intensified with every passing day. The audible rage he had been tortured by since childhood left him no safe quarter; the train roaring up from Mexico seemed to never end, its cryptically encoded letters spelling the mystifying words he heard as he demolished anyone who looked Carolina's way.

"Your losing control, Fully," she told him fearfully one night as she cleaned his wounds in the back seat of the car.

"Control over what?" he asked, holding her close.

"The dark side you told me about," she whispered. "I'm worried you'll take things too far, hurt someone too badly, ruin our future for nothing."

"Sometimes I feel so confused," he admitted. "Why am I so angry? You're all I ever wanted. And I have you."

"Is it my fault?" she wondered aloud. "Am I to blame? Does the way I act and dress draw too many stares? Should I change my style or do something different with my hair?"

"No," he replied firmly. "You're perfect."

"So are you," she cried alongside him, wiping the blood from his hands after each skirmish. "I love your passion. It's something that's always been absent from my life. You make me feel alive. I thrill watching you fight almost as much as I love hearing you sing. It's wrong. And I know it. But I can't change the way I feel."

Thus, their behavior became complicit. Ashamed yet exhilarated, he understood she used her beauty to lure their prey. Night after night, their lips moistened by the blood of their victims, their hands groped and clawed at each other's flesh. Steam on the windows. Sweat on the vinyl. Each night a discarded article of clothing closer to the ultimate and forbidden union the nuns and brothers claimed would damn them to hell. At times—as they swayed rhythmically, teetering precariously on the brink of abandoned release, her eyes ablaze, her curls spilling around their intertwined bodies—they wondered if hell could really be all that bad as long they were sentenced to share its consuming fire forever.

But in the end, Fulgencio's sense of duty would prevail. He'd nudge her gently away and pray for forgiveness, patience, and the will to wait for the day they could be joined as one under God, preserving her honor. Their frustration knew no limits as they were both consumed by desire. Each yearned to be the vast ocean in which the other drowned.

They both were keenly aware that her father fretted about them, but they also recognized that he could never understand the depths of the tumult in which they tossed, like boats ripped from their moors and lost upon storming seas. For at home and at work, Carolina and Fulgencio kept up the appearances of a proper couple destined for the altar in due time. He took her *serenatas* every weekend without fail. She baked him chocolate chip cookies and carrot cake with the help of her withering mother. And Fulgencio toiled more arduously than anyone else in Mr. Mendelssohn's employ.

Still, Mr. Mendelssohn worried, expressing his fears to both of them. First, he asked Fulgencio if something was awry, but Fulgencio played dumb, chalking up his bruises and cuts to football, his mercurial moods to the pressures of applying to college while juggling school, football, work, and Carolina.

"I'm afraid perhaps I made a mistake allowing the two of you to date," Mr. Mendelssohn confided in Carolina, who later relayed the conversation to Fulgencio. "Our society makes it very difficult for people of different backgrounds to be together. I worry your love could bring you great harm in one way or another. But now it's too late to undo what has been done. I know if I tried to separate you, it would only spur you closer together. Such is the defiance of youth. I've lived my life and I won't stop you from living yours. But please, be careful. You're the only daughter we have."

When Carolina repeated the words to Fulgencio, he wept in her arms.

"What's wrong, Fully? Don't you see? He won't try to come between us."

"It's just that. My father could never find the words to reason with us. Instead, he beat us. You, Carolina, are blessed. Your parents see you as a person to nurture, an equal to cherish, not a subject or a slave born to do their bidding."

Carolina rocked him in her arms and kissed him tenderly, assuring him that somehow they would muddle through. "We have to be strong. We have to rise above all of these obstacles. Instead of fighting other people, we have to fight our own demons."

"I want peace," Fulgencio cried. "I just can't find it, even in your arms. I'm afraid there's something wrong with me and I just can't beat it."

"Just remember, Fully," she whispered lovingly. "You're not alone. We're in this together."

"Carolina?"

"Yes, *mi amor*?" she said in a perfect Castilian accent.

"I'm afraid of losing you when I leave for college. What if you meet somebody else? What if you realize you're better off without me?"

She tightened her hold on him. "That's ridiculous, Fully. I'm going to miss you so much. You have all of my love. I promise you. The only thing that could ever come between us is ourselves." To allay his concerns, she kissed him so passionately she made him forget his fears, at least for the moment.

During Fulgencio's senior year, Brother William's football team went undefeated, winning the Catholic school state championship handily. Still, Brother William also sensed that not all was well. Sharing his concern with Fulgencio as they sat alone on the bleachers after practice, he spoke somberly to his pupil. "I feel a hollowness in this line of steel. I don't know everything that's going on in your life, Fulgencio, but I worry for you. I pray tirelessly for God to intercede on your behalf, for the Virgencita to ease your suffering and guide you in the right direction. You are so close to all of your goals, all of the dreams that drove you to me that summer day a few years ago. But I fear there's something threatening to keep you from reaching your destiny. You must not let that darkness lead you off course, Fulgencio."

Fulgencio nodded quietly and drew a deep breath. He knew his mentor was correct. If only he could figure out how to keep it all together just a little bit longer, just long enough to earn that pharmacy degree and wed Carolina. It was all only four more years away, but that span stretched before him like an immutable eternity.

On graduation day, Brother William wrapped his arms around Fulgencio on the Academy's front steps. "Congratulations, my boy. You made it." The headmaster and coach stood back, remarking, "Your smile reminds me of that day in the jalopy as we rode back from our first visit to your ranch."

"I'm happier than I've been in a long time, Brother William," Fulgencio explained. "I saw my father. I think maybe I needed to reconnect with him and my family in order to find peace inside my own heart."

Brother William listened with hope.

"He gave me this!" Fulgencio brandished a large wooden carrying case sitting in the back seat of the car.

"What is it?" Brother William wondered.

Fulgencio's eyes lit up, his face like that of a child's on Christmas morning as he opened the case to reveal a shiny black Remington typewriter. To him, the machine symbolized the great strides he was making on behalf of his family. It was not the tool of a laborer, but that of a professional.

"It's brand new!" Fulgencio exclaimed. "My father never gave me a present before. Never!"

Brother William smiled, patting Fulgencio on the shoulder.

"Tonight, I'm going back to the house for the first time, to have a special dinner," Fulgencio added. "They want to meet Carolina."

Brother William shook his head in astonishment. "My prayers have been answered. We'll have to plan a trip to El Dos de Copas to thank the Virgencita and take her some of that Irish whiskey she so loves. My son, how I have worried throughout this year for you, sensing the shadows cast upon you by the trouble in your soul. But now I thank the Lord for His benevolence. You have emerged victorious yet again."

All at once, Fulgencio fathomed the treacherous depths of the violent darkness in which he had been swimming. He felt ashamed for the sinful tides to which he had exposed Carolina Mendelssohn. And he vowed to repent his ways. He collapsed into Brother William's arms, sobbing, "I've been lost Brother William, but today I think I've finally found my way. May God forgive me."

"That's why they call it *commencement*, Don Fulgencio," Brother William soothed him. "Today you can begin anew. You and your future bride."

"But first, I must become a pharmacist," Fulgencio reminded him.

"Of course," Brother William rolled his eyes, chuckling, "that goes without saying." He patted Fulgencio on the back of his red graduation robe as the young man got into the driver's seat and closed the heavy steel door. "God Bless You, Fulgencio Ramirez!" he called out as his protégé drove away amidst a cloud of dust.

That night, Fulgencio and Carolina huddled close at the

table's crowded edge, in the warm and cozy kitchen on Garfield Street. Carolina radiated magical light like an apparition of the Virgin Mary herself. Ninfa del Rosario served her best refried beans ever, and animated talk filled the fragrant air. Nicolas Junior was still in Korea with the army, but Fernando watched his brother and Carolina enviously from the corner of his eye. Little David rocked his heavy head from one shoulder onto the other, gazing adoringly at Carolina, asking repeatedly when the three of them might escape to the beach again. And Fulgencio's father displayed a side of himself none of his sons had never witnessed. He dressed sharply in a crisp and clean guayabera, white over black slacks. His black *botines* looked shiny and new. His wavy black mane gleamed under the low-hanging kitchen lamp. And he permitted the family to relax and enjoy the evening by locking away the liquor bottles and keeping his part in the conversation to a minimum.

Carolina was delighted to meet Fulgencio's family. She grew hot beneath her white Sunday dress, and her smooth porcelain cheeks flushed with excitement. She grasped nervously at Fulgencio's hand beneath the table as her smile lit up the house.

As the plates were cleared away, Fulgencio's father pushed his chair back and invited silence with his words:

"I want you all to know how proud I am of my son." He looked straight into Fulgencio eyes. "No one gave him this example. No one led him by the hand. He made a man of himself, in spite of my ways. Today he became the first Ramirez to graduate from high school. And he'll be the first to go to college. Your accomplishments, son, make all of our sacrifice worthwhile." Rising to his feet as the entire family gawked in disbelief, he reached his calloused hand out to Fulgencio. As their grip tightened, he added, "I gave you that typewriter so you can use it as you earn your pharmacy degree. Keep it always as a reminder of your old man. I don't know how much longer I'll be on Earth, but I give you both my blessing."

Nicolas Ramirez Sr. turned his eyes on Carolina: "I know that my son will be able to provide for you. Please take care of my boy." Without another word, he walked out onto the porch to smoke a cigarette.

Against Ninfa del Rosario's protests, Fulgencio and Carolina helped her clean up the kitchen. When it was time to go, they all said their goodbyes. And as the family waved from the porch, Fulgencio's father walked the young couple to the car. He opened the door for Carolina and walked around back with his son, opening his door as well.

As the vehicle roared to life, Nicolas Ramirez Sr. leaned in through the window and wrapped his arm around Fulgencio's shoulder, the tough skin and bristles of his face hard against his son's cheek, his smoky breath on Fulgencio's ear as he whispered: "*M'ijo*, for a long time I thought I'd done everything wrong in my life. But now I know that's not the case."

On the Mendelssohn's doorstep that night, Fulgencio gazed into Carolina's eyes. With his left hand he took her right, placing a tiny onionskin sack into her palm. The yellow porch light illuminated a shiny gold chain. Her smile spread at the sight of the dainty medallion of Madonna and Child. She held Fulgencio closely as he placed it tenderly around her neck.

"Soon I'll be going," he said as her eyes filled with tears. "I'm sorry if I've ever done anything which brought you pain, if because of me, you've had a glimpse of hell."

"I'd love you there and back," Carolina replied, her body shaking with emotion.

"Well, I think we're back," he smiled.

Her body went limp in his arms as she sobbed: "I just want *you* back. I want you back from Austin already, and you haven't even left."

"Don't worry," Fulgencio whispered, stroking her hair as they stood in the moonlight. "Time will fly."

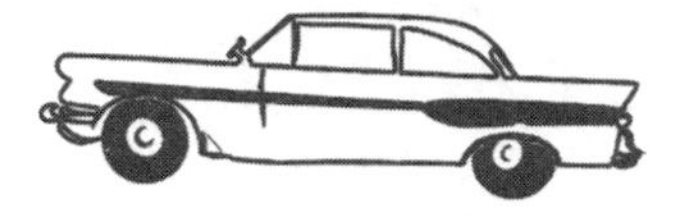

FOURTEEN

The second hand thundered on the wall clock hanging vigil at La Farmacia Ramirez. A tired Fulgencio hunched over his antique Remington, shiny black like the day his father gave it to him. A musty piece of stationary sat blank in the return, his fingers poised to crawl across the keys.

Dear Carolina,

I am sitting here, alone in my pharmacy. Wishing everything hadn't gone wrong. I feel this life has passed me by. And I know you must feel the same way. Why else would you have said I ruined your life? You must have loved me once. You must have regretted the different paths our lives took, when we should have taken one path together.

Thank you for agreeing to see me again. Even if it is months away. At least I have hope that you will remember how you once felt. I hope that you can find it in your heart to forgive me. Because hope is all that has kept me going through these lonely years. Hope in us. Hope that we'd have another chance to make things right.

With love,
Fulgencio Ramirez, RPh

The clicking, ringing, and rolling of the manual typewriter came to a stop. As he folded the letter and placed it in an envelope, he wondered if Carolina would even read it. He handed the envelope to Little David to drop off while out on his deliveries. And he returned to caring for his daily parade of old folks, *viejitos*, pregnant moms on welfare, and, of course, his entourage of hangers-on.

Fulgencio had always attracted followers, from the ranchlands of El Dos de Copas to the streets of La Frontera. A row of metal chairs lined the wall of his pharmacy. There, a steady stream of regulars drifted in and out each day without fail. At least until they died. And even that didn't seem to stop some of them. There was his cousin Primo Loco Gustavo, Eleodoro the Cabrito Man, El Gordo Jimenez, and the list went on. Invariably, one or two of these colorful characters could be found sitting against the wall whenever anyone came into the store to fill a prescription.

Ninfa del Rosario found their presence annoying and unnecessary. She would say indignantly to her son: "Why, Fulgencio? Why do you permit these people to cling to you? Get rid of them. They only bring you down, asking you for money and medicine. You've probably put half their kids through school!"

It was true that Fulgencio had helped more than a handful of families survive over the years, not just by giving them discounts and free medicine when their Medicaid ran out, but also by lending them money he knew would never be repaid. "These are my friends, Mamá," he would say. "Besides, it's none of your business."

"Well, how can it be good for *your* business?" Ninfa del Rosario continued, waving her finger in the air. "When a customer comes through the door, they see this row of paupers, cripples, and dying old men holding up your wall. These people don't look like they belong in a drugstore. They look like they belong in the morgue. In fact, that'll probably be their next stop!"

Fulgencio smiled at his mom's hyperbole. He thought the true reason she hated his bevy of followers was that they reminded her of failure, that they presaged the future of her own beleaguered sons. They reeked of a misfortune she feared might be contagious.

"*¡Ay no!*" She would lament, "*¡Que gente tán fea!*" What ugly people, she lamented, turning her nose up as she strode by them, her scarf wrapped around her hair, her green sunglasses concealing the disdain in her eyes.

Fulgencio enjoyed the presence of his cronies for multiple reasons. First, they kept him company. Company that was alive, at least for the time being. Second, their collective failures made him seem like a shining success, which propped up his tattered ego. Third, he believed they were in need of healing. Not the kind of healing that came in a medicine bottle, but rather a healing of the heart and soul. And that was something they shared in common.

"How funny it is," Fulgencio once commented to Brother William out on El Dos de Copas during that long and torturous year of waiting to finally gaze upon Carolina's countenance. "There we sit in the drugstore, my tired old friends and I. Surrounded by pills and syrups, narcotics and amphetamines, barbiturates and antihistamines, antibiotics and controlled substances. There are drugs on the shelves, over the counter. There are drugs flooding the streets. But none of it can cure what is wrong with us."

"No," Brother William had said forlornly, hurting for his disciple. "Only we can do that."

"What about God, Brother William?" Fulgencio asked. "Can he cure us all? Can we find our salvation in him?"

"If you have not healed your soul from within," Brother William replied as they sat out by the campfire, the flames dancing in the darkness, "even God cannot save you."

In those days, fewer people came into the drugstore. Even Eleodoro the Cabrito Man was filling his prescriptions at the new Walmart on the outskirts of town, and then coming over for coffee and an afternoon of metal-chair sitting, which he seemed determined to refine into a competitive sport so he could at long last be champion of something.

"¡*Pinche* Walmart *te va matar, Ramirez*!" Eleodoro would exclaim. "Walmart's gonna kill you. They're practically giving the drugs away over there."

Fulgencio contemplated his treacherous friend with amusement. Eleodoro wore his standard uniform: khaki pants, white guayabera, straw hat. He was a scruffy geezer with a potbelly. Always red as a plump, overripe tomato. White stubble on his ruddy cheeks.

"What kind of friend are you, Eleodoro? That you buy from the enemy?" Fulgencio pondered.

"They have frozen french fries by the ton too!" Eleodoro cried. "How can you compete with that? At least I bring you *cabritos*. I don't do that for the Walmart."

"They'd throw you out if you walked in there with a dead goat," chimed in El Primo Loco Gustavo.

"He *is* a dead goat," said El Gordo Jimenez, leaning back in his rigid chair.

Fulgencio leaned forward against his high counter, surveying his lowly court.

El Primo Loco Gustavo rocked back and forth anxiously in his seat. He was a gnomelike creature, skin and bone stretched thinly over what had once been a generous frame. His clothes hung limp on him, and he always wore an outdated tie from the sixties, psychedelic colors and swirls of oranges and greens. Heavy black horn-rimmed glasses framed his fishlike face. And a wiry maelstrom of jet-black hair exploded from his head in every direction. He looked like a mad scientist, this cousin of his, a Mexican Albert Einstein. In fact, he kind of was.

El Primo Loco Gustavo had once been Mexico's leading statistician. He hailed from a separate branch of the Ramirez family, one based in the interior of Mexico. Declared a math genius as a child, Gustavo had obtained his degrees while attending the Universidad Nacional Autónoma de Mexico on a full academic scholarship in Mexico City. And as if that were not enough to impress everyone in La Frontera and Nueva Frontera combined, afterward, he had earned his doctorate at MIT.

According to rumor Gustavo had amassed an enormous amount of statistical data while working for Mexico's federal government. This data—irrefutably proving that the nation's political leaders were robbing the public blind—had tormented him through years of research and analysis, deep in the musty basements of an obscure government agency. Finally, one day Gustavo stormed into his superior's office, the vice subminister of internal affairs. Dropping reams of paper onto the bureaucrat's desk he exclaimed, "Here it is! Proof positive that our leaders are stealing from the people. We can put a stop to this madness, borrowing billions from the world to build sewer systems and roads while they simply stash the funds in Swiss bank accounts and spend it on villas, yachts, and movie starlets!"

"Excuse me for a moment, Gustavo," the bureaucrat replied, rising from his leather armchair and exiting his paneled office. "Have a seat," he motioned as he walked out.

Moments later a detachment of presidential police stormed into the room and dragged Gustavo to a grim and dank jail cell where he wasted away for five years. When he came out, his wife had married the bureaucrat and they'd sent his children away to a Swiss boarding school. Even his former servants pretended not to know him. People pointed at him in the streets, laughing and mocking him, calling him *El Loco*—since that time, he'd never been the same. He'd lost it all, including his mind. Now he just languished in the shadows of Fulgencio's drugstore, rocking back and forth, spewing out disembodied statistics, and waiting for his turn to become one of the same.

Fulgencio had repeatedly attempted to put his unconventional healing powers to work in his cousin's favor. As El Primo Loco Gustavo pored over chemical manuals and research results in the back end of the pharmacy, Fulgencio worked furiously, mixing a multitude of vials and powders, measuring and shaking, boiling and cooking, grinding ancient herbal remedies into a mystical compound of modern medicine and ancient cures.

"This could be it, Fulgencio," exclaimed El Primo Loco Gustavo, spouting out ratios and formulas. "My projected results are that after consuming your potion, I should be 92.37 percent more sane than I am now. Maybe I'll be able to get a job again. Get my wife and kids back! Maybe people won't point at me on the streets and laugh!"

"A simple haircut and a new pair of glasses might achieve

the same purpose," Eleodoro noted calmly, watching the frantic machinations of the two cousins with detached amusement.

"Okay, drink this and sit down on your chair until it takes effect," Fulgencio instructed his patient.

El Primo Loco Gustavo imbibed the smoking blue concoction from its glass vial and returned to his usual spot, rocking back and forth as nervously as always. Eleodoro edged away apprehensively as smoke began to waft from Gustavo's ears. As an attractive young woman entered the store, Gustavo's anguished face relaxed into an agreeable repose, his color normalized, his hair fell miraculously into place and his glasses slipped off his aquiline nose, falling neatly into his shirt pocket. His atrophied muscles twitched and ballooned, filling his clothes as he rose to his feet. The girl looked at him sideways as she strode toward the counter in a tight navy-blue short skirt with a white tank top, her auburn hair tumbling down to her waist. Gustavo swaggered up to her as she smiled in anticipation of what this charming scholar might say.

And then El Primo Loco Gustavo began twitching, convulsing, and foaming at the mouth. His eyes bulged like a frog's. His hair stood on end as if he'd inserted his finger into a light socket and he began to rock back and forth on the balls of his feet.

"Five million, six hundred thousand, four hundred thirty-seven," El Primo Loco Gustavo belted out as the girl's face contorted into a visage of fear and astonishment at his stunning transformation.

"What?" She quivered, clutching her purse and backing away.

"Screws," he said, his head bobbing out of control upon his shrinking shoulders. "Screws in the Torre Latinoamericana. Five million, six hundred thousand, four hundred thirty-seven to be exact. That's 25.79 percent more than in any other edifice in the Republic of Mexico. That's a lot of screws!"

"Maybe you should borrow one of them!" the girl yelled as she scurried out the door and disappeared into a crowd.

"*¡Más loco que una cabra!*" yelled Eleodoro. Crazier than a goat.

Fulgencio shook his head in disappointment. He seemed to be getting closer every time, but still it wasn't enough to repair the seemingly permanent damage that his cousin had sustained over years of lunacy.

El Primo Loco Gustavo seemed to have forgotten all about his near recovery and the effort that had gotten him there. He simply oscillated back and forth on his chair, fiddling with his horn-rimmed glasses and counting the bus riders through the storefront windows. "Seventeen," he said. "Seventeen . . . on average, that's 4.538 percent of all people riding a bus in La Frontera."

Fulgencio shook his head and returned to filling prescriptions. The second hand thundered on. Little David limped in through the back door with a broad grin on his face.

"She took the letter," Little David told his brother.

"She did?"

"Yes, right there on the porch. She took it. She said, 'Thanks, Little David.' And she went back inside."

Fulgencio's hopes soared to new heights. He surveyed his pathetic entourage. Eleodoro the Cabrito Man was assembling himself a cabrito taco. El Gordo Jimenez snored sonorously, his triple chin jiggling on his chest. El Primo Loco Gustavo struggled to catch a fly with chopsticks, missing badly because of his incessant swaying.

Fulgencio's eyes landed on the typewriter. This was proving to be a long year, but maybe if he wrote Carolina once a week, it would pass more quickly. He resolved to do so, patting Little David on the back and sitting down at the idle typewriter. He wished it were a week later already. The second hand thundered and echoed.

El Primo Loco Gustavo muttered something about flies outnumbering humans and feasting on their own regurgitation.

Fulgencio sighed: "What the hell, I may as well start writing now."

FIFTEEN

He thought of her that day, at the onset of the blistering summer of '59, as he stood on the blacktop headed north out of town. Arm outstretched. Thumb reaching for sky. His grandfather's worn leather suitcase in one hand. His typewriter case on the asphalt.

He had bid his farewells the day before, making the rounds at 1448 Garfield Street, Mendelssohn's Drugstore, and Carolina's house.

He hoped to leave without much fanfare, promising himself that he would not shed a tear. And he managed as much when he said goodbye to his parents, as well as when he shook Mr. Mendelssohn's hand at the drugstore, refusing to accept the wad of bills his boss pressed into his palm.

"I just want to help you, son," Mr. Mendelssohn said.

"Thank you, sir," Fulgencio replied. "You've helped me enough already. I'm going to do this on my own. I am eternally indebted to you already."

Mr. Mendelssohn shook his head, smiling, "You've always

been different, Fulgencio. Despite what some people may say, that's why I like you."

After a tight embrace, Fulgencio looked him straight in the eyes, "No, Mr. Mendelssohn. That's why you respect me."

As Fulgencio walked toward the door he had first stumbled through three years earlier, the clerks all shook Fulgencio's hand as Old Vera wept over the soda counter. With one hand on the door, Fulgencio turned back and waved, a broad smile on his face. His voice rose like an angel flying homeward to heaven: "*¡Ay, ay, ay, ay . . . Canta y no llores . . . porque cantando se alegran . . . cielito lindo . . . los corazones!*" The store came alive with cheers: "*Eso* Fulgencio! Make us proud! We'll be waiting for you!" The quivering smile on Mr. Mendelssohn's face warmed Fulgencio's heart as he headed out into the punishing sun.

His parting from Carolina was not as easy. His wish to somehow avoid an overt display of emotion proved completely unrealistic. From the moment she opened the door in a simple white dress, his heart ached.

"You look like an angel," he told her.

"An angel who is about to lose her wings," she cried, her tears beckoning his own sorrow forth.

"We swore we wouldn't lose each other," he said. "We have to get through, just this one year."

"And we will." She set her jaw with determination. "I'll be waiting for you, Fully."

He'd never forget her standing in the doorway as he finally left, murky tears and mascara streaks staining her once pristine dress, her grief-filled eyes glistening like shattered amber oozing forth her pain.

The heat rose in waves from the blacktop as Fulgencio wiped his brow. That morning it had still been dark outside when he awoke in the bed next to Bobby Balmori's. His bag lay neatly packed already at the foot of the bed. He dressed himself in the clothes of the day, chinos and a loose aqua-colored bowling shirt with wide white stripes running down either side of the front. His black, wavy mane was slicked back, and he tucked his tortoiseshell wayfarers with the green lenses into his breast pocket. The house still lay in the silence of slumber as he walked out the back door through the yard and into the alleyway. The sun rose as he reached the outskirts of town. And by the time he was halfway to Austin, sitting on the hard, rattling metal bed of a merciful pickup truck, he had changed out of his wannabe college-boy duds into his traditional, cooler Mexican clothes: khaki pants, white guayabera, straw cowboy hat. Few of the boys his age dressed like that. It was too Mexican. His brothers Nicolas and Fernando taunted him, saying he looked like a ranchero. But he didn't care. He was comfortable this way. After all, who cared how he dressed? He was going to the University of Texas at Austin to become a pharmacist, not to win a fashion contest.

The farmer that picked him up on the northern edges of La Frontera was headed to Dallas, so it was no big deal for him to drop Fulgencio off smack in the middle of Austin as the setting sun cast its burning orange glow on the monumental UT tower.

Fulgencio's wide eyes surveyed the town as he walked toward the campus. To him this was a metropolis. The tower was the tallest building he had ever seen. Gleaming cars filled the streets, baby blues with white vinyl, lime greens and chrome, candy apple red. Crisp, clean-cut boys waved and hollered from their ragtops at the impeccable sorority girls with wispy golden hair batting eyelashes in their convertibles.

He marveled at the tall, brick buildings of downtown. He

wondered where he might spend his first night in this new world. And he didn't even notice the puzzled looks on passersby as they stared at this lost manchild from another land.

At the edge of the campus, his eyes lit up at the sight of a massive gate with the University's shield hanging overhead. "Enter here ye seeking knowledge," the stone spoke in chiseled tones beneath the emblem.

Fulgencio looked around. He crossed the street and stood beneath the gate, his head arching backward as he took in the looming shadow of its greatness. He mouthed the words as he stepped through the gateway, "Enter here ye seeking knowledge." He smiled. He felt smarter already. Sure, he was tired, thirsty, and covered by a thick layer of dried sweat and dust from the long ride up, but he didn't feel that now. He felt like a college man, a Longhorn, a pharmacist to be.

From the corner of his eye, he caught a sign in a window, across the street and down about half a block. Amidst a strip of shops and eateries, the blue neon sign called out, "Buzzy's Diner." The red sign in the window spoke the two words Fulgencio was most eager to respond to: "Help Wanted."

The cling and clatter of cheap flatware, the chit and chatter of exuberant college kids recounting the day's adventures, filled the stuffy air at Buzzy's Diner as Fulgencio Ramirez walked in, hat in hand. The place was jammed with students eating burgers and fries, slurping vanilla milkshakes. The jukebox was blaring Buddy Holly. And a grizzled old man, arms emblazoned with tattoos, struggled to feed the hungry crowd. "I can't keep up with 'em anymore," Fulgencio heard him muttering as he passed by, balancing plates up and down his arms with the help of mermaids and dragons. As he passed the observant Fulgencio and turned a corner toward a wall lined with crammed booths, Buzzy's foot caught the leg of a chair, and he lurched forward, plates flying into the air. The old sailor landed on the black and white tiled floor with a grimace of pain carved on his wizened mug as he braced himself for an explosion of cheap china smashing and the inevitable roar of laughter to follow. But it never came.

Fulgencio Ramirez saw the scene unfolding even before Buzzy's foot tripped over the chrome chairleg. His eyes traced the trajectory of the dishes even before they left Buzzy's arms. And as his hat, leather suitcase and typewriter case bounced off the floor, his hands and arms swept beneath the plates floating in midair. Not a scrap of food dropped to the floor. Not a spot upon his white guayabera.

The explosion that followed was one of applause as the stunned diners yelled in disbelief, "Way to go, man! What a catch!"

Buzzy dusted himself off in bewilderment as Fulgencio Ramirez brushed by him and delivered each and every meal to the person who had ordered it.

The old man saw the hat and the cases on the tiled floor. His eyes scanned this stranger with jet black hair and bronzed skin. "How? Wha . . ." Buzzy stammered, still in shock. "How'd ya do that?"

"What? Catch the plates or serve them up?" Fulgencio responded.

"Both."

"I'm not sure. I just did it," Fulgencio smiled. "I see things."

"I see someone I'd like on my side," Buzzy said. "It's a war in here, and I need a lieutenant . . . You need a job?"

"That's why I'm here."

Buzzy pulled the white sailor's cap off his own balding head and plopped it on Fulgencio's, "You're hired!"

Hours later, after countless meals had been served, floors swept, and tables wiped clean, Buzzy and Fulgencio sat at the dimmed counter over cups of stale coffee. Buzzy blew rings of smoke in the air.

"Where ya from, kid?" he growled.

"La Frontera."

"Tough place, long ways from here," Buzzy exhaled.

"Not so far," Fulgencio thought out loud, "I carry it here," he said clutching at his chest.

"Ya always so dramatic?"

"I'm just me."

Buzzy ambled to the cash register and pulled out some bills, slapping them on the counter. "Ya have a place to stay?"

"Not yet," Fulgencio answered.

"There's a room in the back," Buzzy offered. "Storage. Got my old Navy cot in there."

"I'll take it," Fulgencio snapped in Brother William fashion.

"Good, 'cuz I already put your bags back there." Buzzy grinned, his eyes dancing with the reflection of orange cigarette sparks. "What kinda hours can ya work?"

"Mornings and nights, maybe lunch, it depends on my classes," Fulgencio ventured.

"Classes?" Buzzy seemed startled. "What kinda classes?"

"University classes."

"You're going to UT?" Buzzy's eyes widened.

"Yeah, why are you so surprised?" Fulgencio asked.

"Well, I . . . you . . . I've never seen . . . hmm." Buzzy rubbed his eyes and scratched the stubble-like growth atop of his head. "Have you been accepted?"

"I got a letter," Fulgencio replied cryptically.

Buzzy chuckled. "Well, we all have dreams, kid. Tell ya what. Ya sleep 'ere. Ya eat 'ere. Ya open the place. Ya close it. Forget lunch. Ya can eat it 'ere, but don't bother with the rest. You'll need some time for studying, when ya get in, of course. I'll pay ya minimum wage, minus room and board."

"You're a generous man, Mr. Buzzy." Fulgencio smiled in the darkness of the silent diner. "May God repay your generosity a thousand times over and may the Virgen de Guadalupe always keep you safe from harm."

"Ya keep talkin' like that and ya'll be the only one harmed around 'ere!" Buzzy laughed. "Now ya catch some z's."

Buzzy vanished into the alleyway, and Fulgencio stood there all alone, beneath a bare bulb, with all he possessed at his feet. He sat on the edge of the cot and snapped his grandfather's leather suitcase open on his lap. An envelope from the University of Texas sat atop his clothing. Opening it, he read the letter just as he had countless times since receiving it. His eyebrows knit together in consternation. He prided himself on being honest, especially with Carolina, but he had chosen to keep the contents of the letter secret. He hadn't exactly lied, but he also hadn't revealed the entire truth. After years of repeatedly stating what he was going to do, he hadn't had the heart to let everyone down. He had told them all that he had received a letter and he was going to UT Austin. Both were facts. However, the letter had not quite admitted him into the school. What it did say was to come meet with the undersigned college dean at his earliest convenience to discuss his application. So here he was. He'd come well before the start of the school year—despite Carolina's frantic protestations—in order to ensure his admission and secure living quarters. The latter had been quickly accomplished, but he anxiously wondered what type of challenge awaited him at the dean's office.

Folding the letter, he next unwrapped, from a neatly folded shirt, a frame with a yellowed and faded image of the Sagrado Corazón, the Sacred Heart. It was a picture his grandfather had given him as a child.

"*M'ijo*," Fernando Cisneros had said, "before she died, my mother gave me this. Everywhere I ever went I took it with me. It kept me safe. Now I want you to have it. I'm old and I won't be going anywhere anymore."

Fulgencio propped it up on a shelf next to the cot, making the sign of the cross over his chest.

Next, he pulled out a smaller picture, this one of his love. Carolina's yearbook picture in black and white. She had signed it: "With love, to Fully, C. M." This he propped up against the framed image of Jesus. He took a shower in the stall Buzzy had shown him before leaving, pulled the chain to extinguish the bulb, and lay down on the creaking cot in his boxers. It was warm. Somehow he had expected Austin to be cold, being so far north and all. Maybe he could save up and buy a fan. Probably not, since he'd need all his money for tuition and books. He drifted into sleep amidst memories of Carolina.

When his eyes snapped open, it was still dark outside. He showered, got dressed, turned on the lights, and warmed up the grill. By the time Buzzy showed up, he'd served the day's first breakfast to a trucker driving through. And he was studying the tattered old menu, wondering where all the good stuff was: "No *chorizo con huevo*, no *machacado con huevo*, no potato and egg tacos." He shook his head. "Where have I ended up?"

The breakfast rush came and went. And every single regular commented to Buzzy on how much better the food tasted. Buzzy eyed Fulgencio working feverishly at the grill, spatulas in both hands, flipping pancakes with one, omelets with the other. When the crowd had dispersed, Buzzy patted Fulgencio on the back and said, "Why don't you go change for school?"

Fulgencio smiled and ducked into the back room, removing his apron and placing it on the cot. There in the center of the cramped room, shelves lined with multicolored cans, stood a shiny floor fan, beaming chrome beneath the bald light bulb. Buzzy whistled happily to Buddy Holly on the jukebox out front, and the smell of grease and bacon hung thick in the air as Fulgencio readied himself to pay the college dean his long-awaited visit.

SIXTEEN

That first morning, after breakfast, Buzzy shook his head and chuckled as Fulgencio walked out the front door, crossed the street, and strode proudly through the gate to the campus. Khaki pants, sky blue guayabera, tortoiseshell wayfarers and all.

Fulgencio strode into the Dean's office, right past a bewildered secretary in black cat-eyed glasses. There he sat before the feared Dean Bizzell, a legendary man who controlled the fate of thousands. But of course, Fulgencio was not in the least bit afraid, for he knew not who Dean Bizzell was, other than the man who could let him into school.

"How can I help you, young man," Dean Bizzell bellowed, scowling in disgruntlement at the intrusion.

"I received your letter, sir," Fulgencio enunciated respectfully from the leather chair before Dean Bizzell's massive cherrywood desk. Producing the envelope, Fulgencio handed the letter to the dean. As the man reviewed it through his spectacles, Fulgencio turned his head from one side of the room to the other, meeting the gaze of faded, long-dead men hanging in portraits on the paneled walls.

Dean Bizzell pensively stroked his chin, scrutinizing the letter, "You're Brother William's student, from La Frontera?"

Fulgencio perked up, beaming at the mention of his beloved mentor. "Yes! You know him?"

Dean Bizzell peered at him through his diminutive lenses. "I've known him for quite some time. He's somewhat of an institution down on the border."

Fulgencio nodded in acknowledgment, staring expectantly at the dean.

The dean shifted uncomfortably in his chair beneath Fulgencio's unwavering gaze. "Mmm," he grumbled, wetting his lips nervously. "Do we have your application?" He sifted nervously through a stack of papers on his desk. Finding it, he proceeded to hem and haw about Fulgencio's GPA and test scores being below average.

Fulgencio rose slowly to his feet, his shadow enveloping the plump and fastidious administrator. "Dean," Fulgencio spoke calmly, "I have come here from a far away place, a place where GPAs and test scores hold little value. I come from a place where a man's value is his word. And where his actions are no different from the same. I have come here not because someone told me to or because my father went to school here. *No, no señor*, I have come here because it is my will. I am here to become a pharmacist so that I can return home and marry the love of my life. This is my destiny, Dean. The people of La Frontera need someone like me to help them heal, someone who speaks both Spanish and English, someone who understand them and cares about them and their families, not just their money. Tell me, Dean, what must I do to see this through?"

Dean Bizzell's eyes bulged from their sockets. His round, ruddy face looked as if it might burst. Fulgencio was not quite sure whether it was fear, laughter, or rage that the dean struggled to contain.

Slowly, Dean Bizzell rose from his ample chair and straightened his tie, his skin regaining its normal pallor. He glanced over his shoulder at the cross on the wall. His furtive eyes landed everywhere but on Fulgencio's. At last, he regained his composure and spoke, "Mr. Ramirez, for a variety of reasons—not the least of which is Brother William's letter of recommendation which asserts that you are a unique candidate, a matter I now see with my own eyes, I am willing to help you."

Fulgencio sat back down as Dean Bizzell did the same. "What are you saying, Dean, that I can go to school here?"

"Conditionally," the dean replied, filling out a form as he spoke.

"What does that mean?"

"You'll have to maintain a high average, high enough to keep you on the Dean's List. That way, nobody will ever question my decision."

"And what happens if my grades drop?"

"I'm afraid you'd have to leave the school." The dean handed Fulgencio the form he'd signed. "Take this to the registrar's office and enroll. Good luck. And next time you see Brother William, tell him I send my regards."

Fulgencio jumped to his feet, vigorously shaking Dean Bizzell's hand. "Thank you, Dean. You will not regret this decision. I promise you that."

Fulgencio startled the dean's secretary as he ran through her office whooping and hollering in celebration. "I'm a Longhorn!" he shouted as he scrambled ecstatically across the campus.

A few weeks later, Fulgencio was bussing tables at Buzzy's

Diner as Dean Bizzell sat in a booth with a priest. He was on his way to greet the dean and bring him a free iced tea to show his gratitude, but when he overheard the conversation between the two men, he turned his back so he could continue listening.

The dean's voice trembled, "I was sitting in my office when this young Mexican walked in. He spoke with great passion and intensity about wanting to be a pharmacist and a healer. I was trying to decide what to do about his application. His grades were okay, but not stellar. He was a good football player, but not good enough for here. I was leaning toward sending him over to the community college, and then suddenly I saw Her."

"Saw who?" the priest asked, puzzled. "Your secretary?"

"No, Father O'Ginley. I saw *Her*. The boy was standing before me. His eyes were ablaze like the cloak of that Virgin of Guadalupe the Mexicans adore. And then behind him and to his right, a glowing halo just like Hers appeared. As he spoke I heard a choir of angels speaking in unison. And then I saw . . . I saw Her."

"Who, my son, who?" the priest urged, leaning in over the table.

"You're going to think I'm crazy, but I swear I saw the Virgin of Guadalupe standing there next to the boy."

"Who is this boy, Dean? I must meet him!" Father O'Ginley exclaimed, springing to his feet.

"I'm not sure," the Dean murmured, holding his head in his hands. "All I know is I'm so sorry for all the years I didn't believe. I felt so alone, so lost, but now I know. How could I have doubted for so long?"

The priest reached across the table and patted him on the shoulder, consoling him: "It's okay, Dean. You have witnessed a divine intervention. Very few souls are so blessed. I myself, a devout servant of the Lord, have never been so lucky." He paused for a moment, standing over the vanquished dean as he straightened his robes. "Now, tell me who this boy is and where I can find him."

"His name is Fulgencio Ramirez. I admitted him, so he's probably on campus somewhere," the dean mumbled as the priest rushed out the door in search of the affirmation that had always eluded him.

His black robes swept behind him as he hurried toward the campus. So enthralled was he by his pursuit that he failed to look both ways before he crossed the street. A bus careened unchecked through the green light and the driver never even saw what he hit until the holy man was airborne, his crushed body landing at the street corner, steps from the diner's flashing neon beacon.

A crowd formed instantly around the fallen priest, Dean Bizzell crouched fearfully at his side, the students' expressions frozen in panic and horror at the sight.

"Father O'Ginley is dying on the sidewalk," a young woman cried frantically.

No one dared touch the fading cleric as a thick, red pool oozed around him.

Suddenly, the crowd parted as Fulgencio broke through. Without a thought, he turned the priest on his back and looked into his eyes. "It's going to be all right, Father. We've called the ambulance," Fulgencio whispered, holding Father O'Ginley's chilly hand.

"Who are you, boy?" the priest gasped.

"I am Fulgencio Ramirez."

"Ramirez." The pastor's eyes began to turn to glass, his spirit fading fast. "You're just a boy," he whispered. His heart weakening, he could not muster the strength to speak any further. "Where's the Virgin?" He gasped for air. His eyelids fluttered as he strained to see what the dean had so vividly described. "Let me see," he whispered hoarsely, blood trickling from the corner of his mouth. "Let me see something, somewhere, a sign."

Fulgencio shifted slightly to the side to make way for the paramedics. As he did so, the priest's eyes locked on something in the background. Turning to follow his gaze, Fulgencio joined him in seeing white letters on green metal. On the corner, the street sign read, "Guadalupe."

Father O'Ginley died with a smile curled on his pallid face.

As the ambulance carried the body away and the crowd scattered, Dean Bizzell solemnly shook Fulgencio's hand.

"Thank you for comforting him in his final moments," the dean said mournfully before departing with his head hung low.

When night fell, Buzzy and Fulgencio stood in front of the diner. Buzzy smoked a cigarette, blowing wisps of smoke into the autumn wind. Together, they stared at the dried blood on the sidewalk a few steps away. It had been a somber night at the diner, couples consoling each other over the tragic death they had witnessed. Nothing but the sound of gentle weeping and the clinging of forks could be heard since Buzzy had unplugged the jukebox as a sign of respect for the departed pastor.

"Everyone knew Father O'Ginley," Buzzy muttered, "whether they liked him or not." He threw his cigarette butt on the ground and smashed it under the heel of his boot. "I ain't ever cared none for religion myself."

"He asked me my name," Fulgencio said.

"Reckon he wanted to know who he was lookin' at as he crossed the Great Divide," Buzzy pondered.

"He said I was just a boy." Fulgencio scratched his chin as they both continued to stare at the bloodstain. "I wonder why he said that?"

"Well that's simple," Buzzy shot back. "He said that 'cuz he didn't know ya."

"What do you mean?"

"Well, if he'd a known ya, he woulda known jis like everybody else who knows ya," Buzzy drawled. "You're no boy, Fulgencio Ramirez. You're a man."

Fulgencio Ramirez stared at the dried blood of the holy man whose lifeless hand he had held. He wondered if he'd provided any comfort to him in his hour of death. That night, as he kneeled before the images of the Sacred Heart and Carolina Mendelssohn, in the tiny storage room at the back of Buzzy's Diner, he prayed for the priest's safe passage into the otherworld.

As he slipped into sleep beneath the gentle caress of the whirring fan, he dreamt of the Virgen de Guadalupe. Not the colorful one that hung on Juan Diego's vest in the Basilica in Mexico City, but the monochrome one protruding from the mud gray adobe wall of his grandfather's hut. He dreamt he was dancing "el Jarabe Tapatío" with her on the street corner. They tapped their heels on the concrete, chipping away at the dried bloodstain beneath. They danced beneath the street sign named in her honor. They laughed at how funny it was that her name was emblazoned on this street so far from the mountains where she first appeared bearing roses in the snow. And they guffawed at how the gringos mispronounced her name as if it were just another American street name, oblivious to its original meaning.

"Gwadaloop!" they called it. "I'll meet ya'll on Gwadaloop! We'll have a burger at Buzzy's on Gwadaloop! Y'all hear 'bout that priest got hit by a bus over on Gwadaloop?"

Fulgencio and La Virgen wondered if the gringos would ever get it. Would they ever understand that words and their proper pronunciation had meaning? They figured no, but what the hell? Who cared as long as the two of them knew the truth?

La Virgen de Guadalupe and Fulgencio sipped from a bottle of rum Buzzy kept in the storage room, dancing beneath her street sign and the stars in the heavens above until the crack of dawn, when Fulgencio Ramirez woke up from his dream and served *chorizo con huevo* to the truck drivers just passing through, on Gwadaloop.

SEVENTEEN

Day in and day out, Fulgencio toiled and sweat for Buzzy. He kept the grill immaculate, the counters spotless, the tiles beneath the booths devoid of crumbs. He polished the gleaming chrome of the rectangular napkin holders so bright that he could see the very aura of La Virgen radiating from them as the morning rays poured in through the diner's windows. And he revamped the menu to include all of his favorite Mexican specialties. Business had never been better. Buzzy's was the only joint west of Highway 35 that served a good taco. And now not just the kids, but the teachers and merchants were coming in for their meals. Buzzy was convinced Fulgencio possessed a magic touch. And nothing had done more to persuade him than his admission to the university.

Every day after breakfast, Fulgencio crossed Guadalupe Street to go to class. And ever since the day the pastor died, he was not the only one to make a mental note to look both ways before stepping off the curb. His classes were more challenging than anything he'd ever studied in La Frontera. Finding himself behind his classmates in subjects like chemistry, biology, and anatomy, he signed up for tutoring as he struggled to make the grades required to maintain his conditional admission. After closing the diner at night, Buzzy would stay up with him at the counter, making fresh coffee and blowing smoke into his bleary eyes. Books splayed out on the countertop. Formulas and equations floating through the air entwined with the smoke that curled around them.

Buzzy wasn't half bad at math, which was surprising for an old sailor who learned how to count while baking in the galley of a warship during the Great War.

"This is harder than I thought it would be," Fulgencio admitted to his boss as he struggled to solve a practice problem for an upcoming chemistry test.

"Nothing worthwhile is easy," Buzzy reminded him.

Overwhelmed by school and work, Fulgencio barely had time to think of anything else, but Carolina was always in the back of his mind. On Sundays, he lined up quarters atop the payphone by the diner's restrooms, and he called her long distance.

"It's so hard to hear you, but not see you," Fulgencio told Carolina.

"I miss you so much, Fully," she replied, her voice trembling. She sounded so small and so far away. It was as if the distance between them had weakened her. She had always come across so lively and bold. Now she seemed melancholy and afraid.

At times when she shared stories about what was going on in La Frontera, he would sense his jealousy bubbling up from that cauldron of fire deep inside him, the mysterious words rushing into his ears like waves of whitewater channeled through treacherous rocks. He yearned to be in all of her stories. And he couldn't help but fear that someone would take his place.

"You have nothing to worry about," Carolina assured him. "I might as well be one of the nuns the way I'm behaving."

The thought of her in a habit broke the spell of his disturbing jealousies and unsettling insecurities, forcing him to laugh.

"It's not supposed to be a joke!" Carolina chided him. "But I'm glad to hear you laugh. I can imagine your smile and it's contagious."

"I can't wait to be with you," he repeated at the end of every torturous but vital conversation.

That first winter, he hitchhiked back down, his knees knocking—freezing cold—in the bed of a stranger's pickup. He went down to see Carolina beneath the stars that lit the steps to her father's house. There, he held her tight in the damp chill of night, and they kissed beneath the moonlight. Despite the frigid temperature, the Virgencita de Guadalupe willed a single red rose to spring forth on the rosebush beneath Carolina's window, and Fulgencio plucked it for his love.

Together, they prepared to bring in 1960 in the cozy living room of Mr. Mendelssohn's well-appointed home, sitting side by side on the crunchy plastic-covered sofa. After dinner, while Carolina and her mother washed the dishes, Mr. Mendelssohn motioned for Fulgencio to follow him into his paneled study. There they sat in his prized leather chairs, sipping Mexican brandy.

"Fulgencio," Mr. Mendelssohn spoke deliberately, having clearly given great thought to his words. "This year my daughter graduates from high school."

"Yes, sir. I am very happy for her."

"Yes, me too," Mr. Mendelssohn continued. "And then it will be her turn to go to college."

Fulgencio had known this day might come, but he hadn't prepared for it. The Mexican girls from Garfield Street rarely finished high school, much less enrolled in college. Sure, Carolina was different. More young women from her social rung were pursuing degrees. She had even mentioned the idea of becoming a Special Education teacher, to help children like Little David, but Fulgencio had never given her plans much thought. Was that wrong of him, he wondered? As he mulled that disturbing possibility, he recalled that whenever Carolina started speaking of her own dreams, that maddening tide of white noise and incomprehensible words drowned out her voice. And since leaving for college, he had been so caught up working toward his goal that he had forgotten the rest of the world—including La Frontera—continued to move forward in his absence.

"I have a proposition to make to you, Fulgencio," Mr. Mendelssohn said slowly. "If you and Carolina were to decide to marry sometime in the near future, I would be happy to support you both in your academic efforts at the University of Texas at Austin."

Fulgencio sat quietly, tasting the sweet bitterness of the brandy on his tongue and lips, surveying the dignified study, the elegant desk, the books lining the walls.

Mr. Mendelssohn shifted nervously in his chair, the leather squeaking, "It's been a difficult year here for Carolina. More than you might understand. I'm sure she'd never want to tell you this, for fear of hurting your feelings, but she's had to endure some unpleasant comments while holding steadfast to her long-distance commitment to you."

Fulgencio's ears pricked up, "Unpleasant? You mean . . . bigoted?"

Mr. Mendelssohn nodded, frowning, "The truth is, there are

forces at play that don't want to see a couple like you together. Given the best of circumstances, you have to know that if you continue to move forward with your relationship, you may face some very real difficulties. Given all of that, I would rather see your bond legitimized before anything . . ." he paused, clearing his throat, ". . . before anything disgraceful might befall her. As long as you are not yet married, people will torment her, they will cling to hope that they can divide you. But once you are married, maybe you can find peace together."

Fulgencio nodded quietly, listening carefully to his mentor as the sound of the surf and the ancient, unintelligible words swirling through his mind threatened to overtake Mr. Mendelssohn's rational advice.

"My dream would be for you to join me at the drugstore when you both return with your degrees in hand," Mr. Mendelssohn proposed.

"Mr. Mendelssohn," Fulgencio spoke in a low and serious tone. "I am honored by your gesture. But I must make my own way in this world. I must finish what I have begun and earn the right to support your daughter as my wife. I do not wish to hear the whispers of my rivals, the jealous and the greedy, saying that I married Carolina for her money, for the keys to Mendelssohn's Drugstore. *No, no señor.*"

Crestfallen, Mr. Mendelssohn pleaded, "Don't you want all of this, Fulgencio?"

"Yes, but I want to earn it through the sweat of my own brow."

Mr. Mendelssohn slumped back into his chair. "I fear what troubles you might face, or bring upon yourselves, but what more can I do? As always, Fulgencio, I respect you for being your own man."

"What's more, Mr. Mendelssohn," Fulgencio continued, "I

will ask Carolina to not go to the University of Texas if she truly loves me."

"What?" Mr. Mendelssohn nearly spilled his brandy onto his jacket. "But why? That's my alma mater."

"Mr. Mendelssohn," Fulgencio explained, "I work morning, day, and night to earn my keep and pay my way through school. During the little time I have left between classes and work, I study. And it's only going to get harder with all the labs. You know how it is. I haven't told Carolina this, because I don't want to worry her, but I was accepted conditionally at the school. I have to maintain straight As, or my admission will be rescinded."

Mr. Mendelssohn's tone of voice grew troubled as he replied. "I see. I remember the countless hours of study in pharmacy school, but still, Fulgencio, I think you're being extremely unfair to Carolina. Won't you reconsider?" He shifted uncomfortably in his seat, becoming visibly agitated.

"If Carolina came up to Austin, I would be doomed," Fulgencio concluded. "How could I have enough time to devote to all of my duties and still pay her the attention she deserves? How would I be able to afford to entertain her within the crowd she would most certainly run in?" He could picture her, the glamorous sorority girl, waiting for her short-order-cook boyfriend to close down the diner. Her sorority sisters, crisp and clean with long golden hair, teasing and taunting her from their gleaming convertibles. "I just know I'd never make it, Mr. Mendelssohn," Fulgencio stated. "She must go somewhere else."

"I'm afraid you might be making a very big mistake, Fulgencio," Mr. Mendelssohn cautioned, his cheeks turning red as he rose to his feet. "I will not meddle where I am not wanted, not in my daughter's life, and not in yours. But I don't think you're thinking this all the way through. You have to realize that life is not only about your plans and your dreams, but about those of the people you love as well. Turning down my offer of financial support is one thing, but how can you deny Carolina attending whatever school she wants? Do you think that is fair to her?" He shook his head in obvious disapproval, emphatically setting his snifter on the table between them. "I certainly don't think it's right. And I seriously doubt that my daughter will be pleased by your ideas about her future."

Stunned, Fulgencio stared uncomfortably as Mr. Mendelssohn stormed out of the room. He'd never seen him become upset. But he was clearly perturbed now.

Fulgencio remained in his plush leather chair as Mr. Mendessohn hastily left the study. He'd never crossed Mr. Mendelssohn, never disappointed him. This was a strange sensation. He felt a toxic mixture of shame and pride swirling inside of him. What was wrong with him? Was he too single-minded? Was this part of the *maldición* La Señora Villarreal had spoken of? Or was this simply who he was? Following his instincts had gotten him this far, so, why should he doubt himself now?

As her father had predicted, Carolina was stunned by Fulgencio's wishes. "What?" she exclaimed, echoing her father's initial reaction. "Are you nuts, Fully?" She yelped as they huddled in their coats on the doorstep, waiting for the New Year fireworks to light up the sky. "How could you turn down his offer?"

"You will marry a man, not a boy kept by your father," Fulgencio replied.

She shook her head and laughed. "You always speak like you know so much. And I'm supposed to not only wait four more years to be your wife, but I'm also supposed to go to some other school to please your whim?"

"Trust me," he urged, clutching her hand, his eyes boring intensely into hers through the frosty mist. "It's for the best. I can't stay focused and make the grades if you come to the same school."

"You're asking me to sacrifice my education in exchange for yours." She crossed her arms indignantly.

"But when we're married, you won't even have to work. It won't matter where you went to school."

Carolina's jaw dropped. "I can't believe you. All you think about is yourself. I've waited so long to see you, to be with you tonight. My dad had talked to me about this for months. And I thought you would do anything to be with me. Instead, you've ruined everything. Happy New Year, Fulgencio. And if you think you're going to boss me around or tell me what to do, you've got another thing coming."

Rising and swiftly spinning around, she slammed the door shut behind her, leaving him alone on the cold and unforgiving doorstep. This was not how he had expected to bring in the New Year. *No. No Señor.*

Walking slowly through the darkened neighborhood toward the Balmori house, he pulled his coat tightly around his shivering body, exploring his nagging doubts. Was he being unreasonable? Was he making a mistake? He struggled to keep the white noise and the ancient Aztec words at bay. They didn't allow him to concentrate or think clearly. He shook his head in a vain attempt to clear his mind. *Focus,* he pushed himself, but his effort was futile. In the distant sky, explosions crackled and boomed, distracting him from his cumbersome ruminations. Twinkling lights streamed down like glitter, his thoughts dissipating like the ephemeral sparkles in the smoky sky as he paused by the side of the road to admire the fireworks.

EIGHTEEN

Five months later Carolina graduated from high school. Against her parents' wishes and advice, she acquiesced to Fulgencio's stubborn demands, turning down UT in favor of Incarnate Word College, a sleepy school run by nuns in San Antonio, just a couple hours drive from Austin. "My father says I'm making a mistake," she told Fulgencio. "Since I was a little girl, we both dreamt I would attend his alma mater. But I'm an adult now. I've been your girlfriend for four years and someday I'm going to marry you. My biggest dream now is you, Fulgencio. So, for you, I'll put everything else aside."

Although Fulgencio was grateful for Carolina's sacrifice, he still found himself strangely unsatisfied and troubled by their new circumstances. Now that she was attending college in another town, she was away from the sheltered environment of her parents' home. For the first time in her life, she was on her own, going out with friends, and—no doubt—being pursued by other men. He worried he had indeed made a terrible mistake. Had he chosen to protect his college aspirations while putting their relationship at greater risk?

Despite his gnawing fears and doubts, he clung stubbornly to his belief that if they lived in the same town, he would have no choice but to see her every day, rendering himself unable to achieve his academic goals. As he washed the dishes he had loaded with his own culinary creations at Buzzy's, he convinced himself that he'd forced the right decision, that he trusted her, that she would come to see the wisdom of his ways and not harbor any resentment toward him, and that they would survive as a couple.

She drove a 1957 banana-yellow Thunderbird convertible with white vinyl seats, two-tone trim, and white sidewall tires. Her golden curls tossed in the wind with the laughter of her sorority sisters. A couple of times, she drove to Austin to surprise him as he slaved over the grill at Buzzy's. He tried his hardest not to feel embarrassed, but the truth was, he did not enjoy her seeing him laboring like this while she lived in the lap of collegiate luxury. For some reason he could not quite articulate, it felt different than it had back in La Frontera at her father's drugstore. He imagined her sorority sisters' comments behind his back. "Why are you with that fry cook? What do you see in him? Why don't you date one of the frat brothers at Trinity, someone with money, not just a poor Mexican working his way through pharmacy school?"

Still, he'd serve her vanilla milkshakes while she waited at the counter for him to close down. Then they'd drive around the abandoned streets of the slumbering city, her head on his shoulder as he steered her car beneath flickering streetlights keeping time. Later, as the sky was lightening, he'd drive her back to San Antonio as she slept beside him in the car. Dropping her off at her dorm, he'd catch the bus or hitchhike home with the sunrise. Never would he let her stay with him in Austin, despite her insisting. *No, no señor.* He didn't think that would be proper, her sleeping with him in that little cot at Buzzy's. Not proper for a lady like her. Not respectful to Mr. and Mrs. Mendelssohn either. Upon his insistence on those heated nights on the backseat vinyl of her convertible, they would wait until their wedding night to consummate their love. He could not disrespect her, this angel he had placed squarely on a pedestal.

The summer following Carolina's first year in college, she returned home to spend time with her dying mother while Fulgencio continued working and attending summer school. Both of the young lovers yearned across the vast expanse of miles that separated them yet again, straining for each other's warmth and embrace, urgently missing their occasional weekend romps.

At the height of their desperation, they placed their trust in a mutual friend to ferry their love notes and gifts. Miguel Rodriguez Esparza was now attending summer school at UT, driving home to visit his parents every other weekend. He was one of those silly boys the girls all loved to talk to, slight and unassuming. His preppy sweaters hung two sizes too big on his slender shoulders. At San Juan del Atole, he had languished in others' shadows as a backup quarterback that never got his shot at glory. Feeling sorry for him, Fulgencio had taken him under his wing, bailing him out of a few scraps brought on by his tendency to drink one too many and talk way too much.

While in Austin, Miguel frequented Buzzy's Diner, where Fulgencio served him steaming flour tortillas as they reminisced about life in La Frontera.

Fulgencio never felt threatened by Miguel. How could he? Miguel seemed like a weak sliver of a boy. He liked having a friend around, someone who understood where he came from, someone who also found Austin foreign and new.

With every delivery Miguel made that summer, however, he peppered in a comment or two that stuck in Fulgencio's mind long after his departure.

"I didn't get to see Carolina this weekend when I dropped your flowers, Fulgencio," Miguel mentioned, hunched over his coffee at Buzzy's counter.

"Oh?" Fulgencio cocked an eyebrow.

"Yeah," Miguel ventured nonchalantly, "I heard she was out with the old crew, dancing across the border or something."

"Dancing across the border?" Fulgencio scowled. "That doesn't sound like Carolina."

"I know," Miguel replied, "I didn't think it could be true. You know how these rumors are, Fulgencio," he muttered chewing on his potato and egg taco. "You just can't buy 'em. You've gotta have faith, right? Love is blind, no?"

Fulgencio sat alone on his cot in the back room, glowering at Carolina's yearbook photo. "Just rumors," he assured himself. "You can't believe in gossip. You have to keep the faith." He prayed for her love, her loyalty, and her honor. But still, he felt sick to his stomach as he waited impatiently to succumb to sleep, wondering if she was out, dancing with other guys, meeting new people, partying like a decadent rich girl across the border. *No, no, no señor.* It simply couldn't be. He rubbed his eyes in the darkness until he was sick of seeing nonexistent stars. Not his Carolina. She would never stray. She would never let him down.

In his troubled sleep, he saw the serpentine train roaring over the railroad bridge from Mexico, the white letters scrambling and zooming by, and heard the chants of an ancient woman speaking in an unrecognizable but familiar tongue. *Cemmauizcui. Aco. Axcualli.*

He woke to the blaring of a hundred horns ringing in his

ears, bathed in a cold sweat. Turning on the light, he stared at her photo and prayed to the image of Jesus, prayed for protection from whatever demons insisted on haunting him, pleaded for protection from losing Carolina.

In their letters they remained affectionate, but doubt crept between the lines, tempering their passion with the fear of betrayal, the apprehension of letting go and lowering one's defenses at a time of danger.

In his increasingly insecure letters, fed by Miguel's comments, Fulgencio urged Carolina to not go out on the town without him, to not speak or flirt with other men, to spend all her time with her sickly mother.

Swept up in the changing values of the new decade, Carolina chafed at his overly traditional ways, writing back:

Fully,

This is America! It's the '60s now! Don't you get it? You can't own and control me. I can't believe I let you determine what college I would attend! I should be there with you, in Austin. We could have already been married. And then we wouldn't have all of these self-created problems.

Carolina

Stunned, Fulgencio shared the contents of the letter with Miguel, hoping for some reassurance and support from him. "Can you believe it?" he beseeched his friend. "All I asked was that she act the way a girlfriend should act!"

Miguel shook his head disapprovingly. "Fulgencio, the truth is that she's a college-educated Anglo woman. She probably thinks you're too macho, stuck in the ways of *la raza* south of the border."

His temper curdling, for days Fulgencio could not stop thinking about Miguel's response. But his anger was not directed at his friend, it was aimed at Carolina. Their phone calls became less frequent, often turning into tortured arguments driven by Fulgencio's jealousy and exacerbated by Carolina's increasingly independent attitude. He sent fewer letters for fear of making matters worse. And as his writing slowed, so did hers. If only he could see her, talk in person, he told himself. Then everything would be okay. But he simply had too much work on his hands and could not break away for a weekend in La Frontera like Miguel.

On a Saturday evening before the start of the fall semester of '61, Miguel pranced into the diner and said, "Fulgencio, I hear there's a big dance at Incarnate Word this weekend. Why don't we drive down there? Maybe Carolina's already come up for the start of the semester? Maybe you could see her!"

His heart racing to San Antonio faster than his body could, Fulgencio asked for Buzzy's reprieve, threw on his black suit, and jumped into Miguel's car. He couldn't wait to see her, to erase the distance between them.

By the time Fulgencio and Miguel arrived at Incarnate Word, it was dark. They could hear the distorted clamor of music blaring from the school gymnasium. Vehicles crammed the narrow driveways of the campus thick with trees. Couples strolled along the moonlit paths, leaning on the sides of cars, flirting behind the shrubs, and sitting by gurgling fountains.

Fulgencio could hear the pounding of his heart in his eardrums as he threw the doors open and strode into the sock hop with Miguelito scurrying in his shadow. In his black suit and black tie, and his wavy black mane and furrowed brow, Fulgencio Ramirez looked like a villain who had just stepped off the silver screen, ready to pull a gun out from his jacket at any moment and smoke anyone who made the mistake of looking at him in the wrong way. His throat ached. She better not be here dancing. Dancing like he'd heard she did all summer long in La Frontera, while he slaved over a sweltering stove to pay his way through school so he could afford to keep her in the manner she had grown accustomed to as a pharmacist's daughter. He felt a tentative tap on his shoulder. It was Miguel.

"Whatever you do," he quivered, "don't look over there . . ." Miguel raised a trembling finger toward the back-right corner of the dimly lit hall.

Fulgencio's eyes caught the fire in his heart as he stormed toward the scene he'd dreaded in his dreams. Her shoes off, her curls flinging wildly in the air, her lips curled in laughter, Carolina was dancing with not one, not two, but *three* men at once. Frat boys from Trinity, no doubt. Untethered, a tide of rage propelled him toward her as familiar, foaming words surged through his mind . . . *aco* . . . *calactihuetz* . . . *nacaxaqualoa* . . . flinging bodies aside in an unleashed fury, as Miguel stumbled and climbed over them to catch a glimpse.

Carolina gaped in shock and terror as Fulgencio's fists flew into the jaws and chins of her dance partners. He felled them each swiftly and with a single blow, their bodies sliding out of sight on the smooth floor. His accusing eyes burned into her flesh, seared into her soul as he glowered at her, shaking his head.

"How could you?" he growled, his face contorted and unrecognizable, a macabre Aztec mask. For a fleeting instant, he resembled a dangerous demon looming over her fragile form as she cowered fearfully in the corner, whimpering.

He spit on the floor, the maddening chants ringing between

his ears, and then he spit the words into her face like venom sucked from a serpent's wound and spewed out in disgust: "You're not worthy of my efforts."

He spun on his heel and stormed toward the door amidst the throng's horrified glares. As he left a shattered Carolina sobbing in his wake, he heard Miguel consoling her.

"Don't worry, Carolina, I'm here for you. Everything's gonna be alright," Miguel said.

Disgusted, Fulgencio never turned back. He walked all the way downtown to the bus station and took the 3:00 a.m. Greyhound to Austin, fuming in fury all of the way.

NINETEEN

The months that followed were anguished and seemingly interminable for Fulgencio.

A couple days after that fateful fight at the Incarnate Word dance, Miguel had relayed a final message from Carolina.

"I'm sorry, Fulgencio," he said ruefully, "Carolina says she's had enough of you. She's moving on. She said you're too macho. That she wants no more."

Fulgencio nodded stoically before Miguel's scrutinizing gaze, but later—in the storeroom where he slept, he fell to his knees before the pictures of Jesus and Carolina.

"Why?" he cried. "Is this all my fault? Or was it Carolina's? Did she bring this on, or did I?" Fulgencio yearned for simpler days, his early days working at Mendelssohn's Drugstore when all had seemed so clear-cut. He had known what he wanted and he had worked tirelessly to reach for it. Why was it so much harder to hang on to things than it was to attain them? Why did people have to be so complicated? He alternated between feeling justified in his jealousy and rage and ashamed for his insecurity and violence. Had he been right or wrong? Should he move on with his life and try to forget Carolina or crawl back to her and apologize for his actions? As he struggled to think through his quandary, the arcane chants and waves of sorrow he had now grown accustomed to battled his mental faculties, drowning out his ability to reason.

Unable to find a clear path through his dilemma, Fulgencio worked and studied with a rabid fervor. He'd spend his free moments at a gym down the street, pounding the body bag until he could do little more than hang on to it to avoid collapsing onto the floor, his chest heaving in exhaustion. No one dared look him in the eye, and he ruled Buzzy's Diner like a tyrant.

"I'm worried about you, Fulgencio," Buzzy admitted. "Our customers might be showing up simply for fear if they don't, you might hunt them down, drag them here, and force-feed them."

Finally, the night before the schools all shut down for Christmas break, everything changed. The diner was emptied and cleaned. Buzzy had gone home for the night. Fulgencio sat on his cot, the wrinkled and tattered picture of Carolina in his hand, faded by the flow of his tears. His leather suitcase was half-heartedly packed as he weighed whether to bother going to La Frontera. He was at his wit's end and he figured a couple of weeks on El Dos de Copas with his dead grandfather, the Virgencita, and Brother William might help him get his feet back on solid ground. As he finished packing, a delicate shadow slanted across the floor. He turned, looking upward. And he saw her. Hovering in the doorway, an angel dressed in winter white. He could barely find the strength in his legs to stand and greet her. The words refused to fall from his lips as he gaped at her. They both began to weep in shame.

"I love you, Fulgencio," Carolina cried, her voice shaking. "I haven't stopped thinking of you for a moment. I never meant to hurt your feelings."

"I'm so sorry for how I acted," Fulgencio said, shaking his head in shame.

"I'm sorry for making you feel that way. I promise I'll never do it again," she sobbed, edging closer to him. "I thought you never wanted to see me again."

"I believed the same thing! I . . . he . . ." Fulgencio's thoughts disintegrated into unintelligible fragments as he took a step toward her.

She reached out and tenderly caressed his cheek as their bodies met, a shudder rippling through his body as she touched him. Swept together by a surging tide of emotion—the undertow pulling soul to soul, body to body—they embraced beneath the bare lightbulb in the center of the cramped room lined with canned goods. Their lips melded into each other like magnets made of flesh. His hands kneaded her skin and her aching muscles and her inner thighs melted with desire as they poured into each other. The meager cot could not support their passion as they crashed onto the floor, the faded fabric a muddled rug beneath them. Pieces of discarded metal flung aside. Bald bulb burning. Her white dress in a ball at the foot of the collapsed bed. Her soft breasts gently pressed against his firm chest. Her delicate hands groped his taut muscles. The smell of saliva on burning skin. Gasps. Her screams sent chills up his spine. Exclamations of pain and pleasure fused as one. She was his. And he was hers. For once and for all. She swore like she never had before at the letting go, her hair tumbling all around them, the only shelter from the midnight chill in the air. And he wept upon her chest. All the love. All the anger. All the confusion exploded into the love of his life. Their eyes riveted to each other, they moaned and shouted and laughed and cried and all they could say was "I love you" until they fell to pieces. Her naked body covering his. Her head upon his shoulder. His arms nestling her closely. They slept. And they didn't dream in the black of night. They lay in silence amidst the receding chaos.

Her eyes snapped open in the middle of the night and she spoke softly into his ear. "Fully," she whispered, "marry me now. Let's go home and tell my parents. I can't bear to be apart ever again."

He felt the tugging down below, pulling him inevitably toward her. He was drowning in her gaze as he looked at her. This was not how he had planned it, all these years. Her telling him. This indiscretion in a borrowed storage room. But his yearning—for once—outweighed his misguided reason. All he wanted now was to be with her. To vanquish her lust and desire. To feast upon her pure and sumptuous body. To pour his being into her and feel it all melt away. The frustrations of a lifetime. The fear and loathing. The self-hate. To let it all go and watch her absorb it, neutralize it, conquer it and him.

"Yes," he whispered, "You'll be my wife. I'll be your husband. And we'll make love like this for the rest of our lives."

She kissed him delicately. "I love you so much, Fully. Never let me go now."

"Never," he said.

They rested, dreaming of how it would be. Being married. Sharing a home and a bed and a future.

"But we'll still do this on our own," Fulgencio reaffirmed. "I don't want your father's help."

"Fine," she smiled, stroking his hair. "All I need is you."

"It'll be tough," he warned. "I mean . . . I can afford more than this cot with what I've saved up, but not too much more until we graduate."

"This cot did just fine," she giggled. "Well, almost."

They slept soundly, wrapped in the fabric of the defeated cot.

Early the next morning, they woke and straightened the place up, laughing at the aftermath. They drove her banana-yellow Thunderbird convertible to La Frontera. Home for the holidays. Alive with excitement. Eager to make their announcement.

She dropped him off at Bobby Balmori's house and blew him a kiss as she drove away, "See ya tonight at my house!" she called out.

He waved at her, his smile broad as the Stetson hat on his head. He shook his head. God, how he loved her. He loved her so much it didn't matter anymore that he had betrayed his convictions. What did it mean anyway, they would soon be man and wife. He'd labor their way through college if he had to work three jobs, day and night. And then, someday, they'd come back to La Frontera, and he'd buy Mr. Mendelssohn's store fair and square. He'd pay for every penny of merchandise and then some. He'd take good care of her always.

That night, he wore a black suit with a red tie. His hair slicked back, he borrowed Mr. Balmori's '54 Imperial for the drive to the Mendelssohn's home. He stopped to pick up a bouquet of roses at Curiel's Flower Shop.

"*Buena suerte, m'ijo*," Mr. Curiel crackled from behind the cash register as Fulgencio retrieved a splendid bouquet the refrigerator in the cramped one-room shop.

"Tonight's the big night, Señor Curiel," Fulgencio beamed, pulling a tiny black velvet box from his pocket and shaking it.

"A diamond?" Mr. Curiel ventured.

"*Sí señor*," Fulgencio exhaled. He had spent half his savings that afternoon, buying the ring.

As he walked away from Mr. Balmori's gleaming black sedan and up to the Mendelssohn's front door, Fulgencio felt just as he had that first night he picked Carolina up for the homecoming dance. He passed the white picket fence, and his shiny black shoes reflected the moon, clicking on the walkway to the house, echoing in the still Christmas Eve chill. Frosty dew on the soft grass lay beneath his feet as he circled the house toward the back door to the kitchen. He thought he'd surprise her, roses behind his back, diamond in his coat pocket, a smile emblazoned on his face. He crouched over a bush, peering in through the kitchen window, searching for a glimpse of her.

Suddenly, the magic crashed to the ground with the dozen roses he would leave undelivered on the lawn. His jaw clenched in that jarring rage that so possessed him since the days of his childhood when he was roused from dreams by the alarming blasts of brass, the thundering train, the cryptic letters, the chanted words he could never quite understand or even repeat out loud. *Nacaz tzitzica . . . tecocoliztli . . . chochopica.* The taste of blood filled his mouth as he bit his tongue in disgust. She was dancing with another man again, an affluent-looking, Anglo stranger about their age. There in the dining room. He could see her. Her shoes off, her heels kicking high, laughing and clapping in a fitted red dress, diamonds hanging from her ears ten times bigger than any stone he could afford on his meager salary as a short order cook. Had her parents brought in a family friend to finally marry her off to their own kind? Had they tired of his mystifying and maddening ways? He prowled around the corner of the house back onto the front lawn, rubbing his eyes violently, wishing it would all go away, be a cruel trick played on him by his overactive and jealous imagination. But no, there she was doing it still, her pupils glittering with glee as they gazed into her tall dance partner's sky-blue eyes, her bare arms thrown around the man's broad shoulders. The very naked arms that had cradled him the night before. The arms he had melted into. Her bosom now bouncing in unfettered merriment, the breasts he had buried his soul in, born his heart onto, the altar he had sacrificed his morals upon now grazed against another man's chest in the very home where he'd been about to propose on one knee! She had promised to not stoke his jealous rage again. How could she break that oath again, and so soon?

He had opened up, abandoned his defenses, dared to let her see him for who and what he truly was in his most raw and vulnerable state, and she had betrayed him yet again. He had worried so much about whether something was wrong with his own way of thinking, but if what if the real problem was hers? He could forgive and forget once, but not twice. Not now. Not after what had transpired between them. He yearned with every fiber of his being to barge into the living room, tear her smug gringo dance partner limb from limb, and—like a bucking bronco—shatter and disintegrate the furnishings and fine crystal and porcelain knickknacks that adorned the room draped in doilies and lace. A gringo. This is what she wanted? Maybe this was what she deserved, not a *pobre*, *pinche indio* like him, still wet from crossing the river, still tracking mud on his shoes all over her family's fancy carpets. He was about to force the front door open, but—through a herculean effort—he managed to hold back, out of respect for Mr. Mendelssohn and his wife, although who knew anymore if they even deserved it. Certainly not if this new suitor was their doing, a sign that they'd chosen an easier path for their daughter after all. He shut his eyes tightly, letting the ancient words wash over him, like the surf on the beach near El Dos de Copas, drowning everything out, strangely comforting him in their now familiar rhythm, even though he had no clue what they meant. *Cahua. Cel. Cahua. Cel.* A bridge was swept away, the gate to his soul, the threshold to his heart rendered impassable as a mighty river amidst a violent flood. The metallic ring of the car door clanging shut before he drove away would haunt him, echoing for years to come. Scattered rose petals on the lawn. A black velvet box never handed over, left to gather dust in a desk drawer in his drugstore. And the questions left unanswered, unasked.

The shadow lurking in Fulgencio's soul had been there long before, like a congenital birth defect or the scars and trauma of his tortured childhood. And it had taken this chain of events for the darkness to finally consume him. As he walked away from Carolina's house that chilly December night, he felt transported. Not by his own legs or his own will, but as if he were being carried away by the river, flowing out to the Gulf of Mexico. *Amac. Analco. Atlaza.*

He yearned to scream and cry as he drove back to the Balmori's, but he could not find the will. Something inside of him was dying. He sat in their driveway as rain rattled on the metal roof. Forlornly, he watched his old friend and borrowed family share Christmas cheer through the living room window. Searching for something to ease his pain, to soothe his wounded soul, he recalled a bitter song he had heard his grandfather sing. It was called "Error," and he sang it in the cold chamber of the car:

No me habia dado cuenta
(I hadn't noticed)
De mi error
(My mistake)
De la dicha fingida
(The feigned blessing)

De tu amor
(Of your love)
De que fuí tu jugete
(That I was your plaything)

Y te quize
(And I loved you)
Y te sigo queriendo
(And I continue loving you)
Eso es lo peor
(That's the worst)

Mas cuando pase
(But when it passes)
El sopor de mi tortura
(The height of my torture)
Y me olvide de tu embrujo
(And I forget your spell)
De mujer
(Of a woman)

Y comrependa que ese amor
(And I understand that this love)
Fue una locura
(Was sheer craziness)
Te prometo que nunca
(I promise you I'll never)
Te volveré a querer.
(Ever love you again.)

After a heart-wrenching rendition, he fell quiet. He had never bothered to learn the songs that fit this occasion, the dirges that would soon fill his repertoire with sorrow, bitterness, and pain. So he spent the rest of the night sitting silently in the car, pondering the depths of his misery. The next morning, Christmas Day 1961, he hitchhiked his way back to Austin, sitting in his crumpled and soggy black suit in the bed of a stranger's truck, his tears clinging to his face beneath the frigid, streaming rain.

Fulgencio never returned to Carolina's house. He never explained. He never opened her letters or answered her phone calls. He simply wished to forget. Yet he lived to remember.

PART II

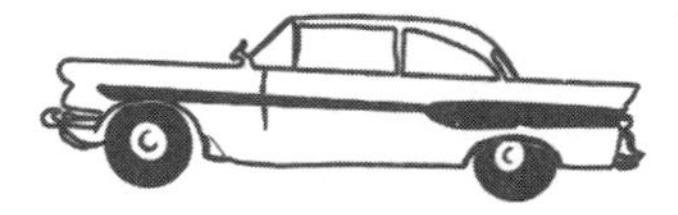

TWENTY

1987

Their eyes met for the first time since that day she waved goodbye from the front seat of her banana-yellow convertible twenty-six years earlier. And although her skin betrayed the inevitable passage of time, her eyes still glowed of gold, and her curls still threatened to emerge, now pulled tight behind her head. She was a beautiful woman, he thought, his black Stetson clutched firmly in his hands as he stood nervously at her door. Clad in black, her delicate figure still held the graceful traces of the girl he had once known and loved. And her ruby lips, only slightly faded, still beckoned as his eternal address.

The long year of waiting had passed. And here he was at last, for his much-awaited audience.

She gazed at him impassively, blocking the doorway with her arms crossed, an unyielding expression on her lovely face. He wondered what she might think of how he had changed over the years. He too was dressed in the color of night. They must have seemed like two ravens contemplating fight or flight,

Fulgencio mused. He still cut an imposing figure, made harder and stronger by the flow of time through his veins. A bit thicker around the waist and chest. Solid. He was still the powerhouse others had feared but she had adored. His weather-beaten skin was cut deep with the carvings of the sun and wind on El Dos de Copas. His eyes remained forever a forest of earth and emerald hues in which she could easily become lost. Even now that she had hardened herself against his advances, she could feel his mysterious pull.

The air hung still around them. The last leaves of autumn plunged from the trees and swirled in the barren lawn. The remnants of the rosebush beneath the window crumbled in the wind.

"Thank you for seeing me," Fulgencio said.

Reluctantly, she motioned for him to enter the darkened foyer, where he spotted his weekly letters lying open and scattered across the entryway table.

"You can thank Little David for me agreeing to this madness," Carolina said. "I felt bad for him when you sent him with your gifts and your letters."

Tentatively, he followed the clicking of her heels into the shadowy recesses of the living room.

The plastic had vanished. The furniture been replaced. Gone were the lace doilies and trinkets. It had become an austere room, the drapes drawn shut in eternal mourning.

She motioned for him to sit on the sofa. Fulgencio assented with his hat clutched on his lap, his knuckles white, fabric buckling. And Carolina sat precariously on the edge of a wingback chair across from him, an uncomfortable distance yawning between the two. Not the distance of a coffee table, but rather the distance of decades of loneliness and yearning, the distance of interminable suffering, the distance of regret, confusion, and misunderstanding. The distance of a death, the death of their relationship so many years before.

"So," Carolina whispered hoarsely, "you're here."

"Yes," Fulgencio managed to utter.

She waited, her face tilting toward the floor.

"It's been a long year," Fulgencio said.

"It's been a long life," she quipped, her lips pursed in a dour grimace he'd never seen on her face in their younger days.

He shifted in his seat, deterred by the bitterness lurking in her voice.

"You received my letters?" he ventured, trying to get something going.

"Yes," she stated. "I never knew the life of a pharmacist could be so fascinating."

He sensed the sarcasm in her tone. He had written the idle musings of his weekly life. He had been wary of releasing too much passion or pent-up love, suspecting it might frighten her after all these years of silence. Sure, he knew the letters were probably boring, but it was the best he could do under the circumstances to keep in touch with her, to try and build some sort of common ground, some sort of foundation to start upon at the end of the year's wait.

He tried again, "Your mom," he asked, "she's okay?"

"Yes, she mostly stays in her bedroom. She thinks this winter will be her last, but she thought that ages ago, as you might recall."

"Yes," he said, "that's why you first came back from boarding school to study here in La Frontera."

"She's lucky I don't hold that against her." Her eyes flashed angrily across his face, burning into his for but an instant.

He'd always wondered if they'd had the blessed fortune of marrying and bringing children into the world, what color their eyes would have turned out.

Reaching deep into his buried soul, he struggled to recapture the magic which had once flowed from within like the Holy Spirit. "Carolina," he said, "I've never understood why you behaved the way you did. You knew how possessive I was, yet you tested me. As I've looked back over the years, I've always regretted my behavior, questioned my reactions and decisions. I've spent years replaying it all in my mind, our last moments together, the last time I saw you. I've wondered if I could have done something differently, something that might have saved us from this wretched life we have led."

A single tear dropped gently from her bowed head onto the rug.

"Do you feel the same way I do?" he beseeched her, raising his hands in the air. "Do you wish things had worked out differently?"

Silence.

He waited for what seemed like yet another eternity, wondering if night had come and gone beyond the cloistered sanctum of those somber walls. Until, finally, she spoke.

"I've wondered too," her voice trembled, "I've wondered what happened. I waited for you that night. You never came. I called. You never answered. I wrote. You never replied." She paused to fight back the tears, salt on her lips. "I gave you everything. I gave you myself. I pledged you my love . . . and you promised . . . but you never showed up. You never came. You abandoned me." Her voice crumbled as she began to sob, hunched over her knees.

He didn't dare reach out to comfort her. Instead, he felt the surge of anger welling up inside of him, as always. He recalled the events of that Christmas Eve, and the fiasco that first tore them apart months before at her college dance. For years he had fought against that rage. He had tried his hardest to accept that it had led to his undoing. He had worked tirelessly to defeat the forces and internal demons that had conspired against his once promising future with Carolina.

He knew he was ultimately to blame for his decisions, regardless of Carolina's actions. And he yearned to not revisit those tortured chambers of his memory. He yearned to begin again, anew, without unearthing all that had ravaged their love. But deep inside he knew—both Brother William and the Virgencita had counseled him—he had to come clean about his tortured feelings and the final actions that had destroyed their relationship in order to earn another chance at friendship, at something only God might prophesize for this stage of their lives.

"Why, Fulgencio?" she cried, looking straight into his eyes. "Why did you leave me after all that we had and all that we dreamt of together?"

He could hear the hard swallowing in her throat, see her delicate neck convulsing in anguish.

Uncontrollably, she screamed in tears, "Why?"

He felt her shriek pierce his heart like a knife as he fumbled to find the words he must reveal, "I came, Carolina," he started. "I came that night . . . here to your father's house. I had a dozen roses for you from Curiel's Flower Shop," he recalled, his eyes searching for meaning in the patterns of the rug. "I had a black velvet box with an engagement ring inside . . ."

She lifted her head toward him, her eyes still swallowing him whole.

"I wanted to surprise you. I came around the side to the kitchen door and there . . . I stopped to look for you in the window." He glanced across the foyer toward the dining room where he had spied her dancing in another's arms. The burning tide of rage threatened to rise again within him, but—unlike in the past—he managed to suppress it. "And I saw you, Carolina. I saw you dancing with another man. Just like the night of the dance at Incarnate Word. Just like I thought would never happen again." He shook his head, dropping it mournfully into his hands.

Brother William had counseled him to go slowly in his explanations as to not come across like a madman, or worse yet, as someone unwilling to recognize his own shortcomings, someone eager to assign the blame to anything and anyone but himself.

Slowly, she reeled him in with a look that snagged the corner of his eye. She looked puzzled and horrified all at once, her lips twisted into a shocked and sickly smile. Her eyes turned to glass for a fleeting instant as she remembered the events of that evening.

"You idiot!" she exclaimed, jumping to her feet.

His eyes searched hers for a clue.

"That was my cousin I was dancing with, *you fool!*"

Shocked, Fulgencio slapped his hand against his forehead in dismay, exclaiming, "What?"

"I couldn't wait for you to meet him!"

"But he was a gringo I'd never seen before." Fulgencio's words fell haplessly from his downturned lips. "He wasn't from around here. He couldn't have been your cousin."

"My mother's sister and her family had come to visit from up north. I hadn't seen him since we were little kids. Since we were both only children, we were like brother and sister. I can't believe it. You're even stupider and crazier than I ever thought you were."

She didn't know the half of it, he thought. Maybe now would not be the best time to tell her the rest of his pathetic excuse. She'd probably laugh at him and call the insane asylum to come drag him away in a straitjacket.

His heart sank into the muted plushness of the oriental rug as the clicking of her heels on the staircase faded upward into darkness. She had left him all alone without another word. The house fell silent yet again. And when no one came, he sheepishly tiptoed his way to the front door. It was dark outside as he exited, casting a final look over his shoulder but finding nothing in his wake. He could have sworn that for an instant someone had been standing there in the foyer, in the door to Mr. Mendelssohn's den, watching him go, wallowing in resigned sadness. But in the absence of onlookers, he pulled the door delicately shut and shuffled morosely to his rusty pickup truck. It was cold beneath the starry blanket of night. And he wondered when he'd see Carolina again, if ever. He wondered if that had been Mr. Mendelssohn himself, watching him go from the doorway to his den, shaking his head in dismay.

What an idiot, indeed, he thought as his drove away. He shook his head in disgust. Her cousin! He had thrown his life away for her cousin! Because she was dancing with her helpless, innocent, *gringito* cousin! What in the world had been wrong with him? Idiot. *Pendejo. Hijo de su chingada madre.* Of course, he knew what it was, as much as he had not wanted to ever fully believe it. *La maldición.*

He pulled the truck to a screeching halt by the side of the road, not far from where he and Carolina had stopped that first night on the way to the homecoming dance. Slamming his fist against the flimsy plastic steering wheel, he cracked it into pieces.

He tore at the sun-bleached vinyl that had once been navy blue. He pulled at his wavy black hair. He climbed out, slammed the door shut, and left the old pickup idling behind him. In the dim glow of the headlights, he kicked at the dirt and litter gathered by the curb. He turned his eyes and arms to the heavens. "Why?" he yelled, a murder of crows rustling from the trees. "*¿Porque*?" he implored the invisible force above and beyond. "All for nothing. I was wrong! I was wrong! My anger! My rage! It was all for nothing! God forgive me . . ." He fell to his knees as a car whizzed by. "Forgive me for this sin. Carolina, forgive me! What have I done?" He lay in ruins, sobbing on the ground, reduced to nothing by the folly and irony of his own grandiose error.

Cipriano always told him, "*El que se enoja pierde.*" He who gets angry loses. Boy, how he had lost. Lost it all. Lost years he could never get back. Lost love he could only dream of rediscovering before the end drew near. And he figured now, it might as well. "*Que se acabe, ay Gran Dios* . . . Let it end, oh great God! Let it end!" He buried his face in the dirt, tasted the bitter chalk of defeat. Sweat and tears stung his eyes as he sat on the curb in the flickering glow of the pale headlights, his voice fighting through the sobs:

Oh gran Dios
(O great God)
Como sufro en la vida
(How I suffer in life)
Por no querer ser menos que nadie
(Not wanting to be less than anyone)

En esta vida todo se acaba
(In this life everything ends)
Por eso quiero esta vida terminar
(That's why I want to end this life)

Ay, cuanto diera por la vida de antes
(What I'd give for the old days)
En cuanto amores a mi no me faltarón
(Loves never failed me)

En este mundo mi Dios todo se acaba
(In this world, my God, everything ends)
Por eso quiero esta vida terminar.
(That's why I wish to end this life.)

Poor Carolina Mendelssohn. How could he have been such a fool? How could he have been so blind to his own flaw, the burden he had secretly, unknowingly, brought with him from Mexico like a smuggler unwittingly sneaking in deadly contraband? He stood up, his tired frame barely able to maintain its balance. His eyes squinted in the face of the pickup's lights. He had worked tirelessly all these waiting years—since unraveling the nature of his spiritual malady—to overcome that fated past, encoded and programmed within him for the sole purpose of bringing about his own ruination. But now he wondered if it would make any difference at all. Just because he was now more capable of controlling his emotions, it did not mean that he could control Carolina's. Nor did he wish to anymore. He desired her love and forgiveness, but it had to flow freely from her heart. He could not blame her for wanting nothing to do with him. And what would she think if he told her the whole truth behind his bizarre, misguided, and hurtful actions? Would she deem him completely *crazy loco*? Exhausted, he dragged his feet back toward the truck. He doubted whether he could even go on. And—before he could reach the door—the truck sputtered and choked. Dead. Out of gas.

TWENTY-ONE

1961

The pickup that hauled him to Austin on that bleak Christmas Day in 1961 pulled to a stop in front of a dark and empty Buzzy's Diner. Beneath a weeping night sky, Fulgencio fumbled with the keys to the alleyway entrance and stumbled sopping wet into the storage room he called home. The scent of gardenias still clung to the air. Her perfume. His heart swam but failed to stay afloat. Her picture, smeared with dry blood, lay next to the shattered frame of the Sagrado Corazón. He sat on the floor in the corner of the room, amidst the fragments of Buzzy's dismantled cot. He stared long and hard at the Sagrado Corazón. He just hadn't had the heart to go out to El Dos de Copas and see his grandfather and the Virgencita, disappoint them with his fiasco. He couldn't face Brother William. He felt like burrowing beneath a rock like a snake and hiding for a thousand years until some paleontologist or archaeologist dug him up, little more than a dust-laden fossil from a distant, faded time.

The Sagrado Corazón, the image of Jesus, seemed sadder than usual. If anyone knew the sting of betrayal, it was Him.

Fulgencio stared long and hard at Jesus, wondering how He could bring Himself to forgive. Forgiveness—Fulgencio knew from the brothers' teachings at San Juan del Atole—was the most sacred of Catholic actions. But still, forgiveness was far from his heart that night on the floor in Buzzy's storage room. His heart froze solid that night. But the hardened look in his eyes still betrayed a fire beneath.

Business resumed, and life went on all around him, and Fulgencio Ramirez pledged himself to getting on with it. He dated a string of women whose names he quickly forgot. He made Buzzy countless dollars by running the tightest ship in town. And he got his degree with the surety of an unstoppable army marching homeward after vanquishing its enemies on the front.

Days turned to weeks, and weeks to months. Stringing them together with little care, Fulgencio felt a hollow in his heart as he packed his grandfather's leather bag for his final trip home. He placed the Sagrado Corazón—wrapped tightly within one of his shirts—squarely in the center of the bag. Carolina Mendelssohn's picture now survived hidden behind Christ's inside the frame. He couldn't part with it, but he could not bear to look at it either, for surely, her absence from his life would drive him insane. His diploma—also framed—he wrapped and placed securely next to the sacred images of his youth.

Buzzy watched with a heavy heart as the typewriter case clicked shut, and Fulgencio stood before him a final time beneath the barren bulb. The old floor fan was neatly stashed away in a corner. Fulgencio had replaced the broken cot with a comfortable new bed for when Buzzy was too tired to go home.

"I wish there was something I could give ya," Buzzy growled.

"Just give me a hug, old man," Fulgencio said, wrapping his

arms tightly around the diminutive sailor dressed in white. Buzzy's cheek felt like sandpaper against his.

He stood back and extended the white sailor's cap to Buzzy. "I'm all done, boss."

"Keep it as a souvenir."

Fulgencio's head turned to either side, surveying the tiny room that had served as his shelter for four long years. "Thank you, Buzzy, for giving me a home."

"Thank you, Fulgencio, for keepin' me company." The short order cook reached up and put his arm around Fulgencio's left shoulder as he walked him out—bags in hand—through the vacant diner.

"Ya know, Fulgencio," Buzzy said, throwing the door open, the tiny silver bell on the handle ringing in Fulgencio's ears. "Ya always kept me on my toes. Ya was always able to surprise me. And that's not easy to do to an old deckhand like me."

Fulgencio smiled as they strolled out onto the sidewalk. The sun was setting, the breeze cooling the concrete.

He continued, "It ain't been easy springin' a surprise on you, though. You're highly alert, a certified Longhorn." Buzzy pointed toward the UT Tower looming in the orange sky.

Fulgencio admired the tower, then scanned the gate he had passed through so many times. Unlike all the others who dashed in and out, oblivious to its message, he had always repeated the words as he passed through its shadow. "Enter ye seeking knowledge," he mouthed.

"So, tell me, Fulgencio, before you go . . ." Buzzy motioned toward the curb, his arm sweeping toward a gleaming, red 1957 Corvette Convertible with white vinyl seats and a matching cove gracing the doors. "Ya surprised?"

For an instant Fulgencio forgot his sorrow and his emptiness as his eyes widened to take in the sparkling sight of the roadster parked before the diner, glowing purplish along its curving lines beneath the neon blue of Buzzy's sign.

Fulgencio ran his hands along the smooth curves and chrome, his mouth gaping in disbelief. No one had ever given him anything of material value, with the exception of the typewriter his father had presented him upon graduating from high school.

"It's your graduation and going-away present!" Buzzy beamed. He had never had children of his own. Never married. Fulgencio was the closest thing to a son he had ever known. "Don't say a word. Just take it and go. Fast and far. And don't look back. A good sailor, like a good cowboy . . . never looks back. We just sail toward the horizon, or ride into the sunset. No regrets. No tears. No goodbyes." Buzzy placed the keys in Fulgencio's hand and folded it shut. "Now go. C'mon! Giddyup!"

Buzzy threw the leather bag into the back seat and closed the driver door as Fulgencio slid behind the three-spoke steering wheel. Then—as Fulgencio adjusted the chrome outside rear-view mirror—he added, "Jis wait a second." He ran back into the store, emerging moments later with a battered, oversized Polaroid camera. "Alright, jis sit there and smile!"

Fulgencio still could not find words to describe his gratitude to this man who had opened his business, his heart, and his storage room to him during these difficult and lonely years of labor and loss. He smiled his first true, warm smile in two years. It hurt as the flash popped.

"Just in case!" Buzzy hollered. And he waved from the curb beneath the sign on Guadalupe Street as Fulgencio Ramirez rode his gleaming steed into the burnt orange sunset.

TWENTY-TWO

He roared into town during the summer of '63 with the top down, his hair whipping in the wind, and his tortoiseshell wayfarers masking the resentment in his eyes. He had harbored mild hopes that perhaps somehow, he could set things right with Carolina Mendelssohn, for he realized that life without her was futile. But the day of his arrival, Bobby Balmori met him with the news of Carolina's marriage, to none other than Miguel Rodriguez Esparza. Fulgencio Ramirez tasted the putrid fruit of betrayal yet again.

"Miguel?" Fulgencio had to sit down at the Balmori's dinner table to process the shocking blow. "Miguel?"

Fortunately, the two were alone in the house, for the torrent of Spanish curse words that spewed from Fulgencio's mouth in response to the revelation was unprecedented.

"It's hard to believe," Bobby said, bringing two cold beers from the kitchen.

The two drank in silence as Fulgencio replayed the events leading up his breakup with Carolina. "Miguel played us. All that time we trusted him. All that time I thought he was my hometown friend up at school. What if all along, he was plotting to divide us? I could kill him!" he shouted, slamming his empty beer bottle on the table.

"Don't do anything you'll regret," Bobby advised him. "You've worked too hard and come too far. You're an educated professional now. You've got to act like one."

"But Miguel?" Fulgencio ran his fingers through his hair in exasperation. "It would make more sense to me if she'd married that Anglo soldier I saw her dancing with in her living room. That would have been what the whole town might have expected. But to marry someone no better than me? Maybe she did it to spite me."

"Well, you disappeared on her. He was there to comfort her."

Fulgencio frowned, glowering angrily at Bobby, "Whose side are you on, anyway?"

"There are no sides, Fulgencio," Bobby tried to explain. "It's over."

From that moment on, Fulgencio went about his business with a vengeance. He realized that Bobby Balmori was right; there were no sides. There would be no competition. It was over. Carolina was a married woman. And the only solace he could draw from the fact that she had wed Miguel Rodriguez Esparza was that he did not have to feel guilt for wishing him an early death. He was a sneak and a traitor and he deserved whatever punishment La Virgencita saw fit to send his way.

He obtained a loan from La Frontera bank where Old Man Maldonado's son now worked as a loan officer. And he found a perfect spot across from Market Square to open his own pharmacy, La Farmacia Ramirez. There, he built a little world where *la raza* could come in and share their woes, get some medical advice in Spanish, and fill their prescriptions, sometimes with little more than a promise to pay. "*Un rinconcito de Mexico en el corazón del Valle*," Fulgencio liked to say. A little corner of Mexico in the heart of the Rio Grande Valley. And in the afternoons, the guitarists would swing by before heading off to their nightly gigs, warm up with Fulgencio, *la voz de oro*, the voice of gold, his heart yearning through the rafters.

The years glided by as he began his morning ritual of scanning the obituaries for those detested twenty-two letters that had ultimately spelled his demise. Though it would be a long time before he fully understood the depth and extent of Miguelito's betrayal, he hated him for marrying her, hated him for punctuating with a period, *punto final*, the most glorious chapter of his life.

Through the ravages of time, the battering of the elements and unrequited emotions, he grew harder and colder. His charm remained vibrant, although his will to live was slowly fading. And what kept him most alive was his pain. He relished and he reveled in it, proclaiming it for the world to hear in the bars and at the dances, in the way he wrung every last drop of emotion from each and every note, every word, in the songs he loved to sing.

One night as he sang "Hoja Seca" at the elegantly appointed Drive Inn across the border, he left the entire ballroom in tears, his words permeating their hearts. In song, he mourned the loss of his love and the impossibility of ever finding another its equal. He proclaimed his faith as nothing but dry leaves, *hojas secas*, killed by pain.

Tan lejos de ti no puedo vivir.
(So distant from you I can't live.)
Tan lejos de ti me voy a morir.
(So distant from you I'm going to die.)

Entré a esta taberna, tan llena de copas,
(I entered this tavern, so full of drinks,)
queriendo olvidar.
(wishing to forget.)
Pero ni las copas, Señor Tabernero,
(But not even the drinks, Mr. Bartender,)
me hacen olvidar.
(make me forget.)

Me salgo a la calle,
(I go onto the street,)
buscando un consuelo,
(searching for a consolation,)
buscando un amor.
(searching for love.)
Pero es imposible.
(But it's impossible.)
Mi fé es hoja seca
(My faith is dry leaves)
que mató el dolor.
(killed by pain.)

No espero que vuelvas.
(I don't expect you to return.)
Ni espero que lo hagas.
(Nor do I expect you to do so.)
¿Pues ya para que?
(What for now anyway?)
Se acabó el romance.
(The romance is over.)

Mataste una vida.
(You killed a life.)
Se acabó el amor.
(The love is gone.)

Si acaso mis ojos
(If only my eyes)
llenos de tristeza
(filled with sorrow)
pudieran llorar.
(could possibly cry.)
Pero es imposible
(But that's impossible)
pues núnca he llorado
(for I've never cried)
por ningún amor.
(for any love.)

Ya que es imposible
(Given that it's impossible)
dejar de quererla,
(to stop loving her,)
Señor Tabernero,
(Mr. Bartender,)
sírvame otra copa
(Pour me another drink)
que quiero olvidar.
(that I wish to forget.)

After his stirring rendition, a group of music executives—passing through en route to Mexico City—offered to sign him to a recording contract then and there, but he turned them down saying he would never again leave La Frontera, not to tour, not to sing, not for anything but the love of one woman, Carolina Mendelssohn, the one he sang for, the one that broke his heart.

He eased his suffering, at times with song, at times in the restless comfort of other women's arms, at times with the sweet elixir of liquor. And he built a fortune, including not just La Farmacia Ramirez, but also a trucking line, a construction company, a produce exporting outfit, a brickyard, a tire recapping plant (similar to the one his father had once had that his brother Nicolas had gambled away), a car wash, and countless head of cattle, sheep, and thoroughbred horses. But no one would have guessed it. He ran it all discreetly from the back of his drugstore. In his prime, El Chotay served dutifully as his right hand man in the field, supervising everything, working tirelessly. And still, Fulgencio lived in his adobe hut, wore his fading guayaberas, drove his clamoring pickup, and grew older.

Of course, he never married. Never had a desire to do so with anyone except Carolina. Never fathered any children either. He concocted his own herbal birth control potion to prevent that tragedy from ever transpiring. For he could not conceive of the thought of bringing a child into this world that was not the result of his union with Carolina Mendelssohn.

Whenever his friends or family needed him, he was there for them, especially his mother and Little David, whom he provided for after the death of his father. He truly felt that he had little else to live for. After all, the promise of Carolina becoming a widow loomed far in the distant future. Sure, he hoped that his wretched foe would die sooner rather than later, but for all he knew, the worthless sap she married would outlive them all. So he went about his life with reckless abandon. Some might have thought he was full of life, but both he and those close to him knew it was quite the opposite: he was overflowing with death. He subsisted in a sort of limbo, waiting for another chance at life with Carolina.

About a decade after his return to La Frontera, while he sat alone in the drugstore at night tallying up the day's receipts, a lone woman came in to pick up her medicine. He recognized her immediately as La Señora Villarreal. Her looks were unmistakable despite the wrinkles that now furrowed her once smooth face, and the strands of white hair that intermingled with her black mane. Her stark, gray eyes still glimmered brightly against the dark backdrop of her sun-roasted skin.

He observed her silently as he filled her prescription, his thoughts on their encounter years earlier in the produce section of Lopez Supermarket.

"Have you looked into it?" she asked, feeling pity for him. She had heard about his mournful singing, his solitary life.

"I'm sorry, Señora Villarreal," Fulgencio replied, counting pills and sliding them into their container. "I'm not sure what you're talking about."

"*La maldición*," she answered. "The one I told you about when you were just a muchacho, standing in the grocery store with your mother."

"No, *señora*. I have not."

"Why not?"

"I'm not sure. I've been too busy."

"Too busy?" Her large eyes opened wider. "Too busy to learn

about the greatest obstacle in your life, the one blocking the path to all those dreams you always had?"

"I still have my dreams. It's all I have these days, really." He placed the container in a bag and slid it across the counter.

"Ask your mother," La Señora Villarreal implored him. "She has to know something. That's the only reason I mentioned it to you back then, because you were together and I thought she would help you with it. We all come from the same lands, you know? From Caja Pinta, way back to when our ancestors landed there on the ships from Spain. Ask her to point you in the right direction. It's the only way you'll ever turn all this around. You can't just wait for that girl's husband to die and then expect her to run right back into your arms, Fulgencio. Life doesn't work that way. It's never that easy, at least not for people like us."

She reached into her purse to pull out her Medicaid card, but he waved it off. "No, Señora Villarreal. Save your Medicaid in case you need something else this month. You've given me more than enough tonight."

After she left, Fulgencio sat for a while contemplating her words and staring at the phone. He picked up the receiver and then placed it back in its cradle a couple of times. Then he finally dialed his mother's number.

"*¿Bueno?*" she answered after a couple of rings. He could hear food sizzling on a pan in the background.

"Mamá?"

"*Sí, m'ijo.*"

"Remember La Señora Villarreal?"

"Yes."

"Remember that day in Lopez Supermarket years ago? Remember what she said? Something about a *maldición*?"

A long pause followed. And then Ninfa del Rosario responded tentatively, "Yes?"

"What can you tell me about that? I saw her just now, and she said I needed to ask you so I could fix it."

"*Ay Dios, esta gente de rancho*. Fulgencio, we didn't move to America so that we could still believe in such things. The past is the past. And the sooner you leave it behind you, the sooner you'll start enjoying life here in the present. Forget about that. La Señora Villarreal is a *gitana*. One of her ancestors intermarried with one of ours at some point along the line, but she is stuck in the old ways and superstitions. Let her believe what she needs to believe. You're a man of science now, aren't you?"

"Yes, that's true, but that doesn't mean I don't believe in *yerbas y maldiciónes*. And you know I talk to people that have left this world all the time. I see them. They're real. So why shouldn't I believe that some sort of curse could be affecting me or our family? Remember when I was a kid and I'd come running to you in the middle of the night? I would hear these strange words, these chants. Remember that? Remember how angry I would get, how violent? Remember how jealous and possessive I was, so much so I left Carolina without even asking her with whom she was dancing that Christmas Eve? Maybe this *maldición* La Señora Villarreal speaks of has something to do with all that."

"*Hijo mio*. You're a man. And you're both a Ramirez and a Cisneros. It's no surprise that you've been the way you are. All of you machos are *imposibles*. I'm sure you'd like to blame your troubles on something else, something you can pay some *curandera* or *bruja* to dispel. And if it makes you feel better, go right on ahead. But don't drag me into your backward quest for answers to all that's gone wrong in your life in the past. My father abandoned me. He left me nothing. He lost everything we had. And some people said the reason my mother died in childbirth was because he was so horrible to her that she did not have the will to go on living. Your brothers have all amounted to nothing. Little David *pues ni se diga*. And you, well, I'm thankful for your help, but we both know you've been miserable for a very long time. So with all that suffering, and all that failure, I've had enough. I don't want excuses about why it's been that way. I just want to move on."

"So, who should I ask? Do you know something and you're just not telling me?" Fulgencio pressed.

She sighed, "Look, *m'ijo*. People out on the ranches, when I was a girl growing up, they always talked about it. Some said they saw a woman standing by the river. I never did. And they spoke of an old curse, *la maldición de* Caja Pinta. But frankly, there were countless stories and none of them ever made any sense to me, so I tuned them out. If you say you talk to dead people, then go ask that grandfather of yours that's now your roommate. He's the one you should be talking to, don't you think?"

"He doesn't say much. He just sits there and plays cards and drinks."

"Well I'm glad to see he hasn't changed," she quipped.

"C'mon, help me out here, Mamá. Give me a break."

"I'm sorry, son. That's all I really know. And, well, there is one more thing."

"What's that?"

"Well, they used to say that the Cisneros men would be unable to hold on to love unless the *maldición* was broken."

Fulgencio nearly fumbled the phone. "What?"

"That's all I know," Ninfa del Rosario Cisneros asserted.

"How could you not tell me this sooner?"

"Because I don't believe it."

"But you mess around with herbs and spells yourself! How can you not believe it?" Fulgencio ran his hands through his hair in exasperation.

"Curing a cold or helping someone with their rheumatism is one thing," she explained. "Dabbling in black magic is another. I don't do that."

"Well, don't you think my brothers and I deserved to know about this *maldición*?"

"No, not really. I considered it when you were kids. I even spoke to El Padre Juan Bacalao about it, asked him if I should tell you. He said I shouldn't. He said that none of that old Santeria belongs in the Christian world."

"Of course he would say that, Mamá. He's got to stick to his script. But if the Padre can make a miracle on the altar every time he celebrates Mass, then why couldn't a *bruja* put a curse on someone?"

"I don't know. Looking back at how everything has turned out for you and your brothers, maybe I was wrong to ignore the curse, but at the time, I didn't wish to burden you with unnecessary doubts about something that you could do nothing about."

"Well, we'll see about that!" Fulgencio declared, a bitter taste creeping into his mouth. "For whatever it's worth, Mamá. Thank you for finally telling me what you know."

"Don't go getting yourself killed over this, Fulgencio."

"I'm already dead inside, Mamá. How much worse can things get? Adios."

That night, Fulgencio sped back to El Dos de Copas, hopeful to extract more information from his grandfather. He found him at his usual spot at the table, playing solitaire before the relief of the Virgen de Guadalupe on the adobe wall.

"*Abuelo,* tell me about *la maldición de* Caja Pinta."

His grandfather sat quietly, palming cards in a hypnotic daze.

"*¿Abuelo?*"

"I don't remember."

"What do you mean, you don't remember?"

"You must forgive me, but my mind isn't what it used to be. My memories are foggy."

"So at one point you knew?" Fulgencio asked, sitting down across from him, searching his solemn eyes.

"I never knew much. There were so many stories and rumors. And I wasn't like you, Fulgencio. I didn't have a talent for seeing the people who have passed to El Otro Lado or talking to them. Some of us do. And some of us don't. *Ni modo*. It was useless for me to try to understand it, so I gave up."

"Why did you abandon my mother? Was it because of the curse?"

"I never abandoned her. Is that what she claims?" Fernando Cisneros kept laying down the most terrible combinations of cards Fulgencio had ever seen. His luck remained abysmal even decades after his death. "Look, now that you mention it, I remember why I gave her to my relatives—El Chino Alasan's family—to raise on their ranch, Las Lomas. The curse has something to do with losing the ones you love, or not being able to hang on to love. After my wife died in childbirth, I was afraid that if I kept Ninfa, she would die before her time too. So I gave her away. I was afraid to love."

"Hmm, so that's why you told me to *not* be afraid to love," Fulgencio recalled. "I didn't fear it, but now I've been in pain because of it most of my life. Why didn't you warn me about all this?"

"I didn't want to burden you with my superstitions. Besides, curses are meant to be broken, *m'ijo*. And maybe you are the one who can finally set our family free from *la maldición*. I remember I once thought I could help you by crossing over to the other side of life and death, but it didn't work out that way. All I've been able to do is sit here. I have not had the energy or power to venture outside these walls to seek the answers."

Fulgencio furrowed his brow, realizing at that moment that this multigenerational *maldición* might be too big for one person to overcome. "I need to tell someone right away, someone who will help me break it," he realized with a sense of urgency. "Someone who will help me figure this out."

"Someone spiritual, Fulgencio. Someone powerful. Someone strong," Fernando Cisneros added.

"Brother William," they both realized at the same time. And the Virgencita began to do an Irish jig on the wall. Apparently, she liked him.

"Yes, Brother William. He's been kind, coming out here often and paying his respects ever since you first brought him when you were still a child."

"I need to go now," Fulgencio said, wishing he'd installed a phone line at the ranch. "Gracias, *abuelito*." He gave Fernando Cisneros a kiss on the cheek and rushed out the door.

That night, huddled over coffee in his office at San Juan del Atole, Brother William took copious notes of everything Fulgencio could recount regarding *la maldición de* Caja Pinta, the collected ruminations of La Señora Villarreal, Ninfa del Rosario, and Fernando Cisneros.

"So, all these years," Brother William asked, "in moments of trouble and anger, you would hear these words you did not understand?"

"Yes, and a thundering white noise that would drown everything else out. But it wasn't just in difficult moments, now that I think of it. It happened at times when Carolina would be talking to me, opening up to me. Instead of listening to her, all I could hear sometimes were these mysterious chants in my head."

"I can't believe you never told me," Brother William shook his head. "Maybe I could have helped you sooner."

"I thought something was wrong with me, that people would think I was crazy," Fulgencio admitted.

"Well," Brother William sighed. "I think we're all a little bit crazy. But once we figure that out, we can start doing something about it."

TWENTY-THREE

Brother William and Fulgencio worked feverishly to unravel the nature of *la maldición*. Each Sunday, they drove out to El Dos de Copas and ventured in every direction within the surrounding ranchlands to interview the campesinos, rancheros, and ejidatarios, recruiting Cipriano to help them as well. Any scrap of information might be of use. Soon, Brother William determined that he would need to keep a journal, one with the multitude of diverging rumors and tall tales. These were possibilities, he explained to Fulgencio, not necessarily realities. As it turned out, there were as many different versions of the story as there were people willing to share. The legends all held Mauro Fernando Cisneros, Fulgencio's great-great-grandfather, at their center. But in each of them, he played a different role. He was by turns a tyrant, a magnanimous leader, a gunfighter, a gambler, a lover of many women, a singer, a humble farmer, an arrogant aristocrat. And in varying accounts, he had either abandoned his wife or killed her, loved her too much or not enough, cheated on her or been obsessed with her, invariably bringing about *la maldición*.

Other iterations claimed *la maldición* had been placed on him and his lineage for stealing lands, for robbing cattle, for taking treasure, for killing *indios*, for fighting the gringos, for helping the gringos, for owning slaves, for freeing slaves, and so on and so forth.

And finally, there was the question of who had cast the hex in the first place. Some guessed the culprit had been his very wife, jealous that he had spawned children with a lover. Others blamed Mauro Fernando's mother-in-law, who had possessed a reputation for practicing *brujería*. Yet others conjured an illegitimate brother cut out of the will and left penniless. Or it might have been a jilted lover, a jealous neighbor, a belligerent nemesis who felt cheated at the card table or in a land deal. So many years had passed that nobody knew the truth for certain. In lieu of a clear narrative, the abundant and self-propagating rumors had circulated those lands as commonly as dust devils and tumbleweed since the mid-1800's. Without many other forms of entertainment, the rancheros and campesinos found it fun to speculate about *la maldición*.

"It's not fun for *me*, Brother William," Fulgencio rued one such Sunday after a dispiriting round of interviews, sipping tequila at the table as his grandfather and his aging mentor played a game of poker. "As if I weren't suffering enough already from losing Carolina. Now I also feel like I could go mad. Every day, having to collect all of this ancient history, and add more and more conflicting and confusing information to it. It could drive me insane. I may have to start taking some of those antianxiety pills that I give my cousin Gustavo."

"Don't cloud your mind, Fulgencio. We need you at the peak of your powers," Brother William urged, spreading a full house across the rough-hewn tabletop, much to Fernando Cisneros's dismay.

The Virgencita leaned in from her perch on the wall and whispered something into Fernando Cisneros's ear.

"Hey, no cheating," Brother William chided. "Is she dispensing gambling advice, Don Fernando? I bet she can see through our cards."

"No, she says you should go talk to the woman," Fernando Cisneros answered sullenly, shuffling the cards in his hand. No matter how he rearranged them, they comprised the worst poker hand imaginable. "*Es por de más,*" he lamented, folding.

"What woman?" Fulgencio pondered out loud.

The Virgencita leaned in again, whispering into Fernando Cisneros's ear once more.

"The one by the river," he explained.

"Why didn't we think of that?" Brother William scratched his head.

"Maybe it's the *maldición* weaving its web," Fulgencio spoke slowly. "It may be clouding our minds, like you just said the pills would do to me."

"You mean it could be affecting me too?" Brother William wondered. "I guess it's possible."

"Maybe this *maldición* is like a living being, Brother William. It protects itself. What do you call it? Self-preservation. It is designed to confuse those affected by it. And now that you're trying to crack it, it may be impacting you too, making both of us ignore those people whose help we need most to end it!"

"That's what I would do," Brother William realized. He rubbed his hands together, his eyes glowing with excitement. "If I were a *maldición*."

Fulgencio laughed. "You're the opposite, Brother William. You're a blessing! And you look the way you did when you were drawing up our game plans for the playoffs back in the day." Fulgencio smiled feebly. "Except this is no game. This is my life."

"Yes, my son. And with a little bit of luck, and help from the Virgencita, we may just figure out how to get that life back on track."

The two lay down their cards, thanked the Virgen and Fernando Cisneros, and headed out into the blazing sun.

Riding on Relámpago and Trueno, offspring of the mighty steeds they had first ridden that summer day so many years before, they headed north toward the river. After a couple hours, they reached its banks. They found her standing on her dune, her long, dark hair flowing in the Gulf breeze. She wore a gray dress that looked like an elegant collection of smooth, silken strips spun by an ethereal wheel, her hazel eyes staring blankly at the opposite side of the river.

"Please tell us your name, tell us who you are," Brother William implored, disturbing her for the first time since that day nearly two decades earlier when he and Fulgencio first glimpsed her on that very spot.

They waited a long time, repeating the question. It was as if she was there, but not there, asleep with her eyes open.

"She's been here a long time," Fulgencio said. "Maybe she's just an apparition, not conscious."

Brother William tried another tack. "What are you looking for? What are you waiting for?"

Nothing.

They sat for a long while in hopes that she would rouse from her trance, but nothing changed.

"We must head back before sundown, Brother William. It has become too dangerous to be out here at night, what with all the *narcos y coyotes.*"

As they mounted and began to ride south, they heard a rustle behind them, and a nearly imperceptible whisper on the wind. The horses started, and the riders turned.

She still stood motionless in the same exact place, staring off into her northern oblivion. They strained, leaning toward her.

And then they heard a faint voice, although her lips did not move.

They both heard her say: "*Yo soy* Soledad . . . Soledad Cisneros."

After that she would say no more, regardless of their efforts to coax more insights from her as to why she was there and whether she knew anything about the *maldición*. They bid her farewell and galloped back to the hut, chased by the quickly advancing blanket of darkness. When they shared their findings with Fulgencio's grandfather, he stared glumly at his cards, as if he longed for them to transform before his tired eyes.

"Do you recognize the name, *abuelo*?" Fulgencio asked.

"Yes, in fact, I do. But I never knew her. And I never saw her spirit as you have today, or as others have witnessed over the years. But now that you speak of her, I know who she is. The woman on the dune looking out over the river, I recognize the name," Fernando Cisneros replied.

"Dear Lord, who is it?" Brother William beseeched him, his patience running out.

For once Fernando Cisneros looked up from his cards and met both their eyes with his fragile gaze. "She is my grandmother."

***

At first Fulgencio and Brother William were buoyed by their discovery. But their enthusiasm dissipated like storm clouds that swept in from the Gulf only to vanish without dispersing rain on the parched terrain.

Fulgencio had always known his grandfather to be an orphan, but he had never given this much thought. His mother had been orphaned. His father had been orphaned. The Mexican Revolution and the constant state of chaos and fighting that ravaged the lands over time seemed to make orphans out of entire generations time and again.

What he now understood, however, was that Fernando Cisneros's direct ancestors, were at the heart of the *maldición de* Caja Pinta. What he could not discern was exactly how they figured into it, and how to figure his way out of it.

Brother William suggested they visit the cathedral in downtown La Frontera and search through archaic birth and baptismal records to lay out Fulgencio's family tree. Perhaps they could find other surviving descendants who could speak to the myths surrounding his great-grandparents and the subsequent *maldición* that allegedly plagued their family.

While he dove into geneaological research, the years began to slip through Fulgencio's fingers as easily as the pills he dispensed to his patients.

The family tree yielded volumes of trivia but despairingly few actionable leads. Mauro Fernando Cisneros had been the owner of Caja Pinta, inheriting the vast Spanish land grant. He had married Soledad Villarreal, who hailed from one of the nearby land grants, of which there had been thirteen bestowed to the area's founding families by the King of Spain in the 1700s. According to the records, in 1848, Mauro Fernando and Soledad birthed twin boys. The eldest of the twins married and had Fernando Cisneros, Fulgencio's grandfather. His surviving relatives included La Señora Villarreal, who was a descendant of one of Soledad's brothers, and El Chino Alasan, who descended from one of her sisters. And what they knew was of little value, aside from the usual conjecture he and Brother William had already encountered in the past.

Their investigation reached an impasse, and time rolled on. During one of those desolate years, a terrible drought struck the region. When the pond on El Dos de Copas dried up, Fulgencio invited Brother William on a cattle drive to take his herd to the river for water. That day they were joined by Cipriano, Fulgencio's *compadre* El Chino Alasan, and a number of ranch hands in the endeavor. Beneath the brutal pounding of the Mexican sun, in a cloud of never-settling dust, wearing Stetsons, the men guided the cows to salvation.

It proved to be the last time that Brother William made the trip from La Frontera to El Dos de Copas. It was well over two decades since their first ride around the property. Brother William had the time of his life. He forgot the worries of a lifetime. He rode a Golden Palomino at the age of seventy-four through a storm of dust straight into the Rio Grande. He looked up at the heavens from his perch on the horse, stretched his arms toward God, and shouted joyously, "Take me, for I am done!" Surrounded by a rush of jubilant cattle splashing into the swirling waters of the river, Brother William laughed like a madman, holding his hat high in the air and yelping like a Mexican, the way Fulgencio Ramirez had taught him. His horse whinnied and reared on its hind legs. And Brother William looked like the perfect image of a charro silhouetted against the setting sun, the land of opportunity behind him on the northwestern side of a bend in the river.

The ranch hands, all sitting on the ground resting and drinking from their canteens, laughed and pointed. El Chino Alasan, Fulgencio Ramirez's distant cousin from Las Lomas, the nearby ranch on which his mother had been raised, flashed his broken-tooth grin, his dark, leathery skin pulling taut beneath the frayed rim of his ancient hat. He rubbed at the thick stubble on his chin as he observed Brother William.

Slapping Fulgencio Ramirez on the back, El Chino Alasan shook his head in amusement, "¡*Gringos locos chingados*!" He laughed. "¡*El Monje Ranchero, hijo de su mal dormida*!" he yelled out, everyone responding with cheers.

Brother William dove off his horse into the cooling waters and he bathed with the cows and sang old Irish songs from his childhood. And later that night by the campfire near Fulgencio's home, he joined Cipriano, El Chino Alasan, and Fulgencio in taking swigs from the bottle of fine tequila they passed around.

"Saving a hundred cattle is a hell of a lot easier and tons more fun than the struggle of saving a single human soul," remarked Brother William to the group in the flickering shadows of the fire.

"The cow is a very noble creature," said Cipriano in his matter-of-fact way, his tan, oval face lit orange by the fire. "No matter how much you do for a person, they can still betray you. Not a cow, though. You can always count on a cow."

"This is true," agreed El Chino. "I can think of a dozen reasons I might want to kill a person, but I can think of only one for slaughtering a cow. That's to eat it!"

Brother William laughed, "What do you think, Don Fulgencio? You're a healer of people."

Fulgencio looked up solemnly from the fire. He thought of Carolina, now married to another man. He weighed his interminable waiting for her liberation and his stalled attempts to unravel the meaning of the curse that haunted him, threatening to derail any future efforts to win Carolina back. His heart felt heavy as stone. "I'd rather cure a cow than a human being. For a cow you can own. A person you can't. A cow you can keep safe in a corral. A person you can't keep shut in a room. You can count on the fact that an animal will never betray you. But a person. Ah, with a person, you can count on the fact that they *will* betray you. Sooner or later, you'll find a knife in your back and a hole in your heart." As he finished saying this, he felt a surge of anger rising like a sudden wave within his soul. Memories of the night he had planned to ask for Carolina's hand in marriage stormed through his mind. With them came the familiar chanting of incomprehensible words echoing in the distance, mingling with the white noise, washing away in the surf. *Chichicatl. Yolchichipatilia.*

"Amen," whispered Cipriano, still wearing his hat beneath the stars.

"People are treacherous creatures," El Chino reaffirmed, stroking the gun at his side.

Brother William ran his hands over his face, pinching his eyes and the bridge of his nose. "After a lifetime of trying to help people save their souls, I am convinced the only soul one can save is one's own."

"And that of a cow," quipped Cipriano.

"Yes. I think I should have been a rancher," Brother William ventured.

"*¡El Monje Ranchero!*" yelped El Chino Alasan, laughing in delight at the nickname he had coined.

"We should write a corrido," noted Cipriano.

Fulgencio got up and pulled a guitar from the back room of the hut. Sitting back down at the fire's edge he began to pluck the strings, playing scales and arpeggios as the Gulf breeze stroked his cheeks.

First, he hummed a melody and then he burst into song:

Este es el cuento del monje ranchero
(This is the story of the country monk)
Que vinó de Irlanda
(Who came from Ireland)
Como Dios se lo manda
(Sent by God)
Para salvar las vacas
(To save the cows)

Esta es la vida de un hombre sincero
(This is the life of an honest man)
Que vino sin nada
(Who came with nothing)
Mas que el Dios quien alaba
(But the God he worships)
Y encontró su destino
(And found his destiny)

Recuerden siempre el monje ranchero
(Always remember the country monk)
Quien reconoció su lugar
(Who recognized his place)
Donde hizo su hogar
(Where he made his home)
Y nunca dejo de ganar.
(And never stopped winning.)

"*¡Ay . . . ay . . . ay-ay!*" The yelps rose as Fulgencio's voice still hung in the air, and he concluded with a flurry of guitar.

Brother William laughed loudly, sipping from the tequila bottle, proclaiming how true Fulgencio's words were.

With the bottle gone, the fire faded, and nothing but the skeletal remains of the roasted pig hanging on the spit over the ashes, the party disbanded. They all embraced and shook hands. And as the red taillights of Cipriano and El Chino's pickup trucks disappeared past the gate, Fulgencio saw Brother William as he'd never quite seen him before. He looked at peace, like a young child who had just discovered an incredibly wondrous place to play, rest, and dream. Perhaps, Fulgencio wondered, that place was within his very soul. He helped Brother William up, and as they dusted themselves off, he offered him a ride back to town given the late hour.

Brother William assessed the old jalopy, barely hanging on after all these years. Then he glanced back at Fulgencio Ramirez. "Do you mind if I stay here?"

"No, of course not. You can have the bed," Fulgencio said, mildly surprised. Brother William visited often but had never asked to spend the night.

"No, listen." Brother William's trembling hand grasped Fulgencio's sinuous forearm, and he repeated the words slowly and quietly. "Do you mind if I stay here?"

At once Fulgencio understood. His heart grew even heavier, plummeting like a dense rock into a deep murky pond. Brother William intended to stay here for good, *para siempre*.

"My work in this life is done, child." His eyes danced with glee (or was it mischief?), like a pair of synchronized fireflies bouncing in the moonlight. "A few weeks ago, I was diagnosed with terminal cancer. I've thought long and hard about it, Fulgencio. And, with your permission, this is where I'd like to pass on. Maybe from El Otro Lado, I can do a better job at helping you solve the puzzle of *la maldición*. Anyway, this place now feels like home to me."

"You know this land is as much yours as it is mine," Fulgencio answered. "Even if you didn't accept it on behalf of the church that first time I brought you out."

"No, son," Brother William said. "This place is too pure for the church. No, let the church own the giant basilicas and ornate cathedrals. Let the church own altars encrusted with gold and chambers draped in velvet. This place is for God and His creatures . . . for you and for me. This patch of salt will be here still after we've all expired, and after the church bells have tumbled to the ground, and after the towers have crumbled and washed out to sea. And even when the sun is silent and nothing but a ball of frozen, burnt-out gas, we'll roam these flowing wisps of grass, your grandfather, Soledad Cisneros, Trueno and Relámpago, Cipriano, El Chino, the cows, you, and me."

"Do they serve Irish whiskey in Heaven, Brother?" Fulgencio smiled, helping his mentor through the low arched door of the hut.

"They will now," he answered, turning and clasping Fulgencio's face with both hands. His watery eyes spoke volumes of his deep affection for his most loyal pupil. He wrapped his arms around Fulgencio and pulled him close to his chest.

As they stepped back from each other, Fulgencio realized for the first time that this man that had once towered above him, now stooped below him, the last strands of white hair clinging defiantly to his balding head. His heart of stone bled like flesh again, and he felt the familiar rage inside him as tears flooded his eyes. So much loneliness. So much death. So much despair. Why did it have to be this way?

"*Todo lo que nace muere*," the ghost of his grandfather Fernando Cisneros recited from the wooden table in the front room. All that is born dies.

"And as the night leads to day, so does death lead to life," spoke the Virgen de Guadalupe from her relief on the adobe wall. So had the Aztecs who conceived her once believed.

"A true champion always knows when to quit," smiled the old coach. "Now let us rest. Tomorrow we begin again."

Fulgencio insisted that Brother William sleep comfortably in the bed, and he excused himself. "Tonight, I will let you rest with the *angelitos*, Brother William," glancing at the Virgen and his grandfather. "I'll string up my hammock and sleep beneath the stars. *Hasta mañana*."

The door to the hut swung shut by its own will as Fulgencio Ramirez walked slowly to the row of mesquites with his hammock slung over his shoulder.

TWENTY-FOUR

"I understand everything now!" Brother William exclaimed.

It was three days after his death and burial beneath the mesquites, when he finally appeared at the breakfast table, looking as young and fresh-faced as he had the first day he arrived at La Frontera.

Startled, Fulgencio dropped his fork onto the packed dirt floor of the hut. Fernando Cisneros chuckled, which was a true rarity. The jaded gambler was pleased to see Brother William in his new form, reaching out and welcoming him with a warm pat on the back.

"Thank God!" Fulgencio pronounced. "I was worried. What if you couldn't return?"

"How could you doubt me?" Brother William smiled ear to ear.

"You're not from these parts. You're not even Mexican," Fulgencio said, picking up his fork and dusting it off. "Who knew whether you'd be allowed across the border?"

"True. How many days was I gone?"

"Three."

"Interesting. Just like Jesus before the resurrection," Brother William mused. "I must admit, with what I've seen since I've been gone, I was tempted to not return. But how could I leave you behind now that I can actually help you?"

"So you learned something?" Fulgencio's eyes sparked with hope and curiosity.

"Everything." Brother William rubbed his hands together just as he always did when he was excited about hatching a new game plan.

"Well? Out with it then."

Fulgencio, his grandfather, and the Virgencita listened intently as Brother William laid out his findings.

***

In 1773 thirteen families had come to the region with their Spanish land grants. Caja Pinta belonged to Juan Jose Cisneros. It was a vast tract of tens of thousands of acres spanning both sides of the Río Bravo (or Rio Grande, as it would come to be known). For generations the family lived on the land, moved back and forth across the river that traversed it, raised cattle, and farmed along the fertile valley. By the 1840's the head of the family was Fulgencio's great-great-grandfather, Mauro Fernando Cisneros, who married Soledad in 1848 amidst the chaos and violence of the Mexican-American War.

It was that same year that the Treaty of Guadalupe Hidalgo designated the Rio Grande the new border between the two nations. In effect, Caja Pinta had been severed in half. On the northern side of the border, gringos occupied Caja Pinta and called it their own. Enraged, Mauro Fernando Cisneros gathered a posse to travel north across the river and claim his birthright by either evicting or eliminating the squatters. Soledad, who was pregnant at the time, pleaded for him to let the land go. She loved him desperately and feared for his life. But, brimming with hubris and machismo, he would not listen.

Mauro Fernando led his men on horseback over the dusty plains and across the river. Soledad followed him, promising that she would wait as long as it took for his return, keeping watch on the dune near the banks of the river. But Mauro Fernando never set foot on Mexican soil again. Once across the border, his men were ambushed. A traitor amongst the men Mauro Fernando had recruited had slipped across the border the day before and warned the gringos of the impending assault in exchange for a small patch of land to call his own, robbing Mauro Fernando of the element of surprise. Instead, the gringos waited concealed within a thicket of gnarled mesquites and brush as Mauro Fernando and his men emerged from the waters and climbed over the dunes. They were shot and killed from a distance, unable to even meet their enemies eye to eye. Overcome by guilt, the traitor ensured that Mauro Fernando was at the very least given a proper burial in his family graveyard. However, that graveyard was located there on the northern section of Caja Pinta, on what was now American soil.

When news of the tragedy reached Soledad, she hurled herself into the river, striving to grieve at her husband's freshly dug grave, but drowning instead. It was by sheer miracle that a woman from the neighboring ranch pulled her limp body from the water and birthed her unborn twins in the muddy shoals.

Incensed by the tragedy, Soledad's mother—Minerva Villarreal—demanded the newborns be given to her, but Mauro Fernando's will stipulated that if he and his wife were to die, his younger brother would be entrusted with the care of his children and the stewardship of his lands until his eldest son reached adulthood. And so it was. But Soledad's mother was not satisfied. Enraged by the loss of her daughter and grandsons, which she blamed on Mauro Fernando's pride and machismo, the powerful *bruja* wove a damning incantation.

"She authored *la maldición de* Caja Pinta." Brother William's eyes glowed with the treasure of his discovery.

"Go on!" exclaimed Fulgencio, salivating at the promise of an answer to what might have contributed to his devastating failure with Carolina. "Please go on."

Brother William explained that the hex was complex. Soledad's mother, who had been part *india* and spoke the native Aztec tongue of Nahuatl, had decreed that all male descendants of Mauro Fernando Cisneros would carry the *maldición* until her demands were met. The *maldición* would always prevent them from hanging on to their love, would doom them to inevitably lose the women they cared for most by echoing and amplifying the same emotions that had led Mauro Fernando Cisneros to cause her daughter's untimely death: machismo, pride, vanity, insecurity, possessiveness, jealousy, envy, and ultimately, rage.

She wove her spell at the mouth of the river where it emptied out to sea, using the fecund waters from the estuary. She chanted powerful words in the Nahuatl language to craft it. And through her dark magic, the *maldición* wove its way into the family's DNA. But because she knew that the curse would befall her own descendants, she felt a tinge of sorrow and regret as she concluded her incantations. And, at the last instant, she included a way for the spell to be broken.

"What way? For God's sake, Brother William. Enough of the past. What must we do to change the future?"

"I found the *bruja* herself. You see, while Soledad haunts the dune on the banks of the *río*, her mother wanders twenty miles downstream at the river's mouth. Every night, she roams the shores of the beach in mournful desolation. They say her wails of sorrow can be heard in the howling of the midnight wind. She will not be allowed to rest, and neither will her daughter's spirit, until the spell and the *maldición* are at last dissolved. She is tired, in fact. So she told me."

"And?" Fulgencio pleaded.

"Well, it's a tall order. There are several steps to breaking the *maldición*," Brother William said as Fulgencio scribbled feverishly in his tattered notebook. "First, you must unify the lands that were torn asunder by the invaders, causing your great-great-grandmother's eventual death. You must do this so that you can then achieve the second step. You see, Soledad is buried beneath that dune and she is anchored to that land. So once you consolidate the lands, you must move Soledad's remains to be with Mauro Fernando's at the family burial ground north of the river."

"Okay, continue," Fulgencio beseeched.

"Third, you must save the life of a living female descendant of Soledad's mother *and*—lastly—grant her the free passage that her own daughter was denied. Since her daughter died trying to get into the United States, you must help another woman in the bloodline achieve Soledad's goal. And not just any woman: a woman in desperate need, a woman who might die otherwise."

Fulgencio stopped writing. He set his pen down, the words *La Farmacia Ramirez* printed neatly across the shiny silver writing instrument. He sat stunned. "That *is* a tall order."

"I told you, but then again, so was winning all those championships back in high school, Fulgencio. I'm confident you can find a way. The most important thing is, at long last you know! You know what the *maldición* is. And you know how to dispel it."

"At last I understand, Brother William. Why I could not control my anger. Why I heard this strange noise between my ears at times, and those words I could never comprehend."

"Those words were Nahuatl," Brother William asserted, pouring a round of tequilas.

"Isn't it kind of early to drink?" Fulgencio asked, as the Brother nudged a shot glass toward him and another toward his grandfather.

"I'm not on the clock anymore, Fulgencio." He smiled. "And we need to celebrate. My gambit worked."

"What gambit?" Fulgencio asked.

"Going to El Otro Lado to find the answers for you," Brother William replied.

He seemed happy to have died, relieved even, thought Fulgencio. And it was fortunate—for both of them—that he was such a powerful spirit that he could roam at will and not be tethered to his bones or to the room in which he perished.

"Thank you, Brother. Now to get to work." Fulgencio felt a sudden surge of adrenaline. He recalled the passion that had always burned in his soul to labor and toil, and he felt it rekindling within him yet again.

The three men raised their glasses, saluted the Virgencita on the wall, and drank to a future that might redeem the past.

TWENTY-FIVE

In the years that stretched between Brother William's passing and Miguelito Rodriguez Esparza's death, Fulgencio set out to accomplish each and every step required to rewrite his fate and position him for his rewewed pursuit of Carolina Mendelssohn.

Utilizing the funds he had amassed through his entrepreneurial zeal, he began to purchase all of the lands required to put Caja Pinta back together in its original form. It was an arduous task, and one that he was glad to have El Chotay fully alive for at the time. El Chotay spent most of his time during those days running back and forth to the courthouse to bring Fulgencio documents on who owned which parcels of land, who owed taxes, who was on the verge of going into foreclosure, anything and everything that might help Fulgencio strike a good deal and recover his family's original lands legally. The pharmacy began to resemble a strange hybrid between drugstore and history museum, as Fulgencio hung maps of the original Spanish land grants on the walls, accompanied by copies of important documents and original titles bearing the royal stamp of the Spanish monarchs. El Primo Loco Gustavo, who knew a thing or two about computers, even created a map of Caja Pinta showing all of the current parcels that it had been divided into along both sides of the river. As Fulgencio acquired each patch of land, he changed the color of that section from red to green on the map and reprinted it. Fulgencio and his minions stood transfixed before the map for hours, strategizing about his next move and discussing the particulars of each land owner's situation and demands. Even Fulgencio's customers became intrigued by his quest, taking the opportunity to learn about the ancient history of La Frontera, something they had not been taught in the Texas history books.

The process of reconstituting Caja Pinta took Fulgencio nearly a decade. When the complex deed was finally done, and he owned all of the vast ranchlands both to the north and south of the river, he commissioned a team of archaeologists from the local university to exhume the remains of Soledad Cisneros from beneath her dune. Fulgencio and Brother William first explained the process at length to Soledad, who nodded silently in agreement before vanishing into the breeze. After several days of careful excavation, the archaeologists discovered her crumbling casket, and—in it—her remains. The move across the river required a bevy of international lawyers, as Fulgencio did not wish to risk simply ferrying the casket across the river in a canoe as Brother William suggested. After an extensive search on the northern portion of Caja Pinta, Fulgencio and the archaeologists located the ancient family burial ground, and within it—hidden beneath layers of dried brush and sand—an eroded gray tombstone bearing a crudely chiseled name, *Mauro*, barely visible upon its pockmarked surface. There, at last, Fulgencio reunited his great-grandfather and great-grandmother. Brother William officiated a brief ceremony and blessed the gravesite once the final shovel of fresh soil had been heaped atop their joined remains.

As he walked to his pickup truck, Fulgencio turned back and saw Soledad, her gray dress flowing in the Gulf breeze. But this time she was not alone. Next to her stood a tall, lanky man with a thick mustache in a white shirt and khaki pants. Their arms entwined. And then, lifting Fulgencio's heart, they smiled briefly and faded into the twilight.

He was halfway there.

***

During those interminable years of waiting, working, and chipping away at the *maldición*, Fulgencio often ran with his compadre, El Chino Alasan, south of the border. Not only was El Chino a distant cousin from the ranchlands near El Dos de Copas, but they had also become compadres when Fulgencio agreed to serve as godfather to his daughter, Elsa, and his youngest son, El Chinito.

El Chino and his clan were an enigmatic bunch. They ruled the ranchlands to the west of El Dos de Copas with more than an iron fist; they preferred the gun. Despite his numerous run-ins with the law, legendary shootouts in gambling dens, and endless land disputes, El Chino had never served time, and he had never betrayed his word or his compadres. He was a man who believed in the law, he asserted, his own. "*Mi palabra es la ley*," he liked to emphatically declare, quoting his favorite macho anthem, "El Rey."

Not long after Fulgencio had accomplished the first two steps in dispelling *la maldición de* Caja Pinta, El Chino threw the door to La Farmacia Ramirez open and strode up to the counter.

"Compadre!" he yelled from beneath his frayed straw hat.

They hugged and patted each other on the back in thunderous fashion.

"*¿Que pasó, compadre*?" Fulgencio asked, knowing full well from the glower in El Chino's eyes that something more serious than a bodily ailment must have driven him to the drugstore that day.

The two men retreated to Fulgencio's cramped office, where they sipped some Herradura Reposado, savoring the smokiness in its texture.

"I need your help, compadre," El Chino said. "Those Guerrero brothers—El Johnny, La Vaca, and Juan Grande—they're squatting on my land. They've taken Las Lomas. I have to boot them out."

Fulgencio surveyed El Chino's scruffy, leathery face, the thick golden stubble, the dark, deep lines. He smelled of sweat, smoke, and tequila. As he assessed his distant cousin, a thought entered his mind. "Are any of your workers—and their families—still out there, trapped on the ranch?"

"In fact, yes, compadre. Two of my ranch hands and their wives and children, as well as our cook and housekeeper."

Despite a tinge of guilt, Fulgencio silently wondered if any of the women might also be descendants of La Bruja. Almost everyone growing up and living on those ranchlands could trace their origins to the original settlers. Might helping El Chino also contribute to dispelling the *maldición*? "Their lives could be in danger," Fulgencio mulled.

El Chino became increasingly animated at the thought. "I should've killed those Guerrero brothers long ago, when they cheated me in that poker game. You know, the one in Piedras Negras. But no. For once I got soft and now look at me. I'm paying the price!"

"The price?"

"People are already saying that El Chino's lost it, getting old.

They say the Guerreros are too tough. Everybody fears them now, especially after what they did to that judge when he sent their father away to the federal prison in Mexico City."

Rumor had it that the Guerreros had tied the judge's head to the rear bumper of one pickup truck and his feet to the back of another and driven them in opposite directions. Right there on their incarcerated father's ranch, El Pedregal. The judge had sentenced him for a murder he didn't commit, the brothers had said, so now he owed them one. If their father was going to rot in prison, then he should be allowed a good, solid murder. And who better than the judge who condemned him? They may not have known the word *irony*, but they sure liked the taste of it—and the sound of it—as the judge's cries for mercy and screams of tortured anguish punctuated the vulture-hanging air.

Now no one stood in the Guerreros' way. People cowered in their shadows. They folded their cards when the brothers even approached the poker table. And they handed over their women if one of the three just happened to look her way.

El Chino jumped to his feet, pumped his fist in the air, and roared, "Those rats have stolen the wrong *queso* this time! We're gonna go in there with guns in both hands blazing! We're gonna blast them so far off the damn ranch they're gonna end up in the goddamn river and float out to sea like boats captained by buzzards. *¡Hijos de su chingada madre!*" He slammed the drained shot glass on the desk. Veins bulged in El Chino's neck, his eyes popping bloodshot, his temples throbbing. Fulgencio worried his compadre might have a stroke or heart attack before he even had a chance to defend his honor. *"Calmados montes, compadre,"* Fulgencio reassured El Chino. "Easy does it."

"We'll ride in on horseback at night firing away like *pinche*

Pancho Villa!" El Chino shouted as El Chotay, who had been lurking in the shadows, struggled to contain his laughter.

"No, compadre, if anything, that's what they'd expect from you," Fulgencio said. "We need a plan, one that spares lives, maybe even saves them. Remember, you have to protect the lives of those workers you have still stuck there on your ranch."

"A plan?" El Chino said, stroking the stubble on his chin. "My idea of a plan is point, shoot, clean up.'"

"Yes, but maybe there's a way we can avoid getting ourselves and a bunch of other innocent people killed. I imagine they're holed up at the ranch, waiting for you to do something, right? We have to think. Why now? Why this piece of land? Why you and not some pansy who would simply roll over and let them have it? They must have had a darn good reason to cross you. After all, you're El Chino Alasan."

"Damn straight, compadre!"

"So, what is it?"

"What's what, compadre?" El Chino shot back.

"Why now? Why that ranch?"

"Hell if I know, *hijos de la puta grande* . . . I'm gonna . . ."

"The bridge." El Chotay poked his head into the tiny office.

"What?" El Chino whirled around.

"There's a plan to build a bridge for tractor-trailers. Some say it'll be on the river near Las Lomas and El Pedregal. They have El Pedregal, which has highway access but no river frontage. They want Las Lomas to reach the river. They'll build a connecting road on the land, lease the road to the government, and sell the land to industrial developers. They'll make a fortune."

Fulgencio's eyes twinkled. He had taught El Chotay well. Funny how a guy who barely finished grade school could see so much.

"There you have it, Chino," Fulgencio smiled. "There's your reason."

"I don't want reasons," El Chino slammed his fist on the desk. "I want solutions!"

"Well, let's hit them where it'll hurt them the most then," Fulgencio strategized, pouring three more tequilas.

"The balls?" El Chino asked eagerly. "That's not like you, Fulgencio, to hit below the belt."

"No, compadre." Fulgencio shook his head. "We'll pretend to take what the Guerreros already believe to be theirs. We'll strike where they feel most safe: El Pedregal. Your land would be worthless to them without El Pedregal's highway frontage, and their plan would be shot."

El Chino's eyes widened. In slow motion he whispered, "El Pe-dre-gal." The glimmer of understanding radiated from his face through the dimly lit room, illuminating them all in its warm, golden glow.

Fulgencio had never been one for chess, but a land dispute, now that he could sink his teeth into. He sketched a rough map of the area on a prescription pad and snapped like Brother William used to when the chips were down and time was running out: "Okay. Expecting you to come in full force, they'll be overcommitted to Las Lomas. Where do you think they'd hole up? The old ranch house? The barn?"

"Well," El Chino said, "they'd probably have two guards at the gate. Someone patrolling the fence. And the rest at the ranch house. They like their cards, booze, and women way too much to stay in that barn. It's not very comfortable, even for the cows."

"So, they probably will have left El Pedregal unprotected.

Who lives out there? Anyone special? Doesn't their grandmother still live there?"

"Yes . . . yes . . . I do think so," El Chino pondered.

"So, here's what we do . . ." Fulgencio started.

"We kill the grandmother and send them her toes!" El Chino exclaimed like a schoolboy guessing wildly on an oral pop quiz.

"Nooo," Fulgencio drawled slowly. "We gather a decoy posse to go in and simulate that we've taken El Pedregal. They won't even have to fight for it. The ranch will be left so unprotected that, most likely, they'll have someone guarding *la abuela* at the house, but no one on the fences or gates. So, we post our men at the gates and fences. Soon enough, passersby will notice and take the news to the brothers that we've commandeered their ranch."

"Yes," El Chino said, "go on."

"The brothers and their men will overreact, fearing for their grandmother's life. They'll abandon Las Lomas in a heartbeat, leaving your workers and their wives and families safe and sound. We'll post a sentinel on the caliche road that leads to El Pedregal, and he'll radio ahead to our decoy posse to scatter when they're coming. By the time the Guerrero brothers get to their ranch and figure out they've been duped, we'll be the ones dug into the superior defensive position at Las Lomas. You'll beef up your defenses, and they won't be so quick to try again now that you're on the lookout."

"Brilliant, compadre! ¡*Eso*!" El Chino exclaimed. "But no one dies," he lamented.

"Precisely," Fulgencio said.

He slumped in his chair. "I don't know, compadre. I don't think this will increase my legend."

"People will think you're smart."

"Something they may not have thought before," El Chotay quipped, dodging the daggers that flew from El Chino's eyes.

"They'll fear you even more," El Chotay said. "A man with a gun is to be feared. A wise man with a gun is to be respected."

El Chino was sold. He shook his head emphatically. "Fine, let's do it then. Besides, I can't afford to get killed yet. El Chinito hasn't even hit high school. I have to see him through at least that. And that sister of his, Elsa. *Dios mio*. I have to keep an eye on her too. Men are after her like *moscas a un panal de rica miel*."

That night the men gathered at El Dos de Copas and laid out the plan before both the real posse and the decoy one. Beneath the cover of night, illuminated by the campfire in front of the hut, they plotted, the smell of roasted cabrito wafting in the Gulf breeze.

La Virgencita approved of the plan, commending its designed lack of bloodshed.

Fulgencio's grandfather, Fernando Cisneros, always the card player, appreciated its gambling nature. "They're gonna buy your bluff and end up folding 'em. It's a winner!" He exclaimed from his table beyond the arched door.

Brother William welcomed any possibility of taking the next step in overcoming *la maldición*. "Remember," he grabbed Fulgencio's elbow as he left, pulling him back from the group. "Practically everyone out here is related to you in some way or another, and to Soledad Cisneros and her mother, La Bruja."

When the decoy posse found El Pedregal's fences and gates unguarded, they posted themselves visibly, creating the outward illusion that the ranch had fallen into El Chino's hands. Meanwhile, the men primed to retake Las Lomas awaited the radio signal, huddled in their pickups, their breath steaming up the cabins in the winter chill.

No one was more surprised than La Abuela Guerrero as her three ogreish grandsons burst through her door, beams of wood and splinters flying everywhere.

While El Chino regained control of his ranch without firing a single bullet, Fulgencio was disappointed to learn that his plan had yielded no progress against *la maldición*. A quick survey of the handful of women who had been held hostage at Las Lomas revealed that they had all come to the borderlands from the interior of Mexico. They were in no way related to the Cisneros clan.

To make matters worse, the success of the endeavor resulted in an unexpected backlash, as rumors spread quickly through the area that the Guerrero brothers had been badly duped by El Chino.

Fulgencio hadn't counted on the Guerrero brothers' reaction. He figured they'd admit defeat and look elsewhere for their next squatting. But he underestimated the hatred the youngest of the three intrepid criminals harbored for El Chino. El Johnny Guerrero was a two-bit hood. He was a drunk and a womanizer. And he would have been dead long ago were it not for the long arms of his brothers.

It had been El Johnny's greatest scheme ever to take El Chino's ranch and now he had humiliated his entire family in the process. To top it off, it was not the first time El Chino had gotten the best of him. He had always admired the long legs of El Chino's daughter, Elsa. It had always burned him that they were not his to touch. Any other man would have let him have her, but not El Chino. And then there had been the infamous card game in Piedras Negras. The one where El Chino had exposed him as a cheater and still managed to leave him shirtless and pantless, skulking out amidst jeers in nothing but his shoes and moth-eaten boxers. This latest embarrassment was simply the final straw. El Johnny snapped.

About two weeks after El Chino had reclaimed his land, right about when those in his camp were beginning to feel safe that the whole dustup might blow over, El Johnny Guerrero walked into the day school in downtown Nueva Frontera where El Chinito was attending math class. Amidst the frightened screams of children and the horrified gasps of schoolteachers, El Johnny yanked the little boy straight out of his desk, carried him by the scruff of his neck right out the front door, and threw him into the cab of his pickup, roaring off in a cloud of smoke and dust. On the way back to his ranch, he made one more stop: at the Nueva Frontera technical college, where he kidnapped El Chino's daughter, convincing her that if she did not accompany him peacefully, then he would take out his anger on her younger brother.

The instant El Chotay burst in through the front door of the drugstore with the news, Fulgencio knew something had gone terribly wrong. By the time they crossed the river and reached El Chino's ranch, a group of men had gathered, all brandishing pistols and rifles.

"*¡Los vamos a matar a los hijos de puta!*" El Chino screamed, taking a swig from a half-empty tequila bottle and waving his twelve-gauge Winchester shotgun in the air. "We're gonna kill the sons of bitches!"

Knowing full well that an all-out frontal attack on El Pedregal would spell the doom of not only countless men, but probably his godson and goddaughter as well, Fulgencio raised his hand in the air. "No," he said. "I will take care of this, compadre. We must think of El Chinito and Elsa."

El Chino sobered up at his compadre's words. There was no one whose intelligence he respected more. He consulted at length with his wife, who harbored a deep respect for Fulgencio ever since his medications had cured her from a terrible venereal disease that El Chino had gifted her years earlier. His counsels also whispered into his ear and—like a tribal chief—El Chino grudgingly granted his consent. "But only because you're their *padrino*."

Fulgencio and El Chotay raced into town, heading straight for the federal garrison. The recently appointed judge quivered at the thought of what had happened to his predecessor when Fulgencio Ramirez explained the situation to him in his spartan office overlooking the Rio Grande.

"Don Fulgencio," the magistrate said, "we must be prudent. Around here the Guerrero brothers wield a powerful influence. We must think of the lives at risk. Both my men and I have families as well."

Fulgencio straightened his back, his shadow looming over the timid magistrate. "I am an educated man, your honor. And that is why I have chosen to attempt to resolve this matter with the help of the proper authorities. If you are going to mock the robes that you wear, I suggest you do so somewhere else. Because if it's death you fear at the hands of the Guerrero brothers, let me assure you, there will be many more deaths at the hands of the Guerreros if you do not intercede."

The magistrate began shaking visibly, his teeth chattering like castanets, his bones like maracas.

"If you won't be a judge," Fulgencio snapped, "at least be a man."

The magistrate rose slowly, his head wobbling precariously upon the tenuous house of cards that was his body. "Very well, Don Fulgencio. We will give it a try. But if I get sent home in a body bag, you will be the one to face my wife and children with the news."

Fulgencio shook the judge's trembling, clammy hand and

stormed out, leaving the frightened *federal* in the wake of his fading aura. Later, when asked why he complied with the request, all the judge would say was it was the will of the Holy Spirit. And El Chotay swore to his wife that night in the darkness of their cramped bed, that from his vantage point on the other side of the keyhole to the judge's office door he had indeed seen the golden mist of La Virgencita glowing next to Fulgencio Ramirez as he spoke.

Between Fulgencio and El Chotay, in the cab of the pickup, sat the Browning 9mm, its magazine loaded to the hilt. They waited in the metal chill, observing through the cracked windshield as the diminutive magistrate and his detachment of soldiers marched past the guards at the gate, straight up the road to the Guerrero's ranch house on El Pedregal. Several minutes passed before they returned, empty-handed. Fulgencio met them at the gate, his gun tucked beneath his jacket.

"*¿Que pasó?*" Fulgencio demanded.

"It was the *abuela*." The judge trembled. "She wouldn't let us in and she said we had no right to be on her land. That we had no proof of any wrongdoing. She denied it all."

Fulgencio's thick black brows knitting into one, he snapped in classic Brother William fashion, "You wait here." Striding past the befuddled sentries at the gate, (who were so stunned at the boldness of this intrusion all that they could do was follow in Fulgencio's shadow) the fearless *padrino* marched straight up to the massive wooden door of the stucco hacienda.

Beneath the swaying palms, Fulgencio stood in his black western suit and black Stetson hat, his matching pistol aching cold for a heated release.

The heavy portal creaked open to reveal an elderly woman spun of iron and earth. Gnarled as an ancient tree, the fire in her eyes betrayed the distant recklessness of her youth, the fervor of her commitment to this band of criminals that had sprung from her loins to terrorize the borderlands.

"¿*Sí*?" she creaked, echoing the door, her scraggly salt-and-pepper eyebrows cocked, the corners of her chapped lips turned downward to the red Saltillo tile beneath her feet.

"Those men have come here to take Elsa and El Chinito Alasan, and your son, El Johnny . . . without any violence. Either you let them do their job, or I'll take care of it myself. And God knows, if you leave it to me, the blood blending into your floors will be your own, the one that runs in the veins of your children."

La Abuela Guerrero was nearly rocked off her feet by Fulgencio's unprecedented statement. Nobody had ever dared speak to her, or any of her family members, this way. Fear flickered behind her unyielding eyes. She nodded and whispered, "Send them again," before disappearing beyond the closing door.

Fulgencio waited by the pickup with El Chotay, as the judge—his heart sounding the cadence for his march—paraded once more up to the imposing hacienda with his entourage of uniformed soldiers all in green with machine guns poised over their shoulders.

After a short while, Fulgencio Ramirez spied them coming around the bend, marching in step with the judge, who brought up the rear. His heart sank to the salt-ridden dirt as he noticed that the men were carrying something in their midst, something small and limp, something much like the body of his dead godson.

The judge's silence spoke in volumes, and the evasion in his eyes assured Fulgencio of just how little the law would do to help him now. He gritted his teeth as the somber troop approached, and he delicately slung the boy over his shoulder, noting that the apparent cause of his death had been the swift snapping of his neck.

"And the girl?" Fulgencio forced the words from his bitterly pursed lips.

"The old woman said she is still alive. El Johnny wants to keep her that way for his . . . needs," the judge timidly replied. All the judge could do was shake his head and face the ground in shame at his impotence as Fulgencio's pickup vanished into a swirling cloud of dust.

First, Fulgencio stopped by El Dos de Copas to pick up Brother William and have the Virgencita give the departed child her special blessing. La Virgencita told him to assure El Chino that his son was already in Heaven surrounded by *angeles* and *santos*. She cried a river of mud from her place on the wall as Fulgencio, Brother William, and El Chotay rode off with the innocent child's broken body. El Chotay sat in the back while Brother William cradled the boy to protect his remains from the bumpiness of the speedy ride.

Neither spoke, but both understood: This was war. All bets were off. The time for thinking was over. The time for vengeance was at hand. It was not even necessary to vocalize the shared understanding that Elsa Alasan, El Chino's daughter and Fulgencio's goddaughter, was also a female descendant of La Bruja.

TWENTY-SIX

El Chino knew the instant he gazed into the desolate valley of Fulgencio's eyes, that the time for cleverness and peace was behind them. Without a word, he discarded the empty tequila bottle onto his porch and summoned his men.

At sunset they gathered their horses in the clearing before El Chino's simple wooden home. Fulgencio sat high in the saddle on Relámpago, while Brother William mounted Trueno. Brother William had donned his preferred fighting uniform, which he only wore when he knew he must do everything possible to inspire his teams with the absolute confidence that God was on their side. His black robes swirled in the blustering winds of night. And though he abstained from wielding a conventional weapon, he instead was proud to carry the banner of their cause, a long and ancient ceremonial cross of wrought silver, gleaming beneath the moonlight. Twenty souls all told, they rode like mad men resurrecting the crusades, Brother William holding the cross on high. Their silhouettes hunched forward over the necks of their steeds as they rushed, manes flowing, toward the looming shadows of El Pedregal. For the sake of silence and the advantage of surprise it held, they didn't waste their shots on the sentries at the gate—they merely trampled over them with a flurry of merciless hooves. Blood and dust coating their horses, they descended upon the ancient house the Guerrero's grandfather had first stolen from a dying cousin decades past. Shots rang out from the hacienda, whizzing by like pesky flies as the men reached the soaring walls of the forbidding structure.

Of the three criminal brothers, La Vaca, dumb and slow as the bovine creature for which he was named, was the first to die in the bare hands of a crazed El Chino Alasan. Screams of men and blasts of fire punctuated the night. The battle ensued in darkness, for all the lights had been extinguished in defense.

With the initial offensive surge, El Chino's forces penetrated the compound, blowing the Guerreros' henchmen from their frontal positions, scattering bodies left and right, and marching over their bloodied corpses in search of the remaining brothers.

Twisting necks, slashing throats with the bloodied dagger he clenched between his teeth as he fired the pistols in his hands, El Chino's eyes illuminated his prey in a blinding, golden haze. He left a trail of destruction in his path as he worked his way through the house, calling out his daughter's name in desperation, "¡Elsa! ¡*Hija*! ¡Elsa! ¿*Donde estas*?"

Furniture smashing. Windows shattering. The howls of dying men formed a chorus of dissonant demons lamenting death like pigs being gutted. Brother William sprayed holy water as he floated through the chaos, blessing the perished, praying over those in the final, lurching throes of death. Amidst the chaos, Fulgencio moved not with the frenzied passion of the enraged Chino, nor with the dogged loyalty of his foot soldiers and henchmen. *No, no señor.* He advanced with the meticulous precision and accuracy of a professional. Clean. Efficient. He risked his own safety to avoid firing his gun, choosing instead to use his fists, his boots, and even the butt of his weapon. He held the memory of Carolina in his mind, hoping it would either protect him or be his final vision before dying.

He also couldn't help but think of El Chinito, whom he had played with years before on the drugstore floor on a crisp December day. El Chino and his wife had stopped by while doing their Christmas shopping in the downtown shops near La Farmacia Ramirez. Fulgencio had laughed from the counter high above, joking with his godson, delicately tossing a rubber ball from his massive hands into El Chinito's tiny ones.

"It's good he has a *padrino* I can trust to look after him," El Chino had bellowed sincerely as he pounded Fulgencio on the back that day. "Maybe he'll follow your example and graduate from college someday. He'd be the first Alasan to do so."

That had not been El Chinito's destiny, Fulgencio regretted sourly, plunging through the maelstrom of the firestorm raging around him. He hadn't made it. But Elsa still had a chance. And now it was her fate that still hung in the balance. It was Elsa whom Fulgencio sought out with every calculated step he took through the cavernous and labyrinthine house. In the utter blackness of the maze, he saw everything in muted shades of green, as if his eyes had suddenly been transformed into sophisticated night vision binoculars.

With the memory of his godson lingering in his mind, he found La Abuela Guerrero, rosary clutched in skeletal hands, kneeling before a giant cross in her monastic cell of a room. One blast, right between her vacant orbs, could have ended her life.

But instead, Fulgencio lifted the woman up deliberately. The candles she had ignited all fluttered out in preparation for her soul to flee her corporeal body and rush toward the pending gates of hell.

Fulgencio's snarling lips curled up against the withered woman's ear as he whispered menacingly, "Tell me where Elsa Alasan is. And I will let you live."

"She is with my son, El Johnny," La Abuela Guerrero answered. "Follow me."

When he set her back down on the floor, she led him down a shadowy corridor, at the end of which she pointed to a barricaded door.

As Fulgencio kicked down the door, Juan Grande, the eldest of the three brothers, fumbled with his gun. His three small children and wife huddled behind him on the bed, sobbing in terror. The brother's shot grazed the brim of Fulgencio's hat before his gun tumbled to the red tile. Dropping to his knees, Juan Grande scrambled for his gun, pleading. "¡*No me mates,* Ramirez! Don't kill me, Ramirez!"

Fulgencio's black boot rammed into the brother's throat, crushing him into the floor amidst the whimpers and squeals of his offspring. "Cover their eyes," Fulgencio instructed their mother as Juan Grande shakily raised his pistol, aiming at Fulgencio.

Fulgencio preemptively knocked the gun from Juan Grande's hand with a swift kick from his shiny black boot. Deftly recovering the weapon, he slammed its hilt against Juan Grande's forehead, knocking him unconscious.

"Take me to Elsa Alasan," he reminded his elderly guide.

Nodding grimly, she stepped around her son's inert body and continued through the room down another long hallway.

Fulgencio peered through green and black shadows. He stepped deliberately through clouds of smoke, ducking into hidden corners to avoid taking heavy fire, the old woman still firmly in his grasp. Emerging behind the yellow light of blasting fire, he heard waves rising up from the depths of his memory, strolling barefoot in the shallow water on a starry night at the nearby beach with Carolina decades ago. He heard the distant whisper of her soft lips brushing against his ear the night he showed her El Dos de Copas, during a brief visit the summer after his first year in college, before they'd gone off and ruined it all. "I love this place, Fulgencio," she had said, her golden eyes muting the stars above, surrounded as they were by broad mesquites and tall wisps of grass, bathed in pale moonlight, strands of golden hair softly caressing his cheeks. "If you wish, someday we can live here, you and me. Forever." *Forever* rang in his ears, drowning out the cries of anguish around him, and suddenly, the familiar sound of the surf rose within his blood, filling his head with foaming white noise and Nahuatl, words which, for the first time, he understood. *Altia. Altia*, he heard. Sacrifice. Sacrifice.

Not feeling the onerous weight of the massive kitchen pantry door, the Abuela Guerrero pointed at with a timorous skeletal finger, he handily pulled it off its rusted hinges and hurled it over his shoulder. Not surprised by the panic in El Johnny's soul at his discovery, all Fulgencio could hear at that moment were the words *altia . . . altia . . . altia*, the chants of a bitter woman roaming the beach at midnight for over a century, adding saltwater to the waves as she wept tears for her lost daughter. Not thinking of anyone or anything else, only Carolina, only *forever*, his head tilted for a moment in puzzlement as he gazed down upon the trembling figure of El Johnny, the killer of his godson, the kidnapper of his goddaughter. Johnny was emaciated from drug abuse, sweating profusely, and desperately clasping a gun in his tremulous hands. *Altia . . . altia . . .*

altia. Sacrifice, La Bruja's chants echoed over the breeze, traversing the lands along the Rio Grande. Sacrifice. He didn't have much time to think about it, although each second seemed to last an eternity. He wasn't sure if she meant for him to sacrifice himself or to sacrifice El Johnny. But surely, if part of his curse had always been to undermine himself by giving in to his emotions, then it didn't make sense to keep doing the same thing.

Elsa Alasan crouched behind her captor, sobbing, her simple white dress scuffed, soiled, and ripped, streaks of blood marring her once-pristine legs. Not even noticing the blade that had bounced off his back as he stood there, the knife the Abuela Guerrero had deviously acquired while gliding through the dark kitchen, Fulgencio found himself awash and insulated within the white noise tide rush of his slow-motion journey through oblivion.

Fulgencio angled his gun toward the cowering El Johnny. *Altia, altia,* the chants kept washing over him. Sacrifice. Sacrifice.

"Drop your gun, or I'll kill her," El Johnny gasped, thrusting Elsa against the wall and shifting his aim, jamming the gun against her temple.

Fulgencio knew if he fired, there was a chance El Johnny might get off a bullet and end his goddaughter's life. *Altia . . . altia . . . altia.* He yearned to sacrifice El Johnny's life in sheer vengeance for El Chinito's. He yearned to unleash the decades of fury pent up in him by emptying his gun's magazine into this depraved criminal's chest. But he knew in his heart, he was not a killer. He was a healer. And in that moment, he knew what he must sacrifice.

"*Altia*," Fulgencio spoke, watching El Johnny's eyes widen in confusion. He abruptly stepped between the crazed drug runner and Elsa Alasan.

Shielding her, Fulgencio closed his eyes as the explosion shook the cramped pantry. Smoke seared his nostrils. He pictured Carolina, wishing her to be his last living thought. He braced himself for the pain to rip through his innards. But nothing came.

As his eyes opened, he was greeted by a macabre smile carved across El Johnny's shocked visage, his eyes like shattered saucers held together by their inert contents. Blood oozed from the corner of El Johnny's mouth as he slid to the floor, a smear of crimson trailing behind him on the wall. El Johnny's gun had backfired, piercing his chest.

La Abuela Guerrero, her mouth gaping in awe, stared at Fulgencio for what seemed like an infinite moment and then crumbled to the ground, her heart giving out.

Elsa collapsed into the safe haven of Fulgencio's arms as they finally found themselves alone in the kitchen. As he ushered her hastily out of the house, eluding the ongoing melee between El Chino's men and the Guerrero loyalists, he wondered what Carolina was doing right then. Was she thinking of him in the darkness of her worthless husband's house while he was out betraying her with some two-bit canteen-loitering *puta*? Were the beads of her perpetually dying mother's borrowed rosary clicking in her hands, susurrating *novenas* for *forever*?

Outside in the cool night air, a silver cross gleamed, floating high above a staff anchored firmly in Brother William's ethereal hand. The Brother's arms opened wide, his black robes swirling around him like enveloping clouds of smoke, embracing Fulgencio and Elsa, then sweeping her away to safety, away from the blazing house, still popping with gunfire.

Fulgencio turned and faced the hacienda, waiting for El Chino and his men to emerge. When they finally did come running, chased by the gunfire of a seemingly endless slew of defenders, he grabbed El Chino by the arm and spoke to him hurriedly as they dashed to their horses, "You can't live here anymore. We have to get you, your wife, and Elsa across the border tonight. This family will kill you, they'll hunt you down and kill you all, unless you go to America."

Back at Las Lomas, Elsa and her mother packed hurriedly as El Chino momentarily resisted Fulgencio's recommendation.

"How can we leave now, after losing so much while fighting for our land and our honor?" El Chino asked.

"Times have changed," Fulgencio urged. "You're an old-world criminal. You made your living honestly and only crossed the law when shooting scum who looked at your wife the wrong way or cheated you at poker. You're a man of honor, not a drug runner adrift without a moral code. These lowlifes will stop at nothing to hurt you and your wife and daughter. Seeking refuge in America is the only way to keep your family safe."

Having witnessed the arsenal and reinforcements hidden within the Guerrero's hacienda, El Chino was forced to acknowledge that Fulgencio was correct. The days of his kind were over. He'd seen his son die at the druglords' hands. He did not wish to have his daughter follow in his footsteps.

"Fulgencio, how will we get across?" El Chino's wife asked, stuffing clothes into a dilapidated suitcase from another era. "Our passports are expired. Ever since El Chino ran into trouble with the law, we haven't been able to renew them, or our Border Crossing Cards."

"You leave that to me," Fulgencio replied. "Do you still have that old Wagoneer?"

El Chino and his wife nodded in assent, and quickly, they piled into the crimson, wood-paneled SUV. Elsa slid into the front passenger seat next to Fulgencio. El Chino and his wife huddled in the second row, their meager belongings piled in the back.

As they approached the Gateway Bridge to the United States, the tension in the vehicle's cabin was palpable. Fulgencio observed that El Chino seemed more afraid of La Migra than of the drug cartels.

At the wheel, Fulgencio glanced at his watch and made a note of the time. In his mind, he ran through the schedule for the customs agent shifts. Then, at the last possible second, he selected the lane farthest to the right as they came over the crest of the bridge.

El Chino's wife made the sign of the cross, her chapped lips moving silently in fervent prayer to the Virgen de Guadalupe.

Two cars out from the checkpoint, they could discern the looming figure of an enormous customs officer inspecting the documents as each vehicle passed. Then he would press a button, and a traffic signal would switch from red to green, allowing the car to pass onto American soil.

Fulgencio's eyes darted to El Chino. "Chino."

"*¿Sí, compadre?*"

"Just one thing before we do this."

"Anything, compadre," El Chino replied, wiping the cold sweat from his brow.

"Promise me if you make it past this officer, that you'll never take the law into your own hands again, compadre. This country is different. If you shoot somebody here, even for a good reason, you will rot in jail, or worse. *¿Me entiendes?*"

El Chino hesitated, his eyes instinctively searching for the nearest exit, his hand quivering on the door handle. But then his wife placed her weathered hand on his forearm, her steely gaze steadying him as he spoke. "I'm not the youngster I once was. If I'm lucky, if

I play by these new rules, maybe I'll live to be an *abuelo*, to experience a taste of something better for Elsa and her children. *Te doy mi palabra*," El Chino replied in a raspy voice. He gave his word.

Fulgencio nodded supportively at his compadre's reflection in the rearview mirror. And when he rolled his window down as they approached the customs officer, he could not contain his smile.

"*¡Mira nada más*!" bellowed the uniformed customs agent, badge (and bald head) gleaming over his navy-blue polyester uniform beneath the plethora of fluorescent lights buzzing like cicadas on steroids high above. "If it isn't Fulgencio Ramirez. San Juan del Atole class of '58. State champs *papacito*!"

"Three years in a row!" Fulgencio pumped the man's hand through the open window. "What's new, Victor, my brother? It's been a couple weeks. Has your grandchild been born yet?"

Fat Victor crossed his arms over his considerable girth and replied, "You're looking at a proud new *abuelo*, believe it or not."

"*¡Que barbaridad*! Are we getting that old?" Fulgencio genuinely pondered. "Congratulations, amigo. *Felicidades.* I want to be at that baptism."

"You better, you son of a gun. I'll bring my guitar, so you better be ready to sing." Fat Victor beamed.

"Anytime."

Fat Victor leaned in and surveyed the weary, dark-skinned passengers in the vehicle. His brows furrowed as his probing eyes identified the hastily stuffed sacks of clothes and the ramshackle suitcases in the cargo area.

"*¿Amigos tuyos*?" he asked Fulgencio, cocking an eyebrow.

"*Familia*," Fulgencio elaborated, staring straight ahead at International Boulevard, a sea of traffic lights blinking like strands of lights strung haphazardly on a Christmas tree.

In those days, the protocol would have been for the passengers to recite the words, "US citizen, sir," or hand over their documents, but the Alasan crew's eyes fell nervously to their laps.

Fat Victor grimaced. His eyes met Fulgencio's for a long second. And then he stood back. "*Pásenle*," he uttered without emotion, patting the roof of the truck and pressing the button to his side.

The light turned green ahead of them, drawing the Alasan's three pairs of eyes like magnets.

And Fulgencio pressed the gas pedal with his bloodied boots.

***

That night, they camped out in the drugstore. The very next day, Fulgencio bought the Alasan family a modest cinder block house by the railroad tracks near the levee in La Frontera. He could arrange for their papers quickly, he said. He had lawyers on retainer that could handle those formalities, the same ones that had helped him secure all the deeds to the lands of Caja Pinta.

Before he left them standing at the doorstep to their new home, Fulgencio looked back and declared, "After the papers are taken care of, we'll get Elsa into community college. You'll see an Alasan earn her college degree. *Palabra*."

El Chino Alasan, his wife, and his goddaughter, all thanked Fulgencio profusely, waving with tears in their eyes as he drove away.

That night when he returned home to El Dos de Copas, Brother William greeted him at the gate.

"It's over," the Brother declared. "Your work is done, Fulgencio. When you saved Elsa and arranged her safe passage to America, you fulfilled the last two conditions to break the curse. I confirmed it with La Bruja herself."

Fulgencio stared solemnly at the ground, wishing he could forget the bloody events of the previous night, the death of his godson. The fact that whomever was left of the Guerrero clan might come after him someday meant he would forever have to carry a gun beneath his western jacket. But the weight of that knowledge was like a feather compared to the burden he felt lifted from his shoulders at last.

He heard the disembodied surf for the last time without being at the beach. As it receded, it left the words *tlaca xoxouhcayotl* inscribed in his mind like letters written on slick sand. On a distant horizon, he envisioned a woman dressed in black wading into the water, disappearing into the Gulf of Mexico, her tangled black curls twisting like serpents and dissolving into nothingness as she became completely submerged beneath the tumultuous waves.

"*Tlaca xoxouhcayotl*," Fulgencio mouthed slowly, his eyes drifting upward from the ground and refocusing on Brother William's.

"It means you are free." Brother William smiled knowingly.

TWENTY-SEVEN

With the knowledge that *la maldición* was finally broken, Fulgencio initially felt an enormous sense of relief and self-understanding. He now believed that if life—and Carolina—granted him a second chance at love, it would be within his power to fight those dark instincts when they reared their monstrous heads. All Fulgencio needed to do was wait for that opportunity. Religiously, he read the obituaries every morning in his drugstore. And, mercifully, only a handful of years later, Miguel Rodriguez Esparza succumbed to the consequences of his debauched lifestyle, perishing of liver cancer.

The way was paved for Fulgencio to try again. But, as he realized after his first meeting with Carolina, there were no guarantees that she would cooperate with his unwavering dream.

***

His knuckle chiseled at the front door of her dead father's house in the crisp, cool noon of a winter day.

About a week had passed since their meeting in the funereal parlor of the house, since he commenced to comprehend the full measure of his youthful and ignorant idiocy. That week seemed more like a lifetime slowly ticking by on the drugstore wall clock as he mentally replayed Carolina's words, agonizing over the fact that he had squandered the better part of his life due to a misunderstanding.

Enrique "El Papabote" LaMarque lurched into the drugstore that week with Fulgencio's repaired steering wheel clutched between his hands and held out in front of him. To Fulgencio, he looked like an overgrown child pretending to drive.

From their row of metal chairs lined against the paneled wall, Eleodoro the Cabrito Man and El Gordo Jimenez waved at El Papabote. El Primo Loco Gustavo jumped to his feet in his hyperanimated fashion, greeting El Papabote and helping him with the wheel.

"Señor LaMarque!" Fulgencio smiled, "It's always a pleasure!"

The wizened old man—grizzled with white stubble on his chin and cropped, white hair on his head—smiled, refusing to hand the wheel over to El Primo Loco. His mechanized voice labored forth from a synthesized voice box in his shredded throat, heavy gasps punctuating his halting phrases.

"Ramirez," El Papabote said. "Your wheel is fixed. *¡Mira!*" He brandished it out proudly, a trophy of shattered plastic pasted back together with superglue in the old man's garage.

"I knew you could do it!" Fulgencio beamed, taking it delicately from his withered and spotted hands.

"Well, you know. I've always been good at fixing things," El

Papabote recited to the synchronized nods of the metal chair gallery. "That's what I used to do . . . before the cancer came." The peanut gallery silently mouthed his words in unison.

El Papabote slowly lowered his tired frame onto the empty metal chair next to El Gordo Jimenez as Fulgencio Ramirez admired the pastiche steering wheel.

"Chotay!" Fulgencio called toward the back of the store as his henchman emerged. "Look what Mr. LaMarque has brought us. Please install this so I can get back on the road."

"No problem, boss," El Chotay said, taking the wheel gently from his hands and vanishing into the shadows.

"*¿Donde esta la troca*?" El Papabote robot-wheezed, his metal chair creaking in rhythm with his mechanized gasps.

"Oh, the truck's out back in the alley. I had it towed over here."

"How have you been getting to work?" El Papabote asked.

"Well, Cipriano has been driving me to the bridge every morning, and from there I just walk. I think I've lost a few pounds this week," he said, patting his stomach.

"So, you're in better shape for love now," El Papabote remarked.

"I'm not sure, Mr. LaMarque," Fulgencio leaned forward on the high pharmacy counter, gazing down upon his court of jesters. "After what happened last time, I'm not so sure I should visit her again."

"You have to, *m'ijo*!" El Papabote became agitated as the tempo of his mechanized breathing accelerated. "That's why I worked so hard on your steering wheel, so you could get yourself over to that young woman. It's your destiny. Now, you must steer your way there!" He pretended to turn an invisible steering wheel in midair.

"Maybe I should wait a little longer," Fulgencio pondered. "Let her calm down. I feel so stupid. Like it was all my fault."

"It *was* your fault, *m'ijo*. So, now it's your *obligación* to fix it," the old man gasped. "¡*Canta*, Fulgencio! Sing your heart out while you still have the voice to do it with." The mechanical box in his throat crackled with emotion.

"You're right, Mr. LaMarque," Fulgencio affirmed. "I must seek Carolina's forgiveness and love."

Fulgencio grabbed his hat and stormed out the back door, leaving his minions in the shadows of the drugstore, lulled by the soothing rhythms of the ticking clock and the gasping of El Papabote LaMarque.

The ramshackle truck clamored through the cracked streets of La Frontera as he made his way to Carolina's house. He wore a khaki overcoat and matching Stetson over a navy blue Western suit with a bolo tie. The repaired steering wheel threatened to crumble in his thick and heavy hands as his hazel eyes surveyed the scenery. Boarded-up shops and gutted movie theaters littered the landscape of what had been a thriving downtown when he returned from Austin in the red Corvette, back in the summer of '63. How the years had passed. Time had passed them by, both him and his God-forsaken hometown. The years filled with bitter song and strange women. El Pedregal in the late '70s. And then the slow muting of his song. He had come to sing less and less often. But when he did, the words still pierced the air like knives and the emotion shot straight through the hearts of his audience. Now, so many years later, he could only hope that his voice could warm her heart, melt its icy core, and earn him a chance at forgiveness and love. At least the *maldición* was behind him. He could finally be a new and improved version of himself.

As the door swung open beyond the echo of his knocking, his voice took to the air, singing the words of "Sin Ti," speaking of the futility of living without her love.

Unmoved, Carolina maintained a stoic visage, her eyes as

static as a doll's, her porcelain face unyielding, but she at least allowed him into the chilly and dark foyer.

As she guided him toward the formal sitting room, he said, "Carolina, why don't we just sit in the kitchen and talk?" He would feel more comfortable there. He didn't want to be distracted by the elusive patterns in the Oriental rug on the living room floor. He didn't want to sit on the absent plastic of the sofas of his youth. He didn't wish to recollect the revelation of his last visit in that room, the overwhelming tide of his wrongdoing as her heels clicked up the stairs.

She obliged him with a blank look on her face. All of her reminded Fulgencio Ramirez of a dainty doll that had not been played with for far too long. He sat at the small kitchen table, stuffed into a corner between a tiny black-and-white TV set on a stand and the phone on the wall next to his head.

She poured some coffee at the stove as his eyes traced the delicate curves of her figure clad in a simple, muted brown dress.

The words poured from his mouth as his eyes settled on the gleaming silver cross hanging over the kitchen sink window. "Forgive me, Carolina. I am sorry for ever doubting you. I am sorry for the mistakes I made."

The china clanged as she lowered coffee cup to saucer, her back still toward him.

"I love you, Carolina. I never married. I never fathered any children. I've lived in a world of waiting and loss. Waiting for you. Losing everything and everyone that ever mattered to me. Please forgive the crazy jealousy of my youth. Please forgive what I have done to us. Please give me a chance to start again."

Silence.

He watched her fragile shoulders rise and fall rhythmically as the waves of grief flowed from within. She hunched over the sink. Frozen. He dared not move.

"Sorry? You're sorry *now*?" Her tortured words echoed through the cold and vacuous kitchen, bouncing off the tile floors pale and yellow.

His eyes traced the lines of the silver cross suspended over her head. He thought of Brother William that night a few years earlier at El Pedregal.

"You ruined our lives, Fulgencio," she sobbed. "With your jealousy and your doubt. You *wasted* our lives."

His eyes fell on the plastic mat in front of him on the table. Tiny fruits and vegetables growing along the edges. Leaves intertwined. Tomatoes, cucumbers.

"How many lives have you ruined, Fulgencio?" she wondered out loud, her head tilted backward as she sought guidance from the cross above. "How much pain did you have to inflict before you saw the error of your ways? I don't think it's me you need forgiveness from. I think it's from yourself and from God." She supported herself with her hands on the sink.

Still tracing the vegetables, Fulgencio spoke, "You are all that matters to me. You are all that has ever mattered to me."

"Then why did it take you all these years to come back for me?" she asked, turning around, wiping her tears away with a dishtowel.

"You married. I waited."

"I never loved that wretched man," she spit out, shirking the rote "may he rest in peace" epitaph.

Fulgencio had waited to hear those words for so many years, to confirm his deepest wishes. He had always suspected she could not have loved another. It surely explained why she had never borne any children with the twenty-two lettered monster. It gave him hope. And it reaffirmed the purity and fidelity of her love toward him.

"Then why'd you marry him?" he asked. "When I came back to town looking for you, I was too late. Bobby Balmori told me all about it. I thought you must have loved Miguel. You must have had your reasons . . . if love wasn't one of them."

She propped herself against the sink with her hands behind her back. She tasted the salt of her tears on her still full lips, a faraway look in her eyes.

"Yes. I had my reasons."

"But you never even cared for him?" Fulgencio queried, wincing in pain at the thought.

"No. Never. It was one of the worst mistakes I ever made."

"What was the worst?"

"Loving you."

He squinted in the golden fire of her accusing eyes.

"You can't mean that," Fulgencio whispered. "We were meant to be together."

"Yes, we were," she said, "but you ruined it."

His head hung low. Onions. Garlic. Heads of lettuce on beige plastic. Coffee getting cold.

"I thought of you often," she managed to say, her voice trembling. "I mourned for what could have been."

"Then give me a chance, Carolina. Won't you forgive me?" he implored. "Spend some time with me. Give us a chance to rediscover our love. I know it burns still deep within you. Just as it does in me."

Her eyes caressed him briefly, a trace of mercy flickering across her face. Its angles softening but for an instant.

Sensing an opening, Fulgencio added, "Search your heart, Carolina. Don't you still care for me, even the tiniest bit?"

Her expression hardened again. "You think you can just waltz back into my life after all these years, and I'll just drop everything for you?"

She had a point, his gaze dropped back to the table mat before him. "I am sorry," he conceded yet again. "Perhaps your work is too demanding for you to make time for an old flame."

She gazed at him intently. "My work has been the only good thing that came of our relationship."

"How's that?" He leaned in, pushing himself to listen and learn rather than think only of his own desires and illusions.

"It was Little David that inspired me to become a special needs teacher. Back when we were dating and I got to know him, I realized how much untapped potential exists in children with disabilities. Then I became a special ed teacher, and I saw just how neglected children with special needs are by our society. But with the right support, they can live much more fulfilling lives. So, you know me. Once I believe in a cause, I speak up and I fight for it. I've been advocating for more resources for special needs kids for years."

"I admire what you've done, caring for other people," said Fulgencio, reflecting on his own choices. "It's a great reminder that we can accomplish more by focusing on the needs of others rather than on our own ambitions. And I'm grateful that because of your connection with Little David, you gave me a chance to see you again."

He felt her studying him. Might she actually believe that he could change? Her eyes searched the deep lines on his weathered face, as if they might form a cryptic map to some unforeseen destination. He could sense her beginning to yield. Perhaps she might still feel compelled—or at the very least, curious—to see him again.

She shook her head as if to clear the cobwebs. "What is wrong with me? How could your spell still lure me?" Disgusted with herself, she brushed by him without another word. The kitchen door swung shut. The perfume of gardenias hung in the air.

His eyes fell back on the illustrated place mat. Tomatoes. Onions. Potatoes. Garlic. Was that a yam? A squash? He was hungry. The wall-hanging phone cord sat on his shoulder like a parrot on a pirate's. He heard the echo of her heels clicking up the staircase. Abandoned yet again. As he tiptoed into the foyer, peering furtively into Mr. Mendelssohn's empty study to ensure he wasn't there, he felt strangely buoyed. His spirits were lifted by something he had seen taking shape in Carolina's delicate visage, in her turbulent wind-tumble haystack eyes. He had caught a blur of motion. Thought. Yearning. A glimmer of giving, melting. Change. Her eyes reminded him of a painting he'd once seen. There had been a special exhibit in Austin, and he happened to be there for continuing education to keep his pharmacy degree up to date. The artist's name had been Van Gogh. *Haystacks in Provence*, he had called his painting. Nothing you wouldn't see out on Las Lomas or El Dos de Copas, the remnants of Caja Pinta before he had reunited those lands torn asunder like limbs dissected from their body. But somehow they'd been different than just dry straw heaped in piles on a field beneath a cornflower sky. They'd been mysterious, full of possibilities. Those were her eyes, suns and stars and haystacks. Carolina Mendelssohn was as captivating as a work of art, but she was so much more than that. She was alive. And her subtle signs, her parting words, hinted that she might allow affection to seep back in through the cracks in her heart, to warm her body and stir her soul with the elixir of forgiveness, with the desire for reconciliation. As the door closed behind him, he walked through the exhaled mist of his own breath.

The faint perfume of roses wafted from the ruins of the bushes beneath the windows. The steering wheel felt scarred but solid in his hands as the truck sputtered to life. Straightening his mustache in the rearview mirror, he saw a surprising sparkle in his eyes, a tingling in his smile. He sensed something was happening. He strained to contain the excitement. He hadn't felt this in ages. It was called hope. He'd sensed it in his youth, and squandered it. But this time, his own greatest obstacles were out of the way.

TWENTY-EIGHT

With her grudging permission, Fulgencio began to visit Carolina regularly. Every morning, before she went to work at the school, he stopped by for a cup of coffee on his way to the drugstore. They sat quietly at the table. Some days they talked. Others, not a word passed between them. At times she smiled. And then again, on what he called the "bad days," she stormed out of the room and whisked up the stairs without a word.

Over time, they came to understand the extent to which they had been played against their love by the scheming Miguel. Fulgencio braced himself for a resurgence of the familiar white noise and Nahuatl chants that had long tormented him, sighing with relief as these failed to resurface. Instead, he found his emotions challenging, but manageable.

As their conversations began to flow, he cautiously attempted to broach his grand excuse, the explanation for his idiotic actions on that distant Christmas Eve. He feared that she would think him incapable of accepting his own shortcomings, transferring the blame to a supernatural third party. But when he at last disclosed the existence of the infamous *maldición de* Caja Pinta and the mysterious hold it had long exerted over him and his male relatives, quickly chasing it with his plea that he hoped she didn't think he was making it all up to shirk responsibility, she simply scoffed and retorted, "Are you kidding me? Of course I believe you! This is La Frontera. I've heard crazier stories."

The tension he'd restrained for years flew out the window with the rest of his reservations. The shared knowledge—about *la maldición* as well as Miguel's conspiracy—cleared the lingering fog of suspicion and confusion which had long tormented them both, enabling them to cut a path through the overgrown weeds of their love's trajectory toward a closer understanding. But still, he could tell she harbored a deeper resentment, a hidden sorrow. And while Fulgencio continued to chip away at the armor which encased her heart, he nonetheless sensed he had reached a barrier of defense she refused to lower. He knew by the way she greeted him at the kitchen door every sunrise—the distant traces of a smile prefaced upon her lips—that she still felt something for him. But was it pity or love? Was it out of respect for what they had once shared or was it out of a desire to be close once again?

Every day, he felt his love grow for her. His yearning gnawed at his innards. He felt the renewed lust of the young man he had once been as his eyes caressed her feminine body, her golden curls, her ruby lips.

Eventually, she came to confess the horror of those long and lonesome years trapped as Miguel Rodriguez Esparza's wife. He was a brute and a ruffian, a spineless, worthless, lazy sap. She had despised him from the day they were wed. But Fulgencio was still puzzled as to why she had conceded to marry him or what had kept her at his side for so long in this era of quickie divorces and absolving annulments.

There must have been something she was not telling him. But he dared not push. He simply hoped that with time, the wall would come tumbling down. The bitterness would melt away. And the resentment he still spied within her would give way to forgiveness, acceptance, and then passionate love unbound, the love that had been dammed up within both of them for all these restless years. Lonely, sleepless nights in cold and empty beds. Staring at the same stars in the sky. Remembering the moments they once shared. Dancing beneath the lights at homecoming. Destroying Buzzy's storage room with the fury of their lust. Cruising back from the beach with Little David asleep in the back seat. Knowing they had been meant to be together . . . forever.

At long last as the first flowers of spring sprouted, and the sun charged the air with its electric warmth, Fulgencio resolved to push their budding relationship to the next level.

One morning, as he arrived for their ritual cup of coffee, she saw him through the kitchen window, carrying a young rosebush in his hands. This he placed among the ruins of the old *rosal* beneath the window to her room. He dug a hole, planted it, and watered it. He was dusting his hands off as she opened the front door for him.

"What are you doing, Fulgencio?" she asked from the doorstep, her hands propped on her hips. She appeared rejuvenated in a white Spring frock.

"Be my date," he said. "Go out with me tonight."

"No," she stated emphatically. "You know how I feel about this. You've asked me before. And the answer is still the same.

If you want to come by here for coffee in the mornings, there's little I can do to stop you. But going out with you in public is another matter altogether. It'll take a miracle for that to happen!"

"Fine, then," Fulgencio Ramirez snapped. "A miracle it shall be. If this rosebush is in full bloom by this evening when I arrive to pick you up, will you be my date?"

She glanced at the young plant. No buds. Nothing but tiny leaves and tender green thorns still supple and soft.

"Whatever," she scoffed, cocking an eyebrow. "We'll see." She shook her head as she headed back into the house. "You're not coming in for coffee today?" she asked, her voice betraying a tinge of disappointment as he walked back toward his truck.

"No, I'll see you tonight," he called out, waving his hat in the air and driving off in a cloud of dust.

That day, Fulgencio prepared a special potion with a recipe his mother had given him and some herbs El Papabote LaMarque procured at the *mercado* across the river.

Wheezing mechanically, El Papabote said, *"Estas yerbas son muy especiales,* Ramirez."

Like a mad alchemist in his laboratory, Fulgencio mixed and boiled green leaves together with a fine brown powder. It was a rare varietal of *yerba buena* and a mixture of cumin with burnt bumblebee ashes. Boiled in a mixture of *mezcal* and olive oil. Mixed with ground rose petals. Pouring the dark, steaming potion into a flask, Fulgencio handed it to Little David.

"Go to Carolina's and sneak beneath her window. Make sure she's not watching. And pour this on the soil where I planted the rosebush."

"Do I say anything?" Little David asked, scratching his head in bewilderment.

"Yes," Fulgencio added. "Say 'In the name of the Virgen de Guadalupe, in the spirit of her miracle in the mountains of the Valley of Mexico, I command you to bloom.'"

By the time sunset was at hand, the rosebush had grown so large and lush, Fulgencio could have scaled its thorns straight to her window. Loaded with red roses in full bloom, it towered like a stalwart tree over the lawn.

Clad in his classic black outfit with a new silver bolo tie and Stetson in hand, Fulgencio Ramirez stood at the front door. Before his knuckle could strike upon the wood, the door swung open.

There stood Carolina Mendelssohn, as radiant as she'd been the night of their first date, in a black fitted dress cut right above the knees, a string of pearls adorning her tender neck, her hair tumbling onto her bare shoulders.

Fulgencio had to remind himself to breathe. Standing in the doorway, her shadow fell across him, seeping into his very soul.

"I brought you some roses." He gallantly extended his arm toward the giant rosebush.

"I saw." Her lips curved upward gently at the corners.

As they stood in the foyer, he helped her with her long black coat. Her soft perfume in the air. Her curls brushing against his hands.

Her eyes glimmered as she looked up at him. His wavy black mane. His angular features. His thick mustache trimmed and neat. "Let's take my car," she said.

"What's wrong with the truck?"

"You told me about that steering wheel."

She invited him to drive. It just would have seemed too strange any other way. Fulgencio Ramirez was a driver, not a passenger.

Of course, always the gentleman, he opened the door for her. There was no way he could avoid the sight of her taut legs tightly wrapped in black nylon.

As they backed out into the street and began to pull away from the house, Fulgencio did a double take, glancing into the rearview mirror. For a flash he could have sworn he glimpsed the silhouette of an older gentleman standing in the doorway to the house.

Rubbing his eyes and shaking his head, Fulgencio focused on the road ahead. Her car was a recent model Nissan Maxima, silver, unassuming. He marveled at the smoothness of the ride, the responsiveness of the engine.

"These new cars feel different," he remarked.

Carolina laughed, "You're a dinosaur, Fulgencio Ramirez."

He had made reservations out on La Isla del Padre, the beach they had frequented in high school, and Carolina opened the car's sunroof so the stars could shine down on them. Neither of them said anything, but they both were reminded of those evenings driving back from the island in the splendor of their youth, Little David asleep in the back seat of Mr. Balmori's car.

"It's like a convertible, but it isn't," Fulgencio mused, fascinated by the opening in the car's roof.

"Where have you been all these years, Fulgencio?" She chuckled.

"Waiting for you. Waiting to live again."

He felt her angle a little closer toward him. In the olden days, the front seat of a car was designed like a bench, he thought. She could have slid over and cuddled up against him then. But now a gulf yawned between them, plastic cup holders and all. They called it a console. Modernity wasn't all it was cracked up to be.

They dined in an elegant room overlooking the Laguna Madre, the narrow bay separating the island from the coast, candlelight flickering across their faces. Like two young lovers out on their first date, she picked at her food demurely, and he swallowed her whole with his ravenous eyes.

"So," Fulgencio ventured, shifting in his seat, "do you think we'll do this again?"

She examined the sparse salad arranged like minimalist artwork on her plate. "I don't know. We'll see."

He frowned, sensing her pulling away. "What's wrong, Carolina? Why do you close yourself off from me?"

She stared at her plate.

"Have you still not forgiven me? Is that it?" he asked. "Because that I could understand. Tell me if it will take more time."

"I don't know, Fulgencio. Maybe some things just can never be forgiven . . . or forgotten."

He could feel her distance growing, tumbling forward into the wake of her receding tide. This is how he had felt over and over again during the past weeks. Every time it seemed he was creeping closer, she would flee. What was holding her back? Could there be another dimension to the *maldición*, a secret clause in fine print that had somehow eluded Brother William?

"Are you afraid, Carolina? Are you worried I'll hurt you again?"

She looked up at him, her eyes glowing in the shadows of the warmly lit room, "No. It's not that."

"What is it then?" Fulgencio rubbed his temples, taking a sip of red wine. "Is it our age? Do you think we're silly trying again after all these years?"

"No, Fulgencio. Just drop it." She looked away. "Some things are better left unsaid."

Fulgencio felt as if he were jammed up against a wall, searching frantically for a crack to stick his fingers into and pry through.

"We've spent time together. We've talked," Fulgencio struggled. "I feel like we know each other better than we ever did in high school, but still something is holding us back. It's something inside of you. Sometimes I'll say something—like the day I was telling you about El Chinito—and you'll leave the room without an explanation. Other times, I see your eyes drowning in sorrow. And I know . . ." Fulgencio's tone hardened, "I know there's something you're not telling me."

"Fulgencio, really," she whispered as heads turned in their direction, "this is not the time or the place. Pass the wine bottle," she said curtly.

He deftly poured more wine into her glass. "Talk to me. Why *did* you marry Miguelito if you never loved him? Why did you never leave him if you didn't love him . . . if you didn't even care enough to bear his children?"

She drained her wine glass and wiped the corners of her lips daintily with her linen napkin. She rose deliberately, looking straight through him, and glided from the room into the night.

Fulgencio slapped a hundred-dollar bill on the table and followed her, leaving the waiter in his wake with their steaming entrees in hand and a puzzled expression on his face. All heads turned, following their abrupt exit.

Outside, it was nippy in the spring Gulf breeze. Carolina stood on a dock, leaning over the wooden railing, looking out over the bay, her golden mane flowing in the wind. Hearing his footsteps falling heavily on the planks, she whirled around, freezing him in his tracks.

Her eyes resembled a pair of shattered honey pots, as the tears welled within the broken glass and the golden fluid spilled out. The wall was tumbling, cracking. Melting. He braced himself for the deluge.

"You want to know, Fulgencio? You want to know *why*?"

He was gripped by both fear and anticipation, clutching anxiously at the brim of the hat in his hands.

"Let me tell you why, Fulgencio. I wanted to spare you the pain that I've lived with each and every day and night for the last twenty-some years!"

He retreated slowly, like a frightened farmer inching away from a rattlesnake poised for attack.

"I didn't marry that pathetic man for love or for money. At first I married him because he made me a promise, an oath to protect my honor. Then I stayed married to him, even after he betrayed his word, because he was the only one that knew . . . the only one that knew my secret, the secret he took to his grave with him. He threatened to tell the world if I ever left his side, trapping me like a prisoner within my own grave, using my own worst nightmare against me like a weapon."

Fulgencio's mind raced alongside his heart, confused, grasping for clarity as she stood with her back to the bay, her arms up in the air, her curls raging around her as the wind ripped at her dress.

Beyond tears now, she was enraged. "You want to know why, Fulgencio? Why I couldn't bear to hear about your compadre losing his son? Because, Fulgencio . . ." She bore down upon him, her eyes ablaze as he quivered in her shadow. "That night you never showed up on Christmas Eve, the night you dropped those roses on the ground and left the ring in your pocket because I was dancing with my cousin, because you were *overwhelmed* by your outlandish *curse*. You didn't just leave your girlfriend. You left your child!"

Fulgencio's heart skipped a beat.

"That's right, Fulgencio," she hissed, standing face to face with him. "I didn't know it yet, but I was carrying your baby.

You never came for us. You left us all alone. And that worthless scum, Miguelito, promised to give our child a name and a home, so I eloped with him. We hid away at his cousin's house in Houston until she was born—our daughter, Fulgencio—and then he forced me . . ." Her body began to shake uncontrollably. "He forced me to give her up for adoption!" She began to weep. "He said I was a fool for ever thinking he'd be the father to your child. And that if I refused to give the baby away or if I ever left him, he'd tell everyone in La Frontera the truth, that I had gotten pregnant out of wedlock with your child. He knew it would have killed my fragile mother and devastated my father. I didn't have the heart to see that happen, to destroy my parents, to raise an innocent child amidst the whispers of La Frontera's small-minded, judgmental people. I was weak. My heart had been broken long before, when you left me. I was young. I was lost and confused. I was scared! So I caved in. I didn't have the will to go on. I crumbled, Fulgencio. And I've lived with the regret of the decisions I made every day since. And that's why I can't forgive. I can't forgive *you.* I can't forgive that dead son of a bitch who promised to give our child a name. And, most of all, I can't forgive myself. I don't deserve another chance at happiness." She pushed him out of the way as she ran to her car, yelling as she got in: "Find you own way home, Fulgencio Ramirez!" Tires spit rubber and sand as her taillights vanished into the night.

Fulgencio stood haplessly on the dock where she demolished him with her honesty. A child? An innocent? The loss he had caused was overwhelming to him before, but now this. The life of a child they had conceived out of love. Another life he had abandoned out of jealousy and stupidity. A rush to judgment. He had executed them all with the swiftness of the guillotine, the roses crashing to the ground like a disembodied head that Christmas Eve outside her window.

Dazed, he went back into the restaurant and bought another bottle of wine from the dumbfounded waiter and walked along the desolate beach. The frigid water soaked through his boots, chilling his feet. Waves crashed. Stars rained from above. He sat with the warmth of the wine—and the anguish—churning in his belly. Sat on the sand, leaning back against a small dune. With the coldness of steel in his bleeding heart, the dagger she had plunged deep into his wounded chest. This verbal assault had not been deflected by his invisible coat of armor. *No, no señor.* It stung like only truth could sting. A child. A poor and pure innocent child of God. Lost in the world without its parents. Two lovers who could have given him the kind of home Fulgencio never had, the home he always dreamt of building with her. His tears stung like ocean water on his cracked lips. Poor Carolina. Now he understood it all. She would have never sought him out and corralled him into marriage by telling him of her pregnancy, though she had indeed written and called with a tone of desperation. Now that his emotions and mind were not blinded by the *maldición*, he understood. *Pobre* Carolina. The burden she had carried alone for all those years. Sitting on the sand, he wondered how he might get back to El Dos de Copas to seek the wisdom of Brother William, La Virgencita, and his grandfather. But he realized he didn't need them to tell him. There was only one road to healing now. They would have to find her. Seek her out and find her. Their daughter. The one she gave up so long ago yet harbored in her heart for all these years with sorrow and regret. *Sí señor.* They would find her and make things right. The final piece which would have completed them, with whom they should have shared that elusive dream of *hogar y familia.*

He rose from the sand, dusting himself off, placed his hat resolutely on his head, and climbed toward the road. He was doing exactly as Carolina Mendelssohn had instructed. He was commencing the long journey, the search, to find his way home.

TWENTY-NINE

In the indigo light of dawn, Fulgencio Ramirez's shiny black boots rustled over straws of golden hay. In the rusty corrugated metal warehouse that he and his grandfather had turned into a stable years past, he shuffled toward a dark and shadowy corner. What seemed like an indiscernible heap of soot-and-mold-covered rags waited ominously for his looming figure. With purpose, he pulled away the giant tarp. The tattered cloth slipped away, revealing his vintage red Corvette. The pristine chrome reflected his image like a warped mirror as he ran his fingers delicately over the long, sloping hood. A rooster crowed in the distance.

Fulgencio almost jumped out of his skin when Brother William bellowed from the doorway. "Going somewhere?"

"¡*Dios mio*! Brother William! You nearly scared me to death. How long have you been standing there?"

"For a moment. For an eternity. What's the difference?"

Fulgencio climbed into the driver's seat, sliding behind the steering wheel, his toughened hands gliding across the vinyl-clad arc. It had been a long time since he fired up the old roadster. The keys still hung in the ignition.

"How many years has it been since you drove this beauty?" Brother William wondered out loud, running his hands along the lines and curves of the chassis, circling it in admiration.

"More than I care to remember," Fulgencio answered.

"Well, fire her up!" Brother William snapped in his old football coach voice. "Let's see what she's made of."

Fulgencio reached for the keys, turning them in the ignition. Nothing. "The battery's dead. The gas is probably ruined. The parts are probably rusted together." He shook his head, leaning back in the seat. "Who was I kidding? This car only looks alive from the outside. But it's dead on the inside."

Brother William leaned in through the window beneath the ragtop. "Let's put the top down." He unlatched it and swung it back with ease.

Fulgencio scrutinized his every move.

"Let's open the gate," Brother William said mischievously.

Fulgencio frowned, his eyebrows knitting together in disapproval.

"Brother William, didn't you hear a word I said? This car is dead. It only looks good on the outside . . . because it's been covered up all these years, hidden away from the elements. But it's dead nonetheless."

Brother William's eyes danced mischievously, "Dead like me? Dead like your grandfather, Don Fernando Cisneros? Dead . . . like you have been for so many years?"

Fulgencio's right eyebrow ascended in unison with Brother William's. "What are you saying, Brother?"

"I'm saying *try again.*" He put his hands on the cool metal of the hood.

As Fulgencio turned the key once more, the engine roared to life, filling the warehouse with the power of its growling. The din resonated through the aluminum walls of the makeshift stables. The horses whinnied and reared, startled by the thundering noise.

The smile on Fulgencio's face hurt. Something deep inside his chest hurt too. He wondered if it was his heart. His heart, breaking for the child he had never known. The daughter he would now seek out upon this mighty steed. He shifted the stick into first gear, and the car rolled into the clearing in front of the hut.

He ducked inside to pack his old leather suitcase and say his goodbyes to his grandfather and La Virgencita. "Wish me well, both of you. I'll need both your luck," he glanced at Fernando Cisneros sitting at the table with his cards spread before him, ". . . and your blessing," he nodded in deference to La Virgen.

"Don't take my luck, *m'ijo. Por el favor de Dios,* make your own," Fernando Cisneros whispered as the Virgen's golden aura pulsated in harmony.

Fulgencio genuflected before her image on the wall, making the sign of the cross. He kissed his grandfather's stone cold cheek lightly, feeling his prickly age-old stubble like sandpaper upon his cheek. And he grabbed his khaki Stetson from the hook next to the door as he walked into the rosy morning light. The car purred as he got in, throwing his grandfather's faded leather bag in the back seat. He wore cozy clothes, for there was a chill in the air: his khaki overcoat lined with fleece, a brown sweater vest. A plaid shirt and khaki pants. He straightened his thick mustache as he surveyed himself in the rearview mirror, the steam from his breath enveloping him.

"God bless you!" Brother William called out, waving his

hand high in the air as the Fulgencio roared away, clamoring over the bumpy caliche road, through the open gates and onto the highway to Nueva Frontera. Fulgencio waved again from the highway as he rode past the ranch. And he honked as he passed El Refugio, a graying Cipriano smiling his chipped-tooth grin from his roadside porch.

He sped through the deserted morning streets of Nueva Frontera, over the bridge, and into downtown. He made a quick stop by the drugstore, where he scribbled a note and pasted it on the front door: "Closed for vacation." Vacation. He'd heard of the concept, but never taken one. *No, no señor.* Work was all he'd known. From a drawer in his desk, he pulled out the tiny onionskin sack containing the fragile gold chain and medallion he had once given to Carolina Mendelssohn. Stuffing it in his coat pocket, he pulled out the leather pistol bag he would carry beneath the front seat just in case. Who knew when one of the surviving Guerrero brothers might seek to reassert their manhood via the grand illusion of revenge?

The light was on in Carolina's kitchen as he pulled up to the curb. As he strode up the walkway, she emerged from the door, still in her bathrobe.

"I didn't think you'd have the guts to come back here again," she said. "And definitely not so soon."

"Then clearly you don't know me that well, Carolina."

Her eyes fell to the doorstep. "I'm sorry about the other night," she whispered. "So many years of keeping that secret. So many years of pain. All alone, Fulgencio. I wish our lives could've been different. That we could have been married and raised our little girl."

"I know," he said. "It's all my fault. And you'll never know how sorry I truly am. But now I am going. Going to find our child, wherever she may be."

She looked up at him in astonishment, her eyes widening. "But Fulgencio," she stammered in shock, "that's impossible. Those adoption records are sealed. We'll never know her unless she seeks us out."

"We'll see about that," Fulgencio said, putting his hat back on, his eyes ablaze with ambition.

"I'm coming with you," she said in a matter-of-fact way.

He waited over a cup of coffee in the kitchen as she packed her bag, arranged for a substitute teacher to fill in for her, and bid farewell to her mother.

Carolina's heels clicked with urgency on the walkway to the red convertible waiting out front. He placed her suitcase in the trunk and opened her door. She looked so young, he thought, nearly as young as she had looked before she even became a mother. She wore black jeans, black boots, and a black leather coat that reached down to her thighs. Her hair was pulled back, cascading over her collar. The fervor of their search invigorated them both.

"What's with the car, Fully?" she asked, crossing her legs over one another and turning her body toward him.

His heart jumped at hearing her call him by his old nickname. "The truck wouldn't make it on this trip," he said. "Besides, the steering on that old junker isn't safe anymore." Internally, he relayed his heartfelt apologies to El Papabote La Marque with all due respect for his sincere efforts.

"I remember seeing you in this car after you returned to La Frontera. I don't think you noticed me, but it made me feel so sad to watch you in it. Anybody else would've looked happy in this car, but you looked so hollow. And I was hollow, too, without you."

"I found no joy in driving it after a while," Fulgencio said. "I had no need for such beautiful things without you to share them with. It made me miss you. Miss Buzzy. Miss life."

As they thundered north on the only highway to enter or leave La Frontera, Carolina's hair flew back in the wind. Fulgencio's antique tortoiseshell wayfarers shielded his eyes. The day felt young. And so did they. For the first time since their moments stolen in the storage room of Buzzy's Diner, they felt liberated, reborn. Free of the secret that had served as a silent tomb for Carolina's soul. Liberated from the walls that had kept them apart over the past months of frustrated reconciliation. Alive with the excitement of new life. Of not knowing what the open road held ahead. Of yearning, of searching, of living yet again. Enveloped in the heated, vibrant roar of the Corvette as they sped away from La Frontera, their hearts were beginning to thaw, even in the chill of dawn.

"Do you think we'll find her?" Carolina's eyes flashed as her hair whipped around her face.

"I know we will," he yelled over the rushing wind, his eyes on the road.

"And where do you think finding her will take us?" she asked.

"Back to where we took a wrong turn. Back to the beginning so we can pick the right path this time. The path to what should have been."

"To what should have been," she murmured, examining herself in the side mirror. "I wonder if she'll want to meet us or if she will resent us for meddling with her life yet again?"

"Don't worry, Carolina," he called out over the wind, "she'll see us for who we are."

"And then what?" she said fearfully.

"And then . . . We'll see."

THIRTY

Pausing at a roadside dive, they crammed into a cozy booth and hunched over *tortillas de harina* stuffed with *chorizo con huevo.*

"How'd you know about this little place?" she marveled, savoring the rich, authentic food.

"My drivers used to come here back when I had the trucking company," he mouthed.

"Trucking company?" She shook her head in disbelief. "I thought you had been a pharmacist all these years. You never mentioned trucking."

"Well, Carolina, it turns out you were right. Pharmacy wasn't enough for me. I always needed more. I felt like something was missing. I tried to find that something in different businesses and entrepreneurial endeavors, but I was looking in the wrong place. What I was really missing was you."

She blushed. "You're still the old romantic, Fully."

"How could a girl resist me?" He grinned.

"Woman," she corrected him.

"Yes, of course, woman!" Ah yes, her brazen, independent spirit had drawn him—like a suicidal moth—from the very beginning. It had even made possible their unlikely liaison.

"Don't make fun of my ideas, Fulgencio Ramirez," she cautioned, waving her fork in the air like a scepter. "Your machismo cursed you way back when and it can still bring you down if you're not careful. *Maldición* or no *maldición*, you know it's still in you to some extent."

"I wouldn't dare," he responded. He didn't mind her modern ways. In fact, in the wake of the broken curse, they inspired him. He discerned a depth in her that he'd been too foolish to fathom the first time around.

Finishing breakfast, they took the scenic route up the Gulf Coast, stopping on a bluff overlooking the sea in the Aransas Pass Wildlife Refuge. They didn't even notice the cold Gulf breeze biting into their skin as they sat up on the backs of their seats, gazing out over the waves crashing below.

"I'd forgotten how beautiful the world could be," she sighed.

"This is just the beginning," he said, gently brushing her hair back with his hand.

By the time they rolled into Houston, the sun was setting, and downtown's imposing skyline loomed against the auburn sky, lights twinkling in the windows.

Fulgencio pointed at a roadside motel on the outskirts of downtown. "Sometimes we used to stay there, the truckers and I, when we brought a big convoy to town. El Chotay thought it was heaven."

She raised a disapproving eyebrow at the dilapidated collection of forgotten shacks. "Is *that* where *we're* staying?"

"No. I think we've suffered enough," he chuckled. "This trip is about ending the pain, not rubbing it in."

Arriving at the Four Seasons hotel, she stepped down onto the red carpet as Fulgencio took her the hand. "I feel like the homecoming queen all over again," Carolina whispered to Fulgencio as the bellman opened the door and bowed. "But I also feel guilty," she confessed as they checked in. "Here we are searching for our daughter and, well, are we having too much fun?"

"No more punishing, Carolina. Whatever happens tomorrow, whatever we find, no more guilt. Just our life."

No one would have guessed it, but Fulgencio Ramirez was a man of money. He had lived a very simple and humble life. In the first months after he opened his drugstore, he had generated sufficient funds to walk proudly into the bank in downtown La Frontera and repay the loan Old Man Maldonado's son had approved. The Spanish-speaking customers loved him, for he was the first and only pharmacist in town who spoke to them in their language. The only one who did not look down on them with disdain from high up behind the counter. The only one that did not hide behind a white lab coat. *No, no señor*, he used to say, sporting his guayaberas proudly and stroking his mustache. He was just like them, but he knew how to heal their ailments. And when the prescriptions didn't work, the herbs and incantations he learned from his mother did. After that, the bank had always supported his entrepreneurial schemes. And since he lived in an adobe hut on his grandfather's ranch, he had managed to amass a vast fortune over the decades, including the reunited lands of Caja Pinta. So much so, that when the Walmarts and the HEBs and the Walgreens swooped into town like buzzards from another world, it was of little concern to him. He didn't depend on the drugstore's income anymore. The many businesses he'd built and sold off over the years could have kept him—and generations to come—living the high life. But still he tended to his dwindling parade of decrepit and senile *viejitos*. He chewed the fat with his assortment of hangers-on. Slowly, these elements filled the yawning vacuum of time as he had waited for another chance to reunite with Carolina.

And now, Fulgencio and Carolina cuddled over candlelight in the hotel's elegantly appointed dining room. While she had bathed and gotten dressed in her suite, he had wandered over to one of the glitzy boutiques connected to the skyscraper via a glass skywalk spanning the busy street below. He walked in a daze, his eyes wide with amazement. He had never seen all this before, this glorious world built by modern man. He had been content retracing his daily steps in the lowly shadows of La Frontera's crumbling downtown buildings. He had even managed to avoid ever setting foot in those windowless hulks of concrete that interloping developers had erected on the outskirts of town in the '70s, the ones they called *malls*. He had also avoided the flashy chain restaurants and stores that had crowded out the mom-and-pop shops on the town's main drags. No Blockbuster Video for him. No Church's Fried Chicken. Rarely, if ever, did he allow himself to cruise along those sign-cluttered neon streets. *No, no señor*, he had found what little comfort he could in the familiar surroundings of the faded downtown. Doing his part to keep Mr. Capistran's Men's Shop in business.

But now, for the first time ever, he felt differently about the new world. As he removed his tortoiseshell frames and allowed the glamour of the shops before him to dazzle and impress, he realized that he liked what he saw. Shortly thereafter, he emerged in a dark olive Armani suit from one of the boutiques with a funny French name he couldn't pronounce. Carolina's jaw dropped before he could catch it with a kiss on the lips as they stood in the doorway to her suite.

They sat quietly, gazing with longing into each other's eyes as the courses came and went. The empty bottle of red wine was retired. And the chocolate mousse was overpowered by the sweetness that enveloped them as their hands touched each other lightly on the crisp, white linen tablecloth. The bubbling of a harp danced around them. And they felt at peace. Relaxed. Settling into each other's shared and sacred space.

At one point, in the midst of their reverie, a large Texan man in a suit and cowboy boots ambled by their table and performed an exaggerated double-take, catching their attention.

"Well, I'll be!" he exclaimed, loudly enough for the neighboring tables to overhear. "How did an amigo like you end up with a gorgeous woman like this? You must be one lucky son of a gun! Did you win the lotto? Woohee!"

Carolina fearfully turned to Fulgencio, her eyes filled with apprehension.

Caught off guard, a surge of electric anger jolted Fulgencio. *Amigo?* He braced himself to feel compelled into action by the man's taunt. But this time it was a simpler wrath writhing through his innards. His ire was stripped of the dense sound of the surf deafening him to his surroundings. His thoughts remained unclouded by the rousing Nahuatl chants urging him to unleash his agitated fury. Instead of reflexively reacting to the Texan's racist jab, he found himself perfectly capable of flipping a switch to activate the training he had undergone after breaking *la maldición*, practicing with Brother William at the ranch and El Chotay in the drugstore as they flung pretend insults at him. Whereas in the past he would have forcibly escorted the Texan outside and pummeled him into the ground with his fists, instead, he sat still, carefully assessing the man, considering what his true motivations might be for such boisterous rudeness. Might he be driven by more than mere prejudice? In the process, he noted a fading band of pale skin on the man's ring finger, a table for one vacant in the corner where the man had dined alone, a drained bottle of red wine next to a single glass where he had sat. He surmised the man was despondent and drunk, either a grieving widower or bitter divorcee.

Suddenly, Fulgencio felt sorry for the Texan. After all, to some degree, wasn't the man right? Hadn't he finally won the lotto? He mentally recited the Nahuatl phrases he had taught himself during his training, aspirations which had eluded him his entire life. *Ihuian nemini. Ihuian nemini.* Peaceful and tranquil person. *Ihuian nemiliztli.* A peaceful life.

"While I don't agree with your style, sir, you're correct," Fulgencio smiled placidly, easing back in his comfortable armchair. "I am very fortunate indeed to be here, sharing this evening with the woman I love."

Taken aback, the man found himself at a loss for words. He stared at the couple for a long, awkward moment, his expression growing mournful.

"In fact," Fulgencio concluded, to smooth over the discomfort and tension lingering between them, "I would gladly tell you how we ended up together, but the story is so long, I'm afraid you'd grow tired and fall asleep."

The man shook his head, stumbling over his words as he replied haltingly, "Well . . . pardon me for my intrusion. My wife passed on recently . . . I'm not quite myself."

"I'm sorry for your loss," Carolina replied soothingly, Fulgencio nodding in agreement.

"You two enjoy each other. One never knows what life holds in store," the man answered, his voice cracking with emotion. He tipped an invisible hat in deference and exited the room with his head hung low, chiding himself for his unwarranted outburst.

Carolina's eyes examined Fulgencio, seeking an explanation for his revelatory change in behavior.

"Poor man," Fulgencio murmured, sipping from his wine glass.

"Fulgencio," she said in amazement. "You've really changed."

Satisfied with the fruit of his labors, he dismissed the accomplishment with modesty. "We all have to grow up sometime, don't we? We can't be ruled by our emotions, and violence isn't the only answer to life's problems."

Smiling reticently, she conceded, "I like who you've become."

"I'm still working at it," he demurred.

Toward the end of the evening, he extracted the little onionskin sack from his coat pocket and slid it across the table, tucking it beneath her cupped hand.

"What is it?"

"Take a look."

He could see the saltwater pooling in her eyes as the tiny gold chain and medallion of the Madonna and Child glided out of the little bag and into the palm of her hand.

She looked at him through her tears, "You kept this all those years?"

"You left it in Buzzy's storage room that night. I found it when I got back to Austin. Sitting on the floor in the corner, behind the broken cot."

"Thank you for saving it," her voice quivered. "Will you put it on?"

He swept behind her and lowered the chain around her delicate neck, lightly brushing against her soft hair, her supple cheek, the fragrance of gardenias lightly perfuming the air. He swooned for a moment but caught his balance, and she pulled him down toward her parting lips. A fire he had not sensed for many years raged within him yet again. As she led him from the dining room and up to their suites on the top floor, he felt a distinct shortness of breath. In the elevator, their lips met again, her back pressed against the mirrored wall. He secretly imagined what it would be like if they pulled the emergency stop button on the control panel and tore each other's clothes off right then and there, between floors.

But no, thought Fulgencio. Tomorrow they would search for the forgotten fruit of their indiscretion. It would surely be a sin and a mockery to reenact the crime the night before. Instead, he escorted her to her door, kissed her gently, and bid her goodnight as he retired to the adjacent suite.

***

Inside his room, Fulgencio leaned back against the closed door. He wondered what Carolina was doing at that very moment next door. What was she feeling? What was she thinking? He no longer dared to assume the nature of her emotions. In a way, he felt liberated from his own controlling ways, and he hoped she felt the same way, free to be herself with him.

Sliding beneath the crisp, cool linen sheets, he slipped into a deep and comforting sleep, dreaming of life with Carolina. In his dream they were young again. They had married and brought their daughter into the world together. They shared a beautiful life, rejoicing as a family, living on the lands of El Dos de Copas. Deep in the muddled fabric of that flight of fancy, he and Carolina walked along a path lined by mesquites. He felt safe and loved as Carolina held his hand. In unison, their eyes landed on a spritely girl skipping ahead of them. Her copper curls reflected the sunlight, and her brown eyes twinkled as she turned and called to them in an angelic voice, "I love you!" The echoes of their harmonious response still rang in his ears when he awoke with the sun streaming through his window the next morning. "We love you too, Paloma," they said. "We love you too."

THIRTY-ONE

Fulgencio Ramirez had never been woken up by anyone other than his mother. And that had been a rare childhood occurrence at 1448 Garfield. *No, no señor.* He was always first to rise, except for maybe El Chotay, who would often sit out in the pickup with coffee and donuts, waiting for Fulgencio to emerge from his hut in the wee hours of the rising day. But that fateful morning in Houston, Carolina roused him with an eager phone call. She was ready to go.

After a quick breakfast, over which Fulgencio recounted his vivid dream to a rapt Carolina, they headed to the County Records Depository.

In the car on the way to their destination, Carolina wondered, “What if the Paloma you dreamt is our daughter, Fully?”

“That’s what it felt like, but our daughter would be a grown woman by now,” he reasoned. “It doesn’t make sense. It felt so real,” he murmured, cautiously navigating the dense Houston traffic.

“Maybe we’ve gotten our hopes up too high,” Carolina worried.

Fulgencio frowned. The last thing he wanted to do was inflict more disappointment and pain on Carolina.

As they approached the low-slung, beige-colored governmental building, Carolina asked, "How are we going to gain access to those records?"

"Leave this one to me," Fulgencio answered, a determined expression steeling his face.

The front desk guard, a handsome African-American man in uniform, scrutinized them as they approached, all clad in black, Fulgencio brooding beneath his black Stetson.

"Y'all ain't from around these parts, are ya?" The guard smiled broadly.

"Not at all, sir," Fulgencio answered, firmly shaking his hand. "We've come a long way." Longer and farther than the man could imagine, Fulgencio thought to himself.

"How can I be of help then?"

"My wife and I are searching from some adoption records," Fulgencio replied.

The guard's eyes shifted to Carolina, who smiled back at him.

"Y'all can find those on the second floor, all the way to the end of the hall. Talk to Mercedes. Tell her Henry sent you up. But unless you have some sort of order from a judge, you and your lovely lady might be plain outta luck."

"Thank you for the information, Henry. Don't you worry, sir. We've got justice on our side," Fulgencio winked back as the guard watched them head up the stairs.

"We'll never make it past this next gatekeeper," Carolina whispered nervously as they approached a high counter at the end of the sterile corridor.

"Have a little faith, *amor*," Fulgencio squeezed her hand.

They waited at the vacant counter for a couple of minutes until a middle-aged woman with gray hair and stylish black glasses appeared from behind a row of shelves crammed with files. The tag on her blouse announced her name as "Mercedes Treviño."

"*Señora Treviño*," Fulgencio spoke in Spanish.

"*Señorita*," Mercedes corrected him.

Fulgencio glanced sideways at Carolina, cocking an eyebrow mischievously. "*Señorita Treviño*, we come on behalf of Henry downstairs. He sends you this . . ." Reaching into his coat pocket he produced a red rose. ". . . and he asks that you come talk to him."

Beaming, Mercedes removed her eyeglasses. In a moment, she seemed transformed, as if she had spontaneously shed ten years due to the pleasant surprise.

Taking the rose from Fulgencio's hand, she quickly maneuvered around the counter, smiling back at them as she fixed her hair. "And who are you?"

"*Somos mensajeros del amor*," Fulgencio answered. "*Buena suerte*."

"I'll be right back," Mercedes promised. "Do you mind waiting?"

"Not at all." Fulgencio smiled. "Take your time."

As she vanished around a corner, Fulgencio and Carolina swept past the desk and ran down a metal staircase.

"How'd you manage that little miracle?" Carolina asked as they descended deep into the bowels of the adoption records.

"A magician never reveals his secrets," Fulgencio grinned, pulling her along.

Organized like stacks in a library, each shelf was numbered by year. It was not long before they found 1962. From there, the files were categorized alphabetically according to mothers' names. Moving hastily, they scanned the archives until they found her name.

In a dank aisle lined by towering shelves bursting with dust-laden files, they rifled through the yellowed papers in the manila folder.

"There!" Carolina exclaimed, pointing at the typed names of the adoptive parents. "Mr. and Mrs. Robert A. Johnson," she read slowly in the dim light. "Here's the address. But what if they don't live there anymore? It's been a very long time."

Fulgencio scribbled it down on a piece of folder and tore it off, replying, "One step at a time."

"This is very illegal," she whispered, stuffing the file back into its place.

"I make my own law," Fulgencio answered as they hurried toward the staircase.

"Still as dramatic as ever."

As they neared the stairs, they heard voices approaching, a man and a woman.

"It's Mercedes and Henry," Carolina hissed.

"They make a good couple," Fulgencio whispered, grabbing her hand and pulling her in the opposite direction.

"Where are we going?" she asked as they broke into a run.

He pointed at the end of the stacks to a red exit sign.

"Hello? Is there anyone down here?" Henry called.

As they reached the exit, Carolina pointed at a sign next to the door. It read, "Open only in case of emergency."

"I think this qualifies." Fulgencio gritted his teeth, pushing the metal bar across the door open.

Fire alarms rang inside the building as Fulgencio and Carolina stepped out into the blinding sun.

***

Robert Johnson squinted as the bright light of day poured in through the door to his home in a featureless subdivision on the outskirts of Houston. He was an elderly man, grayed and stooped by his age. It took him a moment to focus his eyes. But as his faded wife hobbled to his side, an expression of recognition spread across their raisined faces. They smiled knowingly at the couple standing on their doorstep. The large man in the Stetson hat with a mustache. The slender woman with the golden curls and eyes to match. Their hands clasped together, knuckle-white.

"Come on in, chil'ren," Mrs. Johnson coughed. "We've been waitin' for y'all."

As Fulgencio and Carolina stepped tentatively through the doorway into the medicinal air of the house, furnished still in '60s greens, oranges, and yellows, Mr. Johnson piped up in a Texan drawl coated with relief: "We was stawting ta think y'all'd never show up!"

Sitting in the time capsule of a living room, Fulgencio and Carolina listened to the Johnsons, exchanging concerned glances as their story unfolded.

The life of little Holly Johnson had been as quiet and fleeting as the flight of an angel, Mrs. Johnson explained. Adopted by the couple in their fifties after they'd proven unable to conceive children on their own, Holly had filled their home with laughter and light. Her eyes had shone as green as a lush tropical rainforest. "Emeralds is how I used to describe them to my relatives back in Louisiana," Mrs. Johnson recalled.

When her husband brought in an old photo album, the two couples huddled over the coffee table to look at the fading photographs.

A tussle of auburn curls tinged with spirals of gold had topped Holly's tiny head, reflecting the rays of sunlight as she played in the yard with the family dog and ran around the cul-de-sac with the other neighborhood children.

"She was a precious child. She was ma life," Mr. Johnson murmured, a tremor in his voice. "But she was taken far too soon, God bless her splendid soul."

For at the tender age of five, little Holly Johnson had been diagnosed with leukemia. The doctors at Houston's MD Anderson Cancer Center had done their best, but her small body would not accept the bone marrow of another human. And ravaged by the attacking cells of her own blood, she had withered away on a cold hospital bed beneath a maelstrom of tubes, wires and monitors. Her curls gone. The rosy warmth which had once marked her cheeks vanished.

There on that bed, gasping for her last breaths, little Holly Johnson readied to cross the river to the other side, El Otro Lado. Her left hand enveloped by her trembling mother's, her right held tenderly by her father's, she had gazed up at them a final time, her eyes transfixed on a distant point of light visible only to her. "I see them, Ma and Pa. I see them now."

"Who?" the befuddled couple had pressed, desperately clinging to each and every word and thought remaining within her imploding body.

"A man and a woman," her eyes fluttered shut. "They'll come looking for me. He'll be wearing a hat and have a mustache. And she'll have pretty golden curls and red, red lips." She smiled. "Like mine."

Robert Johnson had looked across the dying child at his wife, tears welling in their eyes. They had never mentioned to Holly that she was adopted. They had always figured they would cross that bridge down the road, when she was older and could better understand.

"Tell them I forgive them. Tell them I'll be waiting, Ma and Pa," she whispered. "I'll be waiting for all of you."

The beeping rhythm of the heart monitor had collapsed into a single monotone as Robert and Patty Johnson hunched over Holly's body, now buried in a small and equally featureless graveyard down the road from the Johnson's subdivision.

There, after recounting the sad tale and drying their eyes, the Johnsons limped alongside Fulgencio and Carolina on that sunny but cold winter afternoon. They huddled around the tiny plaque bearing Holly's name and the years of her life, 1962–1967. They prayed. They wept. They held each other upright. And as they prepared to walk away, Fulgencio Ramirez reached deep into his coat and withdrew a single white rose, placing it gently upon his daughter's tomb.

After their visit to the cemetery, Carolina and Fulgencio accompanied the Johnsons back to their home.

"Thank you for letting us share the miracle of the life you created," Mrs. Johnson, a retired English teacher, whispered amidst a series of coughs.

"Thank you for taking care of her," Carolina cried. "We were so young . . ."

"And I was so stupid," Fulgencio shook his head despondently.

"Just remember her message," Mrs. Johnson urged. "She left it with us for a reason."

Through a long afternoon together, Fulgencio and Carolina listened as the Johnsons recounted their favorite memories of their daughter, the ones that still warmed their hearts as they grew old. When Fulgencio noticed that the elderly couple was at last growing tired, he motioned to Carolina that they should leave. Thanking them profusely, Carolina accepted an envelope filled with photos of Holly.

"At last, we can rest." The Johnsons exhaled in unison as they bid the young ones farewell. After a long and drawn-out goodbye, the elderly couple waved from their doorstep.

Fulgencio steered the red Corvette to a quiet spot along the road, pulling over and turning off the engine. There in the silence, the top pulled over their heads, Fulgencio and Carolina held each other and cried. They prayed for the daughter they never knew. They pleaded God for his pardon. And, at last, they begged for the forgiveness they could only find in each other.

"Yes, I forgive you, Fully. I love you more than ever. But do you forgive me for giving her up, for not being there with her when she fell ill?" Carolina sobbed.

"You don't owe me any apologies, Carolina. Of course I forgive you. I left you little choice. And, more importantly, she forgave both of us. It's a miracle simply to know that." He held her close as the sun set, flooding the car's gloomy interior with golden light. "We better get a move on before it's too late."

They drove south toward La Frontera that evening, Carolina's head resting on his shoulder. As they burrowed through the darkness of night, their faces illuminated only by the faint, warm glow of the gauges on the dashboard, Carolina interrupted the silence, her voice tinged by melancholy, "Fulgencio, where did you pluck those roses earlier today? The red one you gave Mercedes and the white one you lay at Holly's grave?"

He stared ahead, his eyes intent on the highway. Deer were abundant in these lands and if he did not keep a watchful eye, he feared one might leap in front of them at any moment, bringing yet more tragedy to the trip.

"We didn't stop by any flower shops along the way," Carolina pressed on. "You couldn't have known about Henry and

Mercedes. We hadn't foreseen Holly's sad fate." She shook her head. "Were they . . . *milagros*?"

After a long while mulling her questions, Fulgencio answered, "To be honest, Carolina, I don't know."

"What do you mean, *you don't know*?"

"I wouldn't call them miracles. Sometimes I feel things or I see them in my mind and suddenly they're there. I don't understand it. It's just the way my life has always been. That's how it was with the flowers. That's how it has been with the spirits that gather around me, like my *abuelo*, Brother William, and El Chotay."

She stared pensively out at the inky night. Outside, the silhouettes of trees flitted by, shadows blurring in the dim moonlight. They drove in complete silence for a long while, working their way down the Texas coastline toward the Rio Grande, until Carolina again broke the hush, crying softly, "I miss her. I yearn for what we lost, all that we could have shared. I feel so sorry for her."

"Me too." Fulgencio nodded, wiping away a renegade tear. "I wish I could do more than make a rose appear. I wish I could change the past, but once someone has gone to El Otro Lado, it is impossible. It's also out of our hands which spirits linger among us."

Nodding, Carolina sniffled, "Losing those you love is so hard."

Fulgencio reached for her hand, squeezing it tightly.

They fell quiet again, plying through the darkness within a somber cocoon of white noise generated by the engine's hum and the wind enveloping the chassis.

"There's something else that fills me with regret," Carolina finally said.

"What's that?"

"How things ended with my father. He was always so loving and accepting. He did everything he could for me, even going against the advice of others." Carolina's voice cracked with emotion. "But I let him down. He never understood my decisions, why I never gave them a grandchild. He didn't complain or judge me, but a distance grew between us over the years and I know . . . I know I broke his heart."

Fulgencio shook his head ruefully, gathering the strength to offer some sort of consolation, "I'm so sorry, Carolina. Your father was a wonderful man, and our daughter was an innocent child. The loss seems as unbearable as it was unfair to you." He paused, searching for some way to soften or ease her pain. "We can't bring them back. And it doesn't change what happened or their suffering. But we can honor their memory. We can attempt to redeem their faith in us. We can begin again."

"Are we crazy to try?"

"We'd be crazy not to . . ."

She lay her head back on his shoulder and joined him in watching the road. As they neared the outskirts of La Frontera, the city lights illuminating the sky in the distance, she suddenly pointed forward, shouting, "Deer!"

Fulgencio abruptly pumped the brakes, pulling the car onto the shoulder and skidding to a stop. About ten yards in front of them, the headlights illuminated a herd of deer—a buck, a doe, and a fawn—bounding gracefully across the desolate road.

PART III

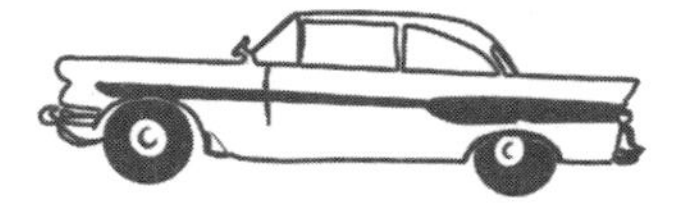

THIRTY-TWO

2006

Through the frosted windowpanes to her dorm room on the top floor of Weld Hall, Paloma Angélica Ramirez watched the snow floating down. Past her ghostlike reflection on the glass, she gazed upon the bundled-up college students frolicking below in the winter's first snowfall, hurling balls of ice and snow at each other, laughing and shouting in innocent glee. The years had darkened and straightened her flowing hair, which, now auburn, framed the moonlike curves of her face, the amber of her eyes, the caramel of her skin. Everything about her betrayed the fiber of her soul: strong, intelligent, proud, passionate, and beautiful.

But she was lonely now. Far from home. Far from family. Far from the river that divided the lands she roamed in the days of her childhood. Turning away from the fun and games below, she crossed her tiny room and pulled a small plastic case from a stack on her desk. From it she extracted a small golden disk.

Smiling wistfully, she slid the disk into her laptop and donned her earbuds. The lush sound of guitars enveloped her as she lay on the brightly colored serape draped over her bed. She listened as his familiar voice rose. The voice that made her skin tingle all over as it reached her heart, warming her. And she crawled beneath the multihued blanket, curling up like a cat, to listen to the sound of her father singing one of her childhood favorites: "Cuatro Vidas." Through the song, her father proclaimed that if he possessed four lives, he would gladly give all four lives for her.

Vida
(Life):

Si tuviera cuatro vidas
(If I had four lives)
cuatro vidas serian para ti.
(four lives would be for you.)

Alma
(Soul):
Si te llevas mi alma
(If you take my soul)
contento la daria por ti.
(I'd gladly give it for you.)

Ser
(Body):
Si te llevas mi ser
(If you take my body)
contento moriria por ti.
(I'd gladly die for you.)

Corazón
(Heart):
En el corazón
(In the heart)
te llevas mi vida, mi alma y mi ser
(you take my life, my soul, my being)

Si tuviera cuatro vidas,
(If I had four lives,)
cuatro vidas serian para ti.
(four lives would be for you.)

The words caressed her softly. The sound washed over her. His voice soothed her, made her feel like a little girl once again, lulled her as she drifted into sleep, her claret lips curving gently into a smile.

THIRTY-THREE

1987

The next night, Fulgencio appeared beneath Carolina's window, which had almost been completely hidden now by the colossal rosebush planted below. Fulgencio was flanked by a full complement of mariachis: thirteen men wielding guitars, violins, and trumpets. All of them, including Fulgencio, were dressed in black mariachi garb, silver buckles glimmering down the sides of their pant legs, broad-brimmed black velvet hats with silver trim crowning their heads. That night Fulgencio sang his heart out. And when she appeared at the doorway, he knelt down at her feet and let his spirit soar with his voice, carrying hers upward toward the stars:

Buscaba mi alma con afan tu alma.
(My soul sought your soul tirelessly.)
Buscaba yo la mujer cálida y bella
(I searched for the beautiful woman)
Que en mi sueño me visita desde niño,
(That I dreamed of since childhood,)

Para partir con ella mi cariño
(To share with her my love)
Para partir con ella mi dolor.
(To share with her my pain.)

Buscaba la Virgen que tocaba
(I sought the Virgin who touched)
mi frente con sus labios dulcemente
(My forehead with her sweet lips)
En el febril insomnio del amor.
(In the feverish insomnia of love.)

Como en la sacra soledad del templo
(As in the sacred solitude of the temple)
Sin ver a Dios se siente su presencia,
(Without seeing God His presence is felt,)
Así presentí en el mundo tu existencia
(Thus I foresaw your existence)
Y como a Dios,
(And like God,)
sin verte te adore
(without seeing you, I adored you.)

Amémonos mi bien en este mundo,
(Let us love each other in this world,)
Donde lagrimas tanto se derraman.
(Where so many tears are spilled.)

Los que viste, quizas los que se aman,
(Those who love)

Tienen un no se que de bendición.
(Have some sort of blessing.)

Amor es empapar el pensamiento
(Love is to soak the thoughts)
Con la fragrancia del Edén perdido.
(With the fragrance of Eden lost.)

Amor es llevar herido
(Love is to have injured)
Con un dardo celeste el corazón.
(With a celestial dart the heart.)

Es tocar los dinteles de la gloria.
(It's to touch the heights of glory.)
Es ver tu cara.
(It's seeing your face.)

Es escuchar tu acento.
(It's hearing your accent.)
Es llevar en el alma el firmamento.
(It's carrying in one's soul the firmament.)

Es morir a tus pies de adoración.
(It's dying at your feet of adoration.)

As the song came to an end with a flurry of guitars and horns, Carolina swooned. She had always loved this song and the way he sang it. "Amémonos," she whispered its title, gazing into Fulgencio's eyes as he looked up at her. Let us love each other.

He said, "Carolina Mendelssohn, will you marry me?" He held out the tiny black box he had saved all those years.

She clasped it in her hands and let the tears rain down upon the shimmering diamond she had waited so long to finally see.

"Yes, Fulgencio. Yes."

They embraced. They kissed. The mariachis yelped, sang, and applauded, plucking at their strings and blowing their horns in jubilation.

THIRTY-FOUR

Clad in a heavy wool sweater, Paloma Angélica Ramirez paced up and down the stairs in her dorm. A chill clung to the air as her mind raced. She was laboring on her honors thesis, a grand architectural project she had envisioned in her sleep. She was designing a futuristic city, anchored on either side of a river that would flow through the center beneath a soaring community punctuated by glass turrets and towers. She had not shared the geographic location for her design with her faculty advisor. It was unnecessary since the vast majority of these projects were an exercise in futility, conceptual whimsies that never came to fruition.

Typically, on move-out day, dozens of miniature models could be found peeking out of dumpsters in Harvard Square. But hers, she knew, was meant to straddle the Rio Grande on the banks north of El Dos de Copas, mending the heart of Caja Pinta. There, she would assemble all the friends and family she so loved and missed during her years on the distant and frigid East Coast. In her mind, she would be uniting two bodies that had been torn asunder by this deep wound which fate had carved between them. She would bridge them together with a vision of love, "the healing power of love" to which her father often referred, glancing tenderly at her mother. Those two pieces of land divided reminded her of the stories they had shared about their misguided youth. Love had mended them. They had built upon it. Now, so would she. She would be the architect of a new world, glorious and brave.

THIRTY-FIVE

Fulgencio and Carolina were wed in a quiet ceremony out on the ranch. They gathered at the edge of the lake beyond the hut, surrounded by a small—but supportive—cluster of close family and friends.

Carolina's mother, her weak voice wavering with emotion, gave them her blessing, saying, "When you were teenagers, you were ahead of your time. Now, you're behind the times! Far be it from me to object if—after all these years—you still love each other."

Ninfa del Rosario—while approving of their union—insisted that the ceremony "did not count" because the officiating minister was no longer among the living. But Fulgencio dismissed her concerns, proclaiming, "Who better than Brother William to unite us in the eyes of God?"

Fulgencio's brothers all wore tuxedos and all managed to bring dates to the event, leading Fulgencio to believe that they too were beginning to reap the benefits of his triumph over *la maldición*. Cipriano, El Primo Loco Gustavo, El Papabote LaMarque, and the dearly departed Fernando Cisneros (playing cards clutched in his hands like a paper rosary) rounded out the guest list. Brother William brandished his gleaming silver cross high above the bride and groom.

As the Brother spoke the ritual words that would formally bind them together, the two lovers barely heard or noticed what was transpiring around them. They held each other's hands tightly, kneeling before the Brother. They gazed into each other's eyes. They felt like children floating in a fantasy

After their wedding, the two lovers escaped to Veracruz, which neither had ever seen. There, beneath the stars and palms, Fulgencio sang the song of the same name, bringing tears to the eyes of all within earshot. The two strolled along the beach, barefoot, hand-in-hand. Lying on a colorful serape that would become a family heirloom, they made love as the waves crashed around them and the water lapped at their feet. They laughed and they cried and they feasted on each other's flesh with desire and regret, with abandon and forgiveness, releasing the burden of their wasted years. There upon the sand, they conceived a miracle of their own. Not one borne of Fulgencio's magic, but rather by the enduring spell of their love.

She was born nine months later in the front passenger seat of the red Corvette, smack in the middle of a traffic-jammed bridge as the two were making their way to the hospital on the US side of the border. When he heard the child's first scream, and he held her up to the heavens, streaked in blood, he saw directly behind her the plaque demarcating the division between Mexico and the United States. The dividing line hung directly over the center of her perfectly spherical head.

Carolina beamed through intermingled tears and beads of sweat as the newborn suckled at her breast. "This is Paloma," Carolina cried. "This is the little girl you dreamt of that night in Houston."

Cars and trucks honked impatiently, yearning for movement, but to Fulgencio the dissonant cacophony sounded like a choir of angels.

"Paloma Angélica," he cooed, leaning over, stroking the infant's tiny wet head and kissing Carolina on the cheek.

And with that, he began to sing tenderly, "Paloma Querida." The song declared that since the day his beloved Paloma had come into his life, his heart had transformed into a dove's nest. In song, he pledged his life and his love to her, a sentiment he knew Carolina shared wholeheartedly.

Por el dia en que llegaste a mi vida
(For the day you arrived in my life)
Paloma Querida
(Beloved Paloma)
Me puse a brindar.
(I began to toast.)

Me sentí superior a cualquiera
(I felt better than anyone)
Y un puño de estrellas
(And a fistful of stars)
Te quize bajar.
(I tried to bring down.)

Y al mirar que ninguna alcanzaba
(And seeing I could not reach)
Me dió tanta rabia
(I was so enraged)

Y me puse a llorar.
(I began to cry.)

Desde entonces yo siento quererte
(Since then I love you)
Con todas las fuerzas
(With all of the strength)
Que el alma me da.
(My soul gives me.)

Desde entonces Paloma Querida
(Since then, Beloved Paloma)
Mi pecho he cambiado por un palomar.
(My chest has become a dove's nest.)

Yo no se lo que valga mi vida
(I don't know what my life's worth)
Pero yo te la vengo a entregar.
(But I give it to you.)

Yo no se si tu amor la reciba
(I don't know if your love will accept)
Pero yo te la vengo a dejar.
(But I come to give it to you.)

The song still ringing in their ears, Fulgencio flashed back to his dream that night in Houston. Walking along the mesquite-lined path from their house to the ranch gate, he felt so safe and loved as Carolina held his hand. In unison their eyes landed on their little girl, skipping ahead. Her copper curls reflected the sunlight, and her eyes twinkled as she turned toward them singing, "I love you!" She heard their shared answer before it even fell from their lips. "We love you too, Paloma . . . We love you too."

It had not been a dream related to the past, he realized. It had been a vision of the future.

THIRTY-SIX

She was packing her great-grandfather's faded and cracked brown leather bag, the same one her father before her had carried to college. Next to it, on her sleek desk overlooking the Manhattan skyline, sat the ancient typewriter case with the black Remington inside. Her father had insisted that she take it to Harvard years earlier, despite the fact that there was a computer in every room. So she had dragged the machine to the Northeast to appease Fulgencio. Unlike her friends who communicated regularly with their parents via Skype, she had come to enjoy the quiet and introspective ritual of pulling out the antique typewriter on silent Sunday afternoons. Sitting in the black and gold armchair decorated with the school's coat of arms, she would click away at the keys on a sheet of stationary pulled from a yellowing stack her father had retrieved from a shelf in his drugstore. Then, when she'd graduated with her master's in architecture, she had lugged it to New York. It had always been a good conversation starter, remaining a fixture on her desks as she ascended from cubicle to corner office at one of the world's most acclaimed design firms. Through those years building a career, she would smile as she shared her thoughts and musings on the events of her week with her parents. It was strange, for although they were older and farther away than most of her peers' parents, she felt a tie much stronger than the ones she sensed between her friends and their elders. She would often thank them for bringing her up with such love, so close to their shared heart. And she appreciated them for always understanding and supporting her vision, even if it did seem quite outlandish for someone from a sleepy border town like La Frontera.

Paloma Angélica would always recall those early years warmly. At first, they had lived on El Dos de Copas, where her parents renovated and expanded the ranch house, preserving at its heart La Virgen's relief and Fernando Cisneros's card table.

How she had admired them. Her father seemed like a gentle giant, singing to her as he taught her how to ride horses, care for cattle, and be a nurturing steward of the land. And her mother was her hero, opening a small school on the ranch for children from the surrounding ranchlands, including those with special needs.

Fulgencio and Carolina also kept the drugstore open after marrying, mostly for sentimental reasons. He had owned it for so long, and it had kept him company through so many lonely years, that he could not bear to part with it. Besides, he would say, what would El Chotay do if he closed it down and the next tenant opened up a women's clothing store! Would the old ghost be forced to hem dresses and fit wigs? And, how could he abandon his parade of misfits and loyalists? Both Carolina and Paloma Angélica agreed.

For Carolina, the drugstore was a warm and fuzzy reminder of her father's own days as a pharmacist, of the times she had spent at the soda fountain in Mendelssohn's Drugstore, her legs demurely crossed, twirling a straw in her fingers, feeling Fulgencio's eyes drilling holes through her back.

And for Paloma Angélica, the pharmacy was a source of boundless human entertainment. She loved the wheezing of El Papabote LaMarque. The rhythmic white noise soothed her as if she were still a baby. And she thrilled at the very thought of playing jacks with El Chotay in the shadowy corners of the store. She delighted at posing trivia questions for El Primo Loco Gustavo to answer. And she savored the steaming *cabrito con guacamole* tacos from Old Eleodoro the Cabrito Man's ever-present bag of foil-wrapped goodies.

Instead of presiding endlessly behind the high counter, Fulgencio now spent time with Carolina and Paloma Angélica, the sources of his joy and rejuvenation. The three were inseparable. In the years before Paloma Angélica left for college, they traveled the world, seeing it all for the first time together. Wandering like three awed children, they held hands as they roamed through the grandiose palaces and cathedrals of Europe, climbed the pyramid of the sun in Teotihaucan, savored the spicy foods of East Asia and India. Learning. Absorbing. Relishing. They explored the world not with the thirst of those searching for meaning, but rather with the appreciation of those who have already found peace. And from their travels they returned with countless artifacts to adorn their homes, both the one on El Dos de Copas and the one across the border in La Frontera.

For when Paloma Angélica began middle school, they moved into the Mendelssohn's sagging and cloistered home. However, it was not proximity to Paloma Angélica's new school that Fulgencio sought, he confided to his daughter.

Over the next few months, Carolina and Paloma Angélica

transformed the decaying home into the warm and wondrous Norman Rockwell portrait Fulgencio had longed for in his youth. Fresh coats of paint, new furnishings and rugs, larger windows and skylights in the stairwell filled the home with life and light. And Paloma Angélica's laughter rang throughout the house.

Carolina's mother was so reinvigorated by the presence of her daughter and granddaughter, that she too underwent a transformation. She worked harder than ever in the gardens, imparting upon Paloma Angélica her vast knowledge of botany and horticulture.

But as the first school year came and went, Fulgencio seemed to grow increasingly antsy. On Valentine's Day, he appeared in the kitchen doorway with two-dozen red roses for Carolina.

Dropping to one knee, he proposed: "Marry me again, Carolina. Marry me right here in this very house."

Her smile illuminated the freshly painted kitchen as if a roaring fire had suddenly been ignited in its hearth.

That summer, the family gathered in the backyard. All of Carolina's uncles and aunts were there, as were all of her mother's friends. Fulgencio's family came as well. Little David was his best man. Nicolas Junior and Fernando brought their new brides and babies. And Ninfa del Rosario thanked God that—at long last—Fulgencio and Carolina would be married officially by a living and properly ordained Catholic priest. (Although she noted that since the ceremony was not taking place within a church, it still might not count.)

The gardens behind the house were sculpted and trimmed to perfection. The wedding scene was set in white. Roses, gardenias, and calla lilies saturated the breeze with their scent. Fulgencio, clad in a black tuxedo, awaited Carolina beneath an arched trellis decorated with white blooms.

As the mariachis began playing the wedding march, Carolina

stood in her white wedding dress at the start of the long runner leading to her groom. Suddenly, she felt a tugging at her elbow. It was Paloma Angélica pulling on her sleeve.

"Mamá. There's a man inside that says he'd like to walk you down the aisle." She pointed toward the house. Standing by the back door, in a perfectly pressed black tuxedo, appeared Carolina's father.

Paloma Angélica would never forget the expression of awe and love that graced her mother's face as she took her father's hand.

As the music played, he walked Carolina slowly down the aisle, toward Fulgencio. When they reached the makeshift altar, he took their hands and placed them together, looking deeply into their eyes.

"Forgive us, father," Carolina said, her voice trembling with emotion.

"Forgive me, sir," Fulgencio added. "It was all my fault."

Arthur Mendelssohn put his arms around them and replied, "Forgiveness has never been mine to give, but I gladly give you my blessing."

So the two were wed again, before the teary eyes of Mr. and Mrs. Mendelssohn who embraced each other with Paloma Angélica giddily pressed between them.

One night, not long after the vow renewal, in the shadows of Mr. Mendelssohn's den with Nat King Cole crooning in the background, Paloma Angélica studied at her grandfather's desk as her parents warmed themselves by the crackling fire and Arthur Mendelssohn lounged in his leather chair.

Holding Carolina's hand, Fulgencio asked his former mentor, "Why did you wait so long to show yourself?"

"I was gathering my strength," he replied. "It wasn't easy. The last years of my life left me somewhat weak and disillusioned. I was tired, but Paloma Angélica came and spoke to me here in this room. She couldn't see me, but, nonetheless, she believed in me. She invited me. She told me how much it would mean to both of you. How could I turn her down?" He shifted, gazing at Paloma Angélica, smiling tenderly. "If it comes from you, it must be good."

***

A faded black-and-white photograph of Arthur Mendelssohn in his navy uniform was the last item Paloma Angélica placed in her suitcase before closing it, right next to the disk containing her father's songs. She stood in the emptied apartment she had once decorated with her drawings and her pictures and her things from home. She marveled at how paradoxical life was. That the things that pained her and hurt her the most all these years away, the things she missed, were also the very ones which held the power to heal her soul, the glue which kept her identity and her vision of the future together. The old typewriter in its case. Her great-grandfather's leather suitcase. The dog-eared black and white image of her grandpa. The voice of her father. And—she clasped the tiny gold medallion of the Madonna and Child—the soothing memory of her mother.

As the taxicab pulled away from the ivy-covered walls of her brownstone, she looked out the window wistfully as her recent past rushed by. Six years in Cambridge. Her bachelor's and her master's in hand, her *papelitos* as her father called them. Then another handful of years in New York, winning awards for her innovative bridge designs, bridges as meeting places rather than simple crossings, bridges as places to exchange and share cultural experiences rather than simply goods and merchandise, bridges as communities, bridges as the cities of the future. She had worked tirelessly, just like her father had taught her. How she had missed Fulgencio and Carolina despite their frequent visits, despite having friends to fill what little free time her work permitted. They were her best friends, she thought, the two lovers who still behaved like children in each other's presence.

As the cab cruised down the West Side Highway, she smiled in anticipation of seeing them again. Sailboats out on the water beneath a perfect blue sky. The downtown towers gleaming like crystal beneath the golden sun. Rolling down the window, she felt the soft breeze on her face and she felt as if she were halfway home already. She remembered her father's words one day as they sat alone in the drugstore. He had said, waving his arms in a grand gesture, "It took me years to figure out that what truly heals is not all these drugs and medicines. *No, no señorita*. Only love can heal. The love between two people. The love of family and home. The love you hear in a song or see in a painting or design. *El amor vive eterno*." Love lives eternal.

As the cabby unloaded her bags at the airport in Newark, she mused, "I'm ready for some of that healing power." She was ready for home.

THIRTY-SEVEN

Fulgencio groomed his white mustache in the mirror as Carolina powdered her face by his side. She was all in white, a light linen dress. He wore a crisp white guayabera and khaki pants. Their youth faded now, they still cut a sharp and beautiful couple.

"You excited?" he asked.

"Yes, my love." She smiled at him in the mirror.

"Our baby's coming home."

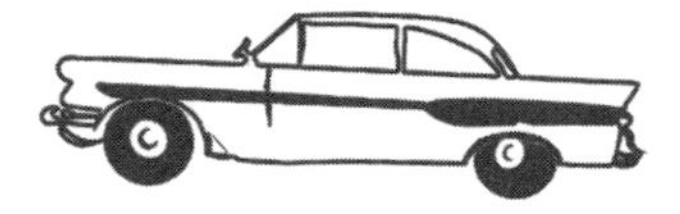

THIRTY-EIGHT

Little David picked Paloma Angélica up at the airport in the antique Corvette convertible. Heading straight to El Dos de Copas, she absorbed the blasting sun as the Gulf breeze rushed through her hair.

When the Corvette pulled to a stop in front of the hacienda she had helped conceive in her childhood, she marveled at the historic integrity of the design. Good work, she had to admit, for a child.

Fulgencio and Carolina stood beneath the arched doorway to the stone house, their smiles lighting up the sky. Paloma Angélica ran toward them, her arms open wide.

Little David pounded the car horn in jubilation as the family shared a joyous embrace. Relatives and friends flowed into the central courtyard before the old hut with the relief of the Virgencita still on the adobe wall. Together, they celebrated Paloma Angélica's return—Fernando Cisneros, Brother William, Cipriano, and the ranch hands. A pig turned on a spit over the raging fire. And La Virgencita danced on the wall to the latest music disk that Paloma Angélica brought for her, headphones over her radiant halo, her fingers snapping beneath her bright green cloak.

Fulgencio cocked an eyebrow and noted to Carolina that La Virgencita had never appeared in color before, but now she looked more vibrant and lifelike than ever.

"First update I'm installing is Wi-Fi," Paloma Angélica asserted. "That way the Virgencita can stream her favorite tracks."

That night beneath the stars, the party carried on with the mariachis playing, Fulgencio singing and the margaritas flowing. In front of the majestic hacienda, cars and trucks gathered, bringing campesinos and neighbors from miles around to the fiesta.

There in the central courtyard, embraced by the optimistic gathering, her face warmed, and illuminated by the flickering campfire, Paloma Angélica revealed her grand plans to build a city upon the river so they could all be joined with their loved ones from El Otro Lado.

THIRTY-NINE

The chants and jubilation of the crowd still rang through the air as Fulgencio and Carolina retired to their bedroom. In the comfort of their bed, they gazed into each other's eyes and smiled.

"She's home," Carolina whispered.

"Yes, and our job here is done," Fulgencio said.

"I always thought our destiny was purely to love each other," Carolina said, "I didn't realize until Paloma Angélica came along that we had an even higher purpose in life."

"*Sí, sí señora*," Fulgencio mused in his now gravelly voice, "It seems we are but part of a greater pattern. I was always too busy stumbling through the maze to see it from a distance, to discern its grand design."

"We have been blessed by her."

"Yes," Fulgencio leaned ever closer toward Carolina, brushing his tired lips against hers. "Tonight, she sounded more like a revolutionary than like an architect."

"But what is a revolutionary . . ." Carolina pointed out, "if not the architect of a new way of life?"

The two fell into a deep sleep, but in the middle of the night, Fulgencio's eyes fluttered open and he heard himself comment: "I don't want there to be an obituary written about us."

Carolina agreed.

"Those things never tell the true story," Fulgencio said. "Besides, I never enjoyed reading them."

"Except for maybe that one day . . ." She smiled.

He remembered the paper falling onto the pharmacy floor, the twenty-two letters that liberated him to pursue their destiny once again.

"Yes, except for maybe that one day," he confirmed. "And since that day, I've known: the end is only the beginning. And so, why put a period on our lives when we will surely carry on?"

She smiled at his confidence in the impending wonder of life after death.

They kissed gently as darkness enveloped them and their souls relaxed within their nestled bodies. Falling deeply. They felt as if they were two glasses of water being poured into one larger container. Swirling and settling in the darkness. Never thought they could be even closer. Two as one. Healing. No distance. No wounds. No borders. No limits. No separation. No vacuum between them. Just unity. Just homogenous continuity. Simply and purely dissolving into each other. One. In the dark. Shadows. Then light. Strolling hand-in-hand along the mesquite-lined path. Young again. Carolina's white linen dress flowing in the breeze. Her smile contagious. And Fulgencio, holding her in his arms forever.

CHAPTER FORTY

As the roosters crowed, Paloma Angélica awoke with the knowledge of what had transpired. She arranged for the burial of her parents by the lake—not far from Brother William's spot—beneath a giant gnarled mesquite tree. One stone, she said. They wanted to be buried together. Their bodies wrapped around each other just as they had been found lying in bed.

Brother William officiated over the brief ceremony, his silver cross gleaming in the high noon sun, his black robes swirling around him.

La Virgencita de Guadalupe tore herself from the adobe wall in the hut and dragged Fernando Cisneros from his card table, cataract eyes squinting in the blasting sun of the courtyard. "It's time we moved, Old Man," she said as they joined the funereal gathering behind the hacienda.

The crowd parted for the Virgencita as she approached the mound of fresh earth that had just been shoveled into place over the lowered coffin. Brother William bowed to her in deference.

And as she opened her flowing emerald cape, an avalanche of roses—red and white—exploded forth, covering the burial site and nearly pushing Brother William into the lake.

La Virgencita looked straight into Paloma Angélica's eyes. And together they knew without speaking what was next. The entire crowd, the same one from the night before, mounted their horses and began to ride quietly north through the meadows toward the Rio Grande.

As they passed a grove of mesquite trees, they heard the laughter of two young lovers dancing on the breeze. Dismounting, Paloma Angélica wandered through the thicket of trees, pushing away the low-hanging branches and leaves, until at last she stumbled into a clearing in the center. It took her a moment to recognize Fulgencio and Carolina, looking just as they did that night of their first date, cuddled on the ground upon a brightly hued serape.

She smiled, "Are you two lovebirds coming?"

From beyond the trees emerged Trueno and Relámpago, the originals, and Fulgencio and Carolina mounted them, following Paloma Angélica back out toward the cheering crowd.

"*¡Beso*! *¡Beso*!" The crowd chanted. And the two kissed fervently, the flanks of their horses pressed against each other.

"Do the honors, Dad," Paloma Angélica gestured north toward the distant river, over the vast lands she had now inherited.

"Let's ride!" Fulgencio shouted, pulling his Stetson from thin air and waving it high toward the sky as he led the small army north toward the banks of the river.

Riding next to her mother and father, Paloma Angélica knew she possessed the resources to build and maintain her visionary city. Now as the banks appeared on the horizon, she was not alone in envisioning the city itself, shimmering like a dream, its spires reaching toward the heavens.

The salty gulf breeze ripped through Fulgencio's black mane. Carolina's joyful laughter filled the air. Brother William shouted in exaltation. And the Virgencita de Guadalupe hung on to Fernando Cisneros's waist as they galloped on the same horse. Shots rang in the air as El Chino Alasan fired his revolvers in celebration toward the sky. And their followers all yelped and pumped their fists in the air.

"¡Viva Fulgencio Ramirez!" they chanted.

He smiled, glancing first to his wife and then to his daughter.

The ground rushed beneath them, hooves thundering as they sped toward the approaching banks, the wind in their faces.

"¡Viva Fulgencio Ramirez!"

Fulgencio shook his head in wonderment as he looked at Carolina, her body hunched over Trueno's neck, racing beside him.

"We're almost there," Paloma Angélica shouted as they neared the river. "This is the spot!"

The horses whinnied and snorted as the group reined them to a stop and dismounted. Brother William jumped into the waters, laughing madly as he had the day he died. The crowd gathered around Fulgencio, Carolina, and Paloma Angélica. Spellbound, their eyes all settled on an apparition on the northern banks of the river. There, a familiar couple stepped to the shore, their toes nearly touching the water. Mauro Fernando and Soledad Cisneros held hands, smiled faintly, and waved back.

"This is the spot!" Paloma Angélica proclaimed, her eyes twinkling with glee.

Fulgencio marveled, "Someone drew a line in the sand, and we crossed back and forth until it disappeared."

"¡Viva Fulgencio Ramirez!" the crowd chanted again.

Carolina gazed lovingly at Fulgencio as they nestled their daughter between them. Paloma Angélica understood that getting here had taken them a long time, not just her parents, but all of those who joined them at the river's edge, the campesinos and the drifters, the *mexicanos* and the gringos, the disinherited and the poor, the misfits and the miscreants, the Papabote LaMarques and Primo Loco Gustavos she glimpsed within the crowd, the Little Davids and the Bobby Balmoris that were bringing up the rear. It had been a long journey for all of them, but they had made it. Fulgencio and Carolina had helped them find their way. And now, she would lead them in building a bridge to the future, anchored deeply on the banks of their past.

"¡Viva Fulgencio Ramirez!"

Fulgencio smiled, gazing upon all of the familiar faces that surrounded him and remembering those that weren't there to share the day: his parents, El Chotay, the Mendelssohns, Buzzy, La Señora Villarreal, and even his mysterious and misunderstood ancestor Minerva, the grieving mother who had cast a terrible spell in her desperate search for justice. At that moment he realized her incantations had proven to be much more than a curse, but rather a blueprint for their communal redemption. He resolved that once the city was built, he would release a flight of doves to seek them all out upon the heavens and call them to this special place they were destined to share.

"¡Viva Fulgencio Ramirez!" the crowd cheered yet again.

He wrapped his arms around the women of his life. He turned his eyes up to the cerulean sky, clearing his throat. The two women smiled knowingly, their hearts overflowing with anticipation. Fulgencio was about to sing in celebration. For at long last, they had all found their way home. And as his voice took flight, they joined the crowd one final time, squeezing the powerful man between their arms as they shouted jubilantly:

"¡Viva Fulgencio Ramirez!"

"Long live Fulgencio Ramirez!"

ACKNOWLEDGMENTS

For inspiration, I'd like to thank my father, who passed away in 2015. Rodolfo Ruiz Cisneros was a larger-than-life person with a will and a spirit that felt destined to live beyond his physical being. His person was deeply rooted in his culture, his region, and his formative era. The vivid stories of his upbringing on the border in the 1950s, and the experiences and tales he shared with me over the years served as the primary inspiration for *The Resurrection of Fulgencio Ramirez.* The songs that Fulgencio sings in the book are the songs my father sung to me as a child. They are classic boleros from what is widely considered the golden age of Mexican music and film. Drawing from memories, dreams, and often murky border history filtered through the lens of time, it seemed appropriate to me to re-create my father's world as a mythical alternate reality set in the fictional border town of La Frontera, which is loosely based on Brownsville, Texas, where both my father and I were born and raised. Memories feed imagination. In this vein, I'd also like to thank my beloved wife, Heather. In many ways, our own love story brought to life the enduring romance at the core of this novel. Heather taught me how to love, and—as Fulgencio says—without love, we're dead. A special thank you to Paloma and Lorenzo, our children. I passionately enjoyed reading and writing since childhood, but it was only when we brought Paloma home as a newborn that I found within me the perspective and the inspiration to write this novel and begin my journey as an author in earnest. The eagerness and sincere joy with which Lorenzo anticipates and reads each and every story I write motivates me to continue honing this often solitary and arduous craft. And, finally, I must thank my mom, Lilia Zolezzi Ruiz, for putting books in my hands further back than I can remember, and always supporting my bilingual and bicultural education, without which I'm not sure I could string *dos palabras* together.

For support in sharing my writing with more readers, I thank Laura Strachan, my literary agent. It took me a long time to find an agent who truly believed in my work and I am very grateful to Laura for actually finding me. I'd also like to especially thank Rick Bleiweiss at Blackstone Publishing, as well as his entire team, for embracing Fulgencio and the magical realism world and characters of La Frontera. I never thought it would take someone near the northern border to help me share my stories of the southern one, but I'm very grateful for the vision and enthusiastic support Blackstone has brought to our partnership.

Finally, there have been many readers, teachers, friends and family that have encouraged and supported my writing over the years. It's not possible to thank them all, but I would love to acknowledge the following people for their support: Professor Efrain Kristal (Harvard, UCLA), Nora Comstock (Las Comadres para las Americas), Teno Villarreal, Jerry Ruiz, Paul Tucker, *Gulf Coast Magazine*, *Notre Dame Review*, *The Ninth Letter*,

Professor Francine Richter (*New Texas*), BorderSenses, Latino Literacy Now (Empowering Latino Futures), Professor Berlyn Cobian (Long Beach City College), Salvador Cobian, and Professor Rodney Rodriguez (LBCC).

For reading, thank you. *Gracias*.

SONG CREDITS

"Don't Be Cruel (To a Heart That's True)"

Words and music by Otis Blackwell and Elvis Presley

Copyright © 1956; Renewed 1984 Elvis Presley Music (BMI)

All Rights Administered by Songs of Steve Peter and Songs of Kobalt Music Publishing

International Copyright Secured, All Rights Reserved

Reprinted by permission of Hal Leonard LLC

"Veracruz"

Words and music by Agustin Lara

Copyright © 1933 by Promotora Hispano Americana de Musica, SA

Copyright Renewed

All Rights Administered by Peer International Corporation

International Copyright Secured, All Rights Reserved

Reprinted by permission of Hal Leonard LLC

"Sin Ti"

"Ojos Cafes"

"Hoja Seca"

"Cuatro Vidas"

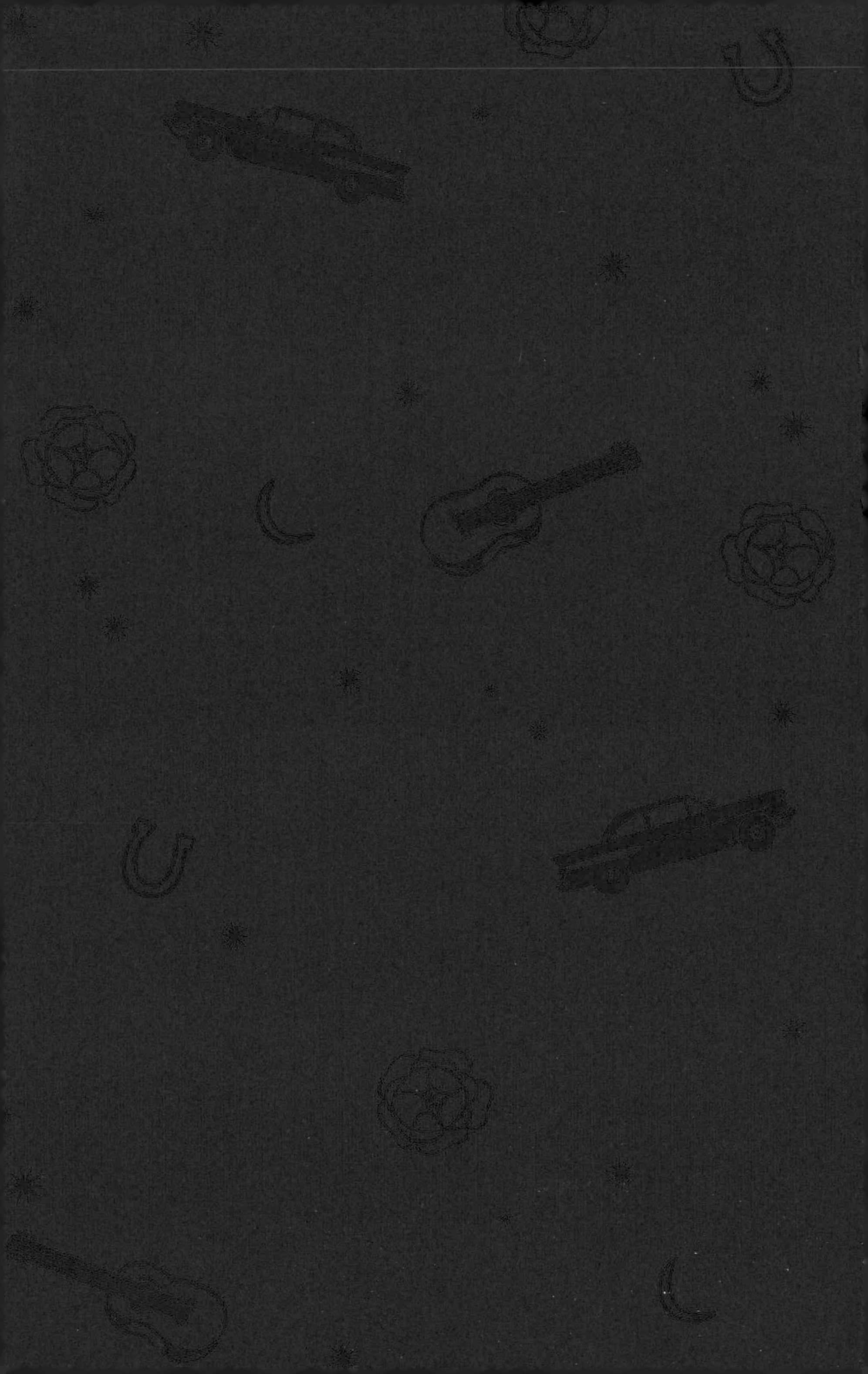